DINOSAUR EXPLORERS

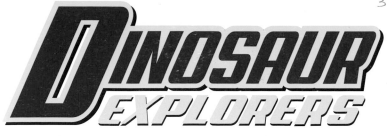

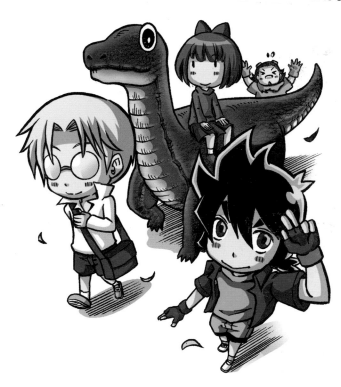

PAPERCUTZ

DINOSAUR EXPLORERS

#4 TRAPPED IN THE TRIASSIC

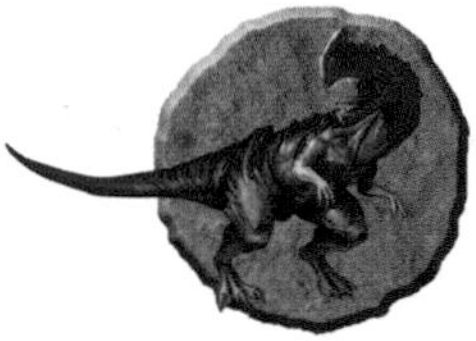

REDCODE and ALBBIE—Story
AIR TEAM—Comics
REDCODE & SAMU—Cover Illustration
MAX—Cover Color
EVA, MAX, FUN, SENG HUI —Color
KENNY CHUA and KIAONG—Art Direction
ROUSANG—Original Design
BALICAT & MVCTAR AVRELIVS—Translation
ROSS BAUER—Original Editor
KARR ANTUNES —Editorial Intern
JEFF WHITMAN—Assistant Managing Editor
JIM SALICRUP
Editor-in-Chief

ISBN HC: 978-1-5458-0205-2
ISBN PB: 978-1-5458-0204-5

Printed in Korea
November 2018

Papercutz books may be purchased for business or promotional use.
For information on bulk purchase please contact Macmillan
Corporate and Premium Sales Department at (800) 221-7945 x5442

Distributed by Macmillan.
First Papercutz Printing.

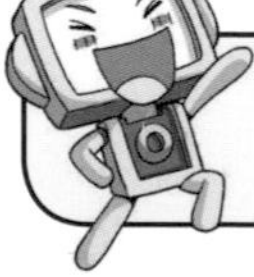

DINOSAUR EXPLORERS Reading Guide
and Lesson Planner available at:
http://papercutz.com/educator-resources-papercutz

DINOSAUR EXPLORERS

#4 TRAPPED IN THE TRIASSIC

REDCODE & ALBBIE – WRITERS

AIR TEAM – ART

PAPERCUTZ
NEW YORK

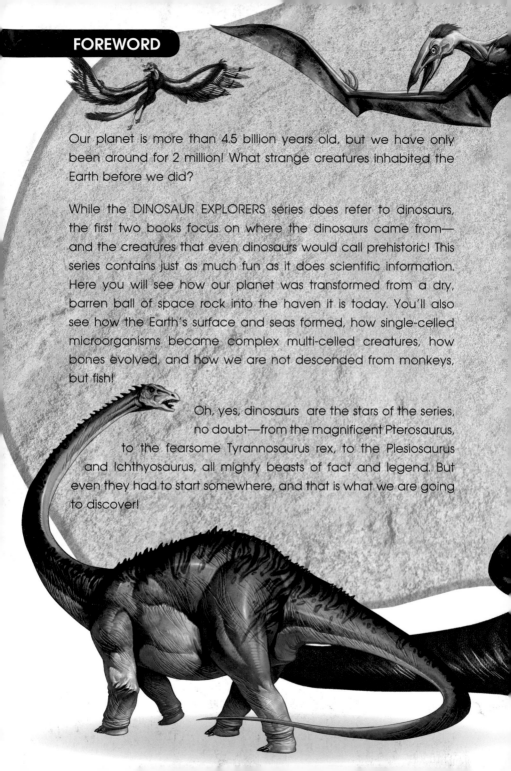

FOREWORD

Our planet is more than 4.5 billion years old, but we have only been around for 2 million! What strange creatures inhabited the Earth before we did?

While the DINOSAUR EXPLORERS series does refer to dinosaurs, the first two books focus on where the dinosaurs came from—and the creatures that even dinosaurs would call prehistoric! This series contains just as much fun as it does scientific information. Here you will see how our planet was transformed from a dry, barren ball of space rock into the haven it is today. You'll also see how the Earth's surface and seas formed, how single-celled microorganisms became complex multi-celled creatures, how bones evolved, and how we are not descended from monkeys, but fish!

Oh, yes, dinosaurs are the stars of the series, no doubt—from the magnificent Pterosaurus, to the fearsome Tyrannosaurus rex, to the Plesiosaurus and Ichthyosaurus, all mighty beasts of fact and legend. But even they had to start somewhere, and that is what we are going to discover!

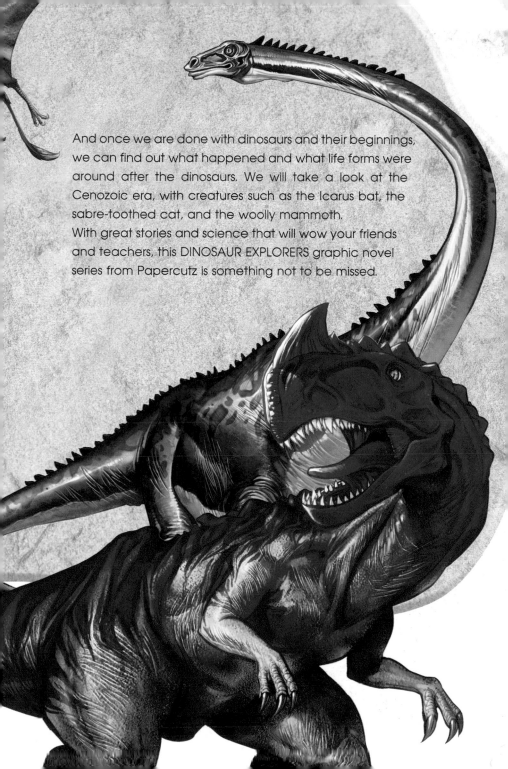

And once we are done with dinosaurs and their beginnings, we can find out what happened and what life forms were around after the dinosaurs. We will take a look at the Cenozoic era, with creatures such as the Icarus bat, the sabre-toothed cat, and the woolly mammoth.

With great stories and science that will wow your friends and teachers, this DINOSAUR EXPLORERS graphic novel series from Papercutz is something not to be missed.

How the Earth was Formed

We know the Earth is the third planet in the solar system, the densest planet and, so far, the only one capable of supporting life. But how did that happen?

1 The Sun's formation

Way, way back, there was a patch of space filled with cosmic dust and gases. Slowly, gravity (and a few nearby exploding stars) forced some of this dust and gases together into clumps–the gases formed into a massive, pressurized ball of heat which became the Sun, while the dust settled into planets, the Earth being one of them.

2 Formation of the Earth

As the Earth formed, its gravity grew stronger. Heavier molecules and atoms fell inward to the Earth's core, while lighter elements formed around it. The massive pressures from the external material heated up the Earth's interior to the point where it was all liquid (except for the core, which was under so much pressure it could not liquify). These settled down into the Earth's 3 layers: the crust, mantle, and core.

While we cannot say for sure just when these dust clouds solidified to form the Earth, nor when they came into being in the first place, we can tell that they took place more than 4.5 billion years ago.

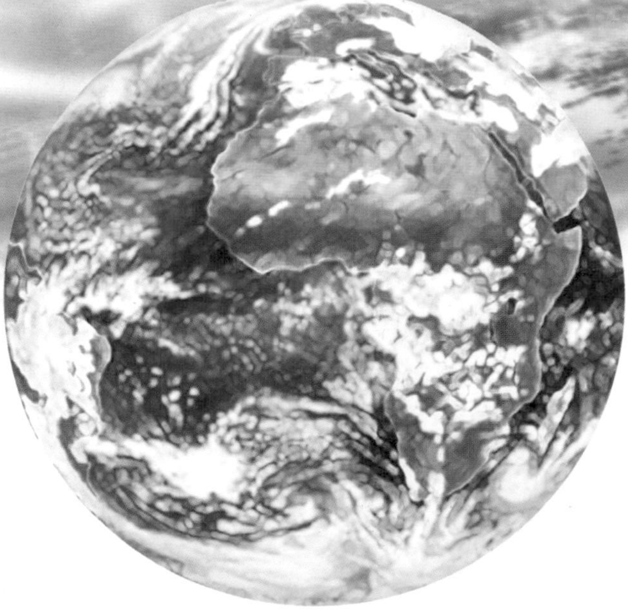

6 The Earth today

Even now, our Earth changes with time; its tectonic plates still move about on the lava bed of the mantle, pushing and pulling continents in all directions.

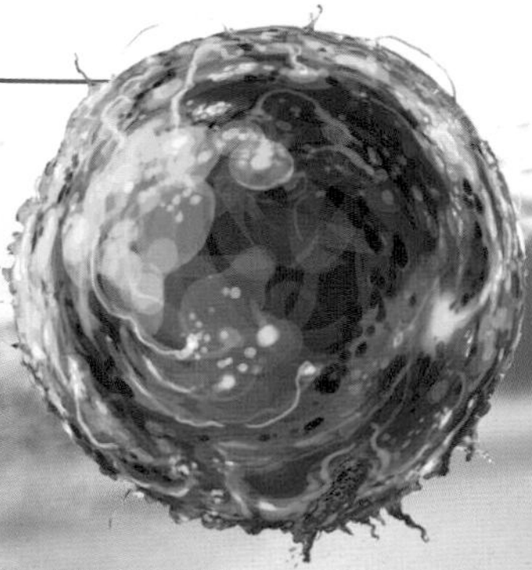

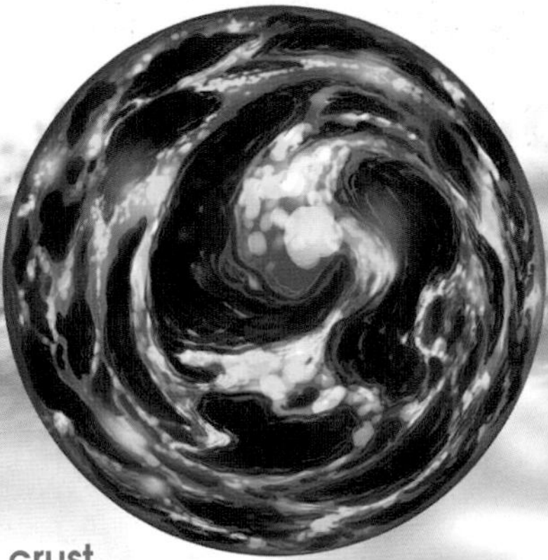

3 The crust

The crust was created around 4 billion years ago, as cooled, solid rock floating on the molten lithosphere merged. Even today, as the continental plates shift away and against each other, some of this rock and molten material might still change place.

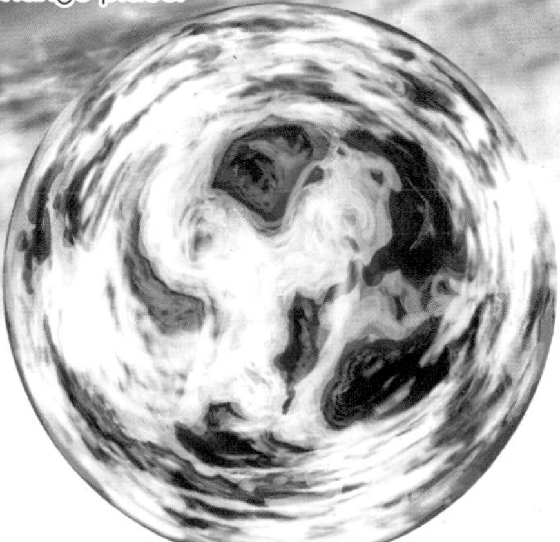

4 The formation of the atmosphere

After our crust solidified, volcanic gases formed our atmosphere. The cooling surface allowed the formation of water vapor and bodies of water.

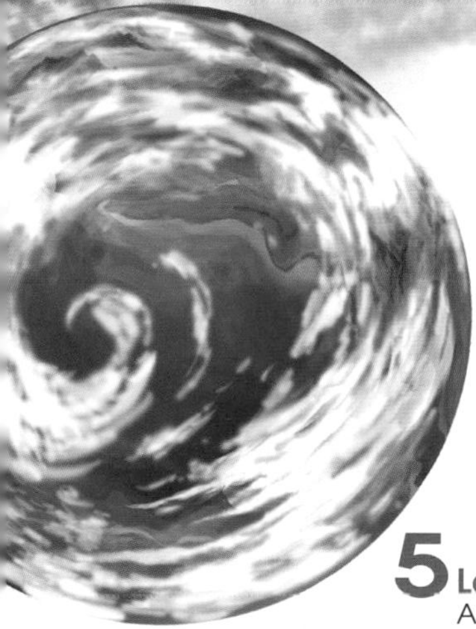

5 Land forms

Around 3.5 billion years ago, several land masses rose above the global ocean, giving rise to the continents we know today.

Geological Time Spiral

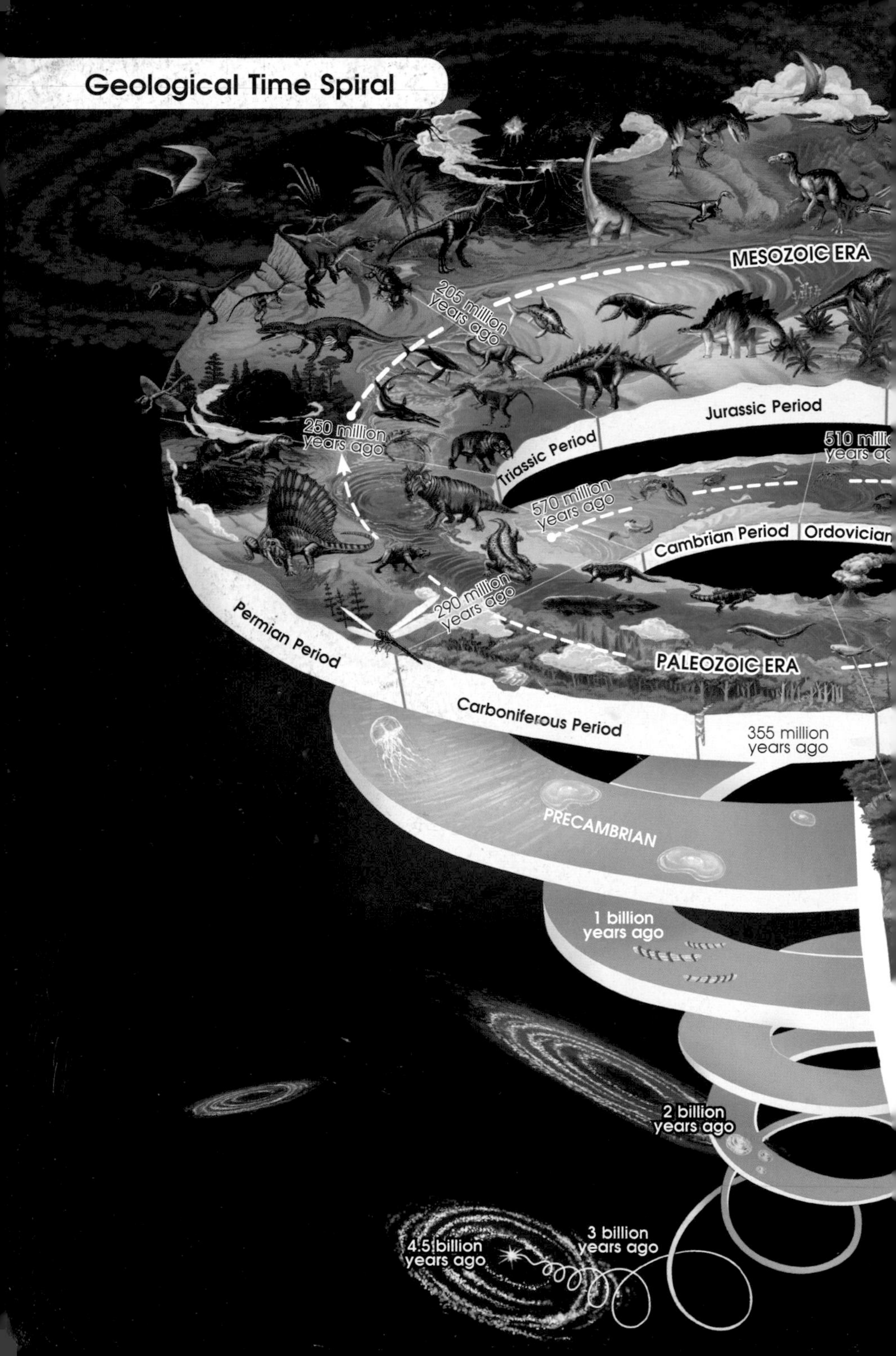
MESOZOIC ERA
205 million years ago
250 million years ago
Jurassic Period
Triassic Period
510 millio years ag
570 million years ago
Cambrian Period
Ordovician
290 million years ago
Permian Period
PALEOZOIC ERA
Carboniferous Period
355 million years ago
PRECAMBRIAN
1 billion years ago
2 billion years ago
3 billion years ago
4.5 billion years ago

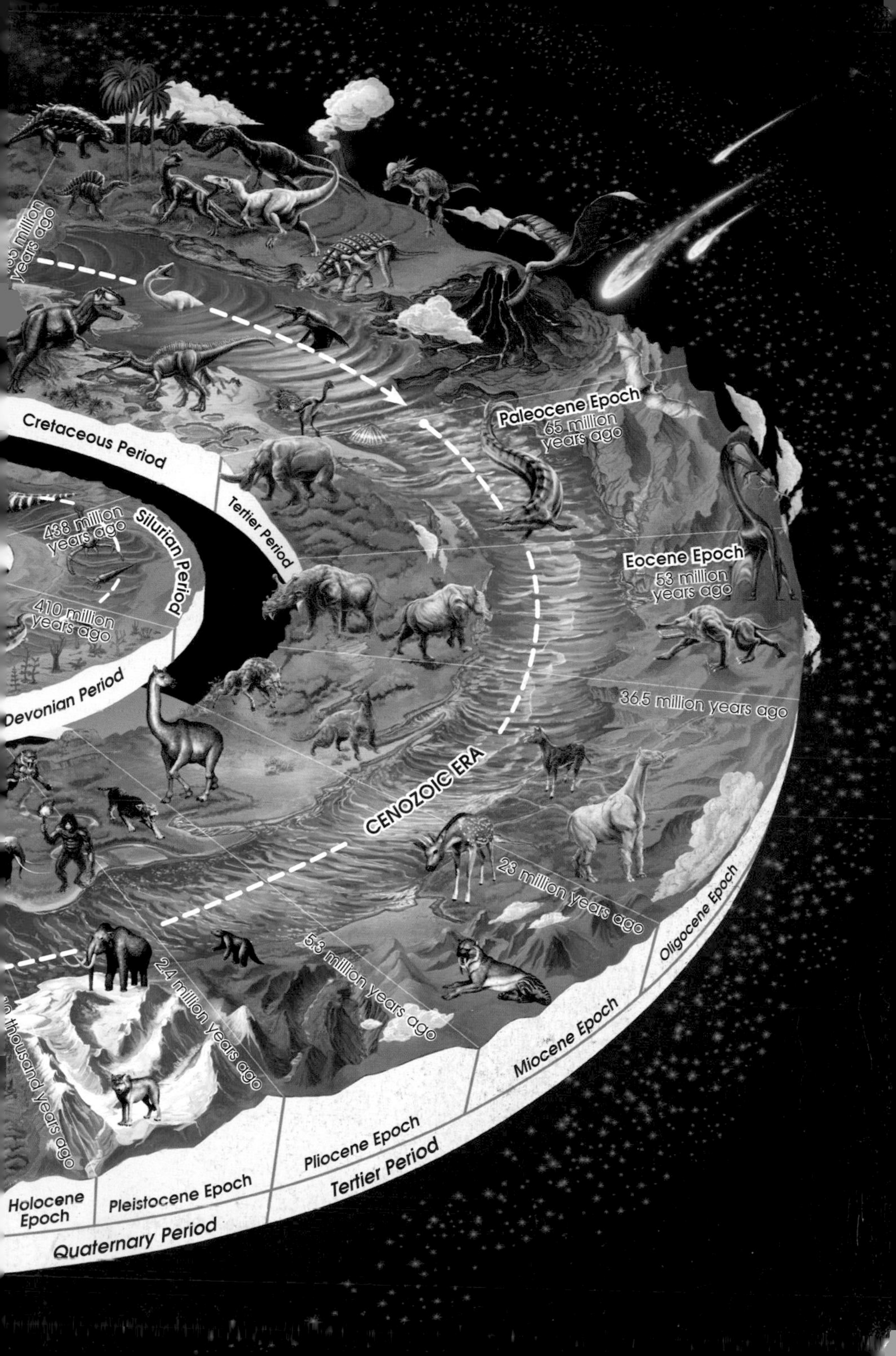

years ago
Cretaceous Period
Tertier Period
438 million years ago
Silurian Period
410 million years ago
Devonian Period
Paleocene Epoch
65 million years ago
Eocene Epoch
53 million years ago
36.5 million years ago
CENOZOIC ERA
23 million years ago
Oligocene Epoch
5.3 million years ago
2.4 million years ago
thousand years ago
Miocene Epoch
Pliocene Epoch
Tertier Period
Holocene Epoch
Pleistocene Epoch
Quaternary Period

GEOLOGIC TIME SCALE

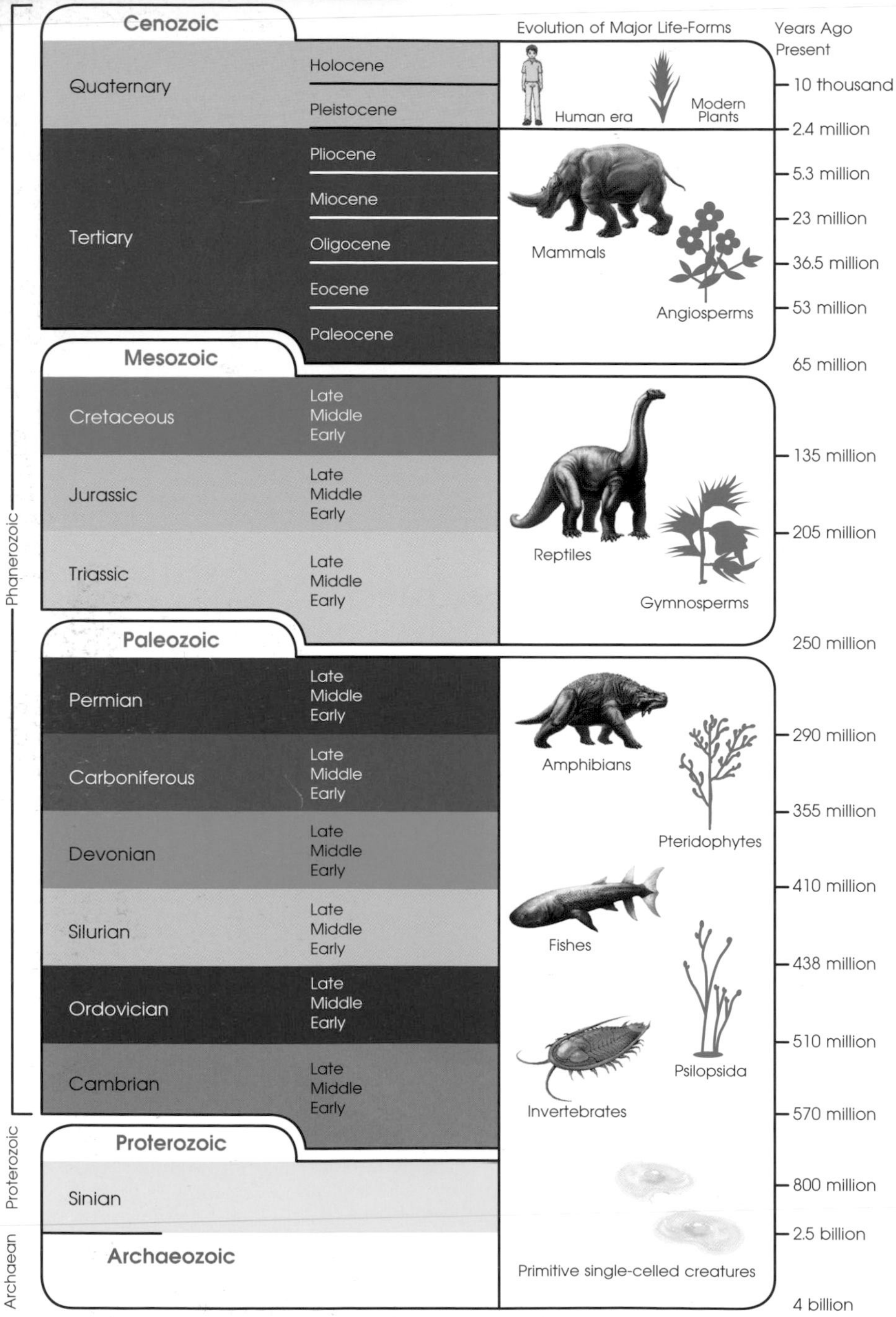

Left margin labels: Phanerozoic | Proterozoic | Archaean

Era	Period	Epoch / Stage	Evolution of Major Life-Forms	Years Ago
Cenozoic				Present
	Quaternary	Holocene	Human era / Modern Plants	
		Pleistocene		10 thousand
				2.4 million
	Tertiary	Pliocene		5.3 million
		Miocene	Mammals	23 million
		Oligocene		36.5 million
		Eocene	Angiosperms	53 million
		Paleocene		
Mesozoic				65 million
	Cretaceous	Late / Middle / Early		
	Jurassic	Late / Middle / Early	Reptiles	135 million
	Triassic	Late / Middle / Early	Gymnosperms	205 million
Paleozoic				250 million
	Permian	Late / Middle / Early		
	Carboniferous	Late / Middle / Early	Amphibians	290 million
	Devonian	Late / Middle / Early	Pteridophytes	355 million
	Silurian	Late / Middle / Early		410 million
	Ordovician	Late / Middle / Early	Fishes	438 million
	Cambrian	Late / Middle / Early	Psilopsida / Invertebrates	510 million
				570 million
Proterozoic				
	Sinian			800 million
				2.5 billion
Archaeozoic			Primitive single-celled creatures	
				4 billion

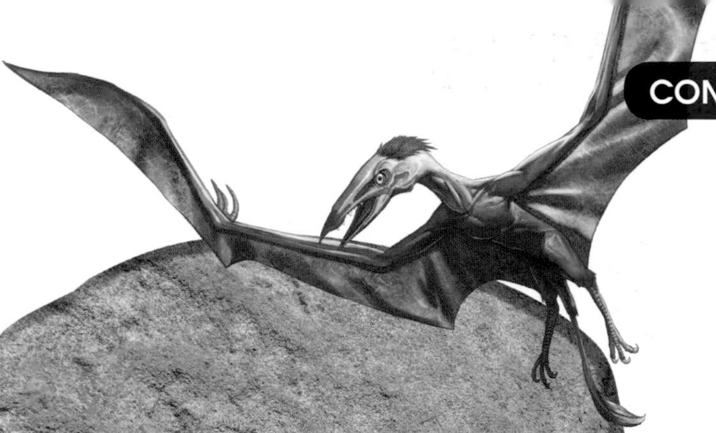

CONTENTS

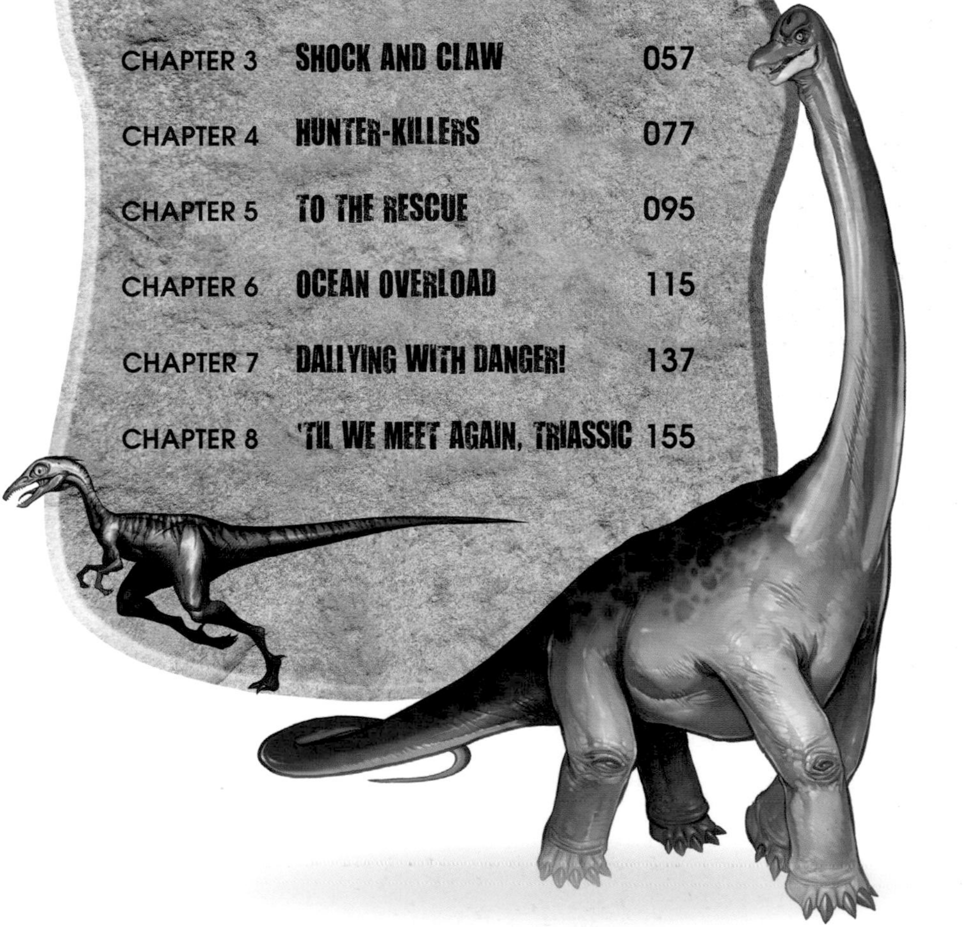

Cast

Sean (Age 13)
- Smart, calm, and a good analyst.
- Very articulate, but under-performs on rare occasions.
- Uses scientific knowledge and theory in thought and speech.

Stone (Age 15)
- Has tremendous strength, appetite, and size.
- A boy of few words but honest and reliable.
- An expert in repairs and maintenance.

STARZ
- A tiny robot invented by the doctor, nicknamed Lil S.
- Multifunctional; able to scan, analyze, record, take images, communicate, and more.
- Able to change its form and appearance. It is a mobile supercomputer that can store huge amounts of information.

Rain (Age 13)
- Curious, plays to win, penny wise but pound foolish.
- Brave, persevering, never gives up.
- Individualistic and loves to play the hero.

Dr. Da Vinci (Age 60)
- A professor at the National Scientific Research Institute.
- A genius inventor.
- Highly knowledgeable, loves adventure, but lazy by nature.

Diana (Age 30)
- Research-based Administrator, the Doctor's helpful assistant.
- A mature, beautiful, and capable lady.
- Good at problem solving.

Emily (Age 13)
- Smart, responsible, and adaptive.
- Calm under pressure, slightly vain.
- Computer savvy.

Particle Transmitter
- One of Dr. Da Vinci's most important inventions.
- Able to teleport the team to any period of time and space to execute their missions.
- Able to send urgently needed items to the team at any time.

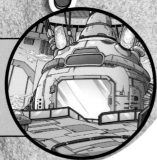

PREVIOUSLY...

A massive earthquake sent the DINOSAUR EXPLORERS millions of years into the past, and when they first emerged in the Cambrian, they had no idea what to do! Though they managed to jump away in time (literally!) to avoid sinister Silurian sea life, they found that their Particle Transmitter only allowed them to travel several million years at a time—a problem when you are over 500 million years in the past!

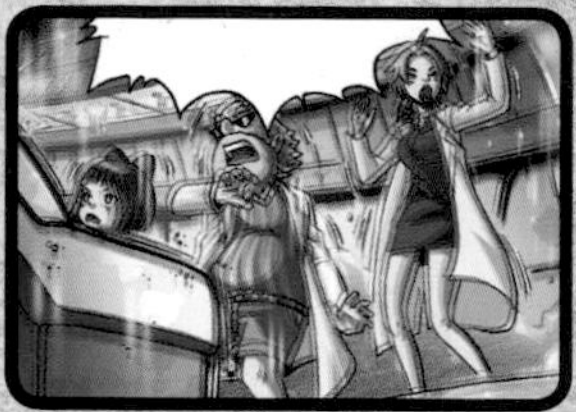

Cambrian

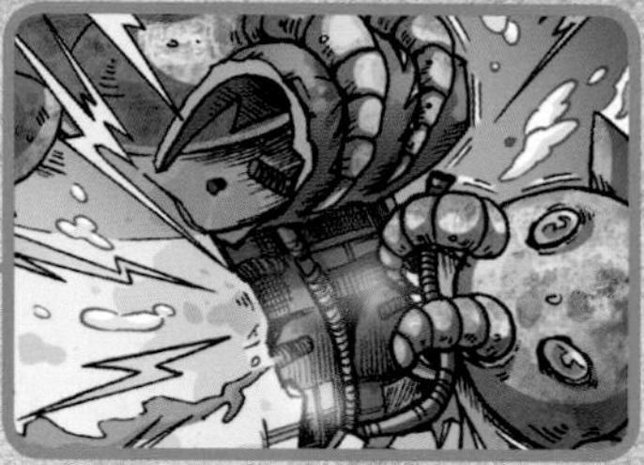

Ordovician

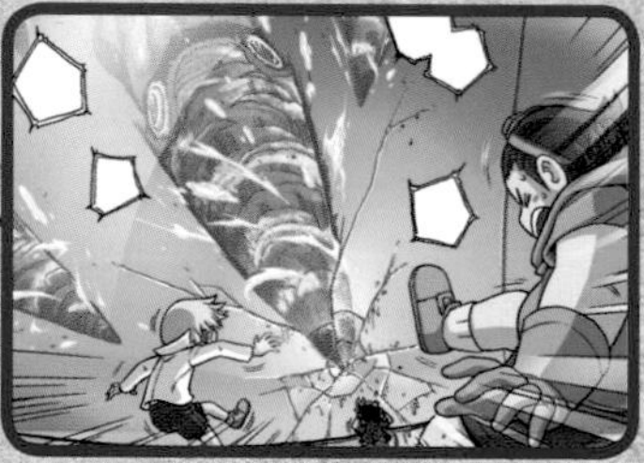

Silurian

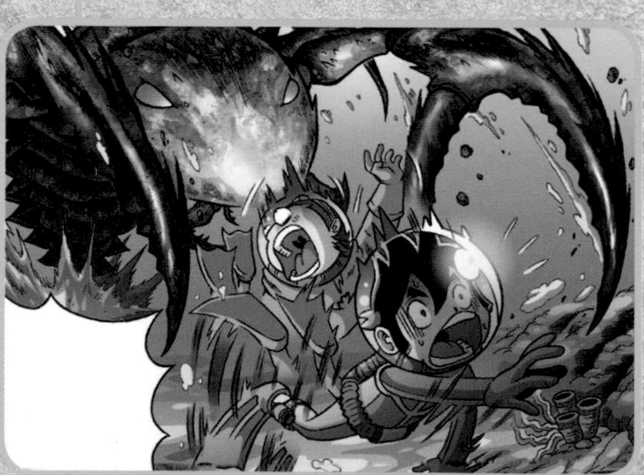

This came to a head in the Silurian when their worries and despair drove them to fighting among themselves. Incensed by Rain's jibes, Emily decided to set out with the DINOSAUR EXPLORERS to prove herself—and prove herself she did, facing everything from giant squid to sand-burrowing sea scorpions with guts and gusto!

Our heroes, heroines, and Dr. Da Vinci managed to escape the Silurian, only to end up facing the Devonian's major maulers, the Ichthyostega and Placodermi! Only a large dose of luck and dried fish saw them make their escape!

Things got bad in the Carboniferous when our protagonists and Dr. Da Vinci nearly became "Happy Meals" for some super-sized bugs! Giant spiders, giant dragonflies, and giant frogs (they might not have been bugs, but they were BIG!) all stood in the way of their attempt to study and escape the Carboniferous!

Devonian

Carboniferous

Permian

Triassic

Jurassic

Cretaceous

Tertiary

Quaternary

They then found themselves in the Permian, stuck with the proto-reptiles whose species would evolve into dinosaurs! Things only got more complicated when the Explorers discovered that their latest assignment included dino babysitting. Though not fans of escort missions, our heroes successfully pulled it off in time to travel... to the Triassic!

*The size of this graphic novel's dinosaurs are exaggerated, and do not really represent the true sizes of the creatures. Hey, it makes for a more visually exciting story!

CHAPTER 1

TRIASSIC TRANSPORT

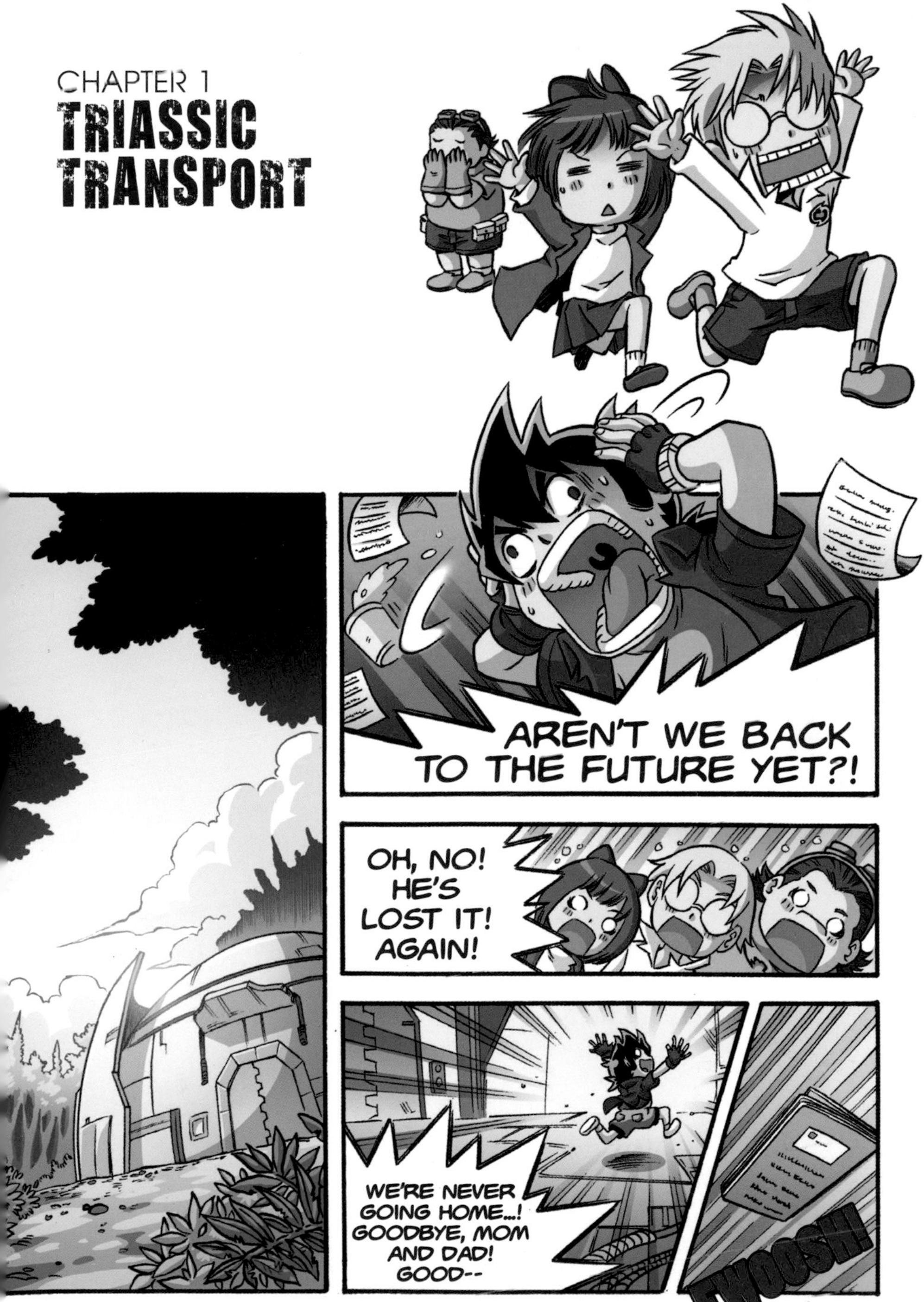

AREN'T WE BACK TO THE FUTURE YET?!
OH, NO! HE'S LOST IT! AGAIN!
WE'RE NEVER GOING HOME...! GOODBYE, MOM AND DAD! GOOD--
FWOOSH!

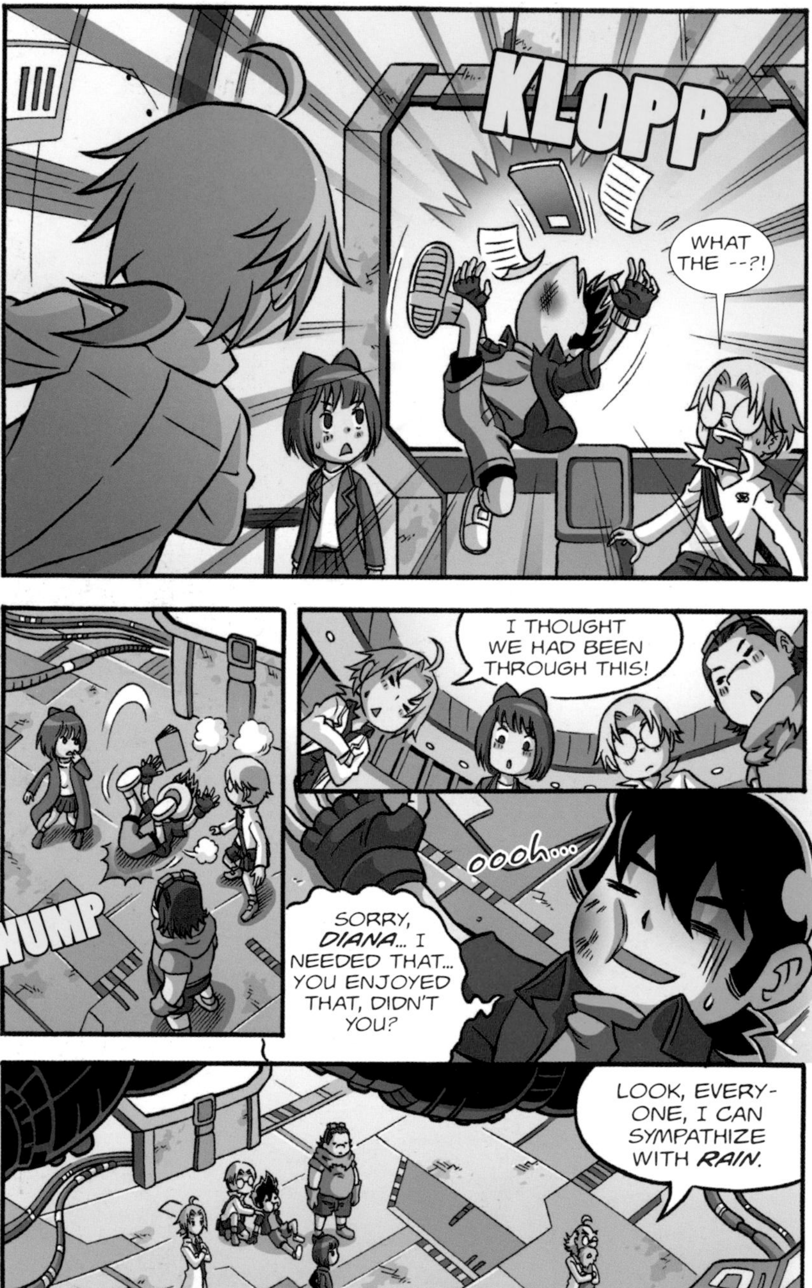
KLOPP
WHAT THE --?!
WUMP
I THOUGHT WE HAD BEEN THROUGH THIS!
oooh...
SORRY, DIANA... I NEEDED THAT... YOU ENJOYED THAT, DIDN'T YOU?
LOOK, EVERY-ONE, I CAN SYMPATHIZE WITH RAIN.

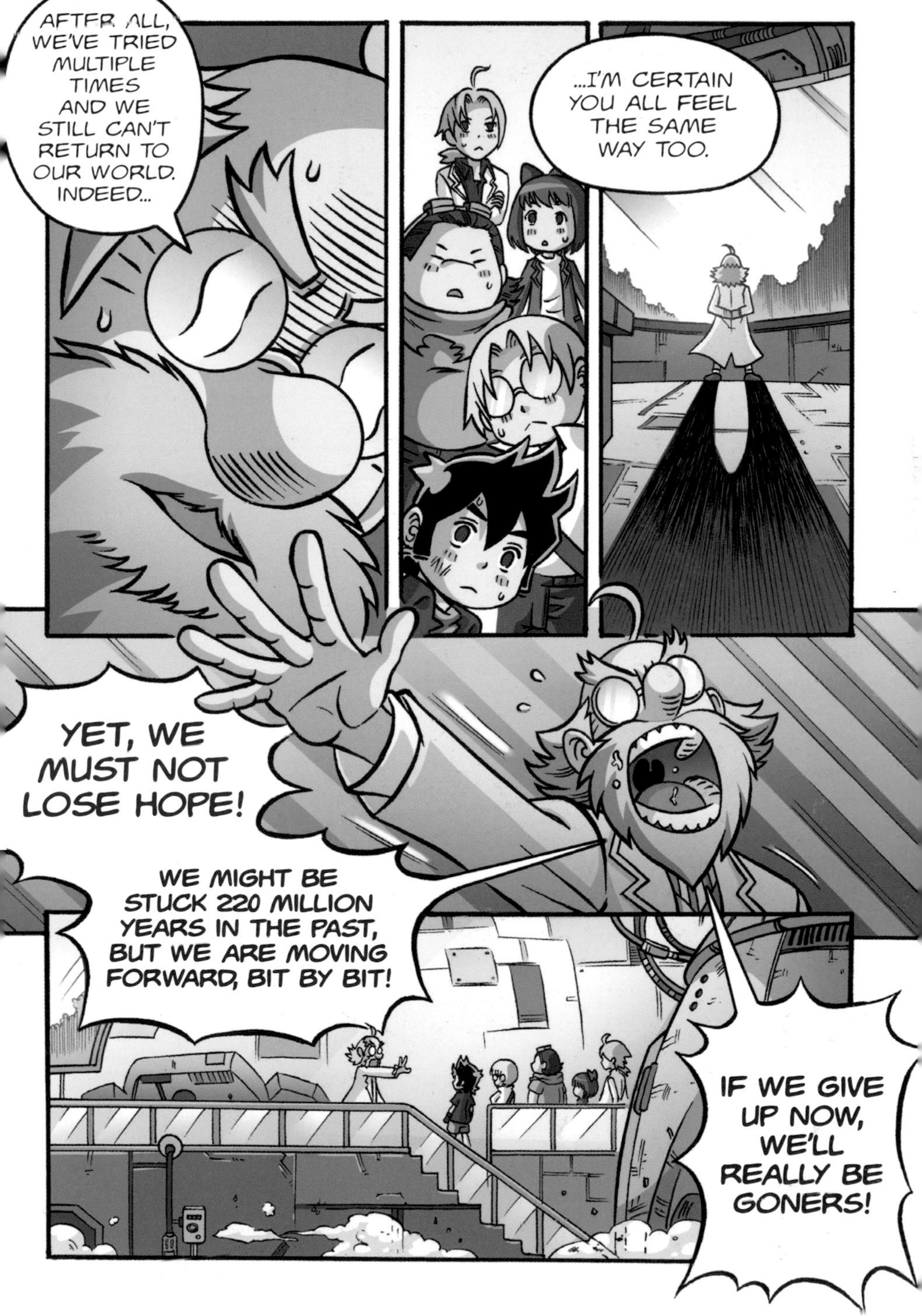
AFTER ALL, WE'VE TRIED MULTIPLE TIMES AND WE STILL CAN'T RETURN TO OUR WORLD. INDEED...
...I'M CERTAIN YOU ALL FEEL THE SAME WAY TOO.
YET, WE MUST NOT LOSE HOPE!
WE MIGHT BE STUCK 220 MILLION YEARS IN THE PAST, BUT WE ARE MOVING FORWARD, BIT BY BIT!
IF WE GIVE UP NOW, WE'LL REALLY BE GONERS!

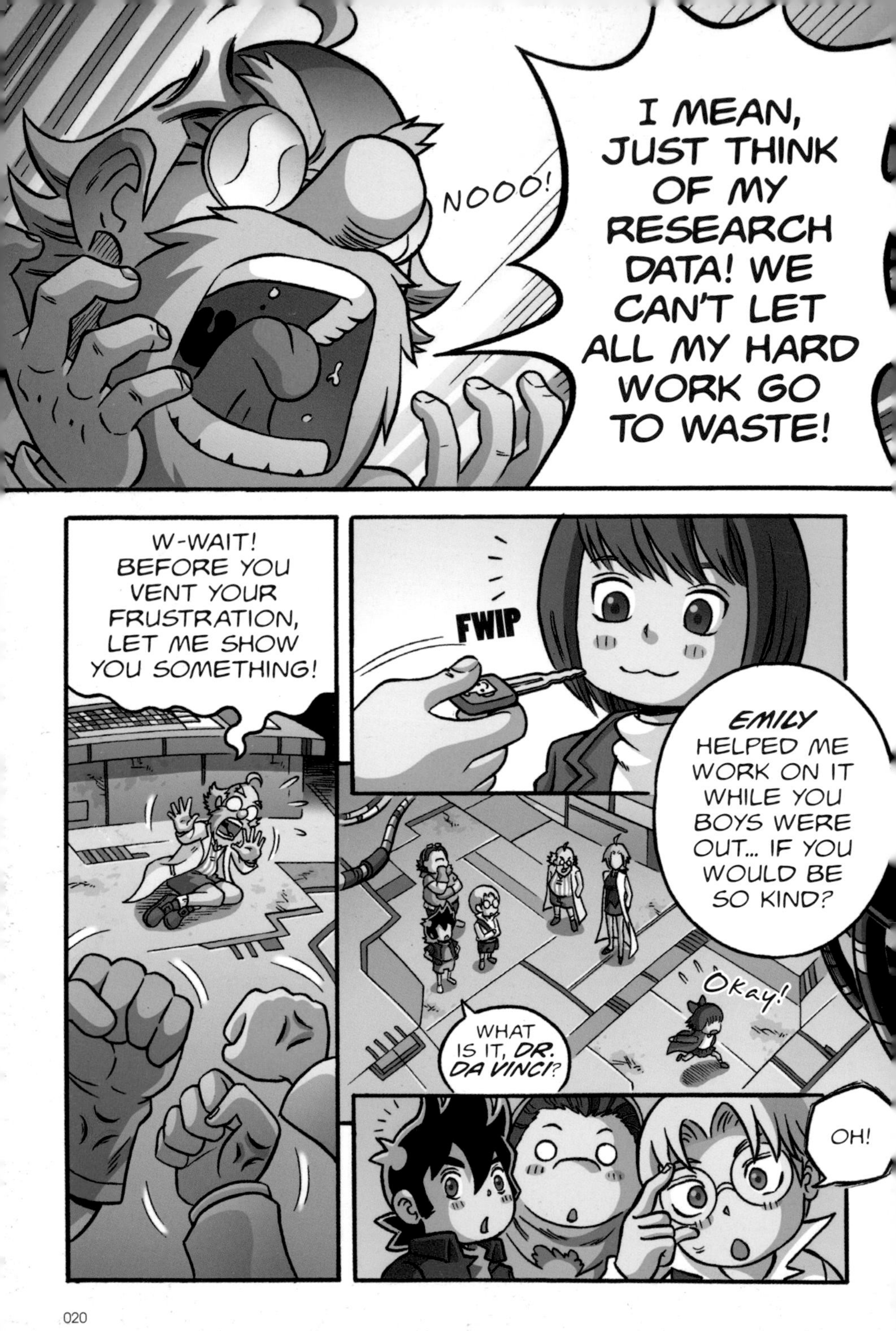
NOOO!
I MEAN, JUST THINK OF MY RESEARCH DATA! WE CAN'T LET ALL MY HARD WORK GO TO WASTE!
W-WAIT! BEFORE YOU VENT YOUR FRUSTRATION, LET ME SHOW YOU SOMETHING!
FWIP
EMILY HELPED ME WORK ON IT WHILE YOU BOYS WERE OUT... IF YOU WOULD BE SO KIND?
Okay!
WHAT IS IT, DR. DA VINCI?
OH!

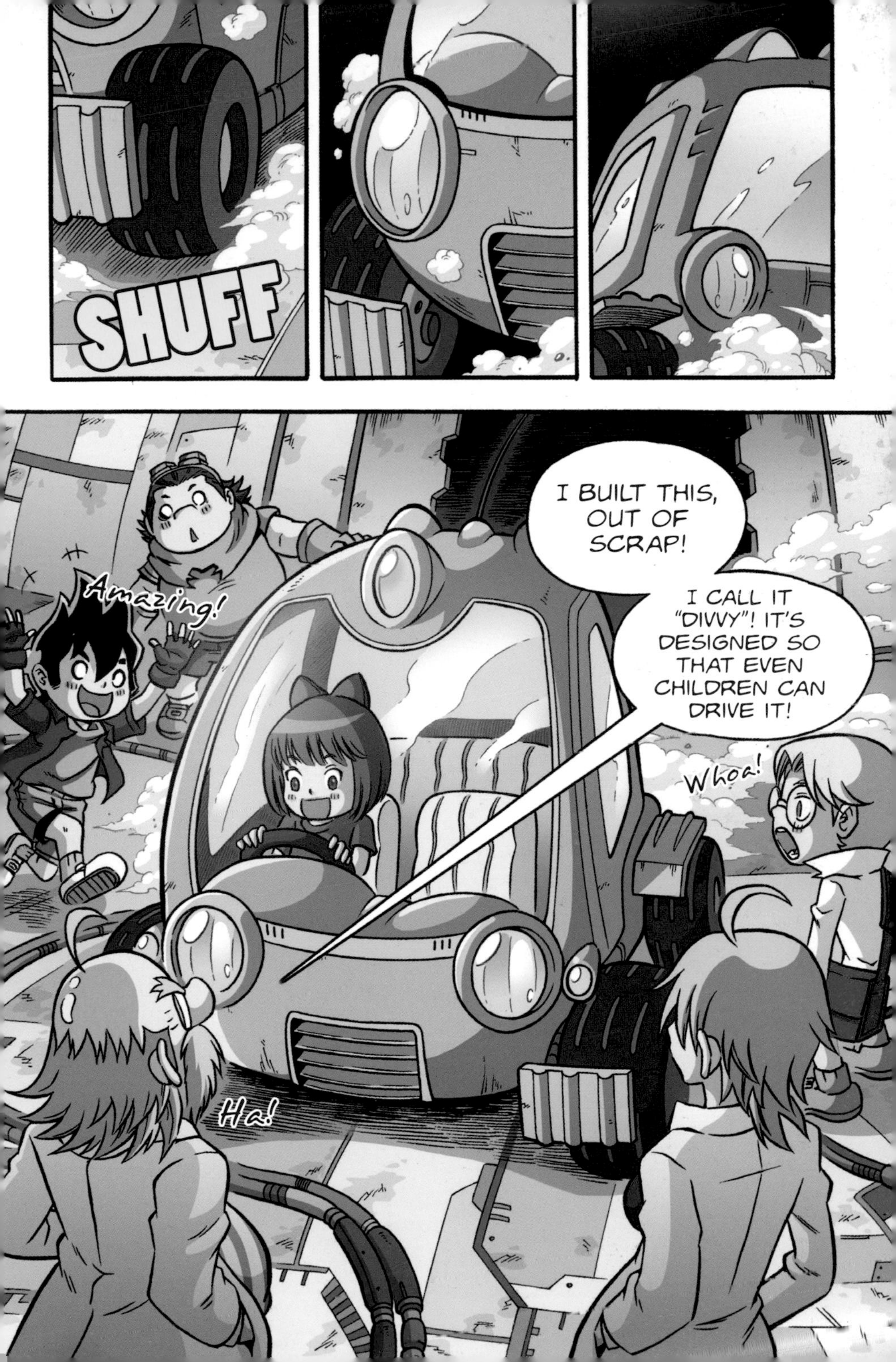
SHUFF
Amazing!
I BUILT THIS, OUT OF SCRAP!
I CALL IT "DIVVY"! IT'S DESIGNED SO THAT EVEN CHILDREN CAN DRIVE IT!
Whoa!
Ha!

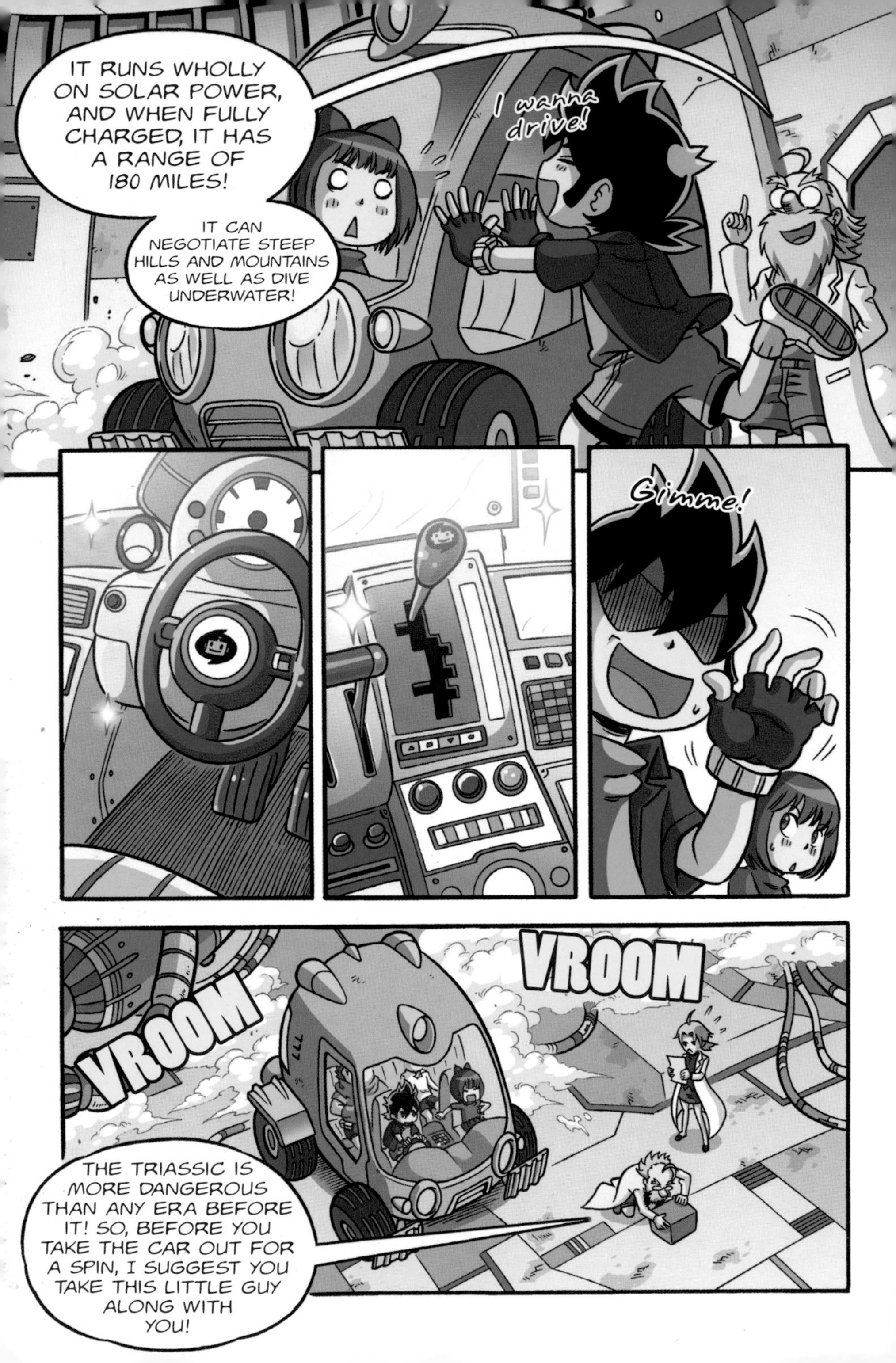
IT RUNS WHOLLY ON SOLAR POWER, AND WHEN FULLY CHARGED, IT HAS A RANGE OF 180 MILES!
IT CAN NEGOTIATE STEEP HILLS AND MOUNTAINS AS WELL AS DIVE UNDERWATER!
I wanna drive!
Gimme!
VROOM
VROOM
THE TRIASSIC IS MORE DANGEROUS THAN ANY ERA BEFORE IT! SO, BEFORE YOU TAKE THE CAR OUT FOR A SPIN, I SUGGEST YOU TAKE THIS LITTLE GUY ALONG WITH YOU!

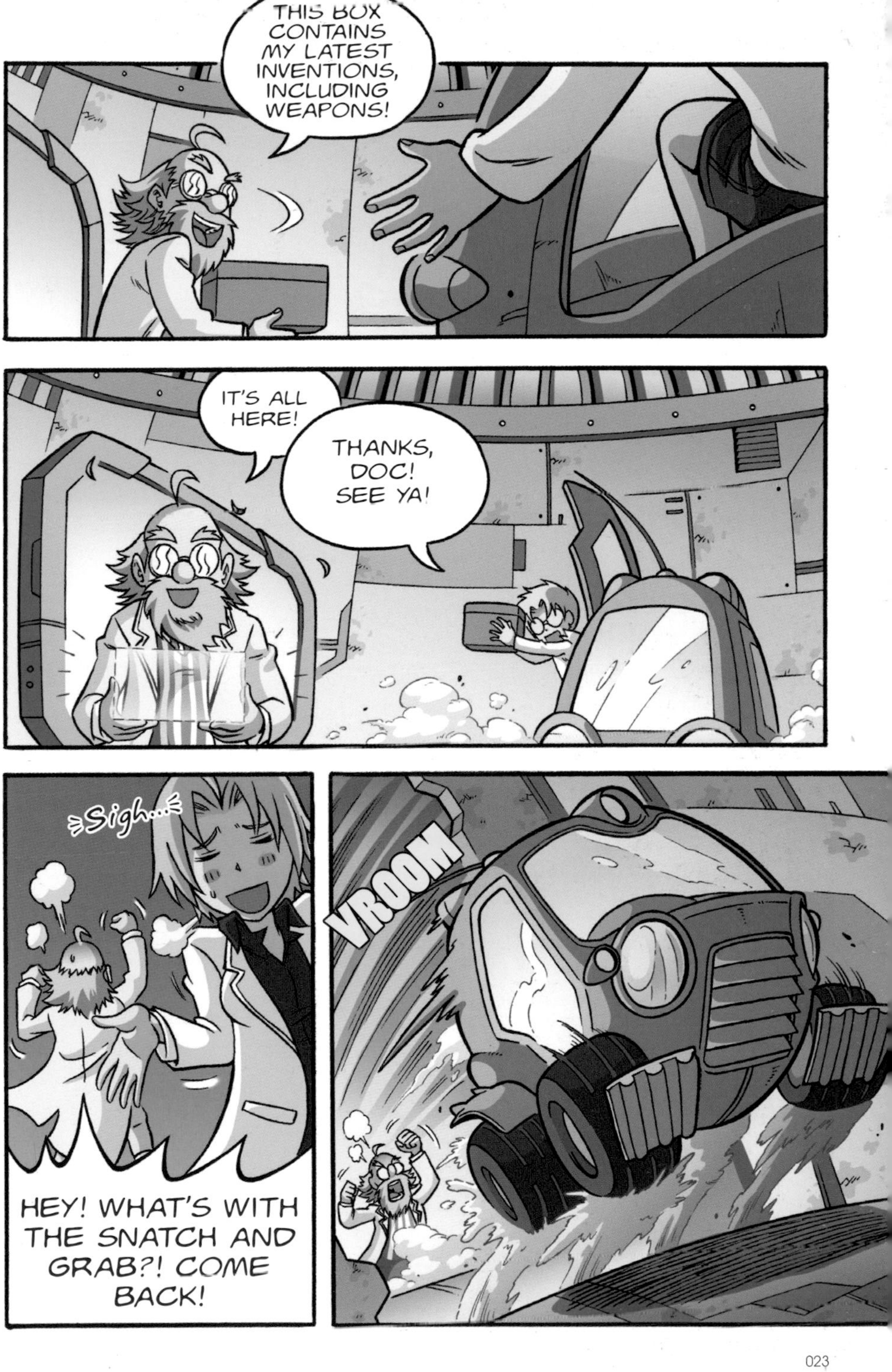
THIS BOX CONTAINS MY LATEST INVENTIONS, INCLUDING WEAPONS!
IT'S ALL HERE!
THANKS, DOC! SEE YA!
Sigh...
HEY! WHAT'S WITH THE SNATCH AND GRAB?! COME BACK!
VROOM

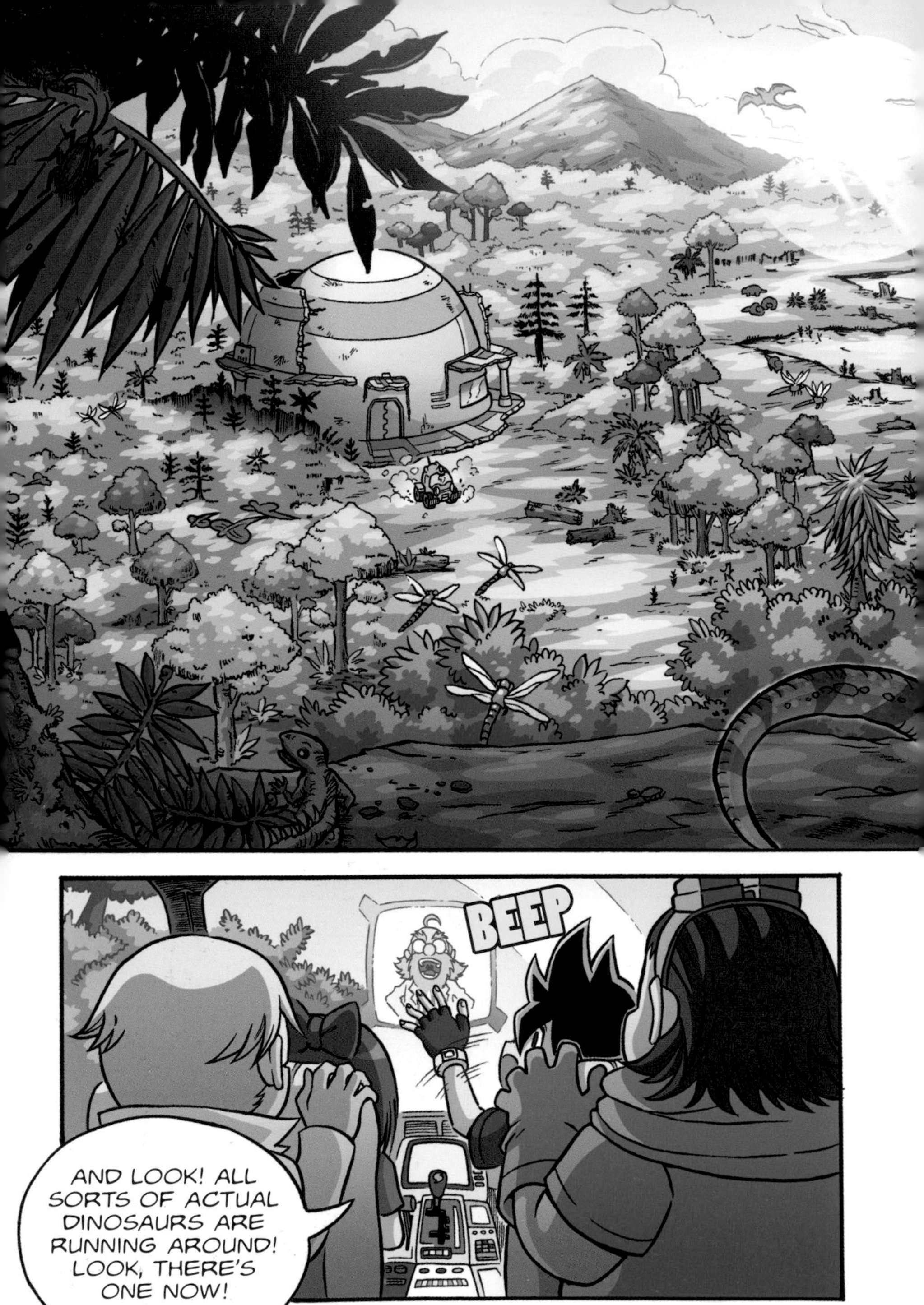
BEEP
AND LOOK! ALL SORTS OF ACTUAL DINOSAURS ARE RUNNING AROUND! LOOK, THERE'S ONE NOW!

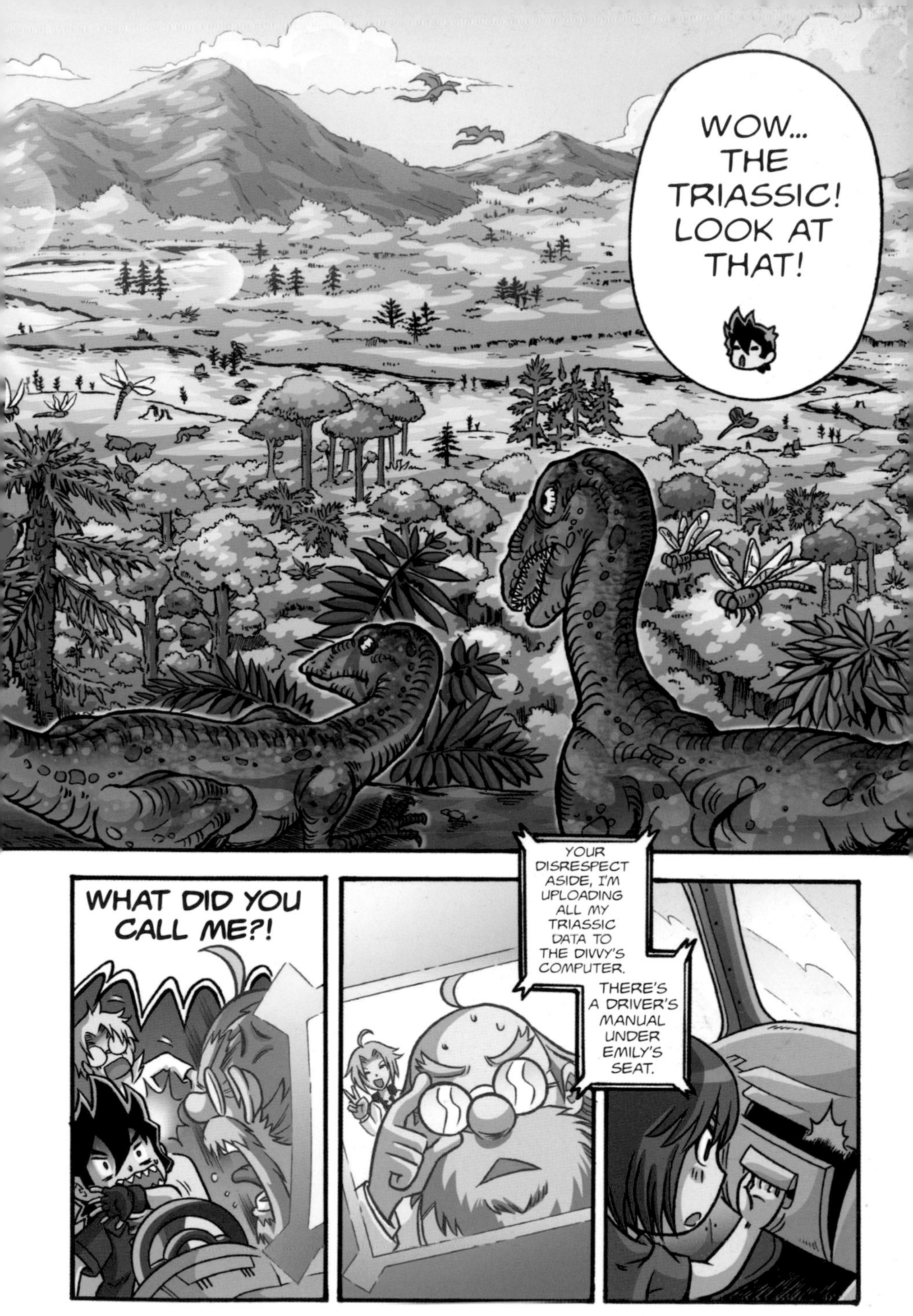
WOW... THE TRIASSIC! LOOK AT THAT!
WHAT DID YOU CALL ME?!
YOUR DISRESPECT ASIDE, I'M UPLOADING ALL MY TRIASSIC DATA TO THE DIVVY'S COMPUTER.
THERE'S A DRIVER'S MANUAL UNDER EMILY'S SEAT.

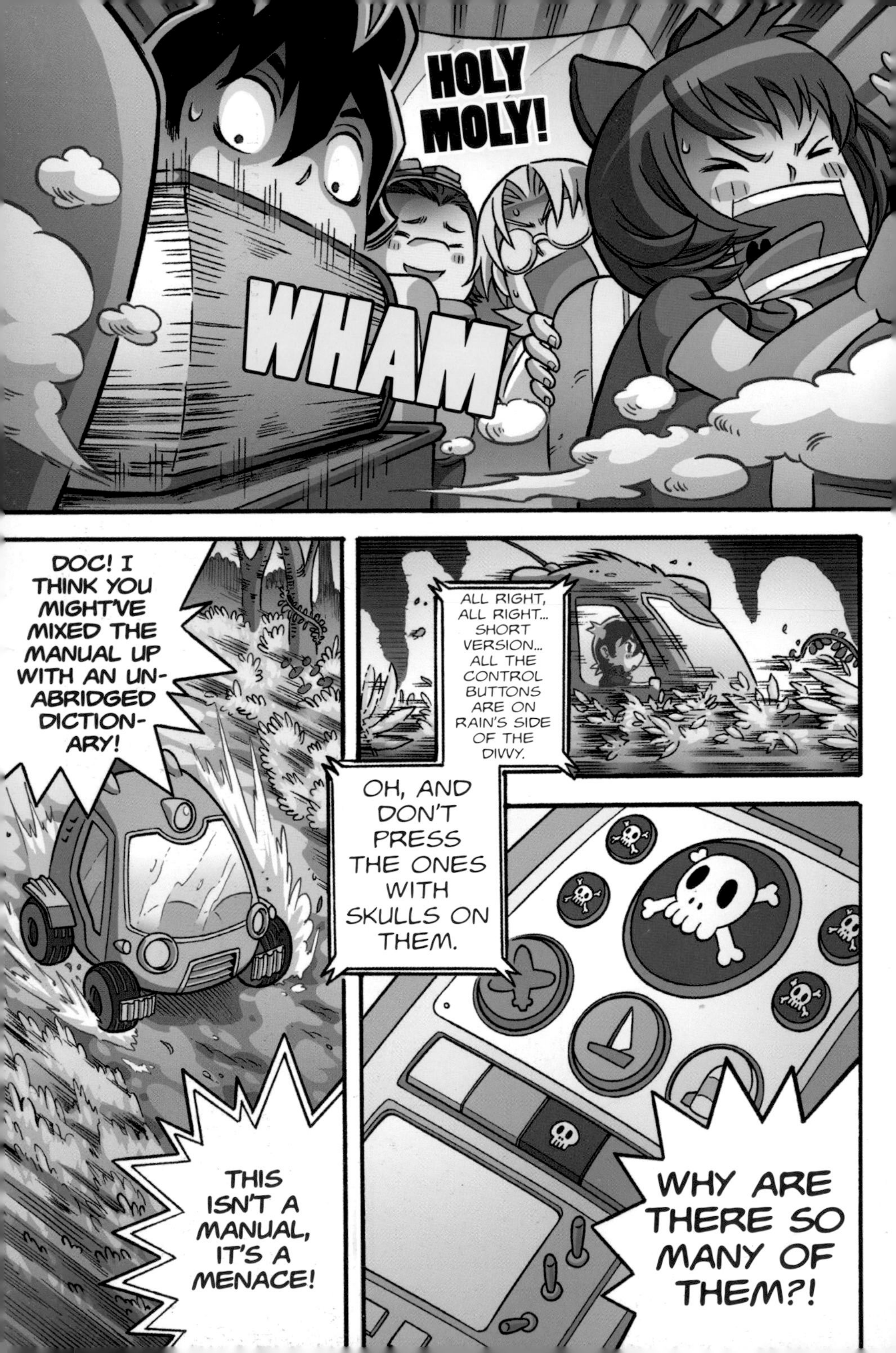
HOLY MOLY!
WHAM
DOC! I THINK YOU MIGHT'VE MIXED THE MANUAL UP WITH AN UN-ABRIDGED DICTION-ARY!
ALL RIGHT, ALL RIGHT... SHORT VERSION... ALL THE CONTROL BUTTONS ARE ON RAIN'S SIDE OF THE DIVVY.
OH, AND DON'T PRESS THE ONES WITH SKULLS ON THEM.
THIS ISN'T A MANUAL, IT'S A MENACE!
WHY ARE THERE SO MANY OF THEM?!

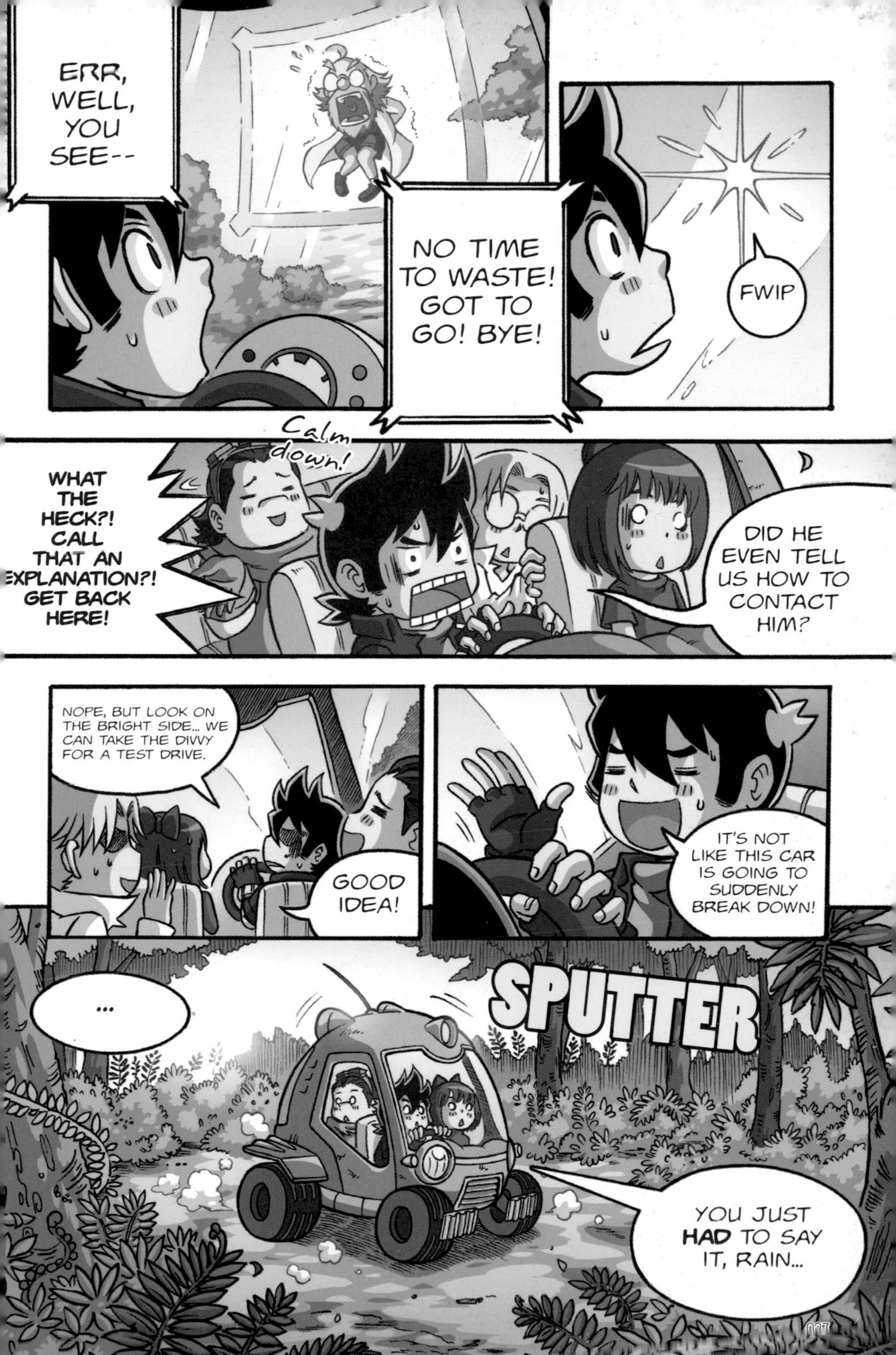
ERR, WELL, YOU SEE--
NO TIME TO WASTE! GOT TO GO! BYE!
FWIP
Calm down!
WHAT THE HECK?! CALL THAT AN EXPLANATION?! GET BACK HERE!
DID HE EVEN TELL US HOW TO CONTACT HIM?
NOPE, BUT LOOK ON THE BRIGHT SIDE... WE CAN TAKE THE DIVVY FOR A TEST DRIVE.
GOOD IDEA!
IT'S NOT LIKE THIS CAR IS GOING TO SUDDENLY BREAK DOWN!
...
SPUTTER
YOU JUST **HAD** TO SAY IT, RAIN...

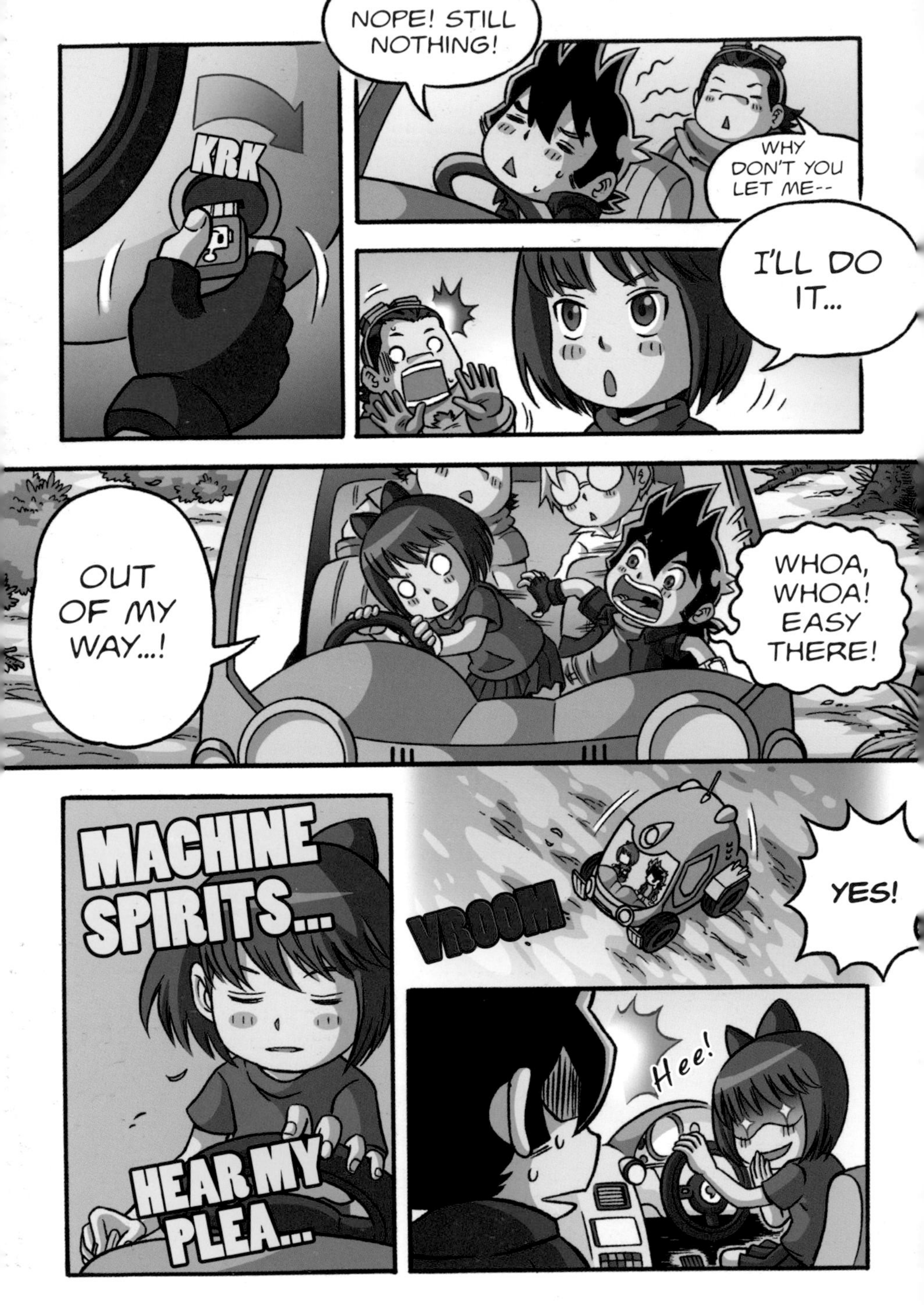
NOPE! STILL NOTHING!
KRK
WHY DON'T YOU LET ME--
I'LL DO IT...
OUT OF MY WAY...!
WHOA, WHOA! EASY THERE!
MACHINE SPIRITS...
HEAR MY PLEA...
VROOM
YES!
Hee!

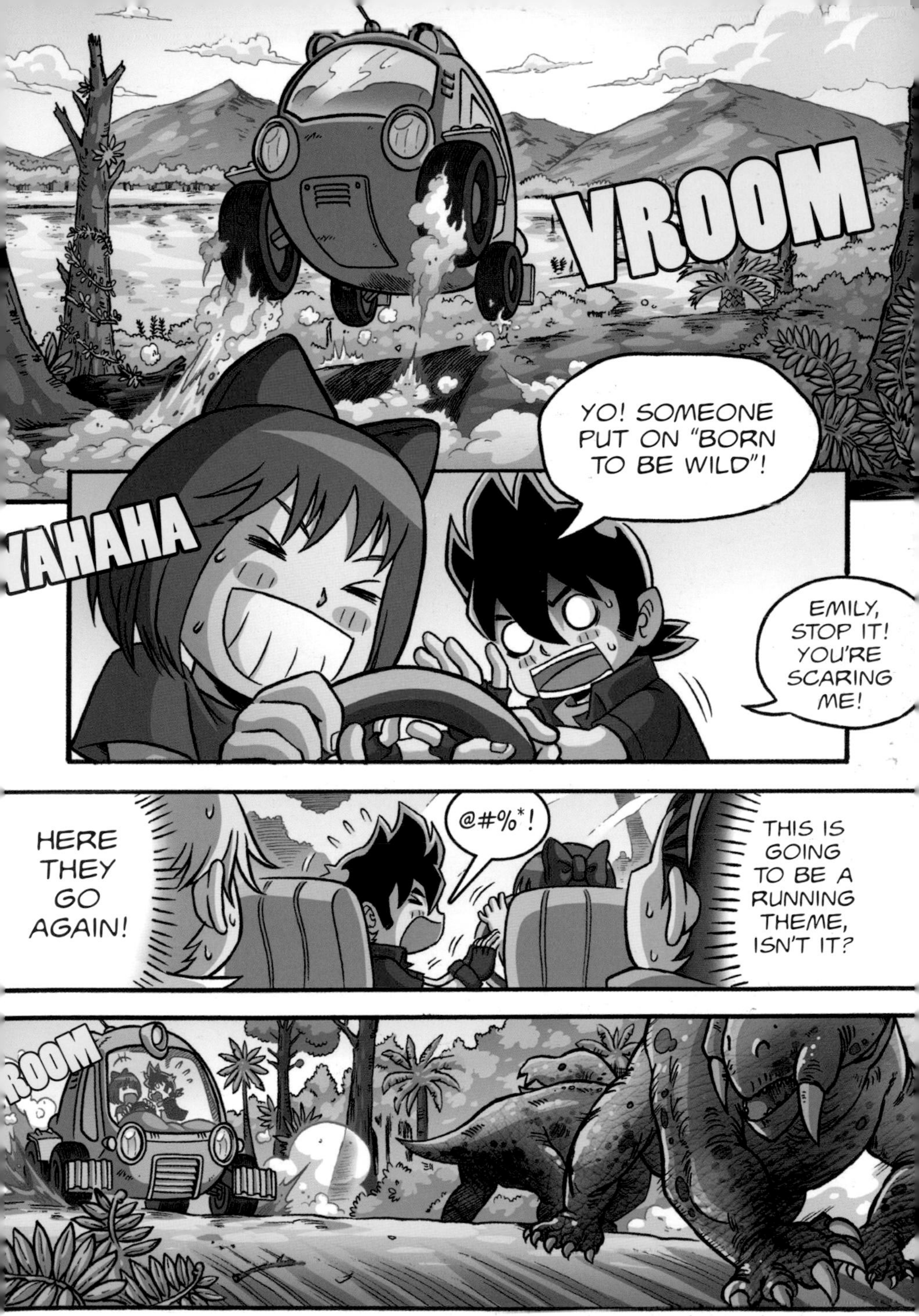
VROOM
YO! SOMEONE PUT ON "BORN TO BE WILD"!
YAHAHA
EMILY, STOP IT! YOU'RE SCARING ME!
HERE THEY GO AGAIN!
@#%*!
THIS IS GOING TO BE A RUNNING THEME, ISN'T IT?
ROOM

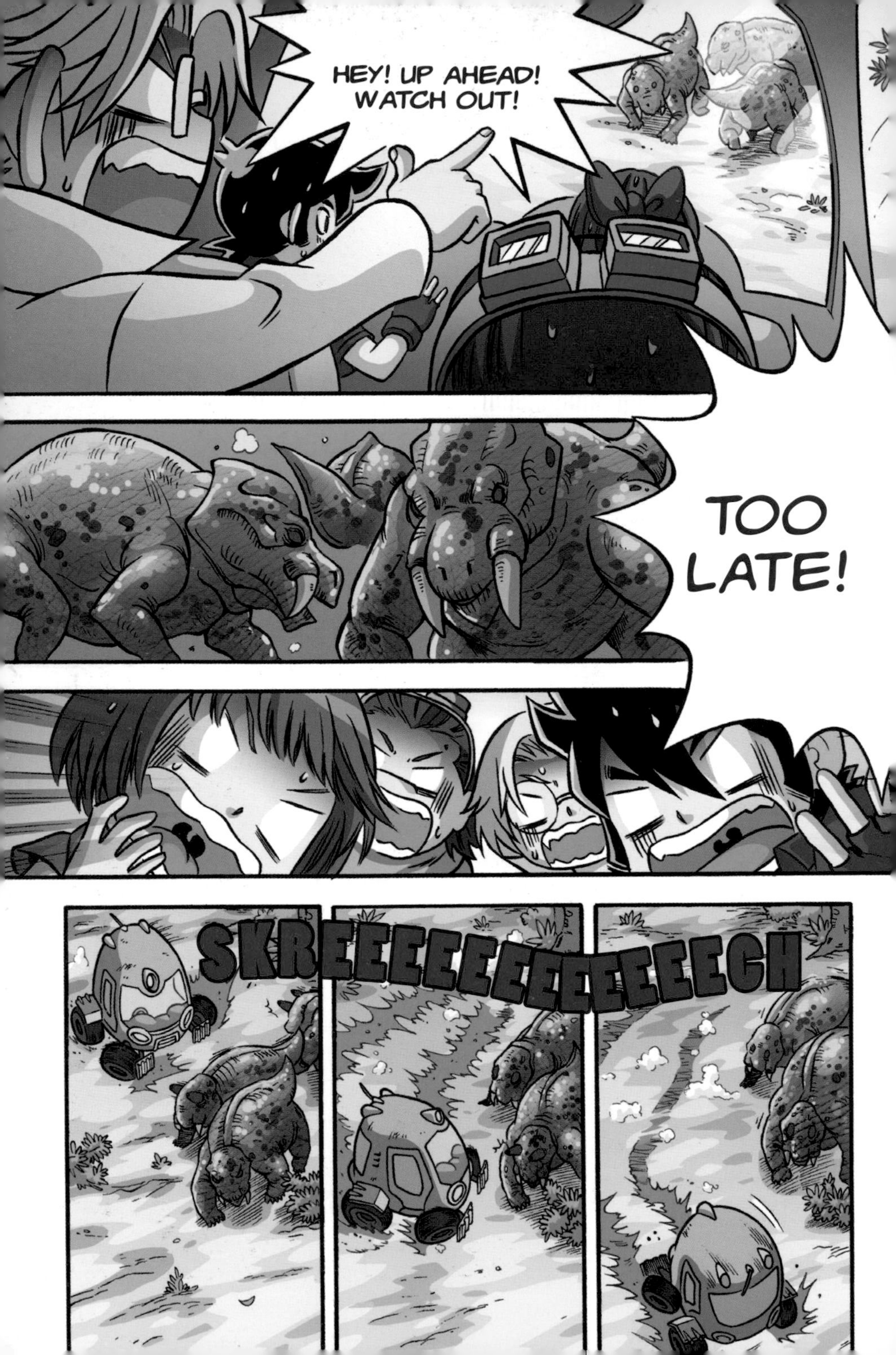
HEY! UP AHEAD!
WATCH OUT!
TOO
LATE!
SKREEEEEEEEEEEEECH

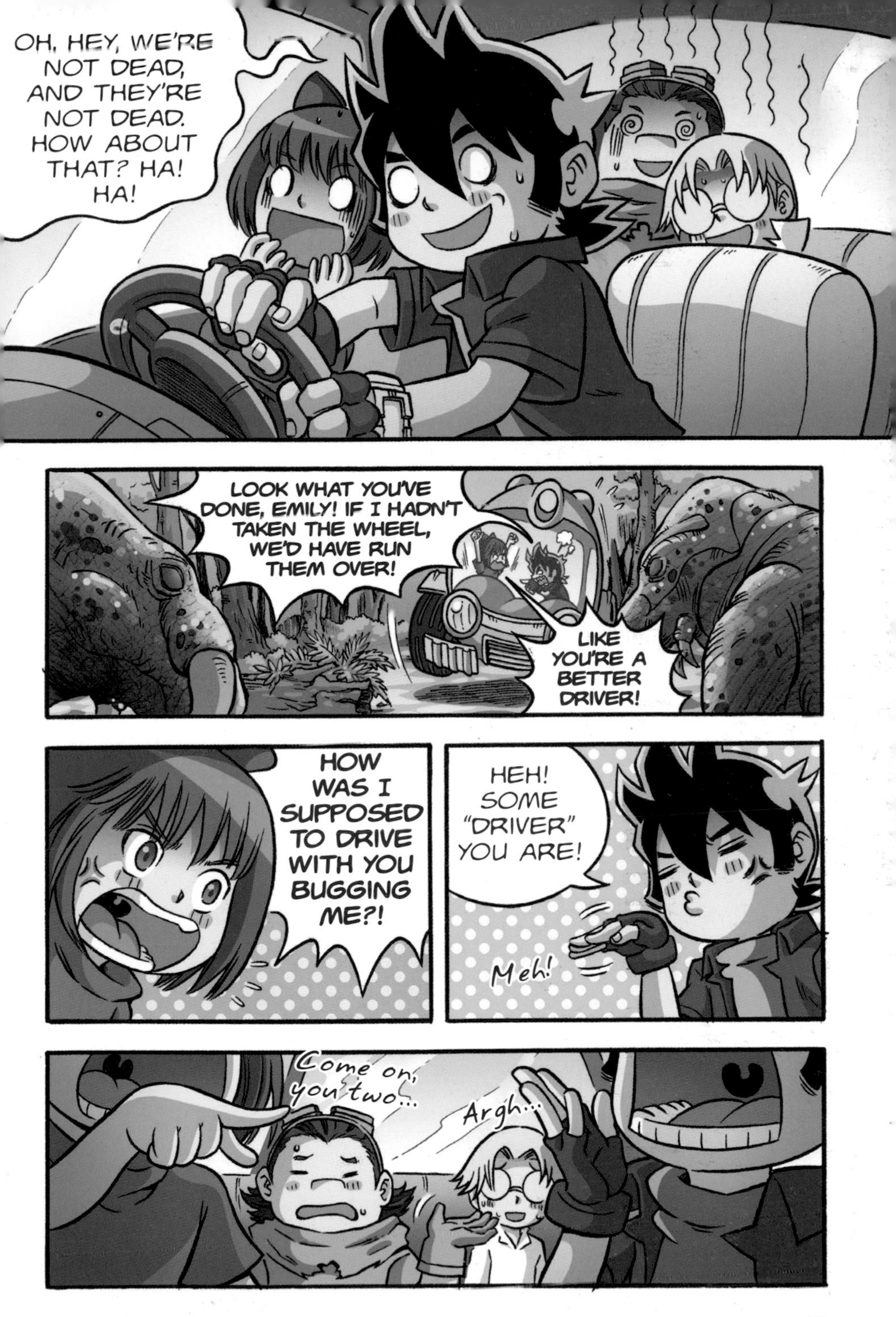
OH, HEY, WE'RE NOT DEAD, AND THEY'RE NOT DEAD. HOW ABOUT THAT? HA! HA!
LOOK WHAT YOU'VE DONE, EMILY! IF I HADN'T TAKEN THE WHEEL, WE'D HAVE RUN THEM OVER!
LIKE YOU'RE A BETTER DRIVER!
HOW WAS I SUPPOSED TO DRIVE WITH YOU BUGGING ME?!
HEH! SOME "DRIVER" YOU ARE!
Meh!
Come on, you two...
Argh...

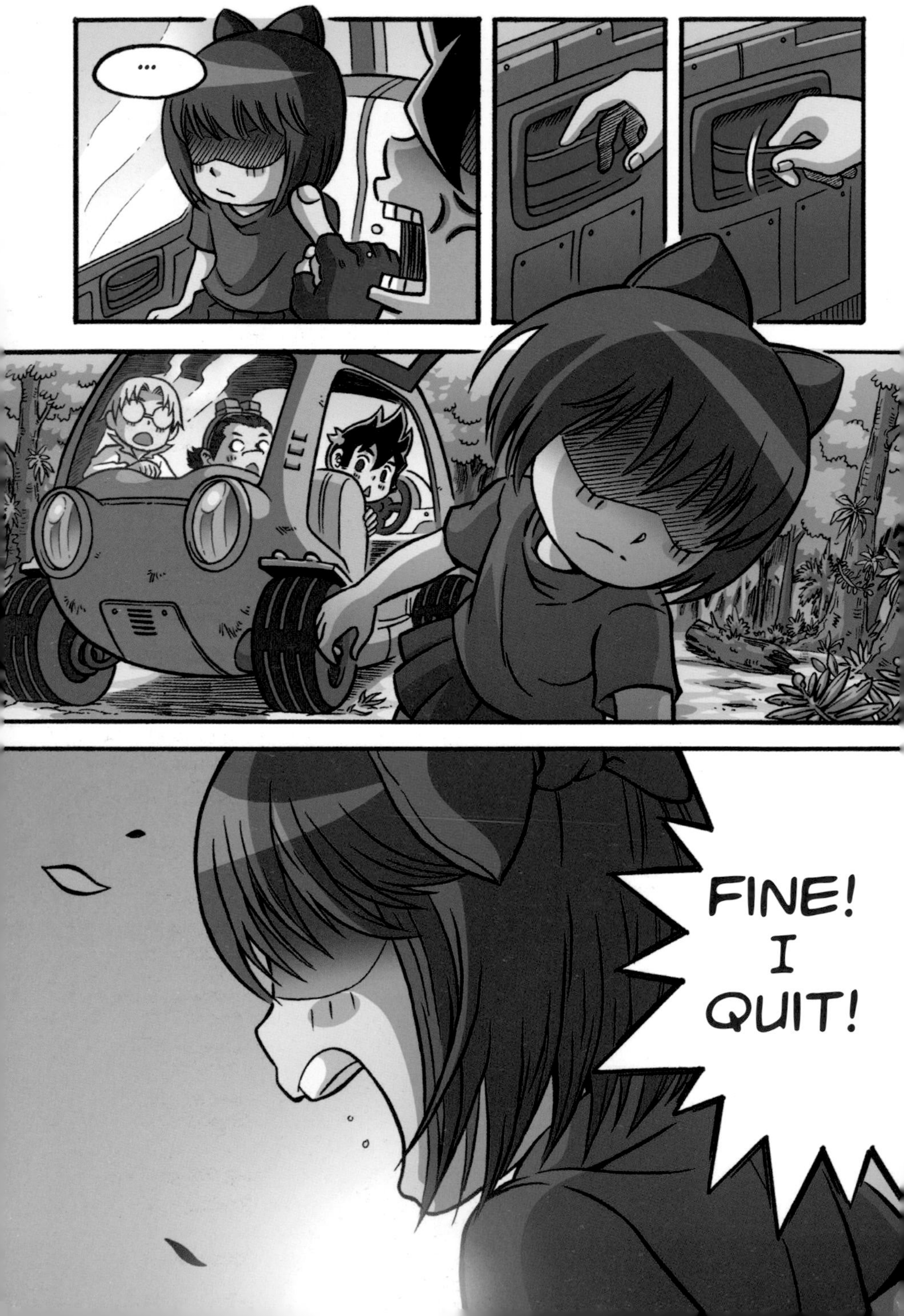
...
FINE! I QUIT!

CONTINENTS OF THE TRIASSIC

During the Triassic, the only land on Earth was the supercontinent "Pangaea," which was located at the equator and connected the North and South Pole. A narrow sea separated what would be today's North American and European continents, and the Tethys Ocean submerged much of the European continent. Through the Mid-Triassic period, the shape of the modern world gradually became more evident, hinting of the split of the Pangaean supercontinent.

Tethys Ocean
Pangaea

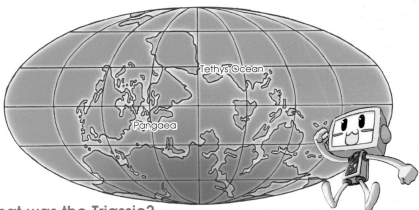

What was the Triassic?

The Triassic was the seventh period in the Earth's geological time scale, and the first of the Mesozoic era. This era began approximately 250 million years ago and ended around 203 million years ago. Additionally, this era was marked by two mass extinctions which occurred just before the Permian-Triassic extinction event and right after the Late Triassic extinction event. There was also a great change in the environment due to the super continent slowly separating. The vast global Panthalassic Ocean surrounded the supercontinent of Pangaea, and was thought to be larger than all oceans of today combined.

I SHALL CALL IT-- **THE TRIASSIC**!

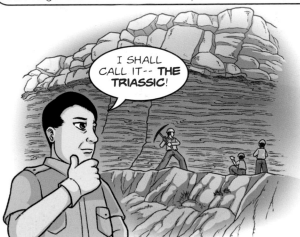

Origin of the name "Triassic"

In 1834 the German geologist Friedrich August Von Alberti named the period after the three geological layers present in sedimentary deposits throughout northern Europe.

Was the environment of Pangaea suitable for plants?

Only the coastal areas; due to its huge expanse of land, winds from the sea were unable to carry moisture deeper into the interior. As a result, the center of Pangaea was largely desert, and compared to other geological eras, the climate was much warmer and drier. As continents combined, what were once originally coastal areas became land, stranding many marine creatures. While Pangaea's general environment worsened over time, however, stronger creatures prevailed, eventually evolving to fill the niches extinct species had left behind, populating the Triassic with new life forms.

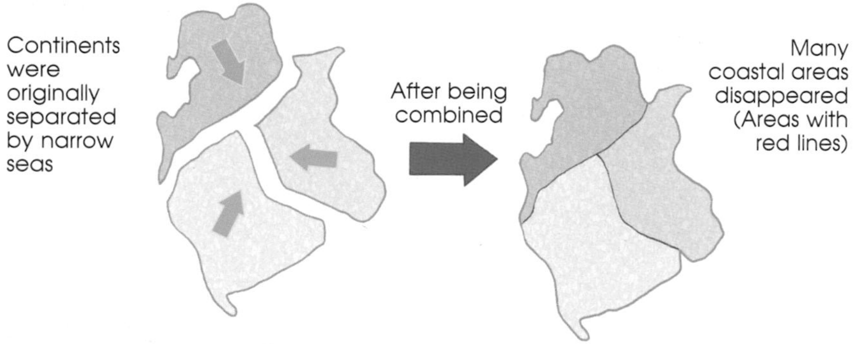
Continents were originally separated by narrow seas
After being combined
Many coastal areas disappeared (Areas with red lines)

What plants existed in the Triassic?

Most of the plants in the previous era went extinct in the Triassic; it was a time when evergreen plants thrived. In areas close to the sea and with ample amounts of rain, one would have discovered large quantities of ferns which gave way in the late Triassic to cycads, conifers, and ginkgoaceae. Furthermore, flowering plants (angiosperms) began to appear during this period.

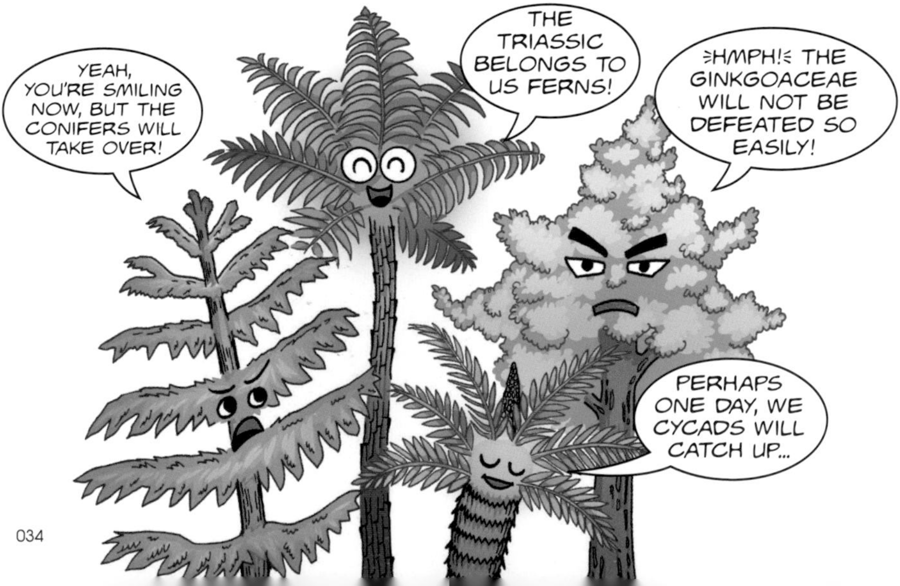
YEAH, YOU'RE SMILING NOW, BUT THE CONIFERS WILL TAKE OVER!
THE TRIASSIC BELONGS TO US FERNS!
≶HMPH!≶ THE GINKGOACEAE WILL NOT BE DEFEATED SO EASILY!
PERHAPS ONE DAY, WE CYCADS WILL CATCH UP...

What could be found in the Triassic sea?

During the Triassic, the first modern corals appeared, forming small reefs. Prehistoric marine creatures were eventually replaced by the Actinopterygii, early sharks, and rays. As for marine reptiles, the ichthyosaurs of the Triassic had adapted to underwater life, capable of surviving in the sea for long periods of time.

The Triassic occurred between two mass extinctions; was it a hard place to live?

Though many species died off in the Late Permian mass extinction, stronger species prevailed. Indeed, by sheer virtue of survival, these species were now able to withstand more demanding environments, becoming the early ancestors of modern life. As for the Late Triassic mass extinction, though many species died out, this also left the Earth bare enough to accommodate dinosaurs.

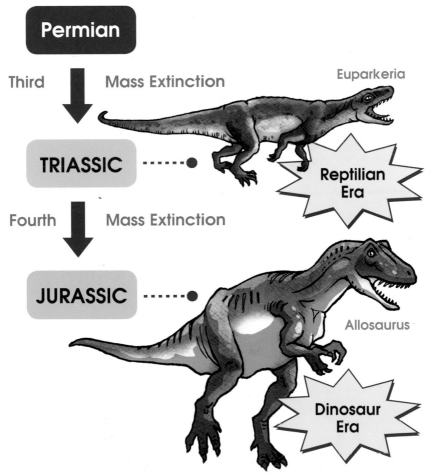

Permian

Third Mass Extinction

Euparkeria

TRIASSIC ······●

Reptilian Era

Fourth Mass Extinction

JURASSIC ······●

Allosaurus

Dinosaur Era

Did the terrifying Dimetrodon survive the Triassic?

Unfortunately not. Most of the land vertebrates of the Permian, including the Dimetrodon, disappeared after the Permian-Triassic extinction event. Nevertheless, the Triassic remained an era of reptiles, with many signs of their existence. Not only did early crocodiles and tortoises begin evolving, but pterosaurs and other dinosaur species as well.

Did the dinosaurs appear in the Triassic?

Yes, the dinosaurs finally emerged in the Triassic Era. The climate and environment, however, were quite singular, not enough to drive dinosaurs into different routes of evolution. Hence, there were only few dinosaur species during this era and their sizes were not comparable to those that emerged later. Truly gigantic dinosaurs and a wide variety of species only appeared in the late Triassic.

Similar dinosaurs of the Triassic

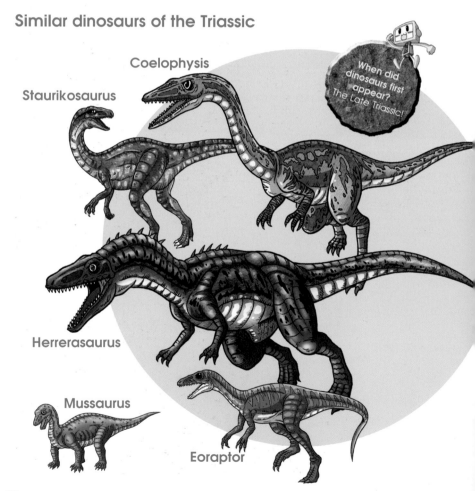

Coelophysis

Staurikosaurus

When did dinosaurs first appear? The Late Triassic!

Herrerasaurus

Mussaurus

Eoraptor

CHAPTER 2
ROCK OF AGES

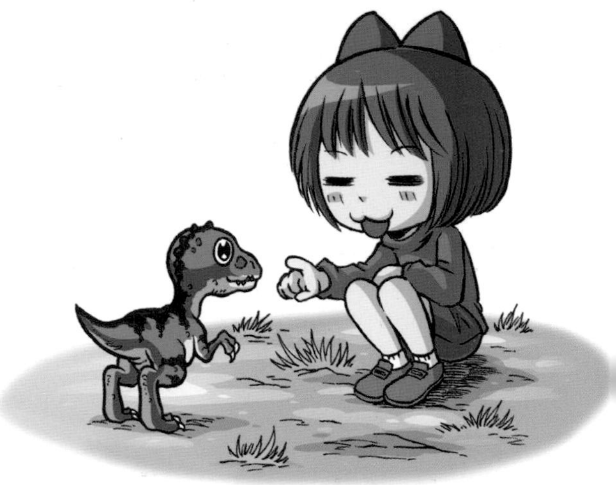

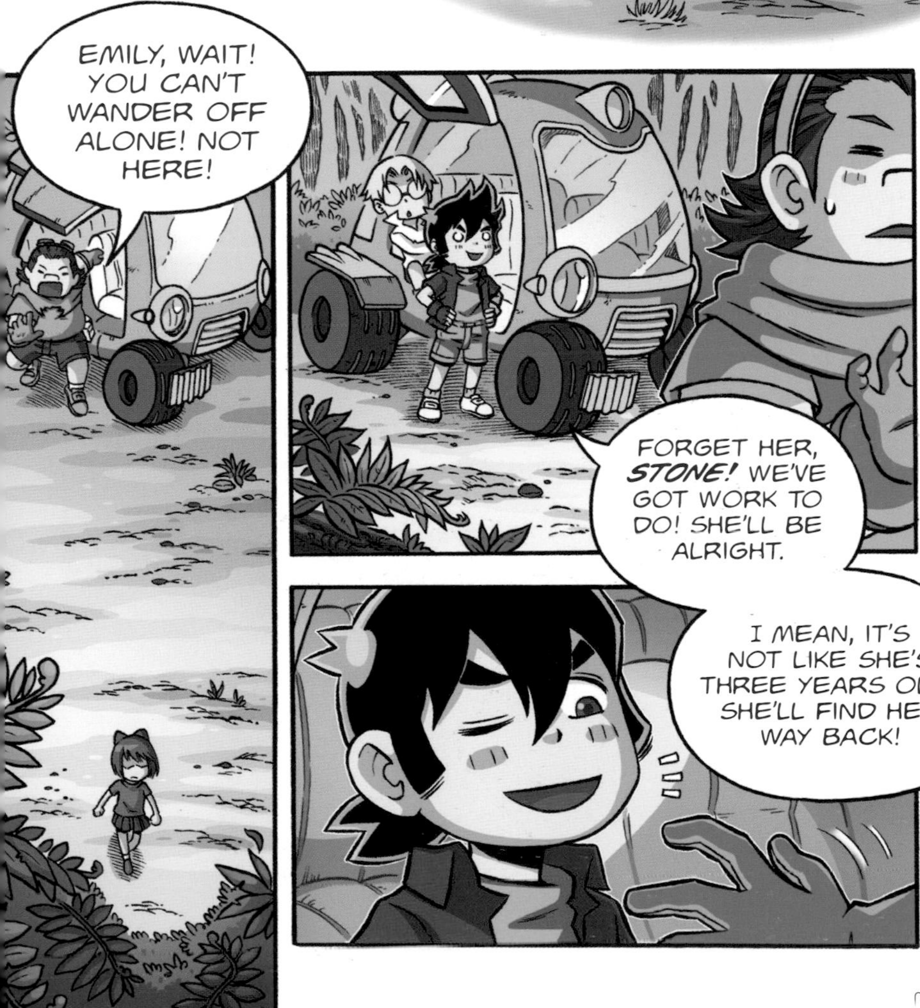
EMILY, WAIT! YOU CAN'T WANDER OFF ALONE! NOT HERE!
FORGET HER, STONE! WE'VE GOT WORK TO DO! SHE'LL BE ALRIGHT.
I MEAN, IT'S NOT LIKE SHE'S THREE YEARS OLD... SHE'LL FIND HER WAY BACK!

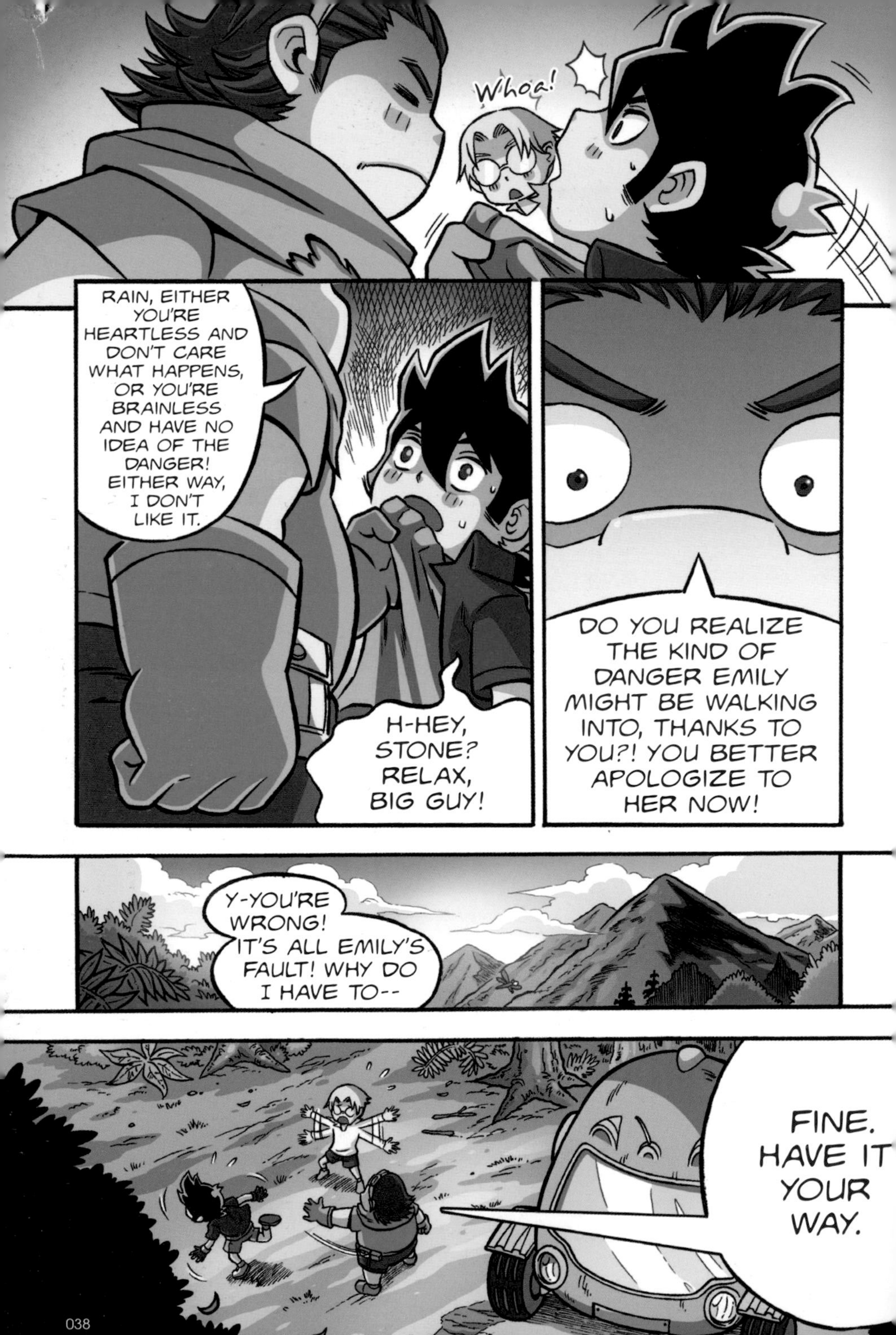
Whoa!
RAIN, EITHER YOU'RE HEARTLESS AND DON'T CARE WHAT HAPPENS, OR YOU'RE BRAINLESS AND HAVE NO IDEA OF THE DANGER! EITHER WAY, I DON'T LIKE IT.
H-HEY, STONE? RELAX, BIG GUY!
DO YOU REALIZE THE KIND OF DANGER EMILY MIGHT BE WALKING INTO, THANKS TO YOU?! YOU BETTER APOLOGIZE TO HER NOW!
Y-YOU'RE WRONG! IT'S ALL EMILY'S FAULT! WHY DO I HAVE TO--
FINE. HAVE IT YOUR WAY.

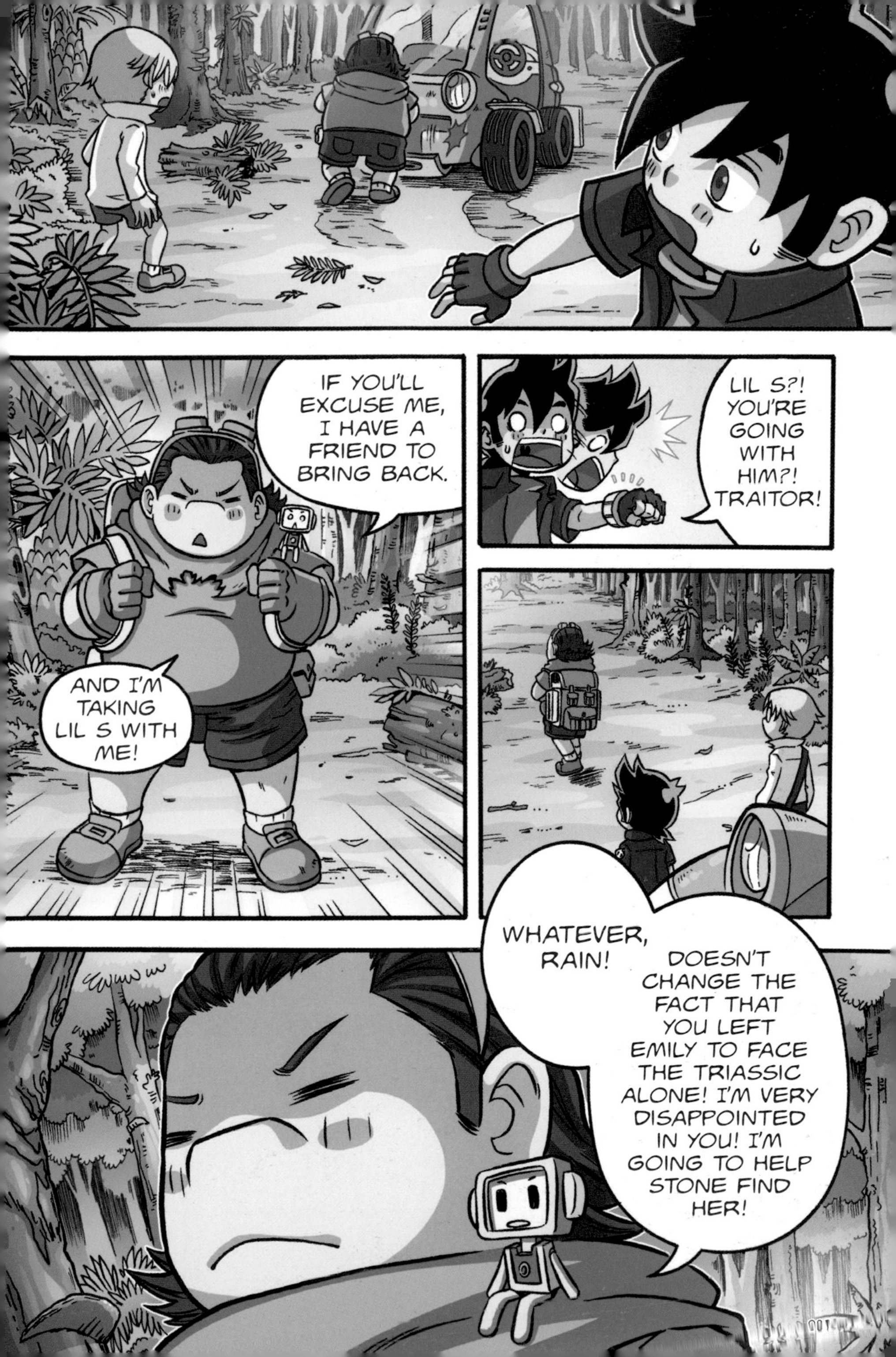
IF YOU'LL EXCUSE ME, I HAVE A FRIEND TO BRING BACK.
AND I'M TAKING LIL S WITH ME!
LIL S?! YOU'RE GOING WITH HIM?! TRAITOR!
WHATEVER, RAIN!
DOESN'T CHANGE THE FACT THAT YOU LEFT EMILY TO FACE THE TRIASSIC ALONE! I'M VERY DISAPPOINTED IN YOU! I'M GOING TO HELP STONE FIND HER!

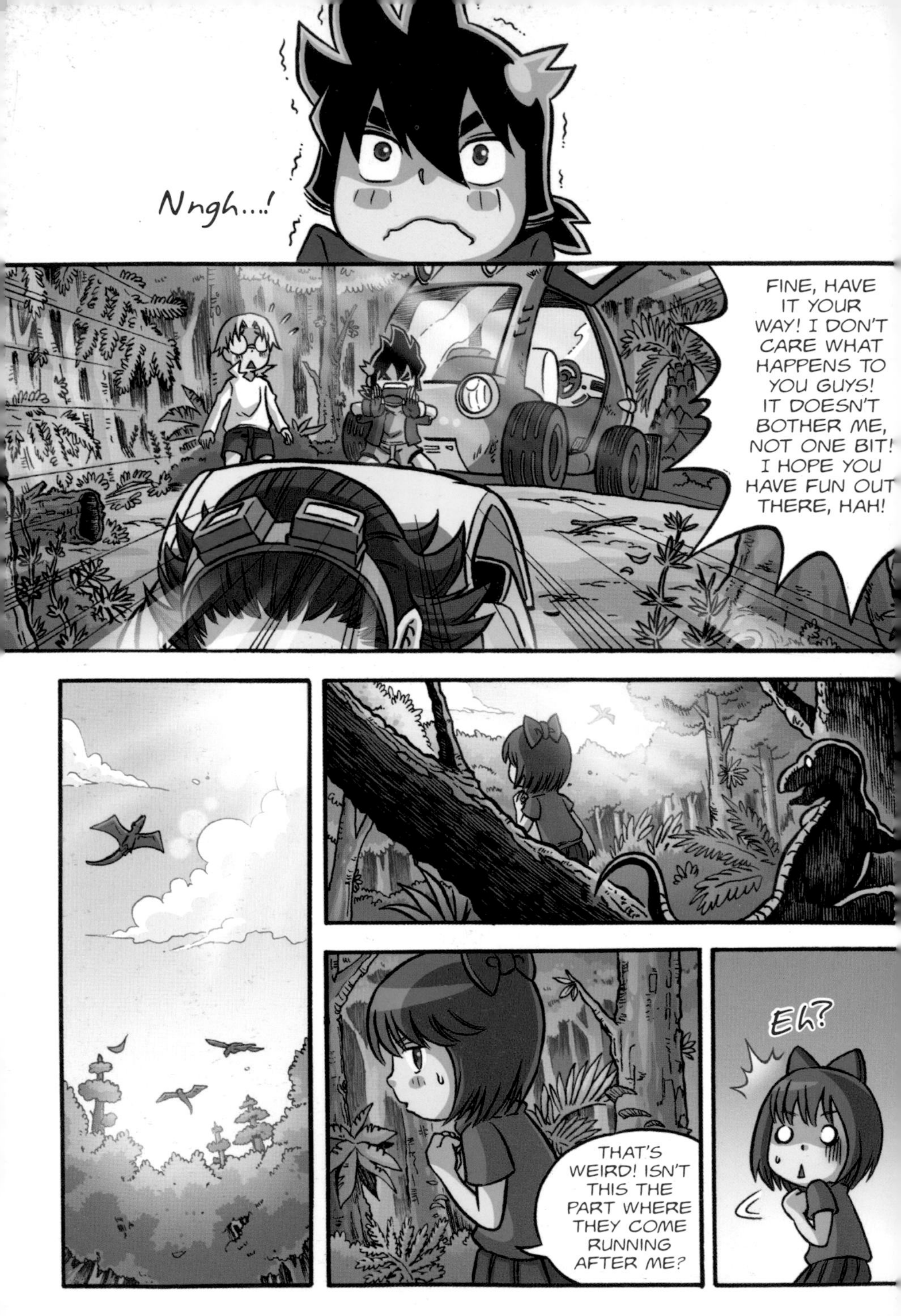
Nngh...!
FINE, HAVE IT YOUR WAY! I DON'T CARE WHAT HAPPENS TO YOU GUYS! IT DOESN'T BOTHER ME, NOT ONE BIT! I HOPE YOU HAVE FUN OUT THERE, HAH!
THAT'S WEIRD! ISN'T THIS THE PART WHERE THEY COME RUNNING AFTER ME?
Eh?

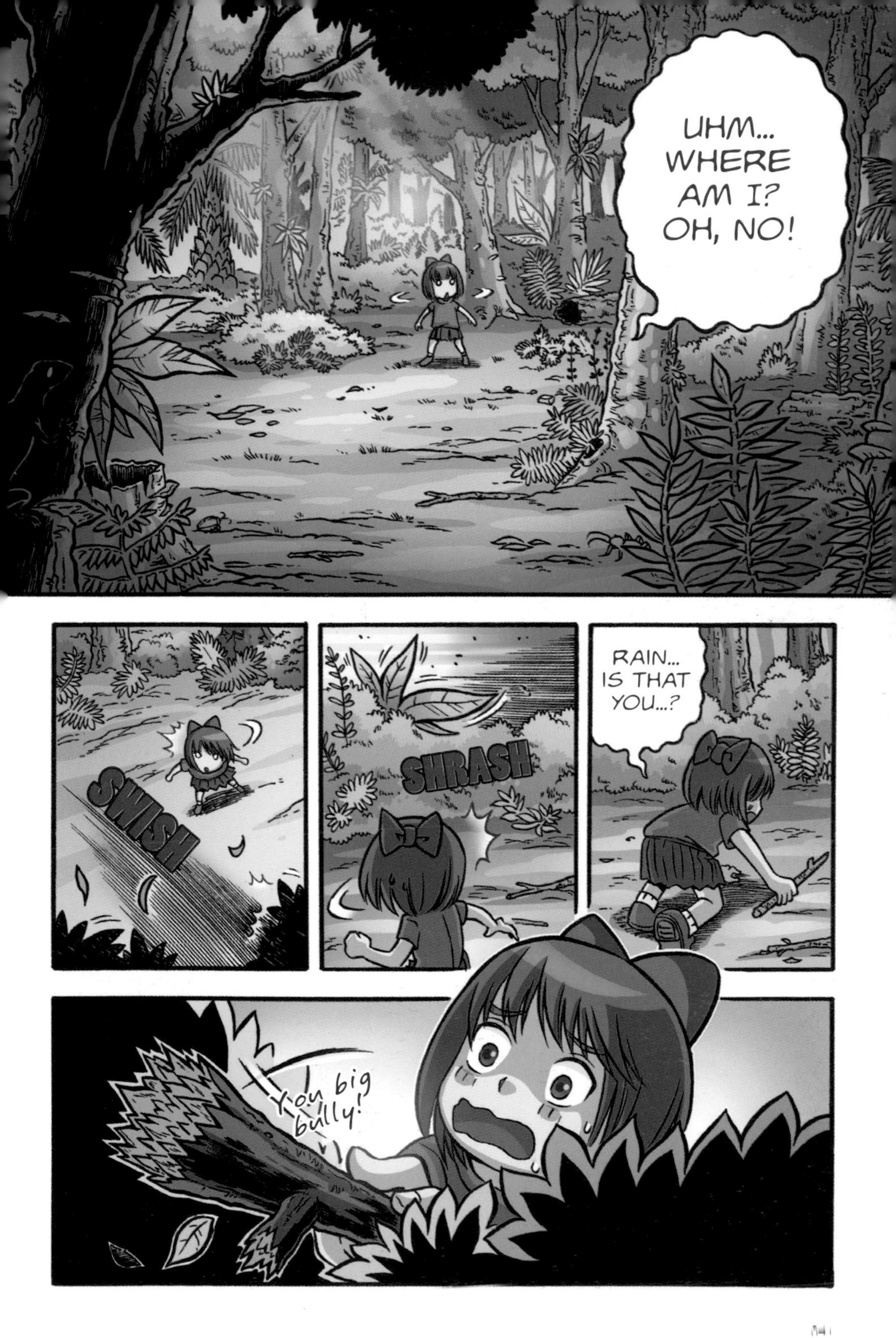
UHM... WHERE AM I? OH, NO!
SWISH
SHRASH
RAIN... IS THAT YOU...?
You big bully!

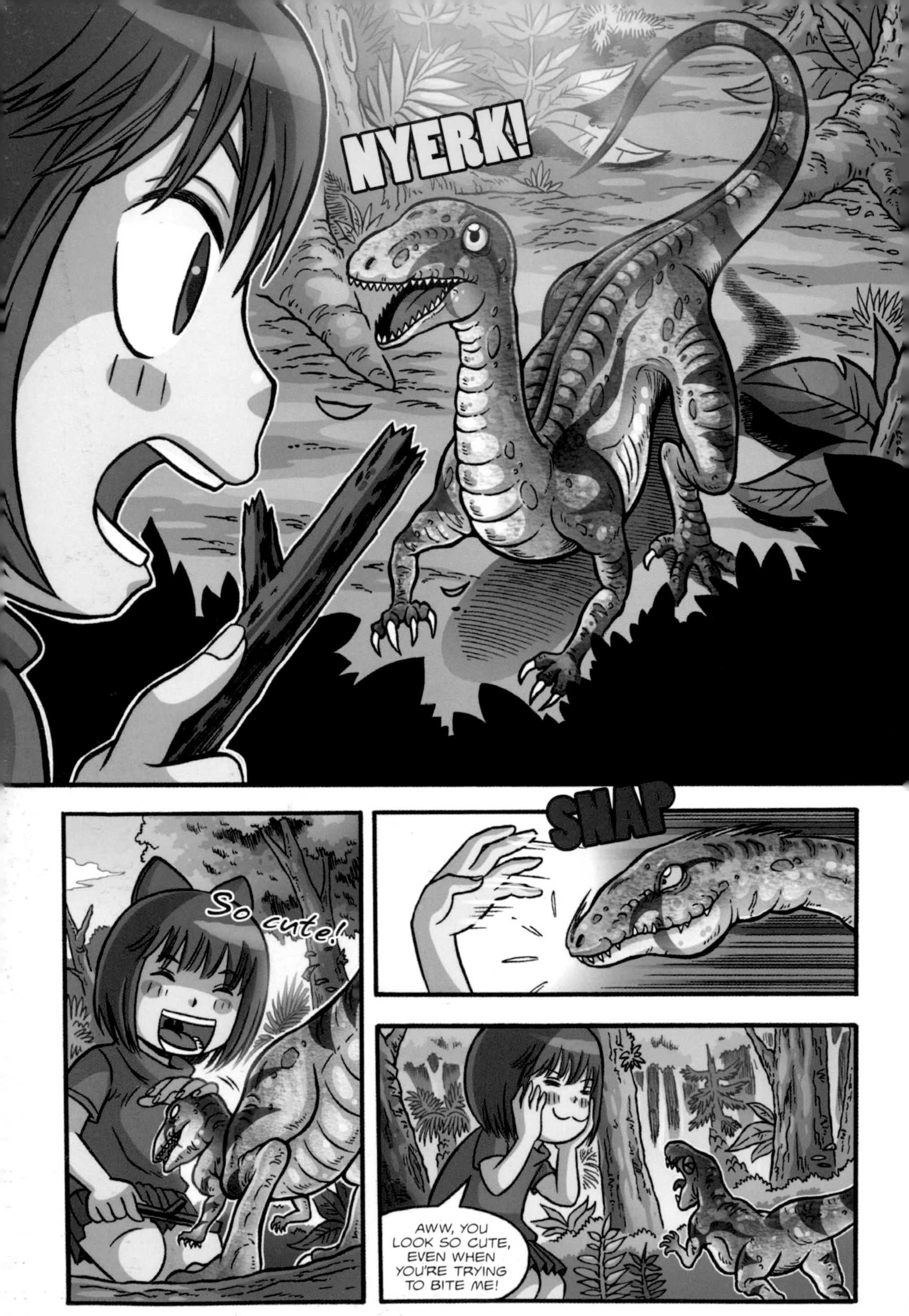
NYERK!
So cute!
SNAP
AWW, YOU LOOK SO CUTE, EVEN WHEN YOU'RE TRYING TO BITE ME!

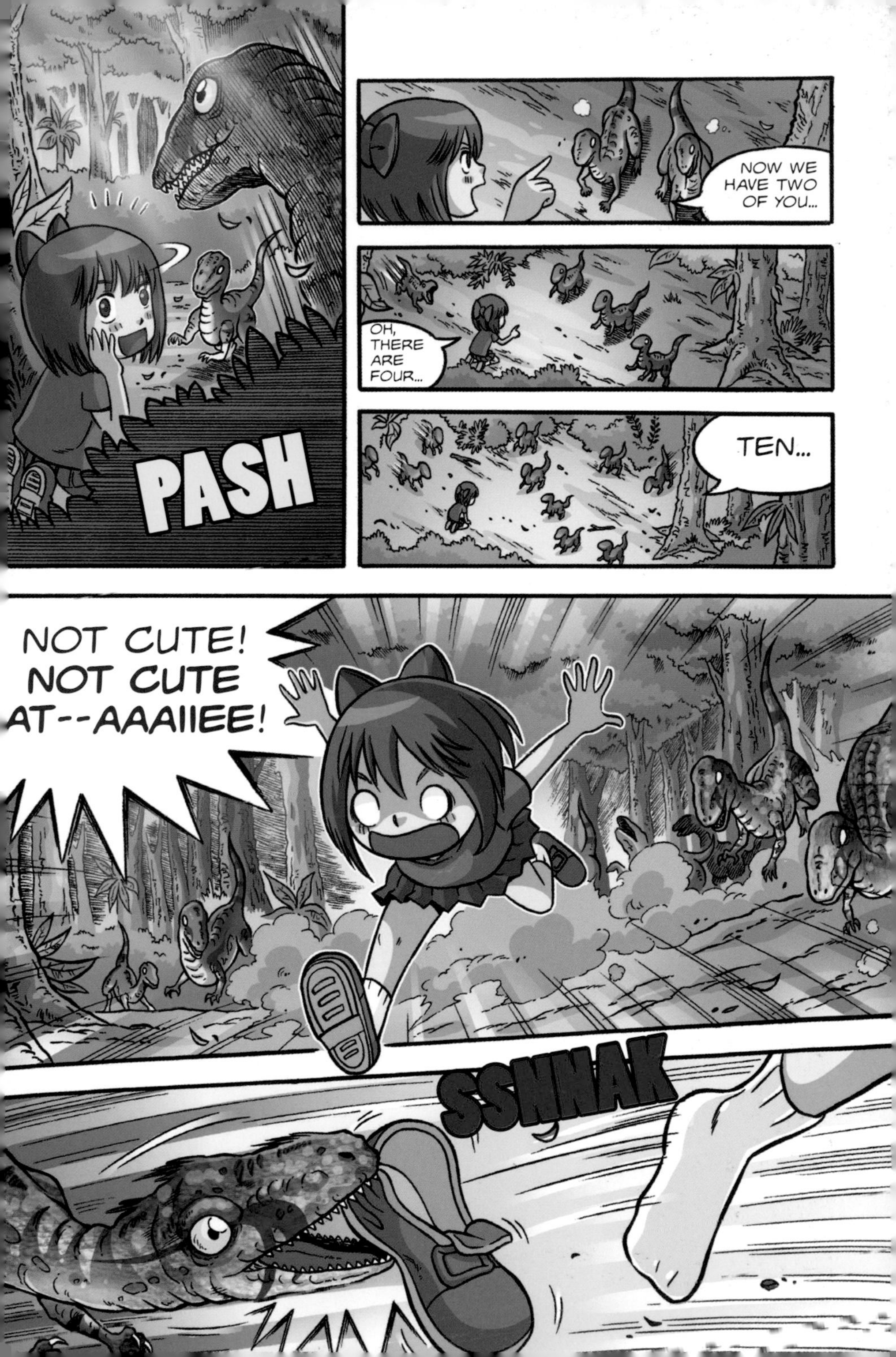
PASH
NOW WE HAVE TWO OF YOU...
OH, THERE ARE FOUR...
TEN...
NOT CUTE! NOT CUTE AT--AAAIIEE!
SSHNAK

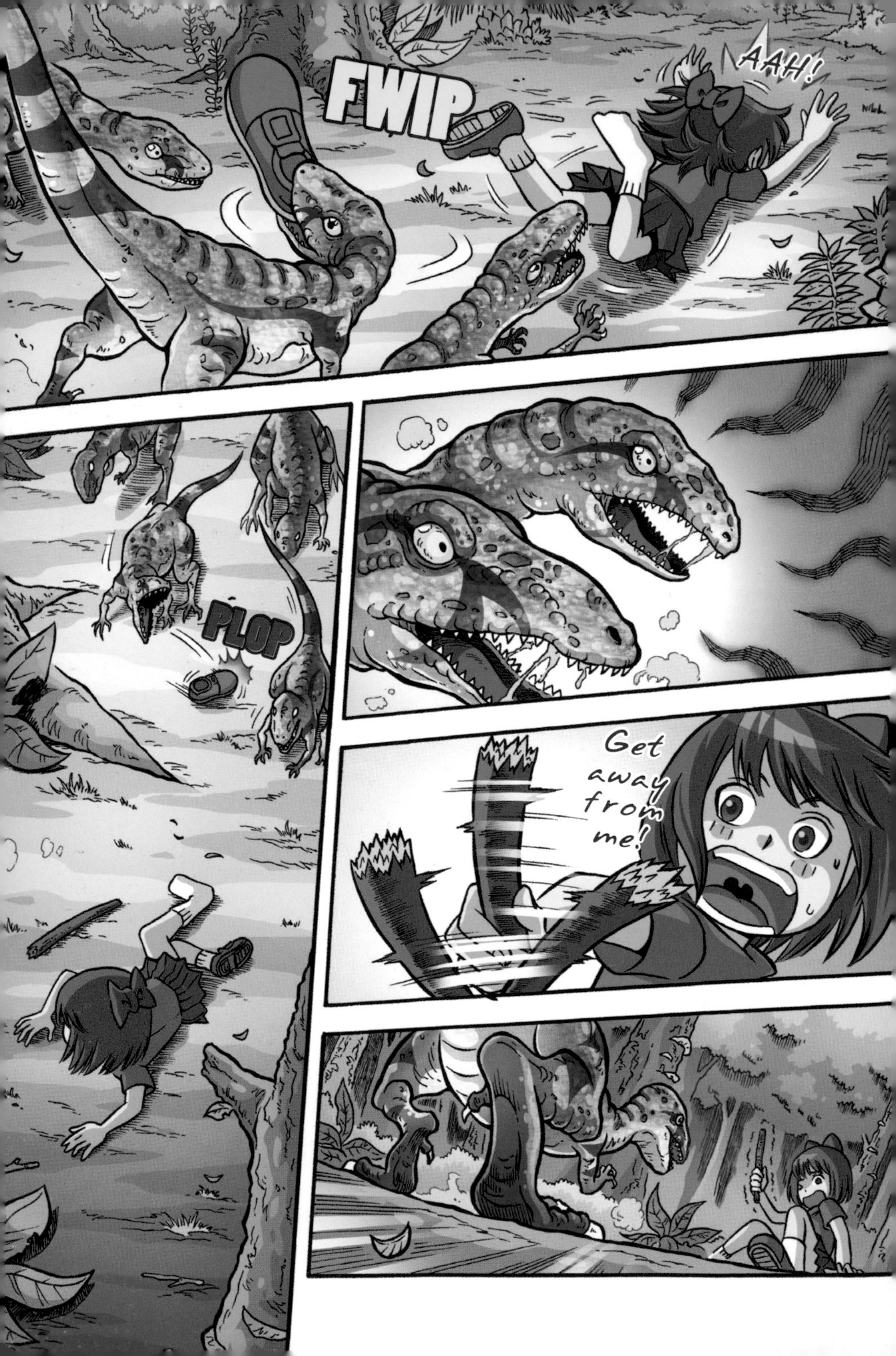
FWIP
AAH!
PLOP
Get away from me!

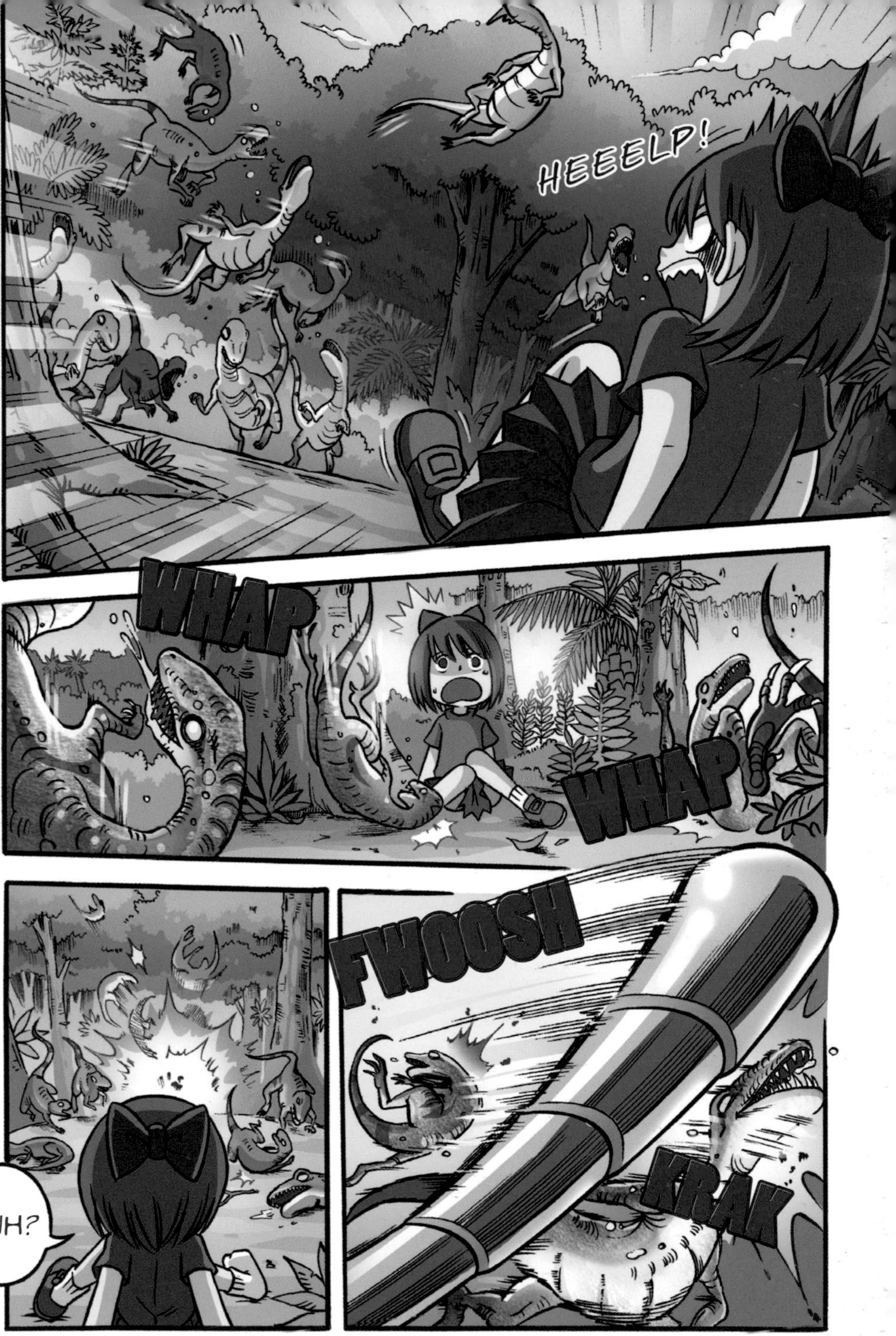
HEEEELP!
WHAP
WHAP
HUH?
FWOOSH
KRAK

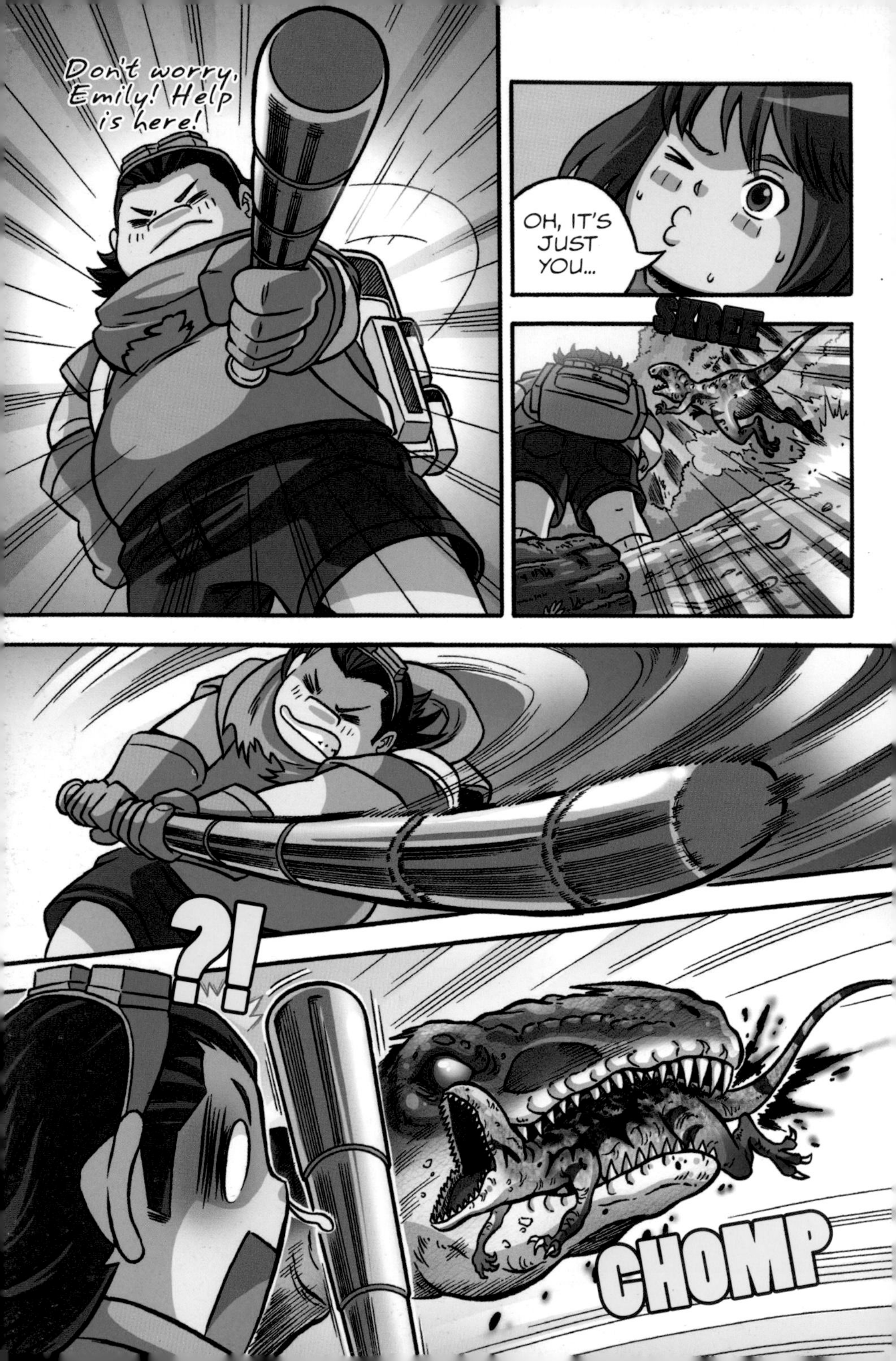
Don't worry, Emily! Help is here!
OH, IT'S JUST YOU...
SKREE
?!
CHOMP

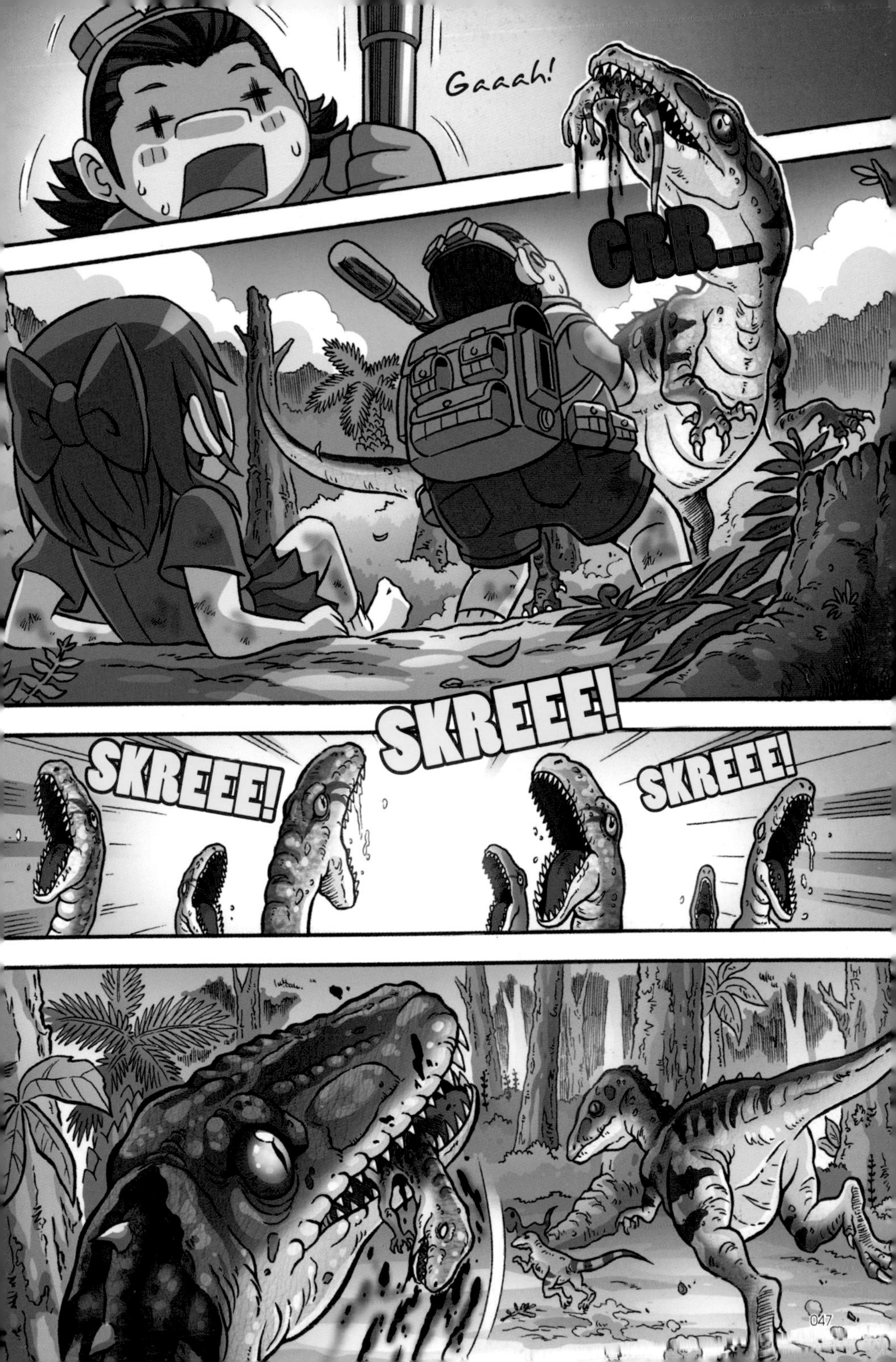
Gaaah!
CRR....
SKREEE!
SKREEE!
SKREEE!

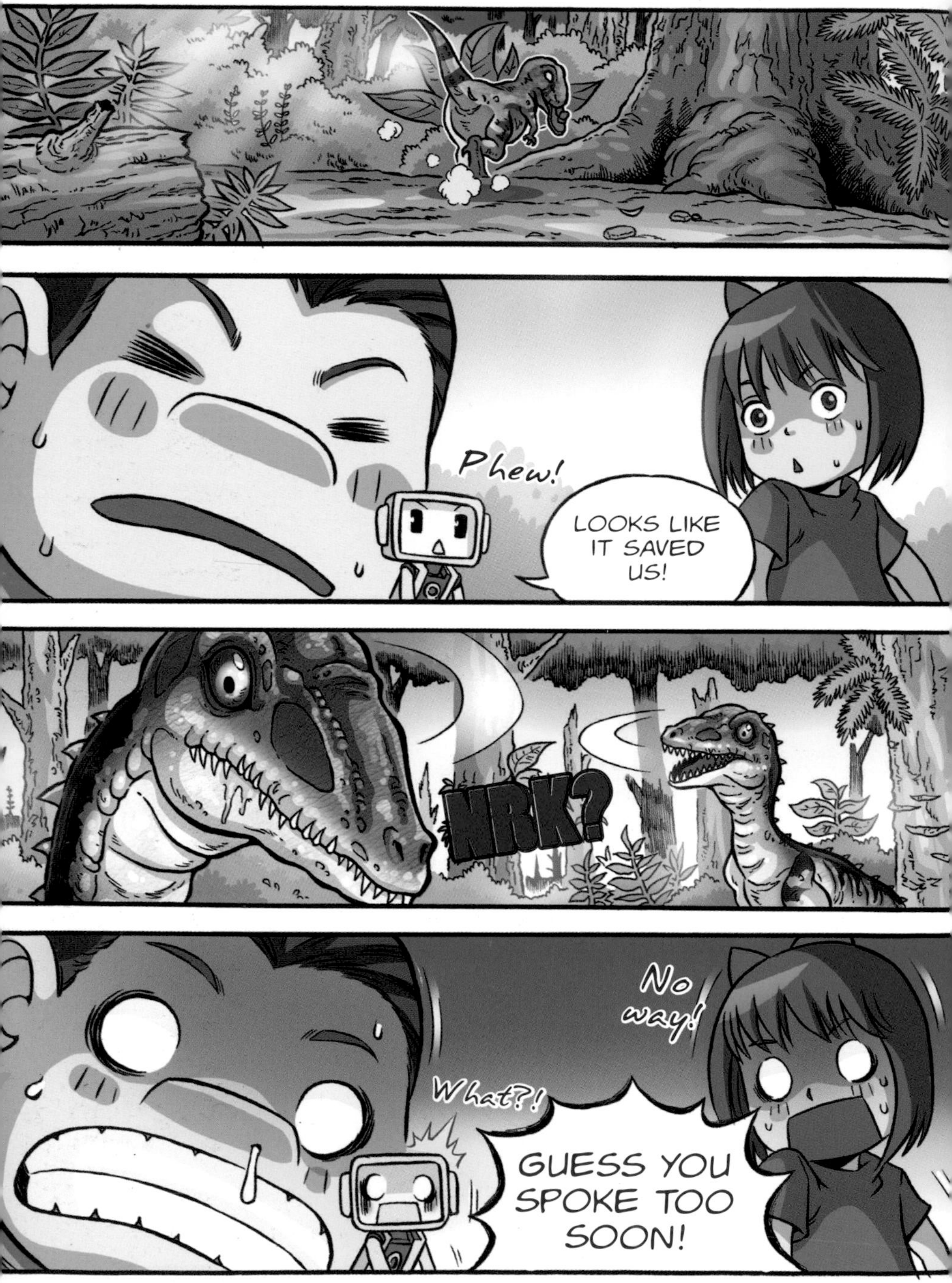
Phew!
LOOKS LIKE IT SAVED US!
NRK?
No way!
What?!
GUESS YOU SPOKE TOO SOON!

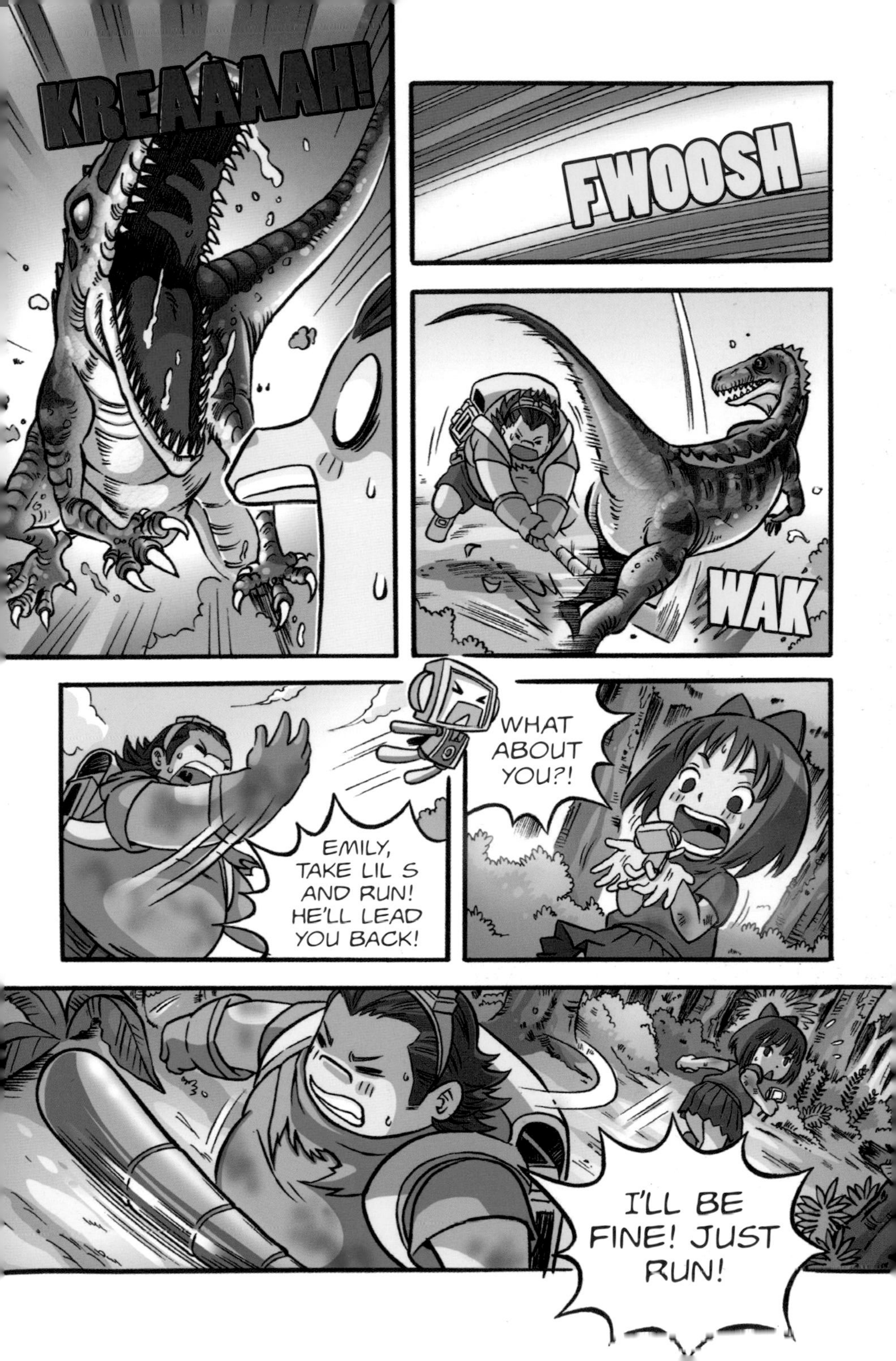
KREAAAAAH!
FWOOSH
WAK
EMILY, TAKE LIL S AND RUN! HE'LL LEAD YOU BACK!
WHAT ABOUT YOU?!
I'LL BE FINE! JUST RUN!

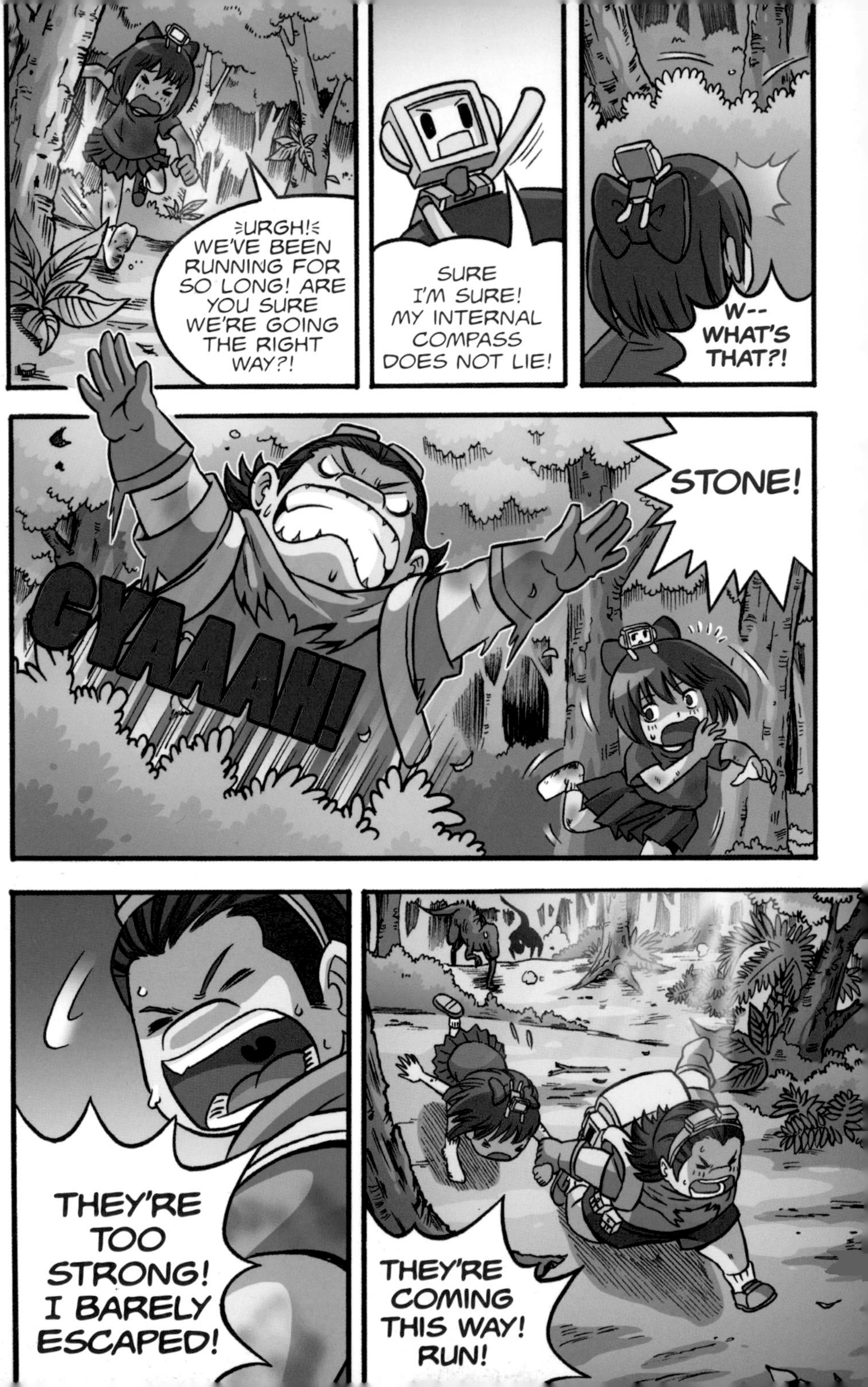
≶URGH!≶ WE'VE BEEN RUNNING FOR SO LONG! ARE YOU SURE WE'RE GOING THE RIGHT WAY?!
SURE I'M SURE! MY INTERNAL COMPASS DOES NOT LIE!
W-- WHAT'S THAT?!
STONE!
CYAAAAH!
THEY'RE TOO STRONG! I BARELY ESCAPED!
THEY'RE COMING THIS WAY! RUN!

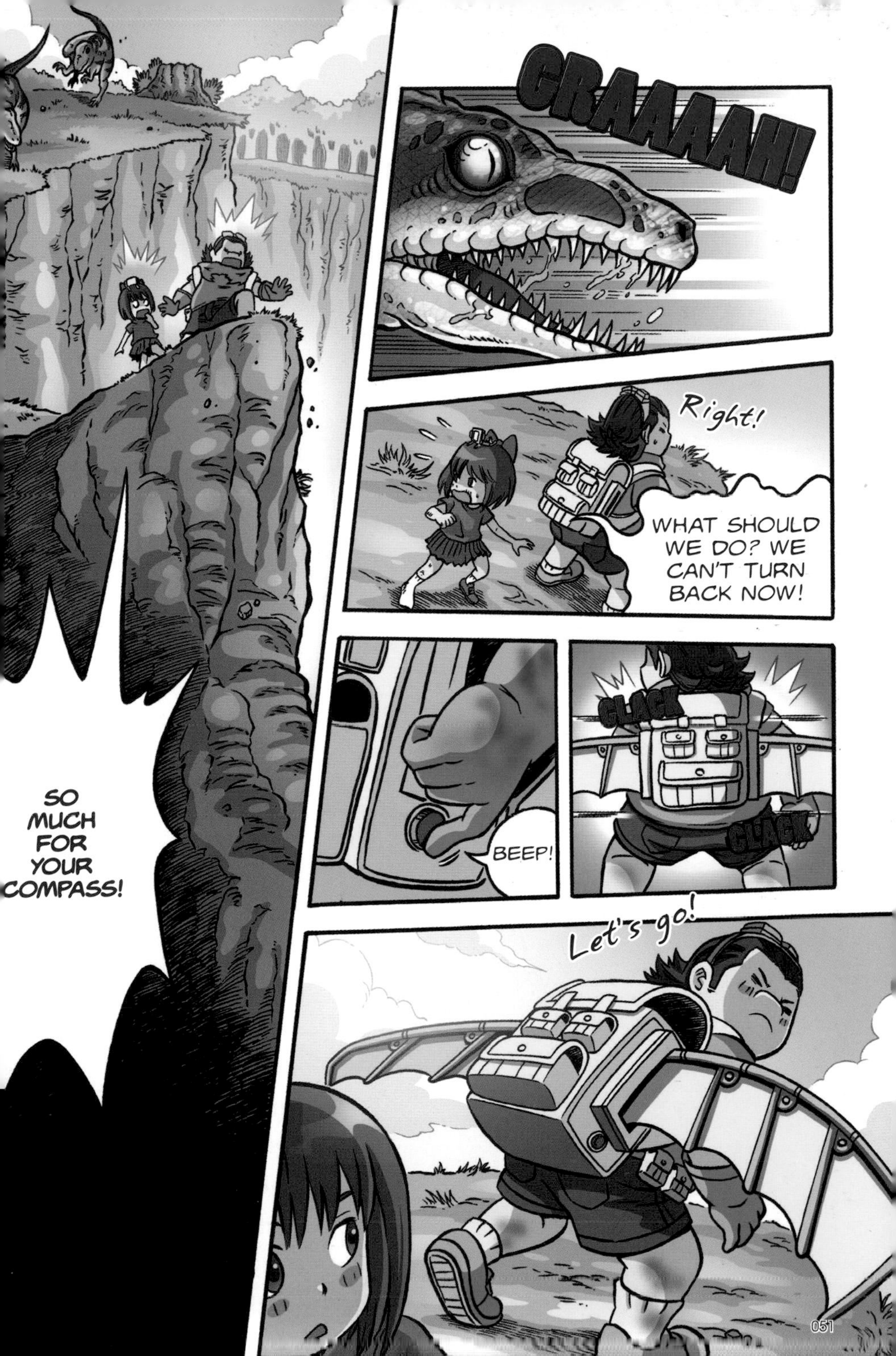
SO MUCH FOR YOUR COMPASS!
GRAAAAH!
Right!
WHAT SHOULD WE DO? WE CAN'T TURN BACK NOW!
BEEP!
CLACK
CLACK
Let's go!

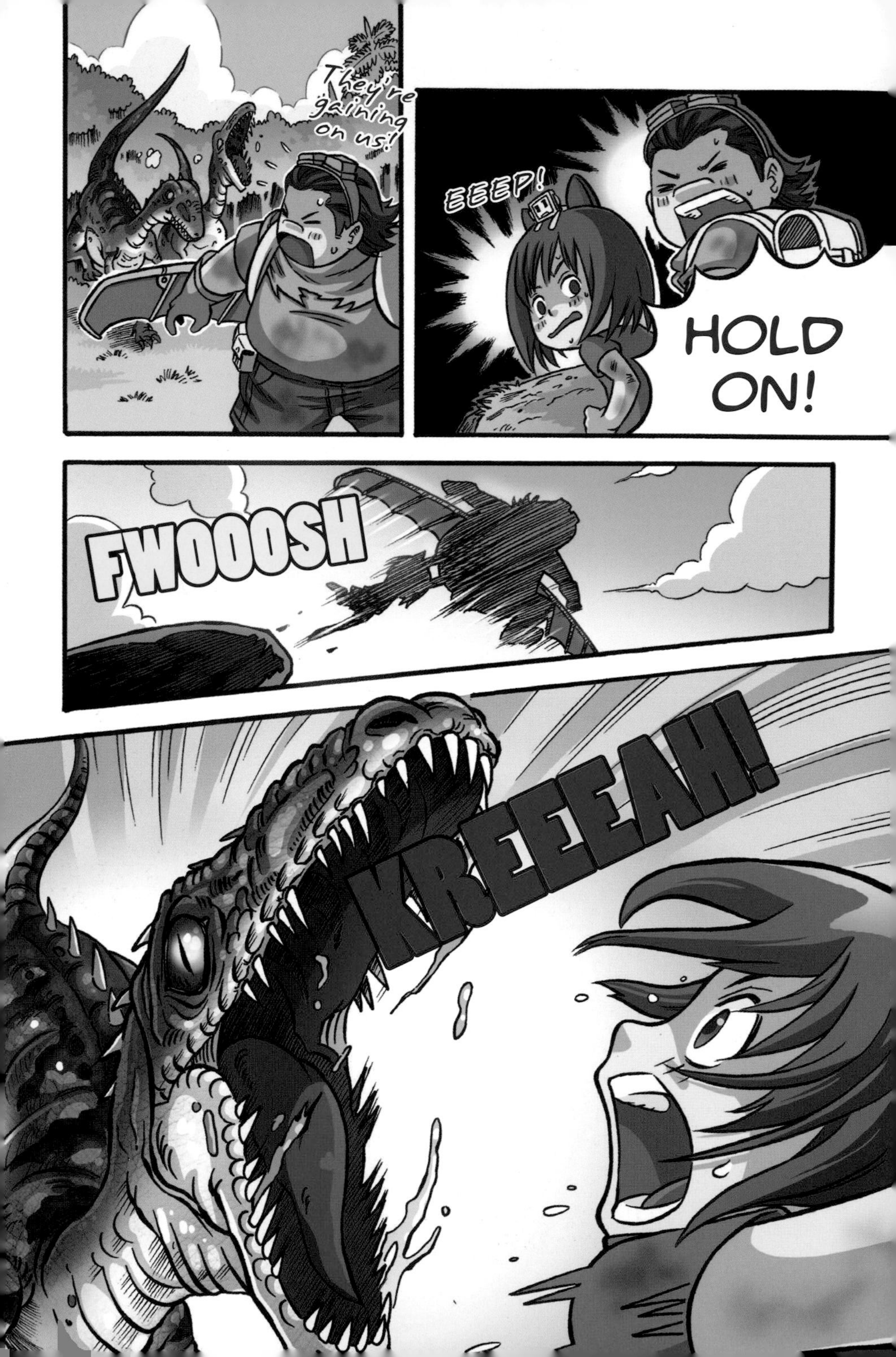
They're gaining on us!
EEEP!
HOLD ON!
FWOOOSH
KREEEAH!

TAKING IN THE TRIASSIC
Thrinaxodon

Thrinaxodon possessed attributes of both mammals and reptiles. It had incisors, canines, and molars with a jutting snout and a body that could have possibly been covered with fur. Its chest and lower back were divided by a diaphragm to help its breathing. Based on all these characteristics, it has been suggested that Thrinaxodon was closely related to early mammal ancestors.

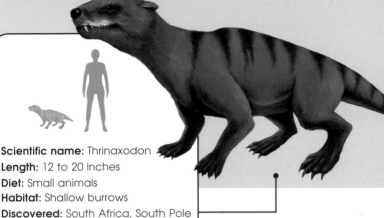

Scientific name: Thrinaxodon
Length: 12 to 20 inches
Diet: Small animals
Habitat: Shallow burrows
Discovered: South Africa, South Pole
Era: Early Triassic

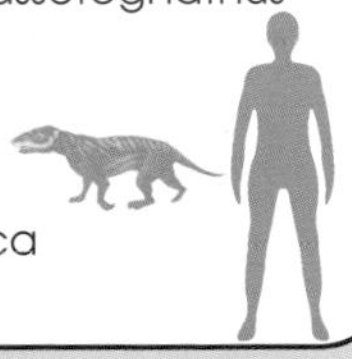

TAKING IN THE TRIASSIC
Massetognathus

Scientific name: Massetognathus
Length: 20 feet
Diet: Plants
Habitat: Unknown
Discovered: America
Era: Middle Triassic

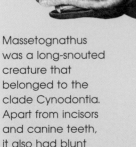

Massetognathus was a long-snouted creature that belonged to the clade Cynodontia. Apart from incisors and canine teeth, it also had blunt molars, suitable for grinding food. Its clawed feet were similar to those of a dog, and its overall appearance was mammal-like.

TAKING IN THE TRIASSIC
Eozostrodon

Eozostrodon was one of the earliest known mammals; despite the fact that it laid eggs, females still used milk glands to feed their young— a major mammal trait. It was thought to have had fur on its body as well. Its teeth were typically mammalian, heavy, and sharpened. Today, paleontologists opine that its large eyes indicated that it could have been a nocturnal.

Scientific name: Eozostrodon
Length: 3 inches
Diet: Insects and other small animals
Habitat: Forests
Discovered: West Europe, South Africa
Era: Late Triassic to Early Jurassic

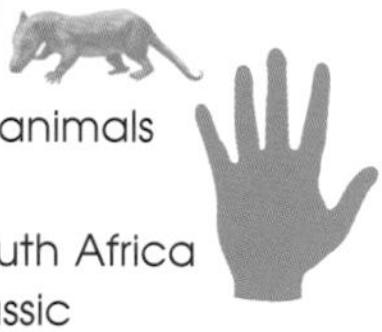

TAKING IN THE TRIASSIC
Placerias

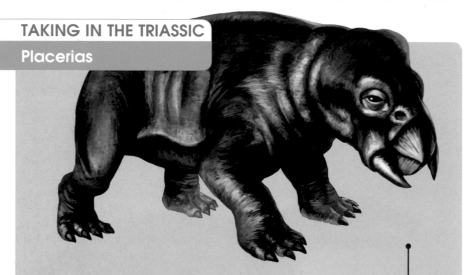

Placerias was one of the last existing dicynodonts during the Late Triassic. Its most notable features were its beak-like mouth and the protruding tusks which helped in chewing tough vegetation. Its tusks could also be used for digging, allowing it to reach the water-filled roots of ferns.

Scientific name: Placerias
Length: 10 feet
Diet: Vegetation
Habitat: In the wild
Discovered: America
Era: Late Triassic

TAKING IN THE TRIASSIC

Lystrosaurus

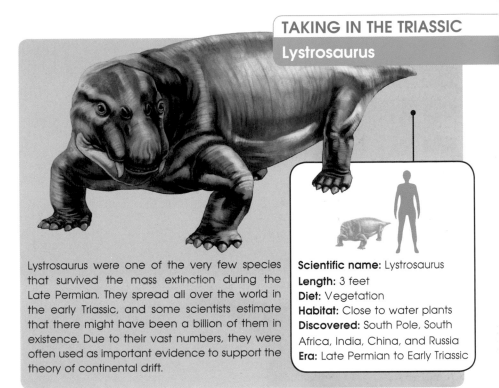

Lystrosaurus were one of the very few species that survived the mass extinction during the Late Permian. They spread all over the world in the early Triassic, and some scientists estimate that there might have been a billion of them in existence. Due to their vast numbers, they were often used as important evidence to support the theory of continental drift.

Scientific name: Lystrosaurus
Length: 3 feet
Diet: Vegetation
Habitat: Close to water plants
Discovered: South Pole, South Africa, India, China, and Russia
Era: Late Permian to Early Triassic

TAKING IN THE TRIASSIC

Longisquama

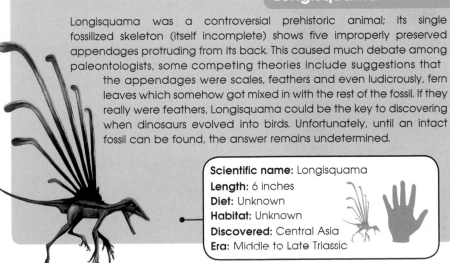

Longisquama was a controversial prehistoric animal; its single fossilized skeleton (itself incomplete) shows five improperly preserved appendages protruding from its back. This caused much debate among paleontologists, some competing theories include suggestions that the appendages were scales, feathers and even ludicrously, fern leaves which somehow got mixed in with the rest of the fossil. If they really were feathers, Longisquama could be the key to discovering when dinosaurs evolved into birds. Unfortunately, until an intact fossil can be found, the answer remains undetermined.

Scientific name: Longisquama
Length: 6 inches
Diet: Unknown
Habitat: Unknown
Discovered: Central Asia
Era: Middle to Late Triassic

TAKING IN THE TRIASSIC

Hypsognathus

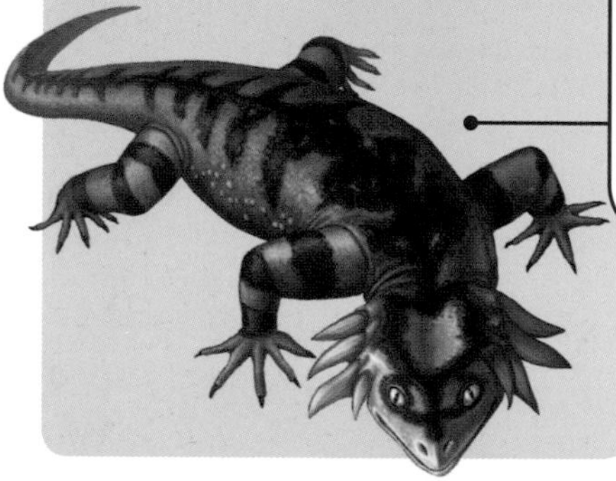

Scientific name: Hypsognathus
Length: 12 inches
Diet: Vegetation
Habitat: Unknown
Discovered: America
Era: Late Triassic

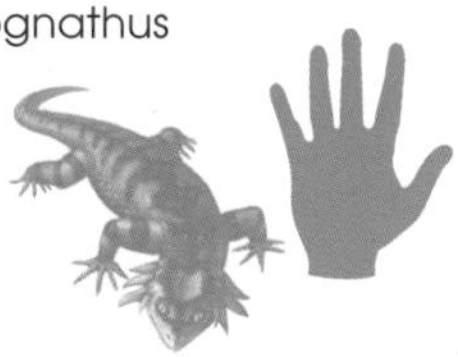

The lizardlike Hypsognathus was not closely related to its latter day counterpart. It had a low, short body with a relatively short tail. A notable feature was the frill of spikes on either side of its head, which was thought to be used as a defense to ward off predators.

TAKING IN THE TRIASSIC

Mastodonsaurus

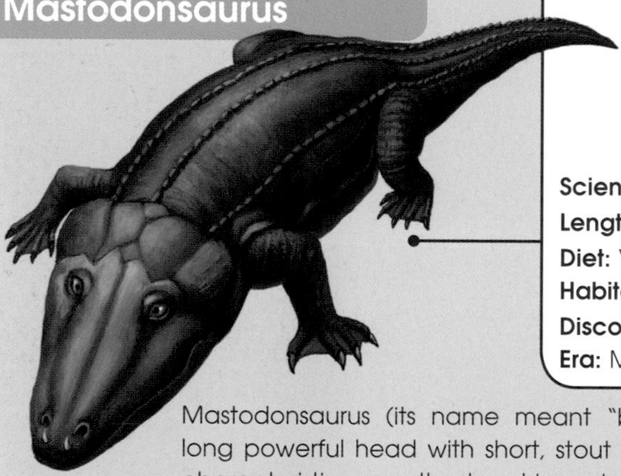

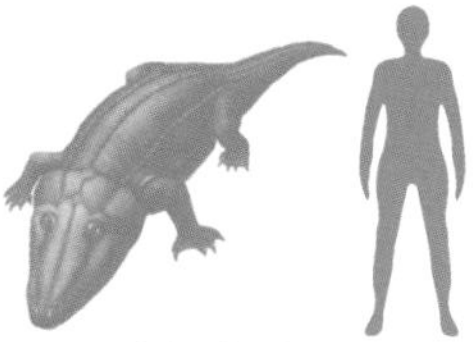

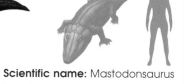

Scientific name: Mastodonsaurus
Length: 7 feet
Diet: Vegetation
Habitat: Unknown
Discovered: America
Era: Middle Triassic

Mastodonsaurus (its name meant "breast tooth lizard"), had a long powerful head with short, stout limbs, but its most interesting characteristic were the two triangular tusks which slotted through the openings on its palate and projected through the top of its snout when its jaws were closed.

TAKING IN THE TRIASSIC

Aeger

Scientific name: Aeger
Length: 5 inches
Diet: Unknown
Habitat: Unknown
Discovered: Around the world
Era: Triassic to Jurassic

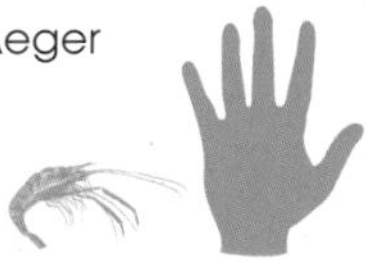

Aeger had 10 legs, long antennae, and a tail. Physically, it bore close resemblance to modern prawns.

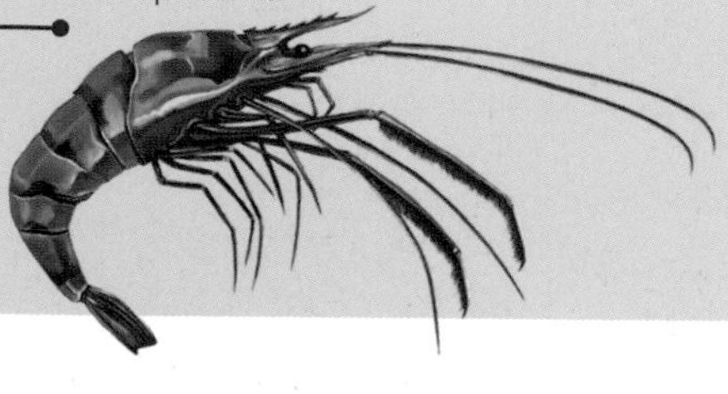

CHAPTER 3

SHOCK AND CLAW

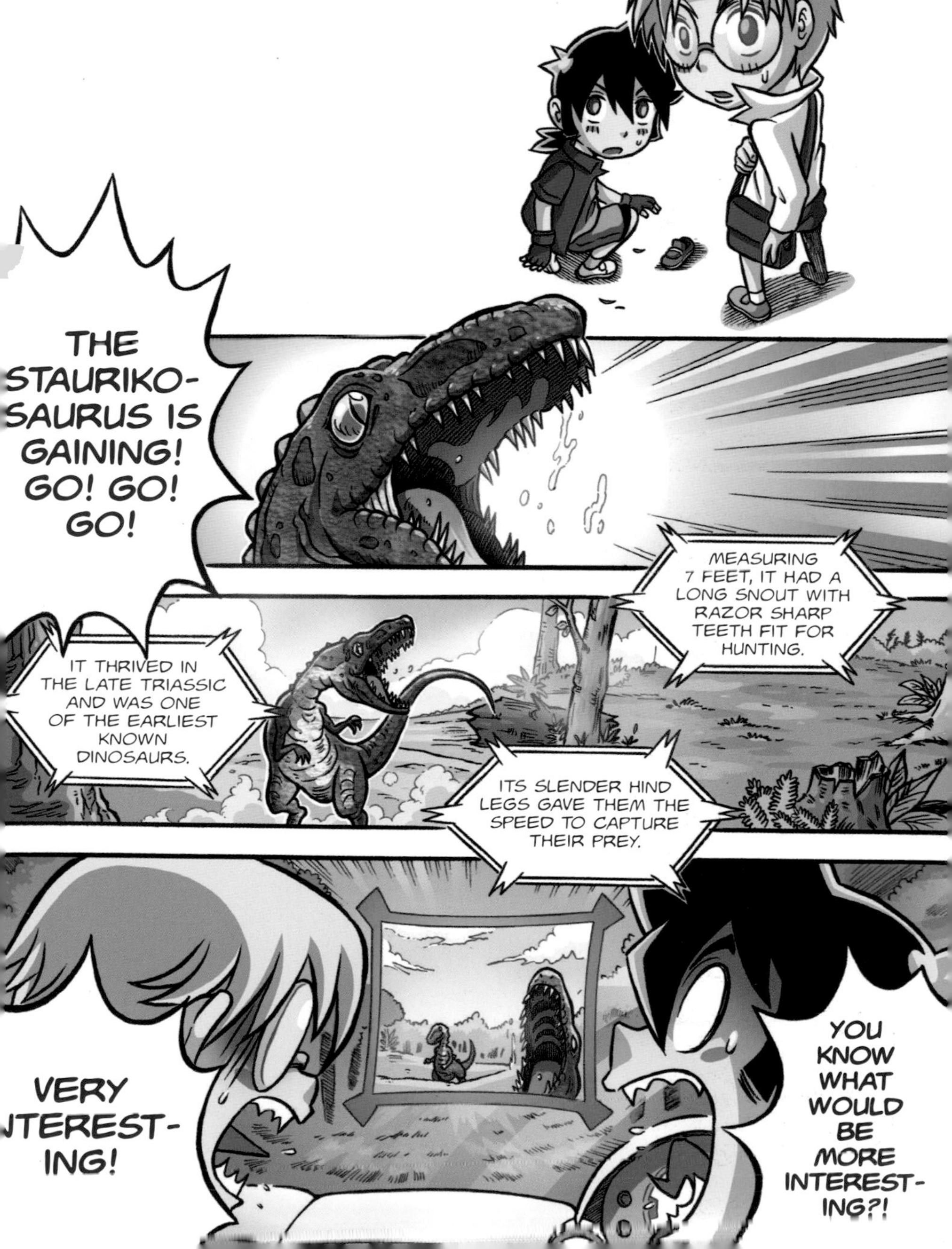
THE STAURIKO-SAURUS IS GAINING! GO! GO! GO!
MEASURING 7 FEET, IT HAD A LONG SNOUT WITH RAZOR SHARP TEETH FIT FOR HUNTING.
IT THRIVED IN THE LATE TRIASSIC AND WAS ONE OF THE EARLIEST KNOWN DINOSAURS.
ITS SLENDER HIND LEGS GAVE THEM THE SPEED TO CAPTURE THEIR PREY.
VERY INTEREST-ING!
YOU KNOW WHAT WOULD BE MORE INTEREST-ING?!

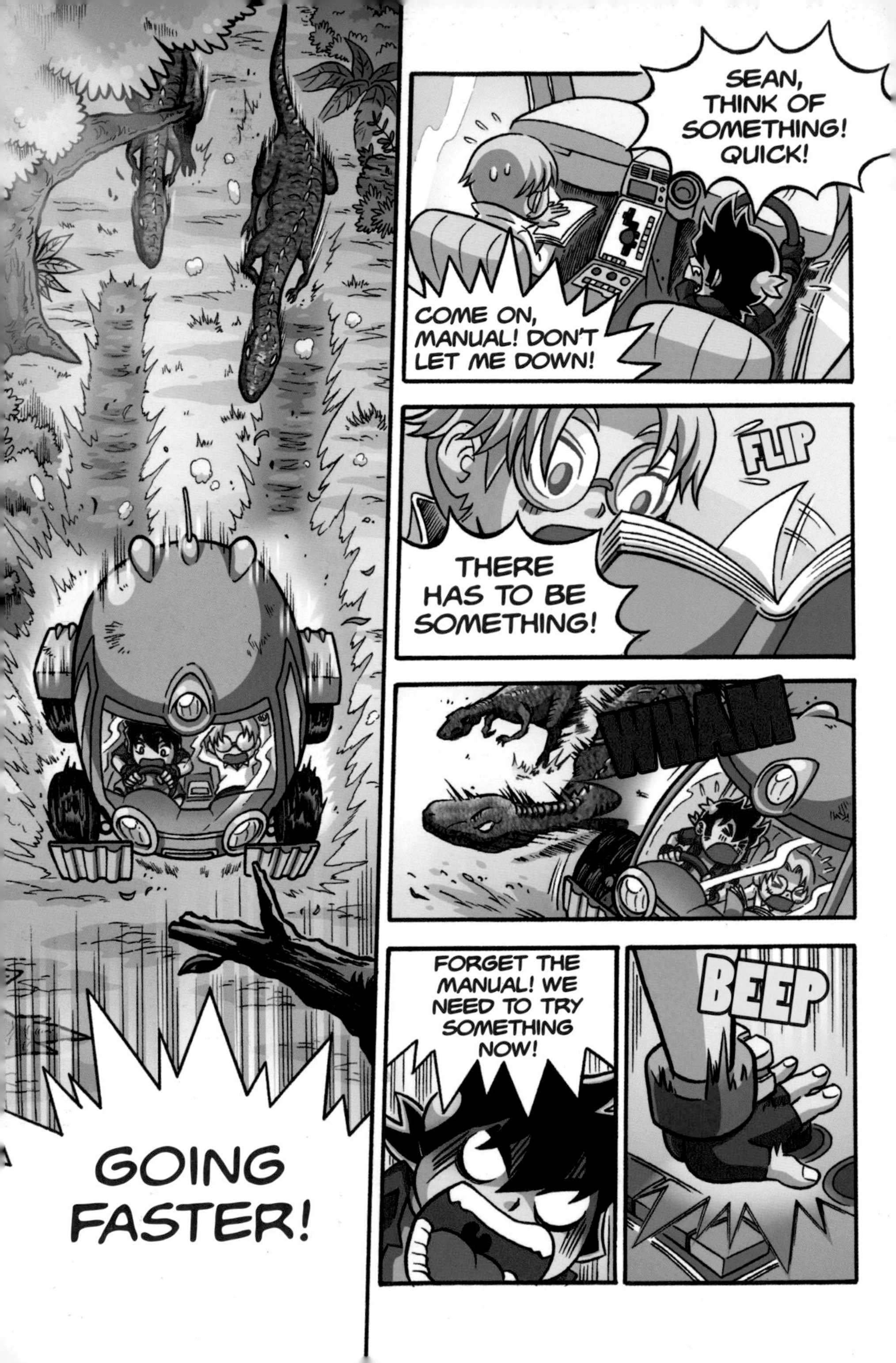
GOING FASTER!
SEAN, THINK OF SOMETHING! QUICK!
COME ON, MANUAL! DON'T LET ME DOWN!
FLIP
THERE HAS TO BE SOMETHING!
WHAM
FORGET THE MANUAL! WE NEED TO TRY SOMETHING NOW!
BEEP

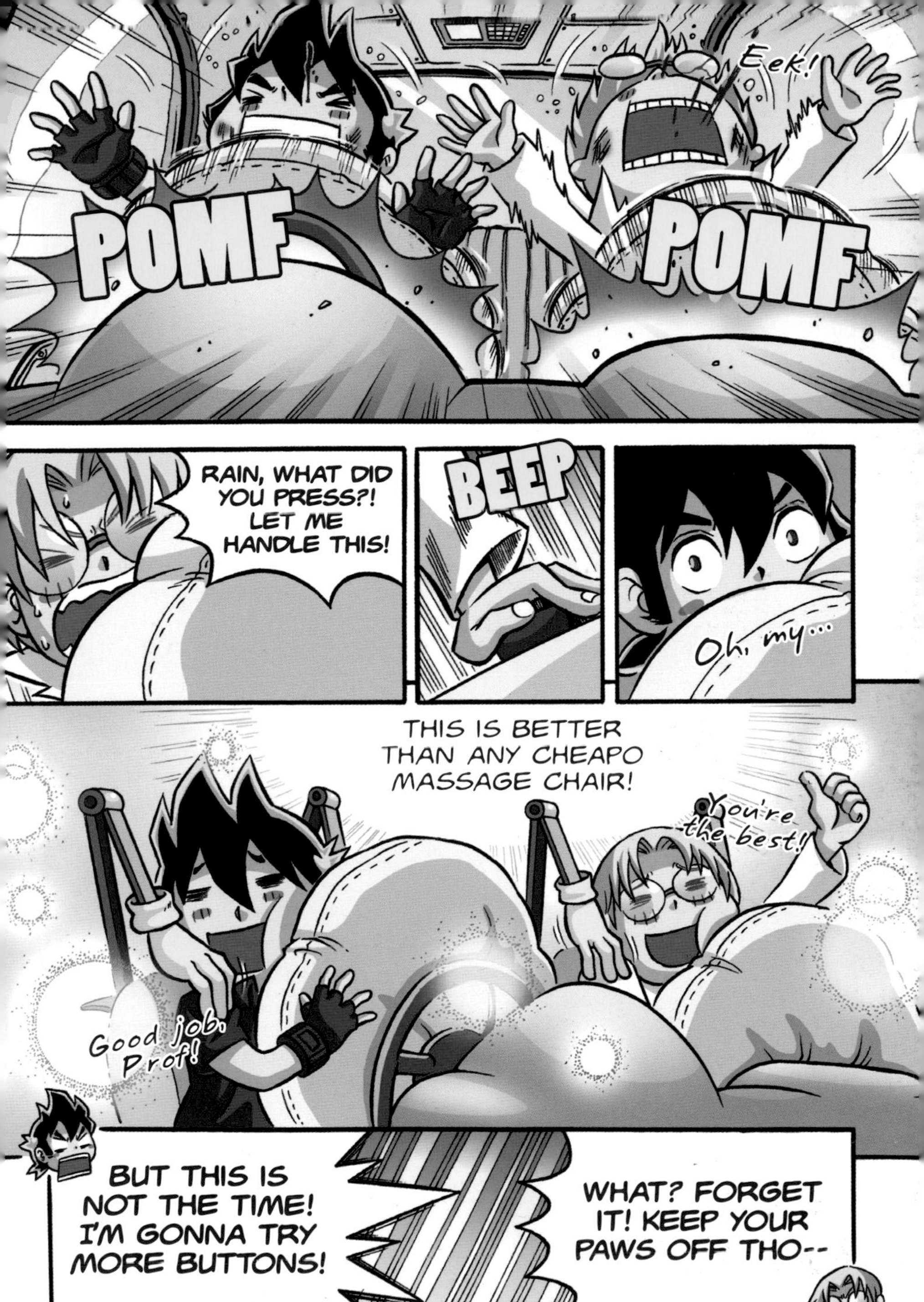

Eek!
POMF
POMF
RAIN, WHAT DID YOU PRESS?! LET ME HANDLE THIS!
BEEP
Oh, my...
THIS IS BETTER THAN ANY CHEAPO MASSAGE CHAIR!
You're the best!
Good job, Prof!
BUT THIS IS NOT THE TIME! I'M GONNA TRY MORE BUTTONS!
WHAT? FORGET IT! KEEP YOUR PAWS OFF THO--

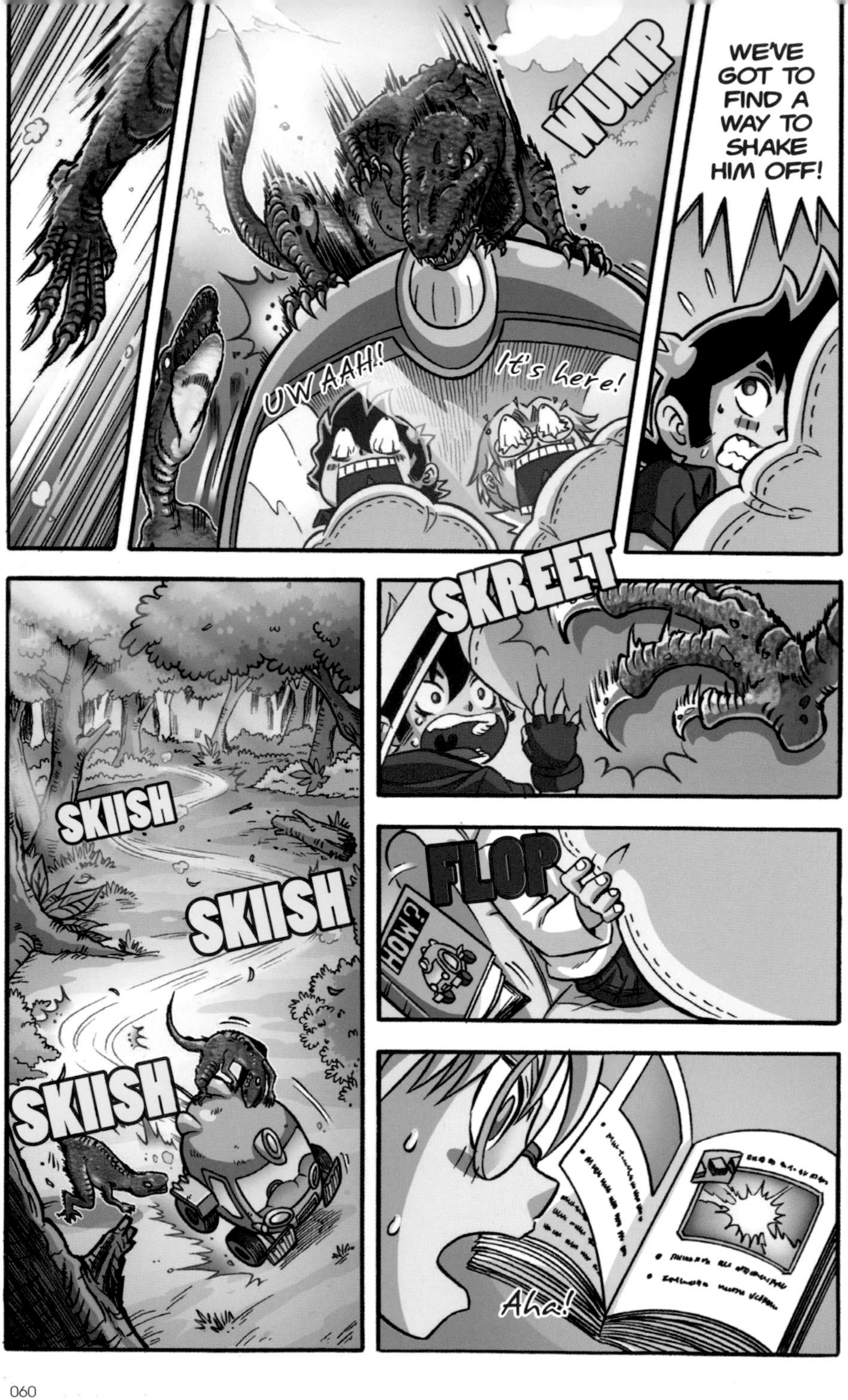
WUMP
UWAAH!
It's here!
WE'VE GOT TO FIND A WAY TO SHAKE HIM OFF!
SKIISH
SKIISH
SKIISH
SKREET
FLOP
HOW?
Aha!

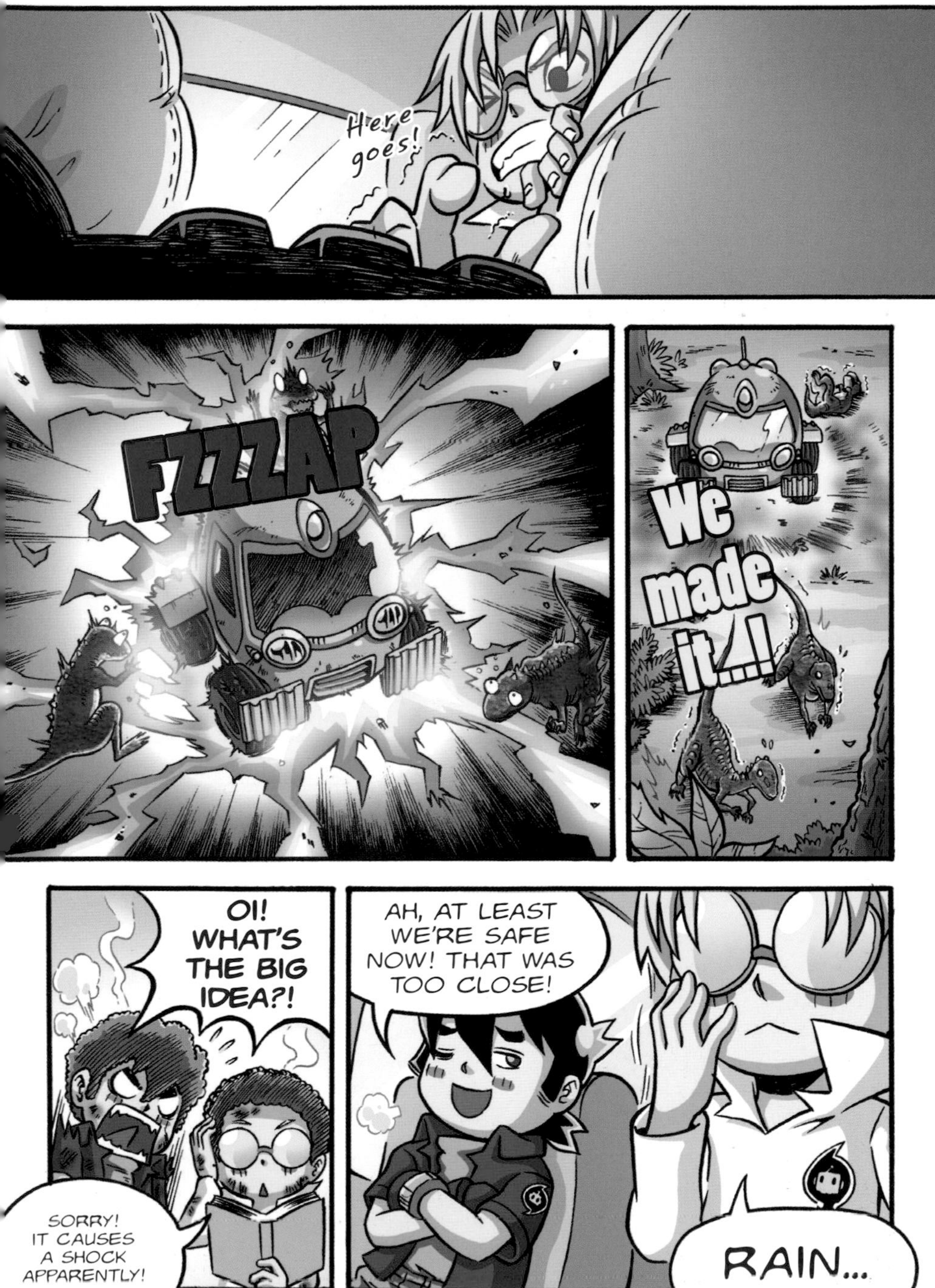
Here goes!
FZZZAP
We made it...!
OI! WHAT'S THE BIG IDEA?!
SORRY! IT CAUSES A SHOCK APPARENTLY!
AH, AT LEAST WE'RE SAFE NOW! THAT WAS TOO CLOSE!
RAIN...

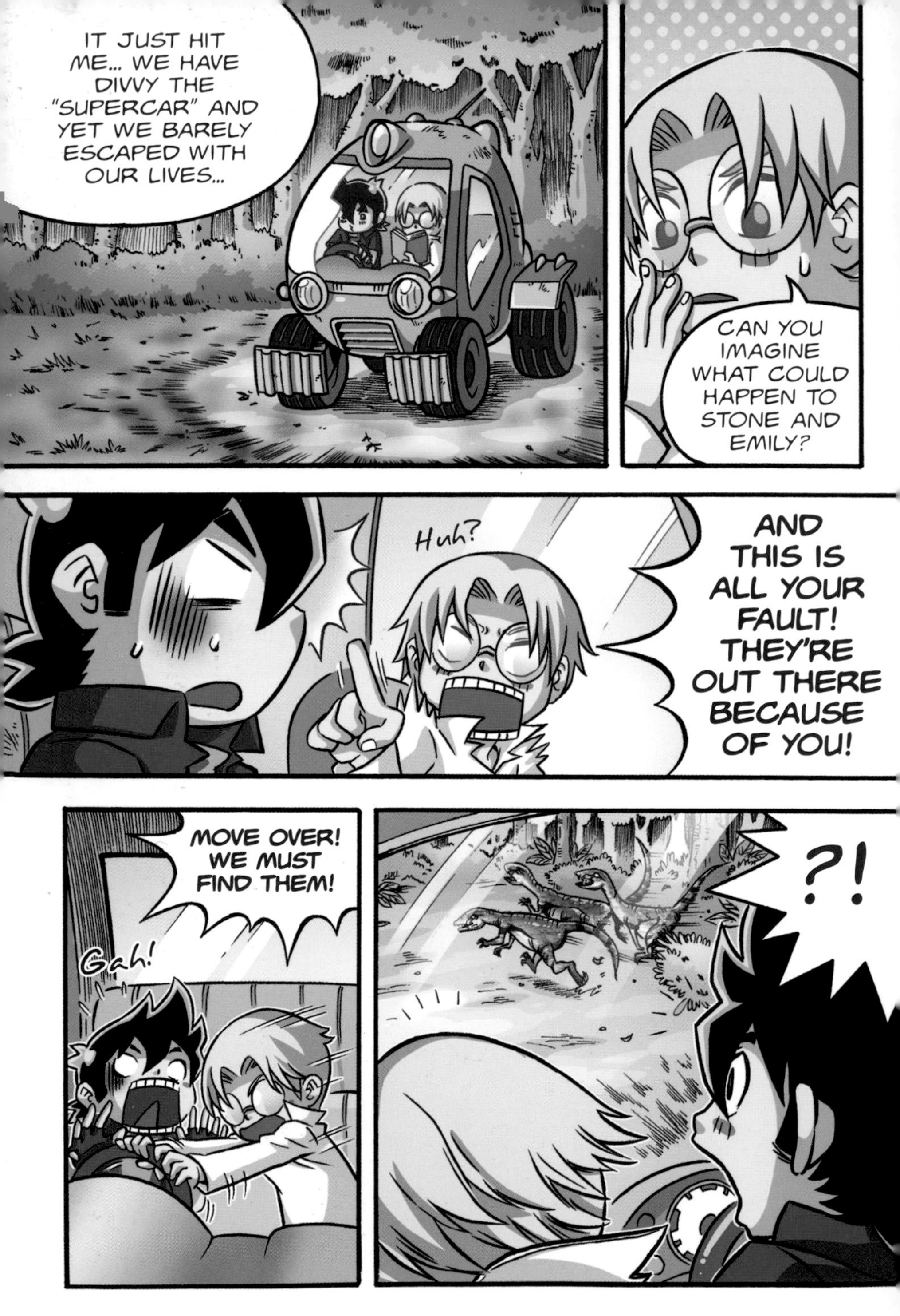
IT JUST HIT ME... WE HAVE DIVVY THE "SUPERCAR" AND YET WE BARELY ESCAPED WITH OUR LIVES...
CAN YOU IMAGINE WHAT COULD HAPPEN TO STONE AND EMILY?
Huh?
AND THIS IS ALL YOUR FAULT! THEY'RE OUT THERE BECAUSE OF YOU!
MOVE OVER! WE MUST FIND THEM!
Gah!
?!

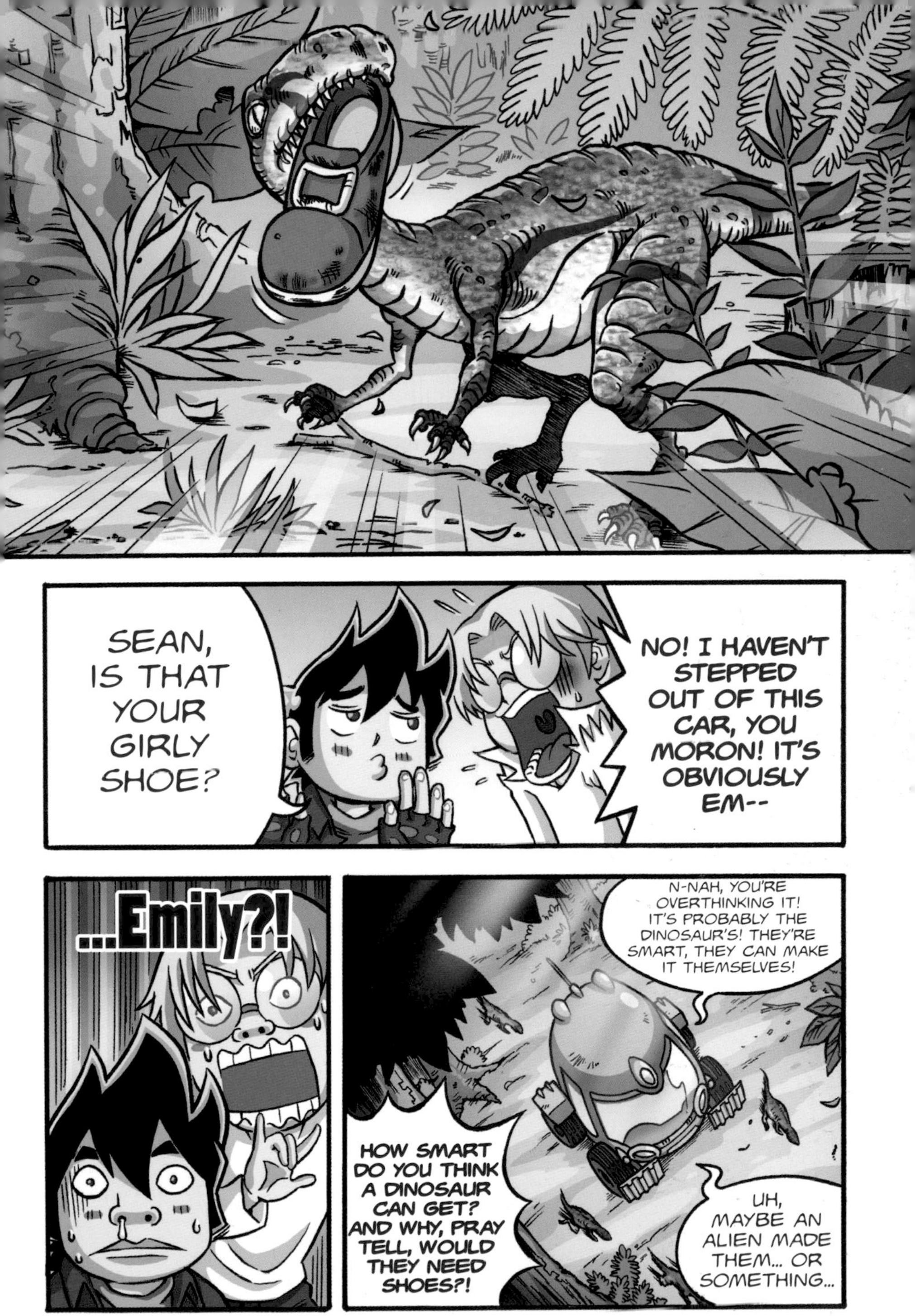
SEAN, IS THAT YOUR GIRLY SHOE?
NO! I HAVEN'T STEPPED OUT OF THIS CAR, YOU MORON! IT'S OBVIOUSLY EM--
...Emily?!
N-NAH, YOU'RE OVERTHINKING IT! IT'S PROBABLY THE DINOSAUR'S! THEY'RE SMART, THEY CAN MAKE IT THEMSELVES!
HOW SMART DO YOU THINK A DINOSAUR CAN GET? AND WHY, PRAY TELL, WOULD THEY NEED SHOES?!
UH, MAYBE AN ALIEN MADE THEM... OR SOMETHING...

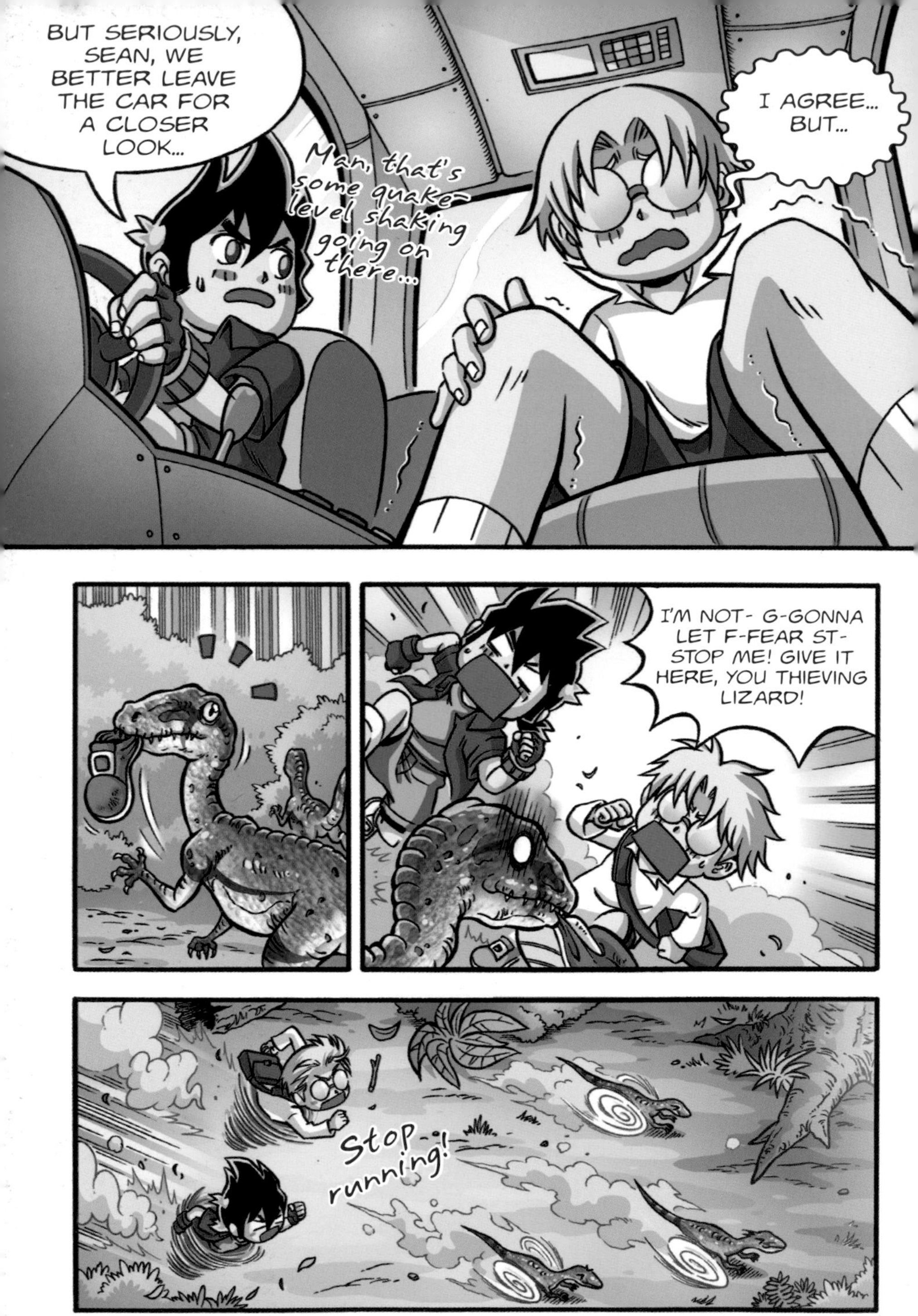
BUT SERIOUSLY, SEAN, WE BETTER LEAVE THE CAR FOR A CLOSER LOOK...
Man, that's some quake-level shaking going on there...
I AGREE... BUT...
I'M NOT- G-GONNA LET F-FEAR ST-STOP ME! GIVE IT HERE, YOU THIEVING LIZARD!
Stop running!

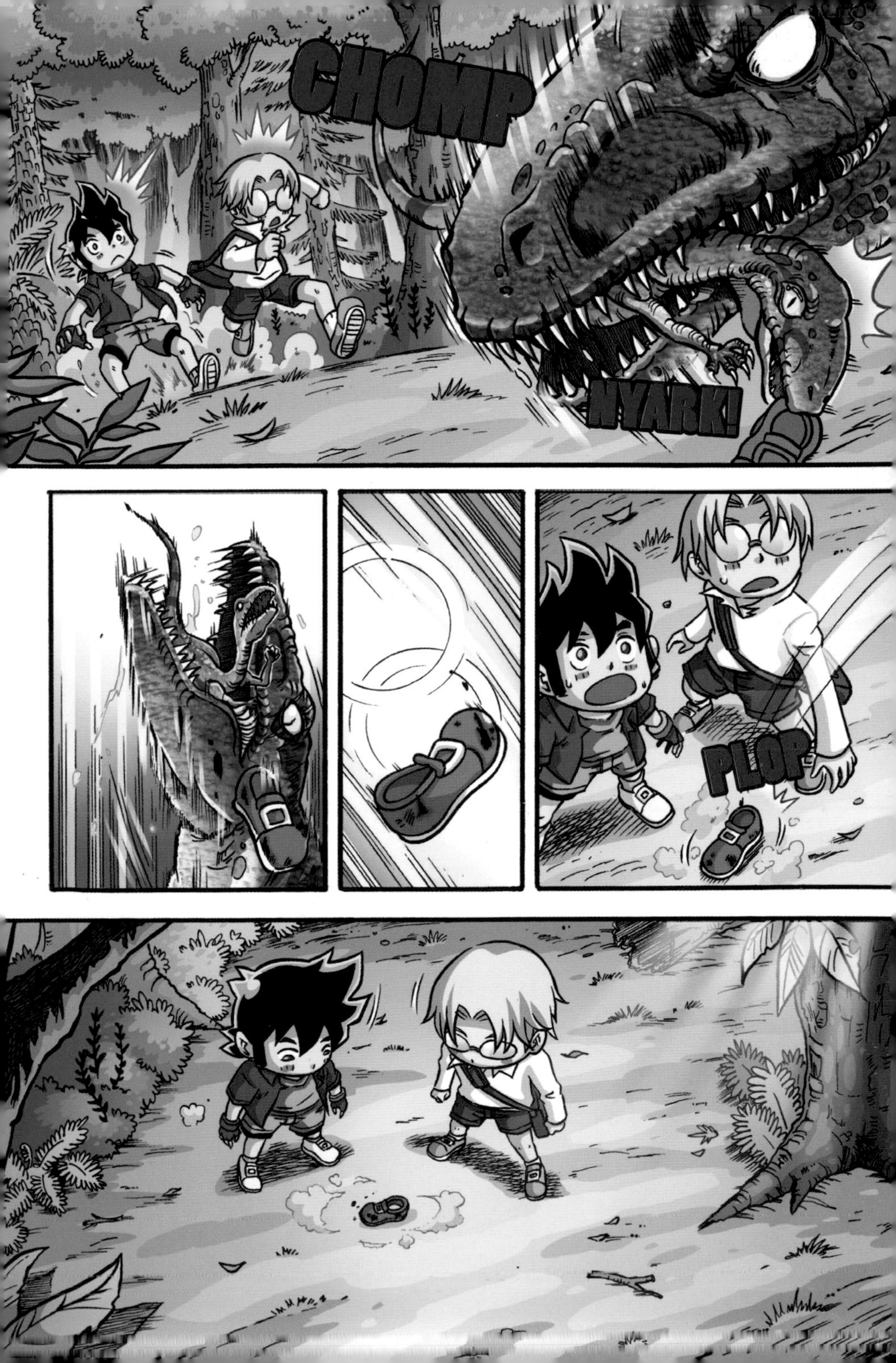
CHOMP
NYARK!
PLOP

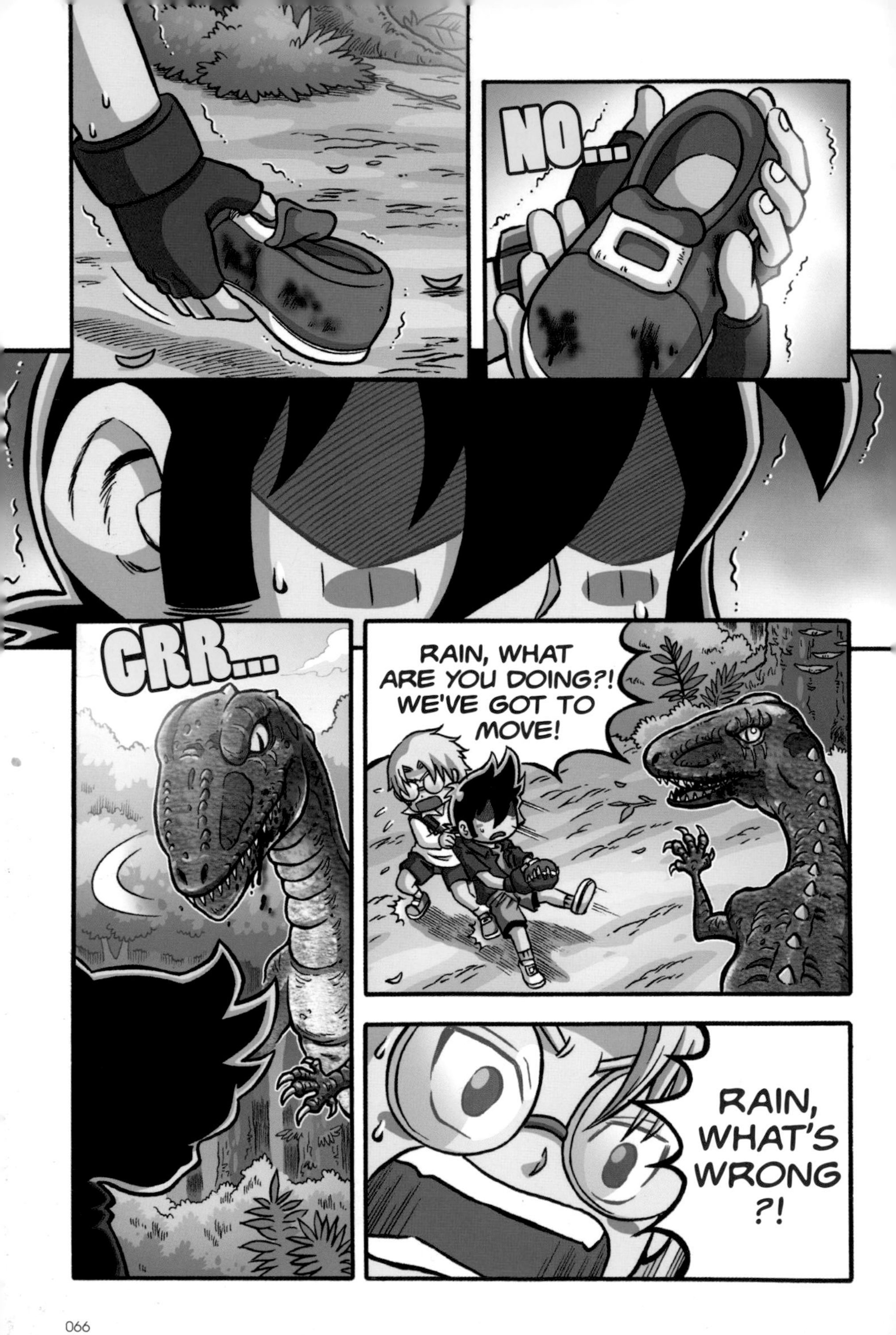
NO...
CRR...
RAIN, WHAT ARE YOU DOING?! WE'VE GOT TO MOVE!
RAIN, WHAT'S WRONG ?!

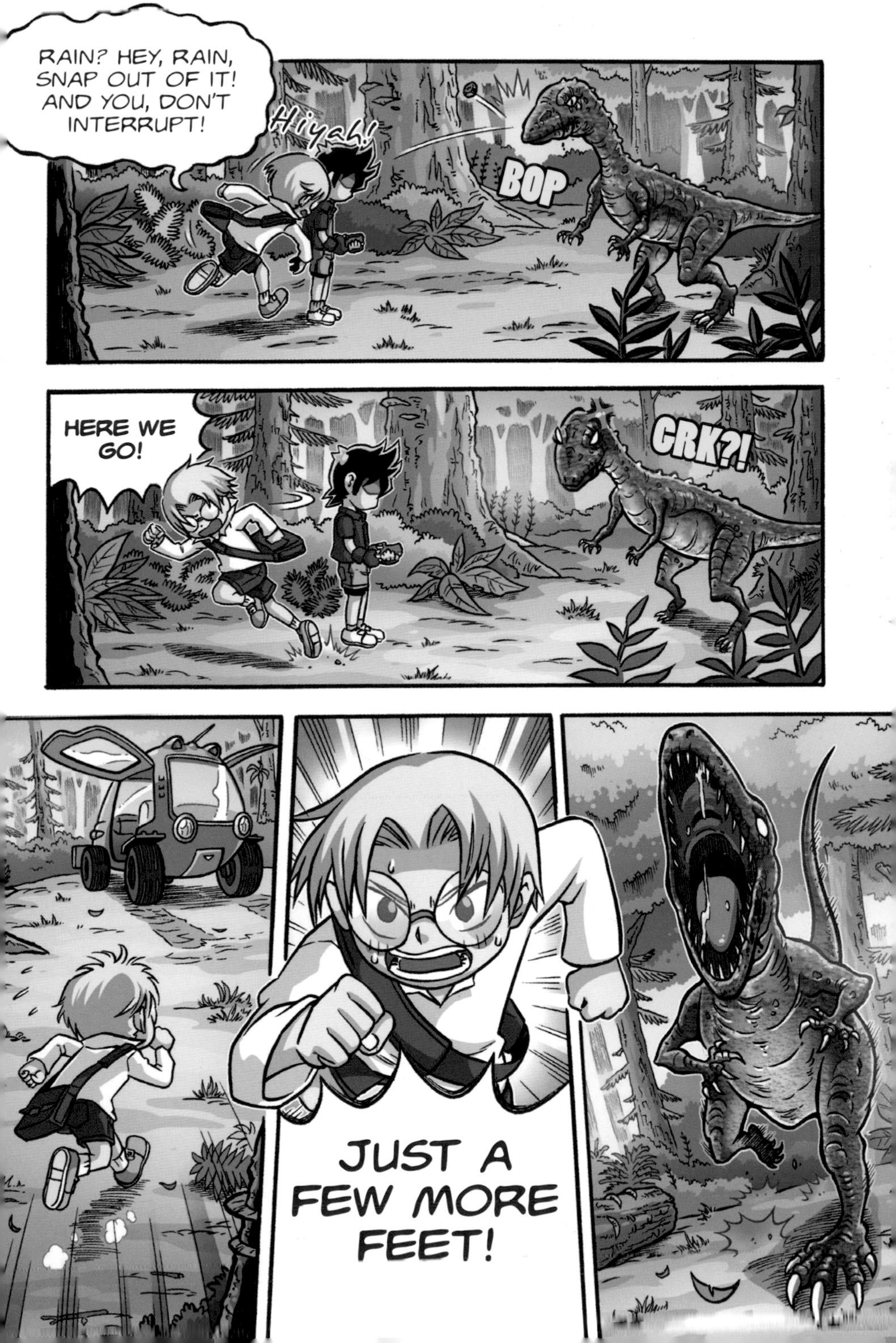
RAIN? HEY, RAIN, SNAP OUT OF IT! AND YOU, DON'T INTERRUPT!
Hiyah!
BOP
HERE WE GO!
CRK?!
JUST A FEW MORE FEET!

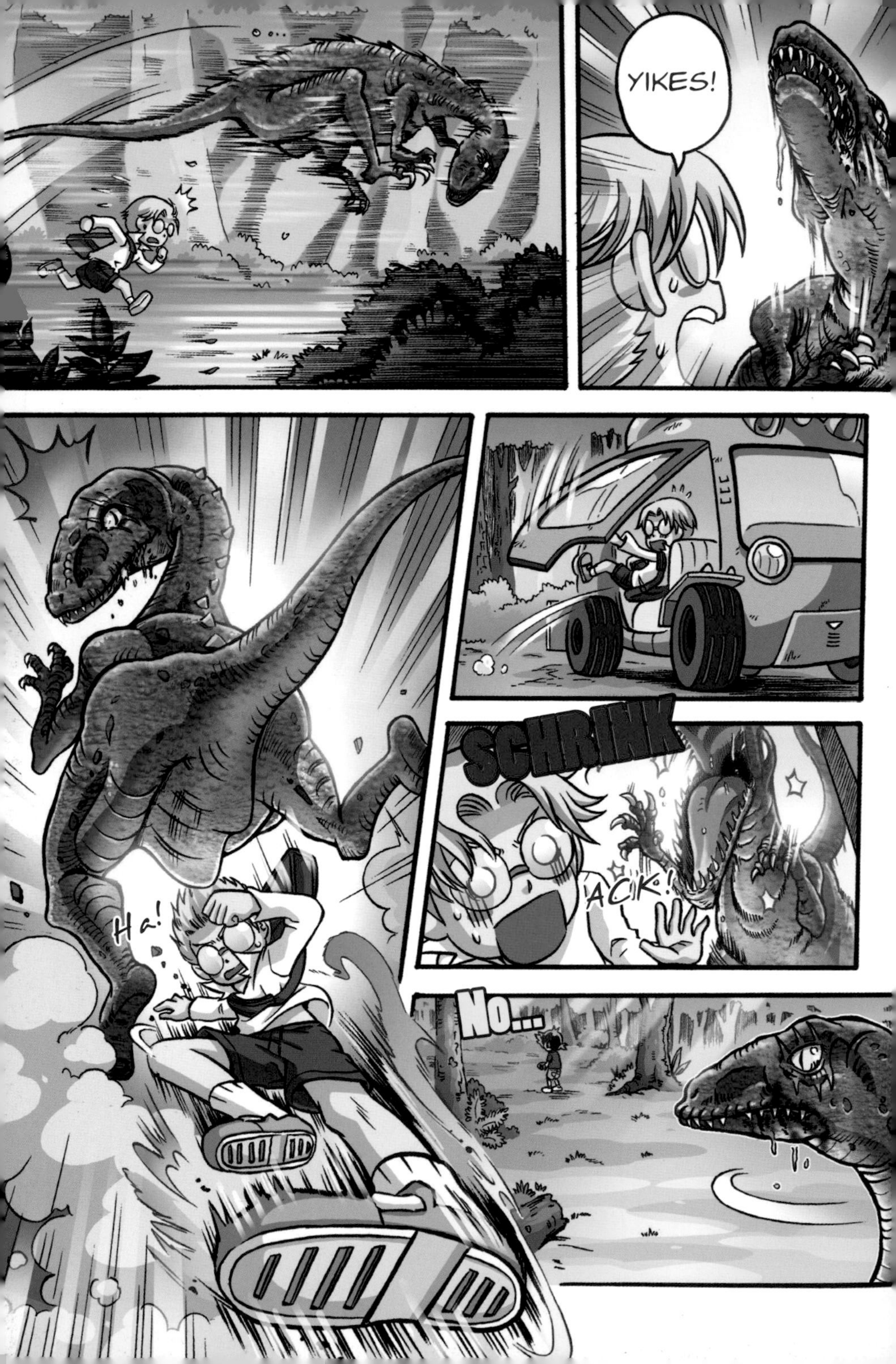

YIKES!
Ha!
SCHRINK
ACK!
No...

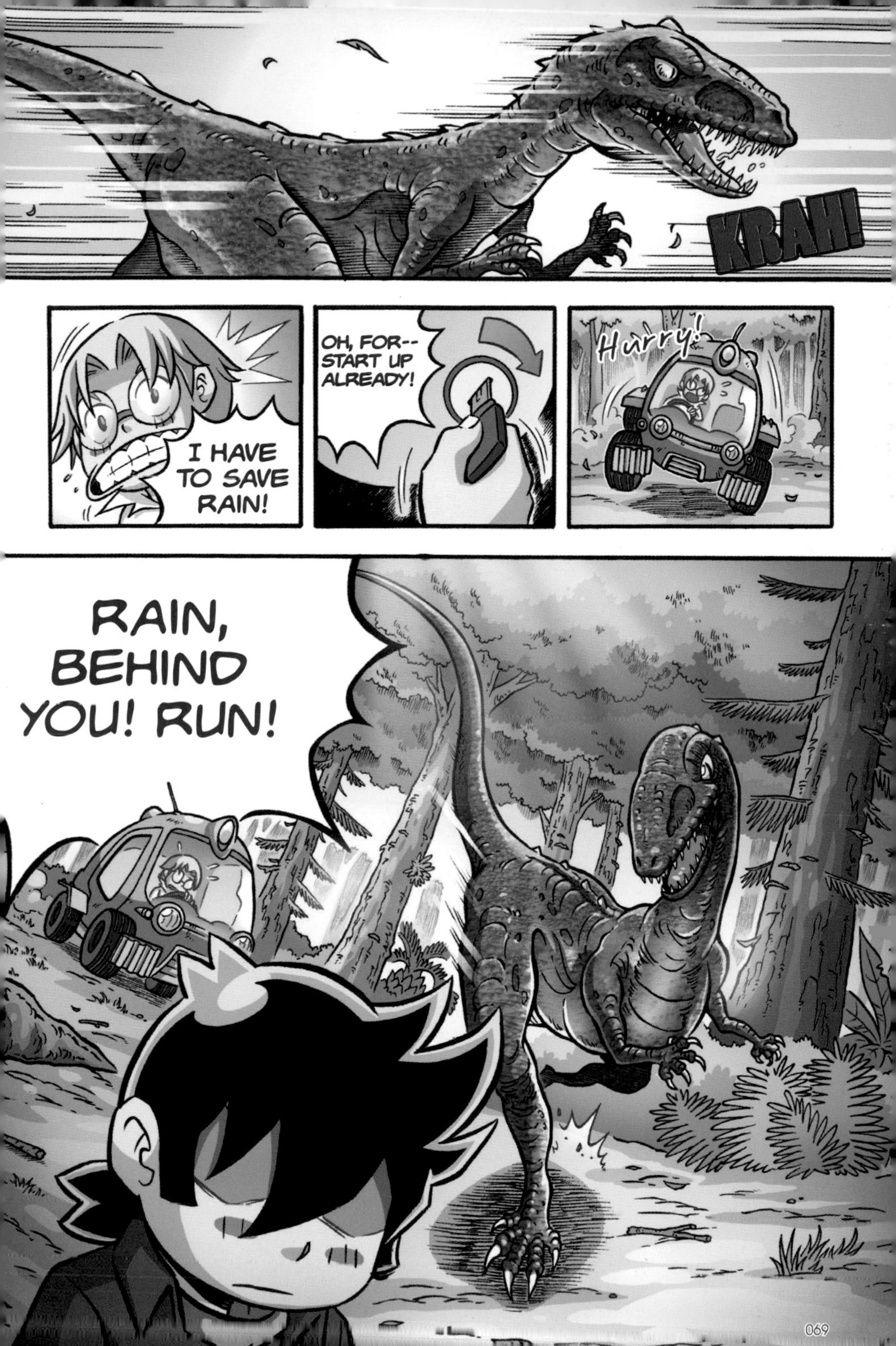
KRAH!
I HAVE TO SAVE RAIN!
OH, FOR-- START UP ALREADY!
Hurry!
RAIN, BEHIND YOU! RUN!

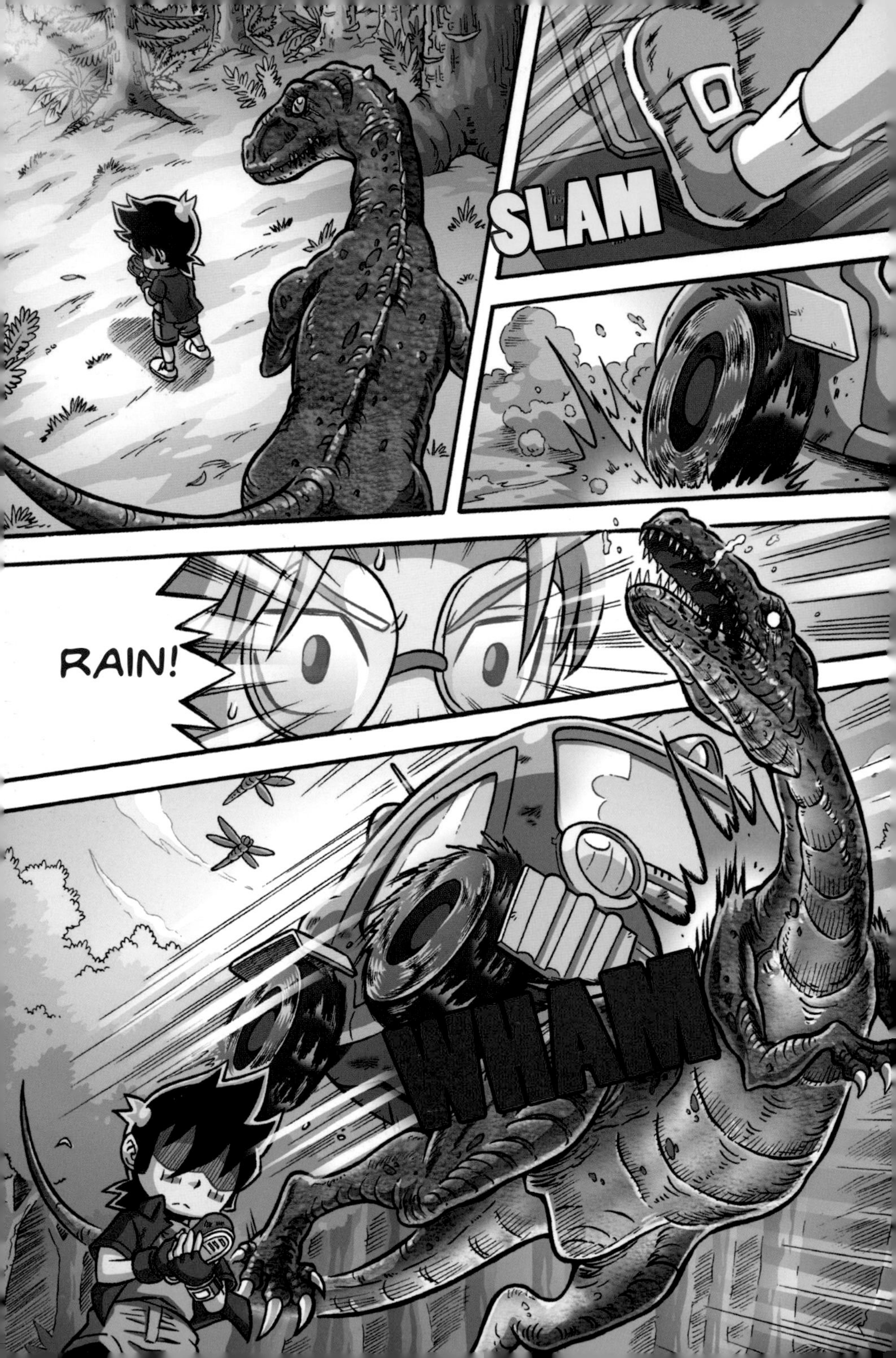
SLAM
RAIN!
WHAM

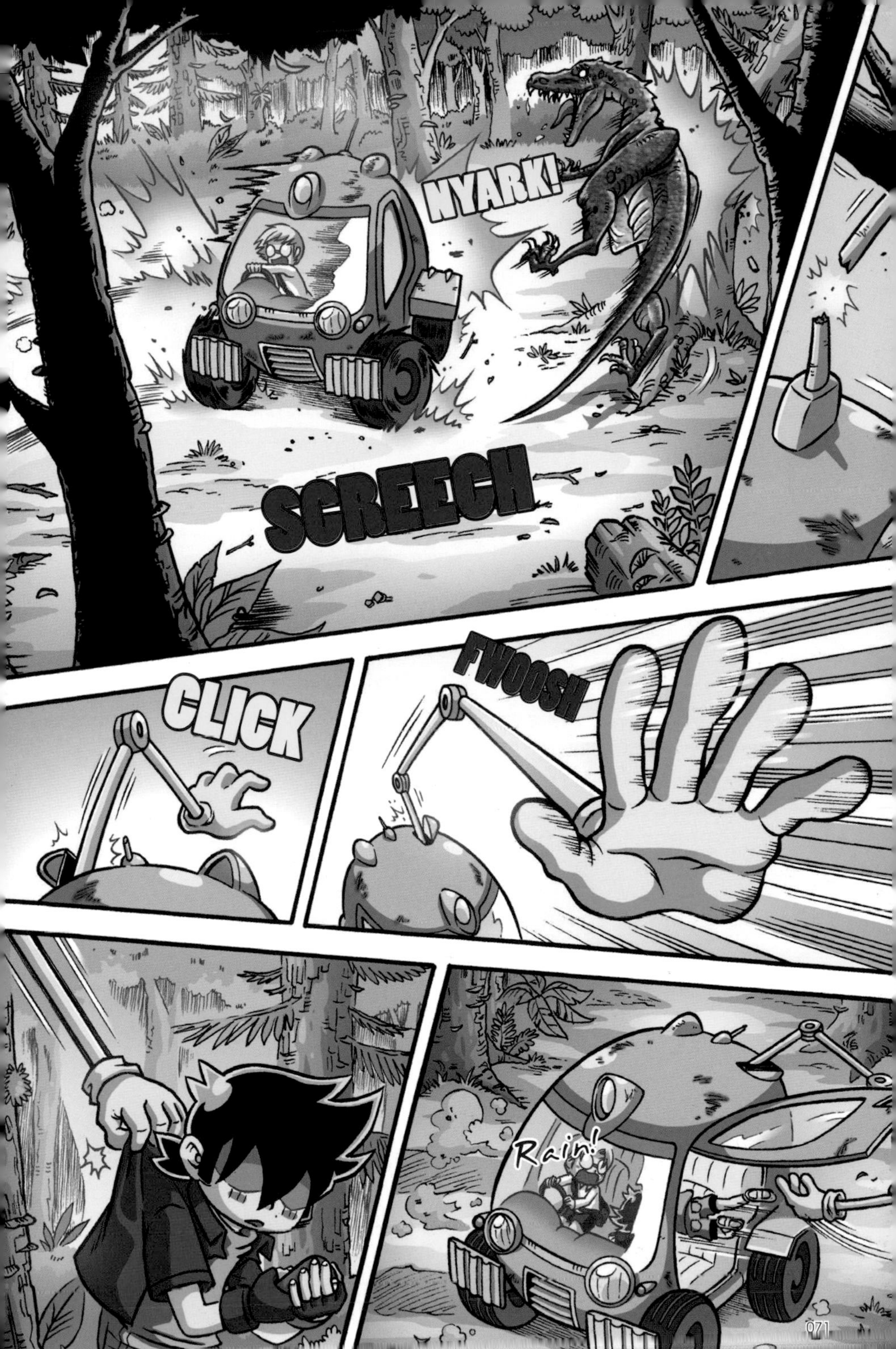
NYARK!
SCREECH
CLICK
FWOOSH
Rain!

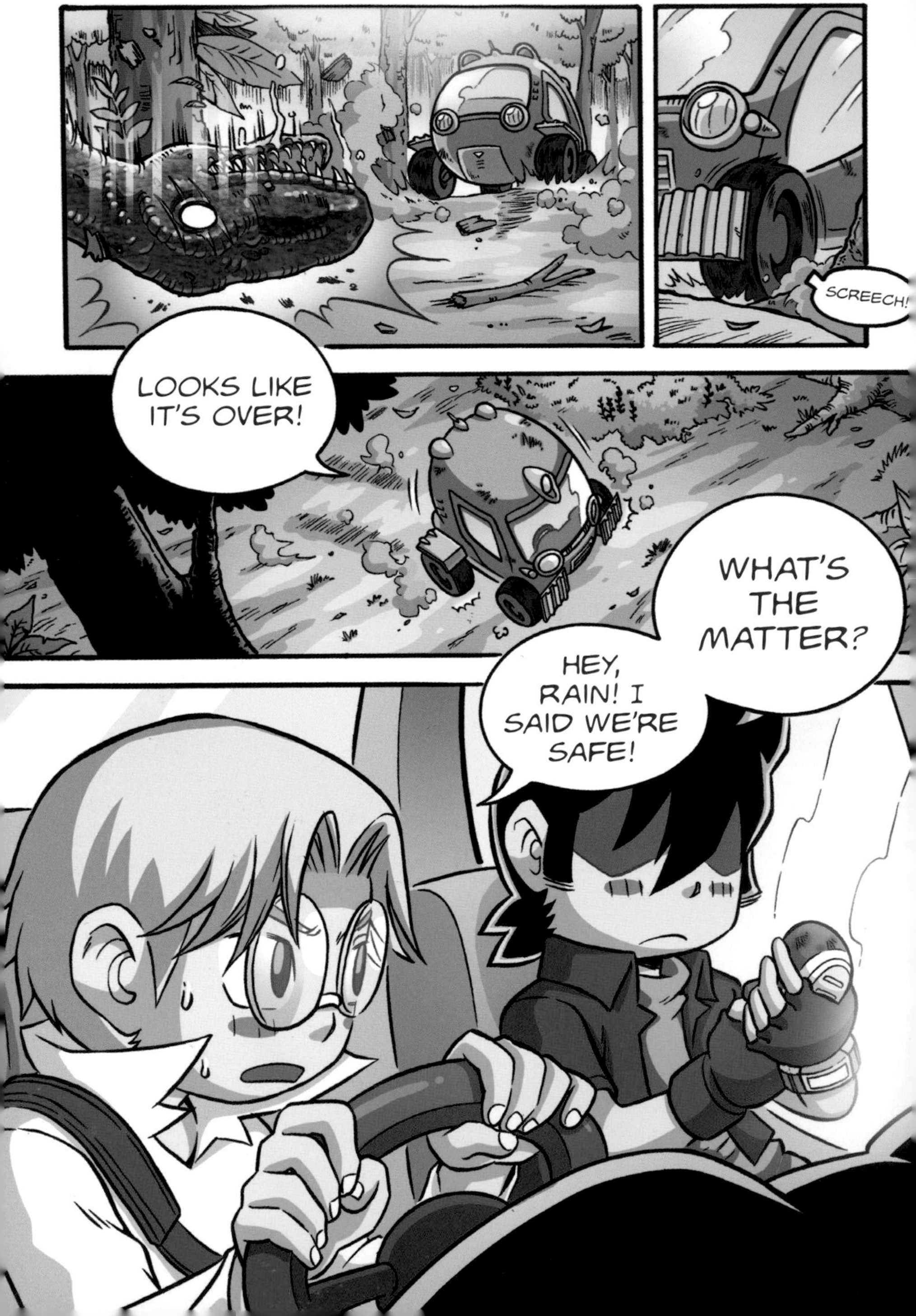
SCREECH!
LOOKS LIKE IT'S OVER!
WHAT'S THE MATTER?
HEY, RAIN! I SAID WE'RE SAFE!

DINOSAURS DIVIDED

The superorder Dinosauria (basically, a general term for all dinosaurs) was divided into the two suborders; Saurischians (lizard-hipped) and Ornithischians (bird-hipped). The differences between the two groups were the bone structures of their pelvises.

Saurischia

Viewing it from the side, the Saurischians's pelvis structure had a three-pronged shape, with the pubic bone extending forward underneath the ilium while the ischium pointed backwards. This structure is similar to that of reptiles!

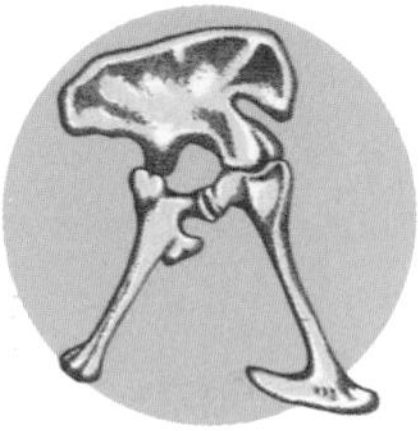

SAURISCHIA

Prosauropods

Prosauropods such as Plateosaurus were a group of small to mid-sized dinosaurs that lived during the Late Triassic. They had sturdy bodies and could walk on two legs (bipedal).

Era: Late Triassic.
Completely extinct by the Early Jurassic.

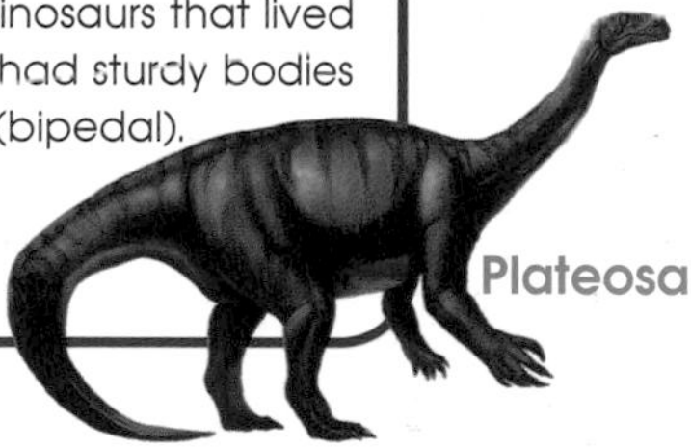

Plateosaurus

Sauropodomorphs

Sauropodomorphs evolved from the Prosauropods and most of them were large herbivores. Their common characteristics included their small heads, long necks and tails and spatula-like teeth.

Era: Jurassic to Cretaceous

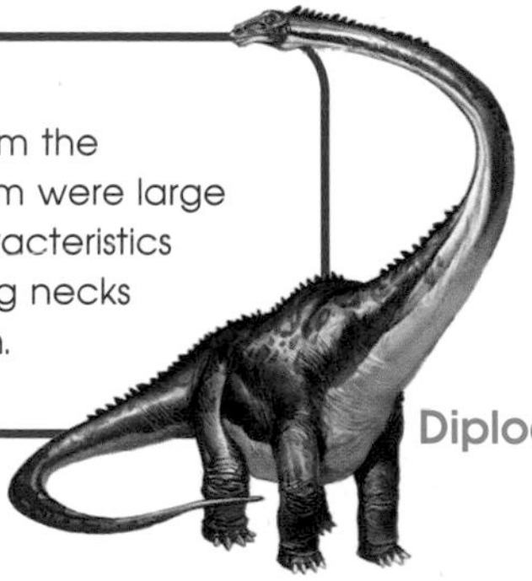

Diplodocus

Theropods

Theropods were not only the earliest, but also the most successfully evolved dinosaurs. They were bipedal with long sharp claws, and sharp jagged teeth with serrated edges.

Era: Late Triassic to Cretaceous

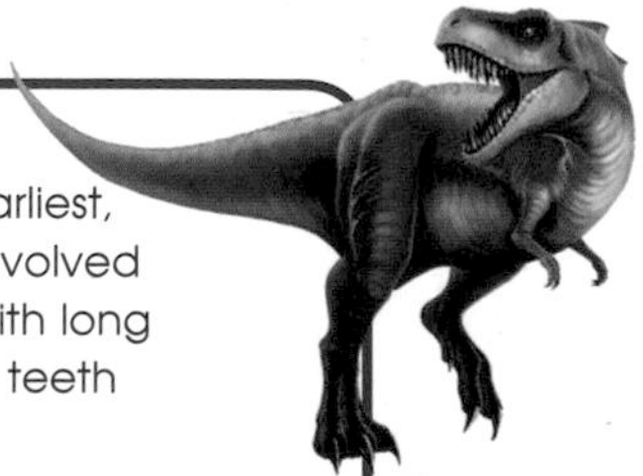

Tyrannosaurus rex

Ornithischia

For the Ornithischians, their ilium was greatly expanded with their pubis jutting forward. Looking at it from the side, their bones seemed to extend in four directions. These bones can be divided into the front and back halves of the ilium; one part of the pubic bone was connected to the ischium while the back and other parts of the pubic bone provided support.

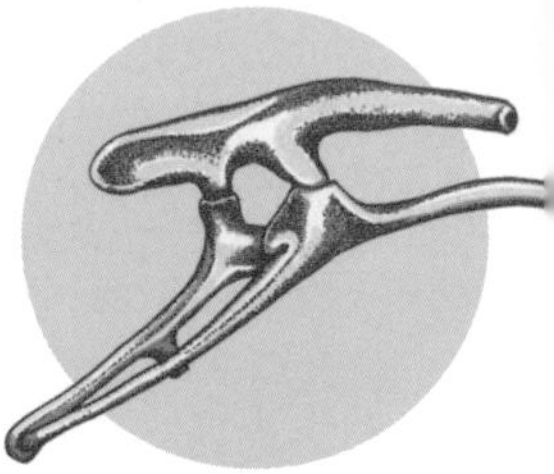

ORNITHISCHIA

Ornithopods

Ornithopod fossils comprise the vast majority of fossils discovered. They were all herbivores, with some being bipedal and others quadruped.

Era: Late Triassic to Cretaceous

Iguanodon

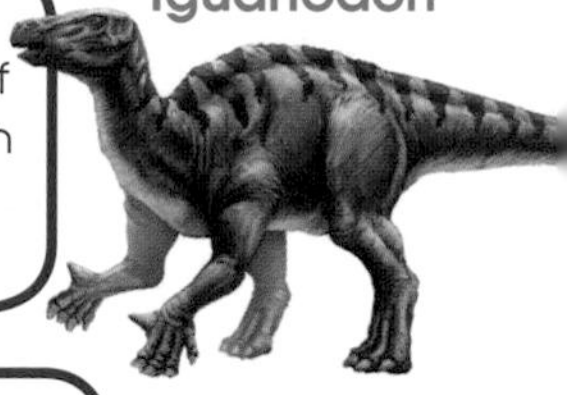

Stegosauria

Stegosaurs were herbivores which first appeared during the Jurassic, lasting until the early Cretaceous. They walked on all fours with a series of straight plates and spines on their humped backs, and also had a pair of spikes near the end of their tails.

Period: Jurassic to Early Cretaceous

Stegosaurus

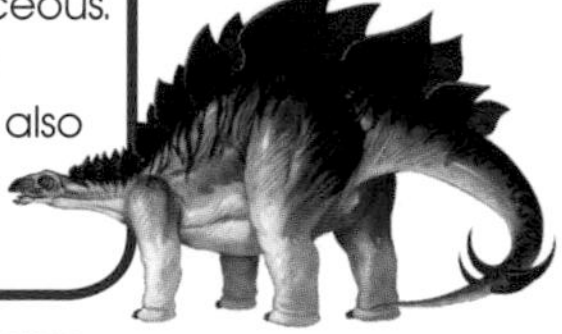

Ankylosaurus

Ankylosaurs were dinosaurs with short, sturdy bodies covered in heavy plate armor. They had four short limbs, with their hind limbs longer than their front limbs, causing them to move slowly.

Era: Cretaceous

Hylaeosaurus

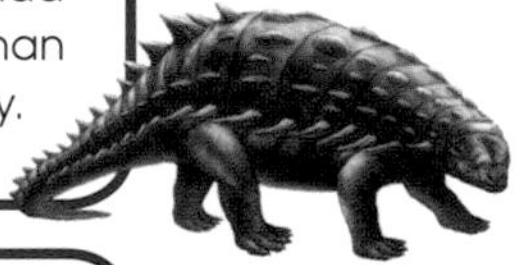

Ceratopsia

Ceratopsids were dinosaurs exclusive to the Cretaceous Era. The back of their skull flared out rearwards, extending the parietal and squamosal bones of the skull roof to form a neck frill which was triangular-shaped.

Era: Cretaceous

Triceratops

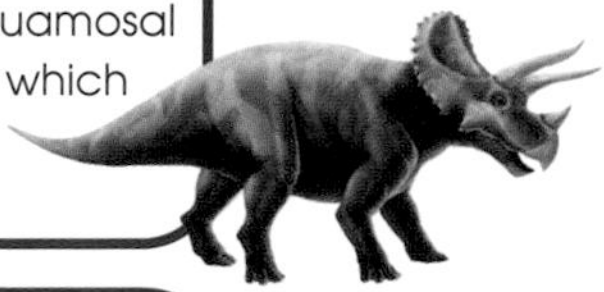

Pachycephalosauria

The most notable pachycephalosaur features were their thick dome-shaped skulls and closed temporal holes. Their pubic bones were crowded out by their ischiums, forming their acetabulums.

Era: Cretaceous

Pachycephalo-saurus

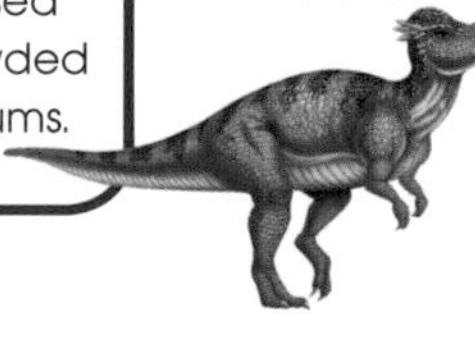

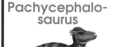

Lagosuchus

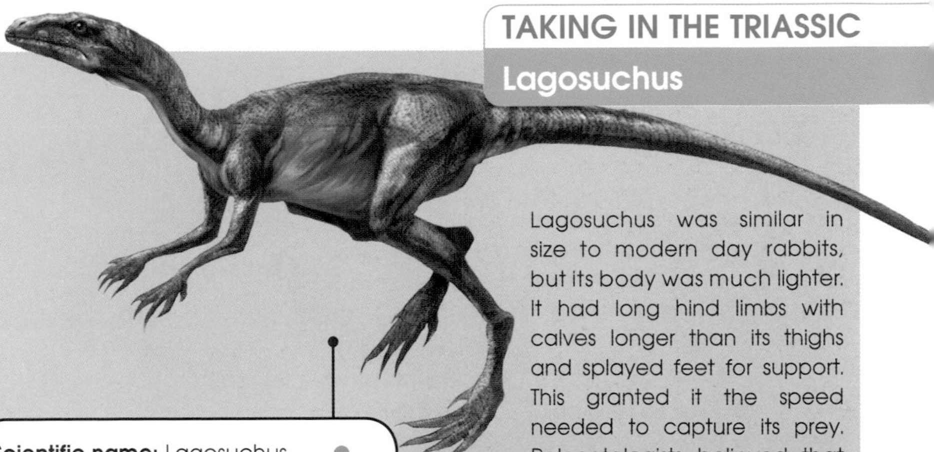

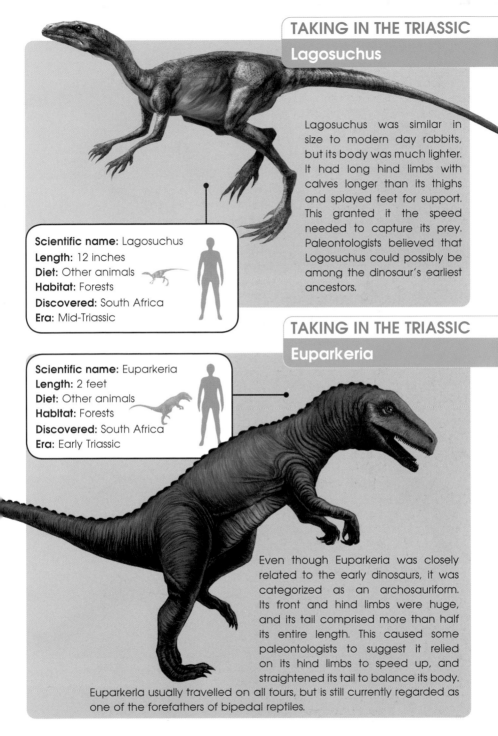

Lagosuchus was similar in size to modern day rabbits, but its body was much lighter. It had long hind limbs with calves longer than its thighs and splayed feet for support. This granted it the speed needed to capture its prey. Paleontologists believed that Logosuchus could possibly be among the dinosaur's earliest ancestors.

Scientific name: Lagosuchus
Length: 12 inches
Diet: Other animals
Habitat: Forests
Discovered: South Africa
Era: Mid-Triassic

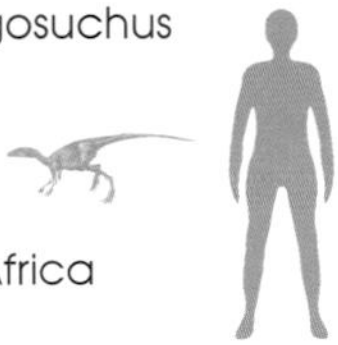

Euparkeria

Scientific name: Euparkeria
Length: 2 feet
Diet: Other animals
Habitat: Forests
Discovered: South Africa
Era: Early Triassic

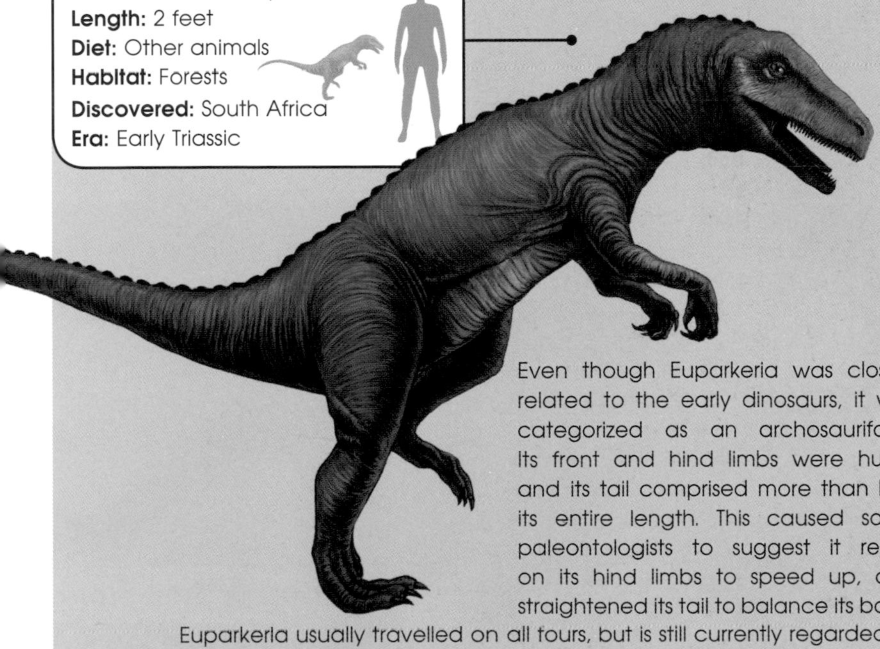

Even though Euparkeria was closely related to the early dinosaurs, it was categorized as an archosauriform. Its front and hind limbs were huge, and its tail comprised more than half its entire length. This caused some paleontologists to suggest it relied on its hind limbs to speed up, and straightened its tail to balance its body. Euparkeria usually travelled on all fours, but is still currently regarded as one of the forefathers of bipedal reptiles.

TAKING IN THE TRIASSIC

Mussaurus

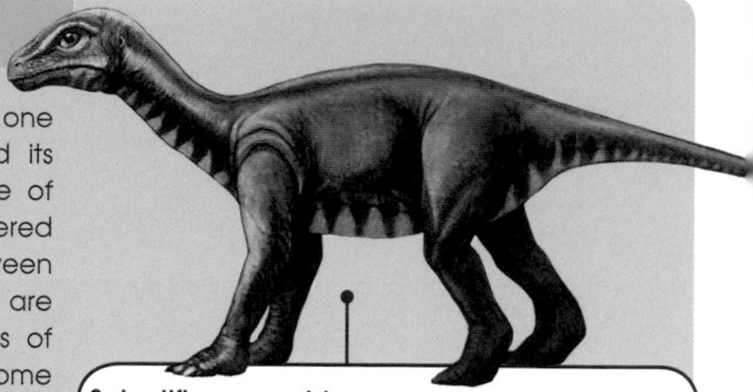

Mussaurus was recognized as one of the earliest dinosaurs and its fossil remains were also some of the smallest; all fossils discovered so far have measured between 8 to 15 inches. As such, they are suspected to be the remains of newly birthed hatchlings. Some paleontologists estimate that the Mussaurus could have reached a length of up to 10 feet.

Scientific name: Mussaurus
Length: 8 to 15 inches (currently known)
Diet: Herbivore
Habitat: Unknown
Discovered: Argentina
Era: Late Triassic

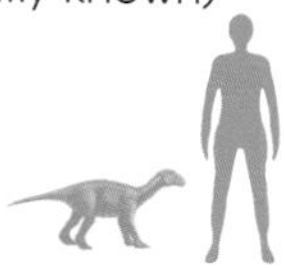

TAKING IN THE TRIASSIC

Lufengosaurus

Lufengosaurus was one of the first complete dinosaur fossils to be discovered in China. It was a mid-sized prosauropod dinosaur that measured around 7 feet upright—about the size of modern-day horses. It had a small head and forelimbs that were half the length of its hind limbs indicating it could have been primarily bipedal.

Scientific name: Lufengosaurus
Length: 20 feet
Diet: Herbivore
Habitat: Forest
Discovered: China
Era: Late Triassic to Early Jurassic

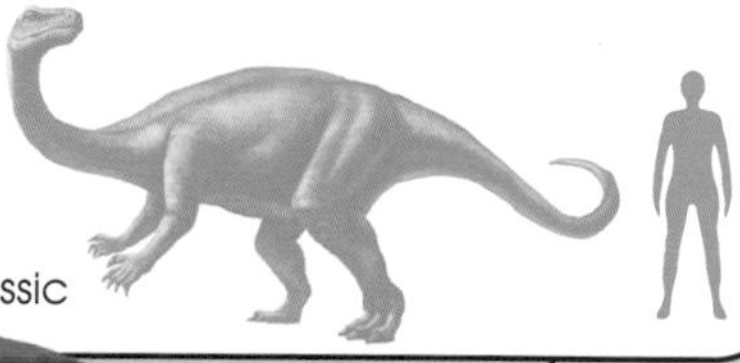

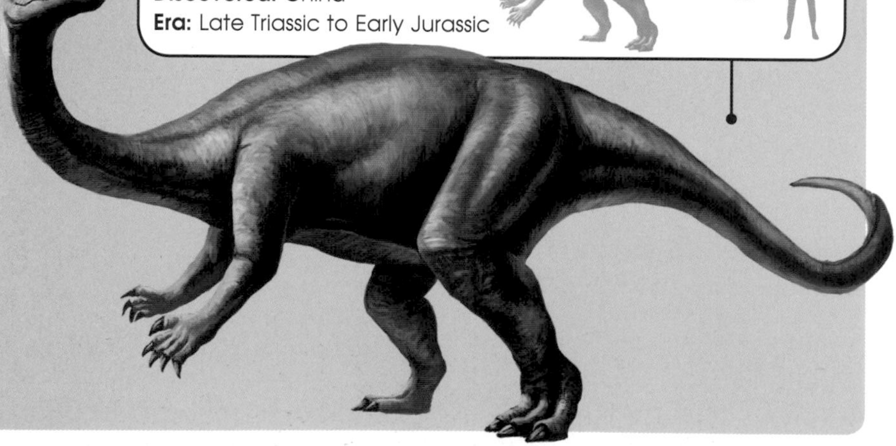

CHAPTER 4
HUNTER-KILLERS

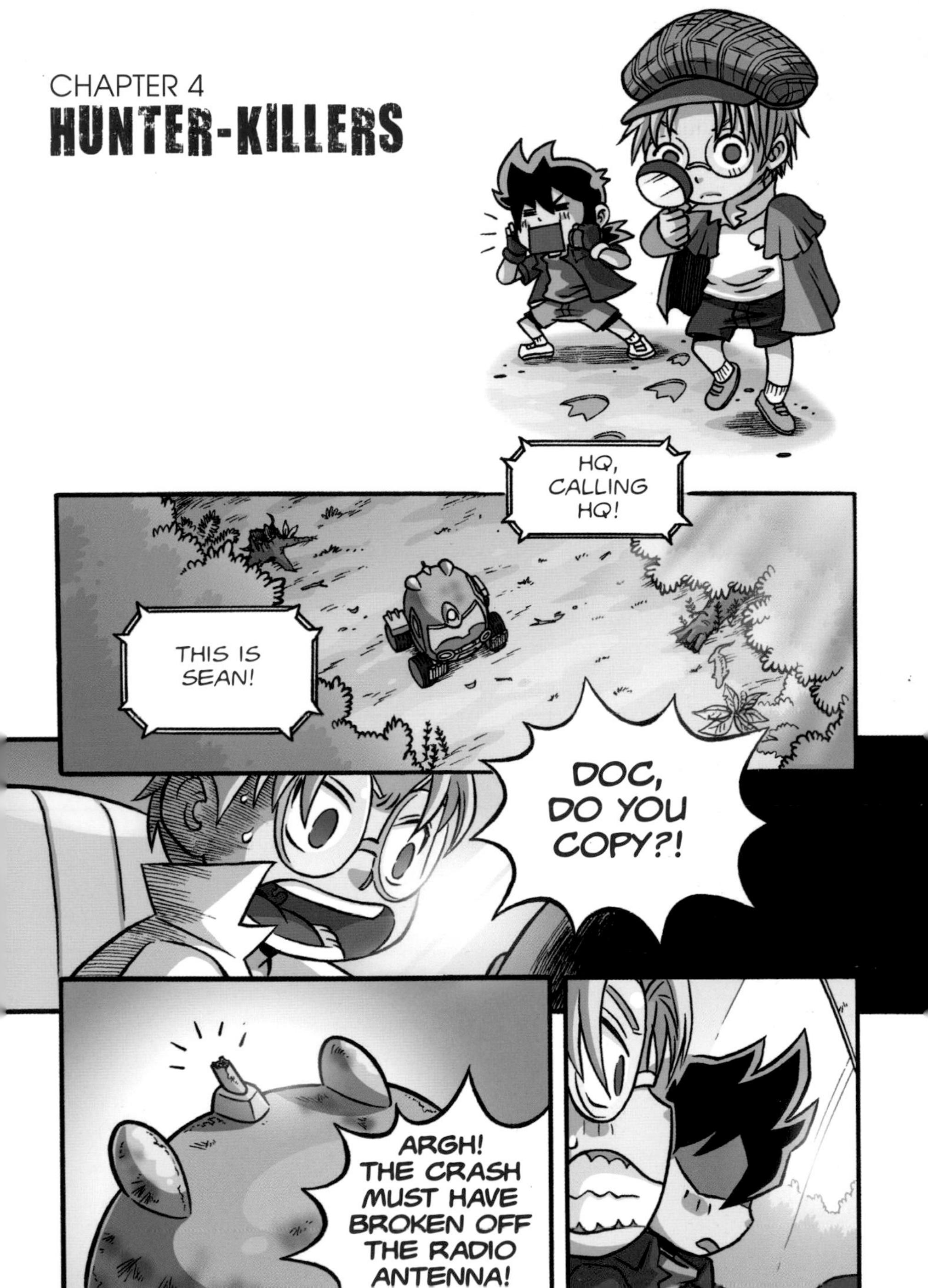
HQ, CALLING HQ!
THIS IS SEAN!
DOC, DO YOU COPY?!
ARGH! THE CRASH MUST HAVE BROKEN OFF THE RADIO ANTENNA!

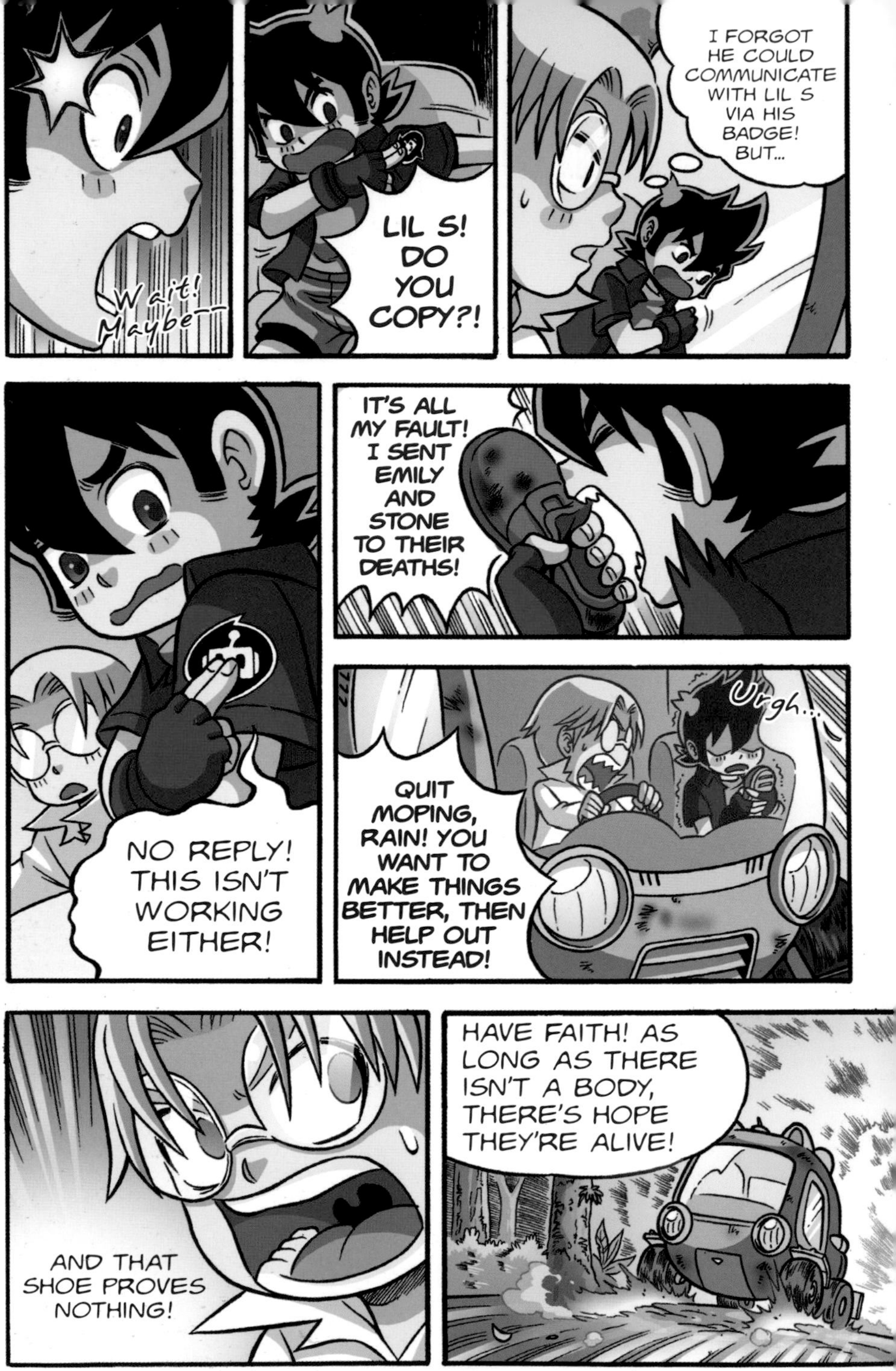
Wait! Maybe--
LIL S! DO YOU COPY?!
I FORGOT HE COULD COMMUNICATE WITH LIL S VIA HIS BADGE! BUT...
IT'S ALL MY FAULT! I SENT EMILY AND STONE TO THEIR DEATHS!
NO REPLY! THIS ISN'T WORKING EITHER!
Urgh...
QUIT MOPING, RAIN! YOU WANT TO MAKE THINGS BETTER, THEN HELP OUT INSTEAD!
AND THAT SHOE PROVES NOTHING!
HAVE FAITH! AS LONG AS THERE ISN'T A BODY, THERE'S HOPE THEY'RE ALIVE!

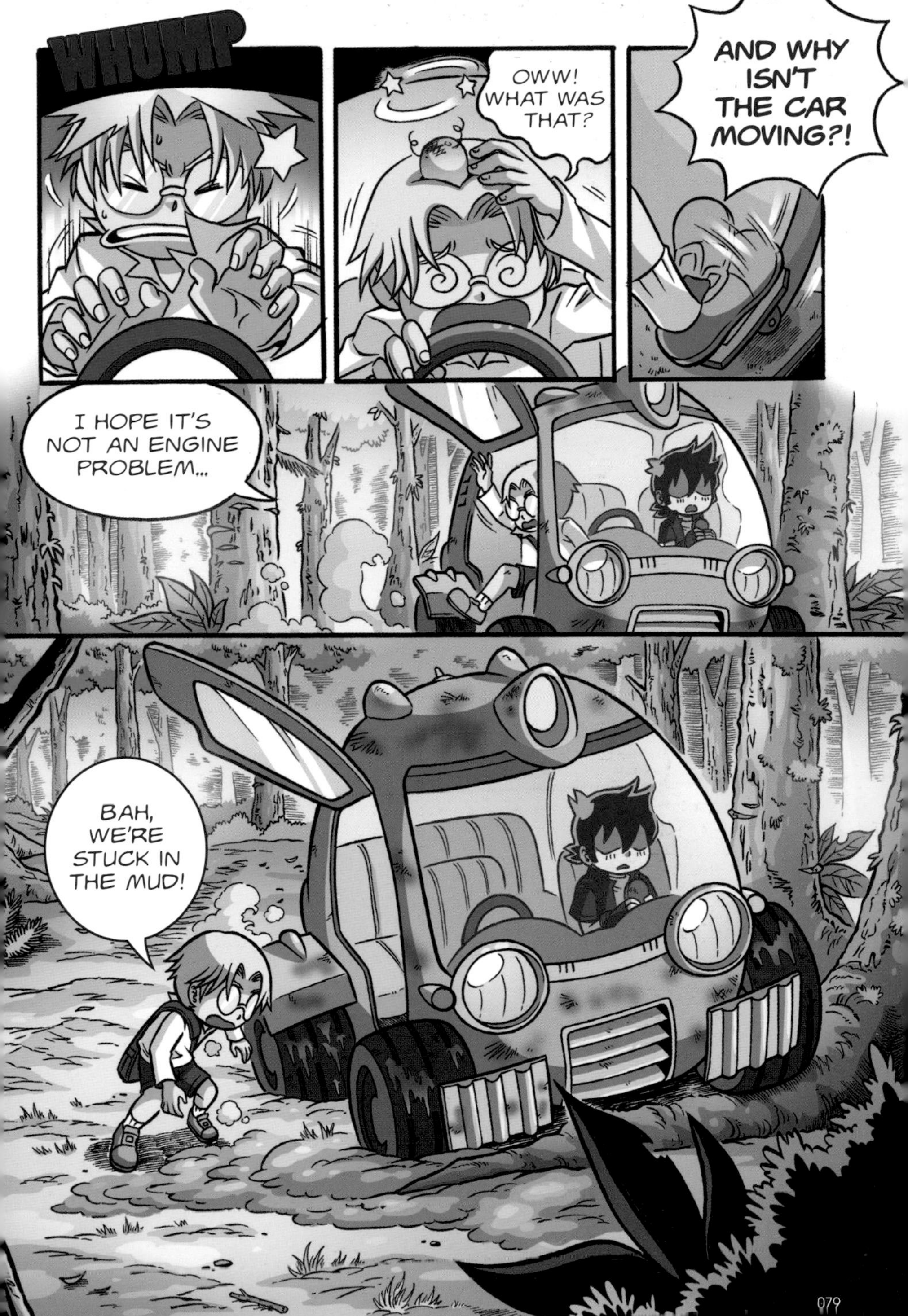
WHUMP
OWW! WHAT WAS THAT?
AND WHY ISN'T THE CAR MOVING?!
I HOPE IT'S NOT AN ENGINE PROBLEM...
BAH, WE'RE STUCK IN THE MUD!

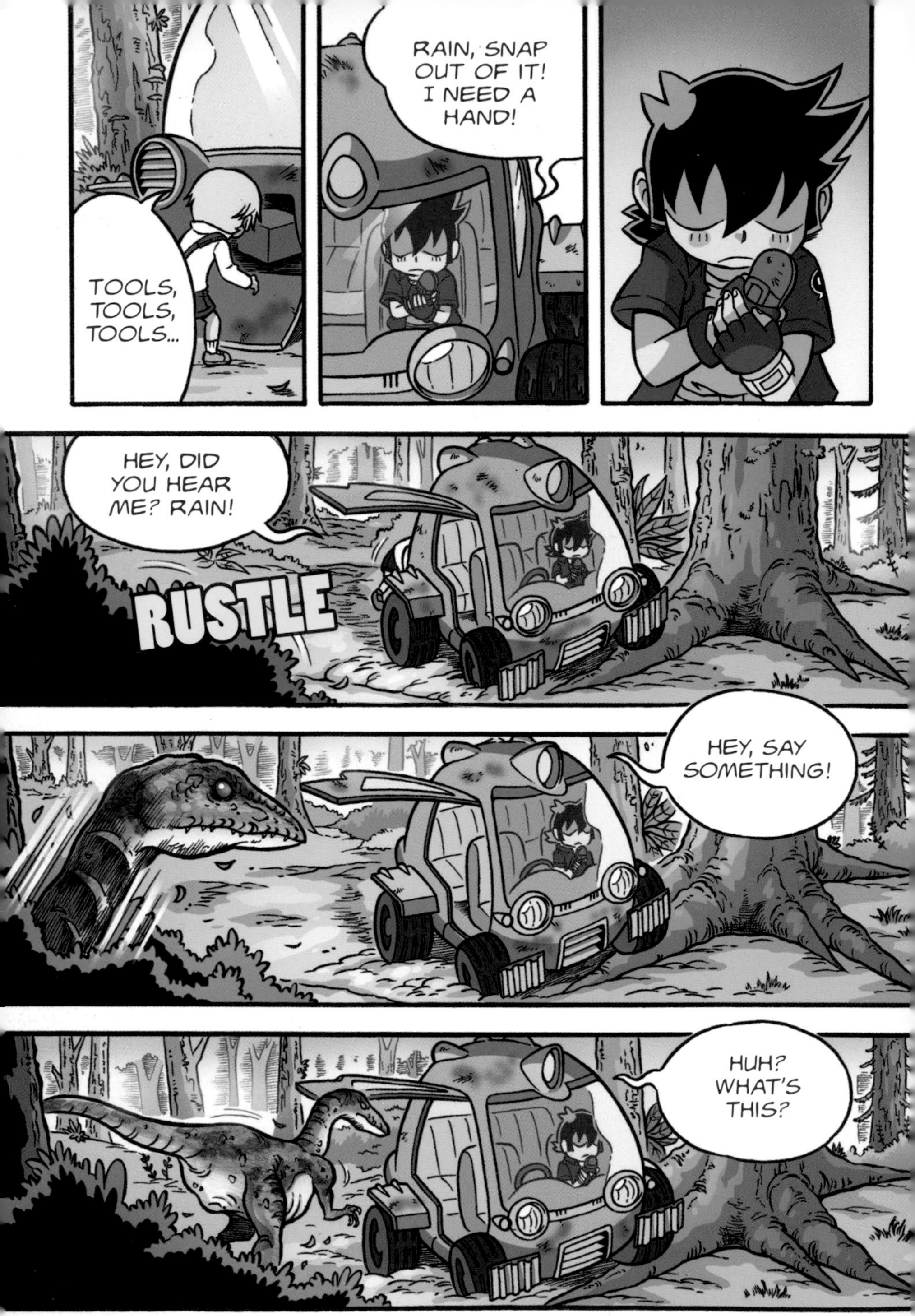
TOOLS, TOOLS, TOOLS...
RAIN, SNAP OUT OF IT! I NEED A HAND!
HEY, DID YOU HEAR ME? RAIN!
RUSTLE
HEY, SAY SOMETHING!
HUH? WHAT'S THIS?

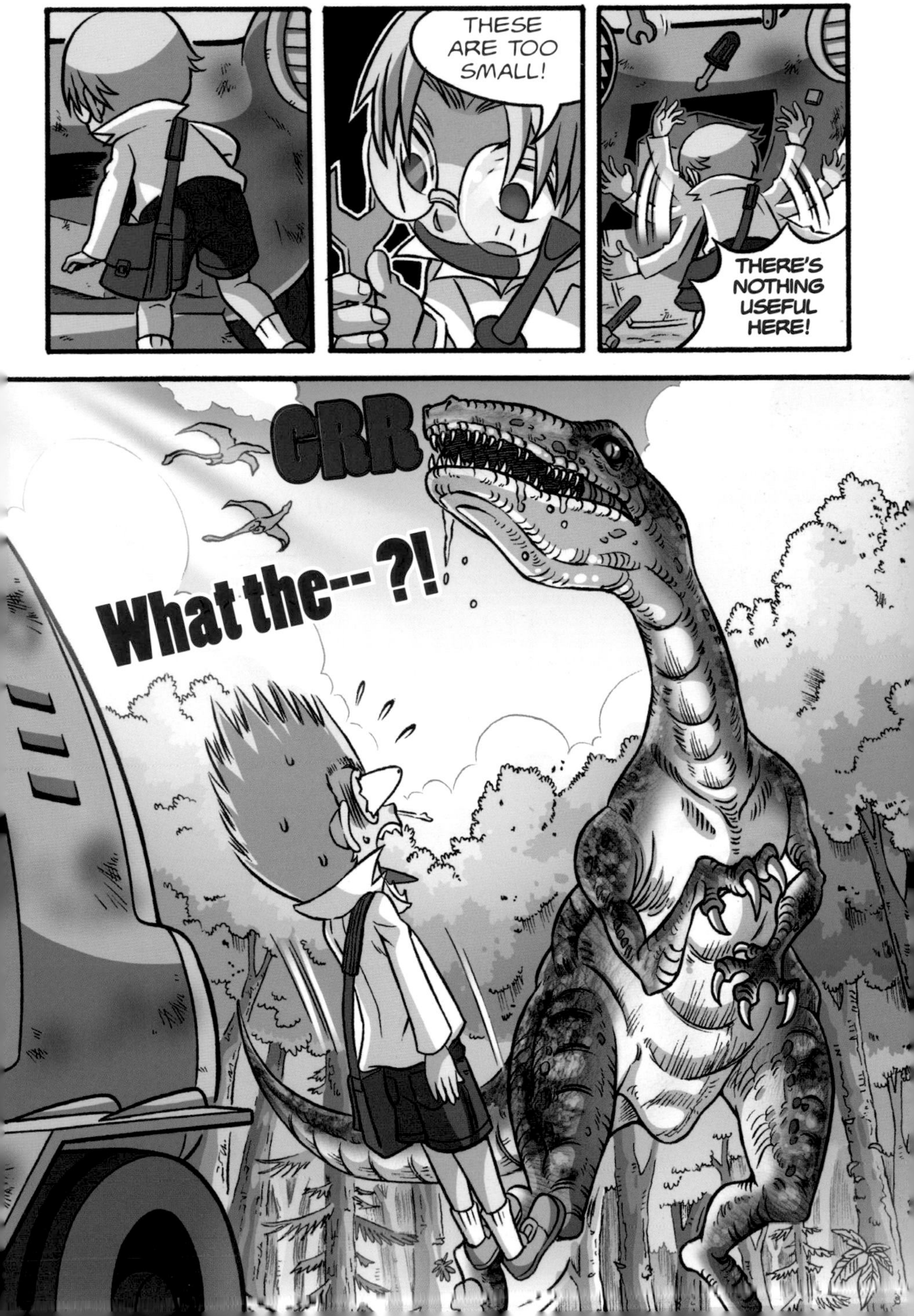
THESE ARE TOO SMALL!
THERE'S NOTHING USEFUL HERE!
CRR
What the-- ?!

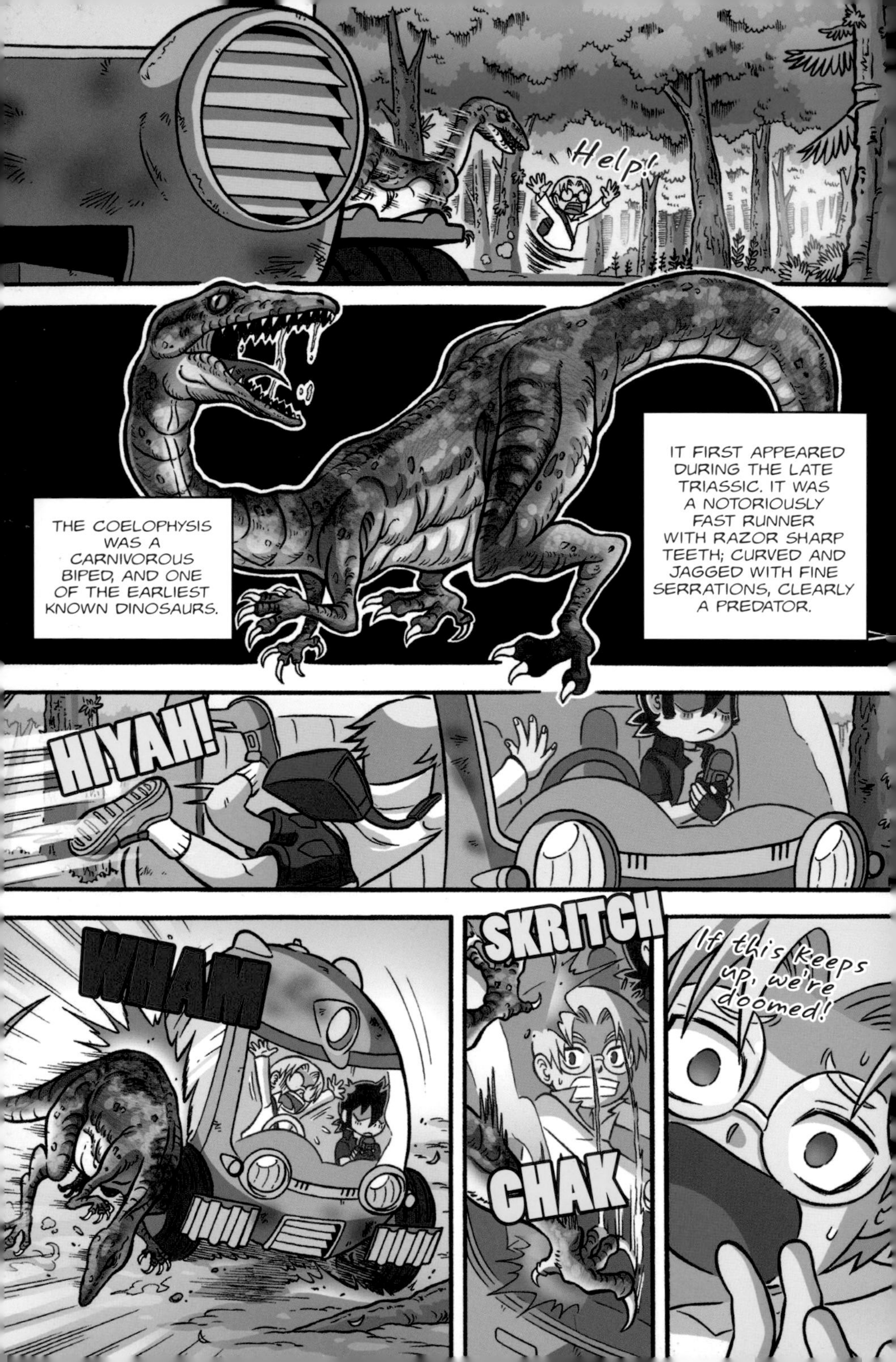
Help!
THE COELOPHYSIS WAS A CARNIVOROUS BIPED, AND ONE OF THE EARLIEST KNOWN DINOSAURS.
IT FIRST APPEARED DURING THE LATE TRIASSIC. IT WAS A NOTORIOUSLY FAST RUNNER WITH RAZOR SHARP TEETH; CURVED AND JAGGED WITH FINE SERRATIONS, CLEARLY A PREDATOR.
HIYAH!
WHAM
SKRITCH
CHAK
If this keeps up, we're doomed!

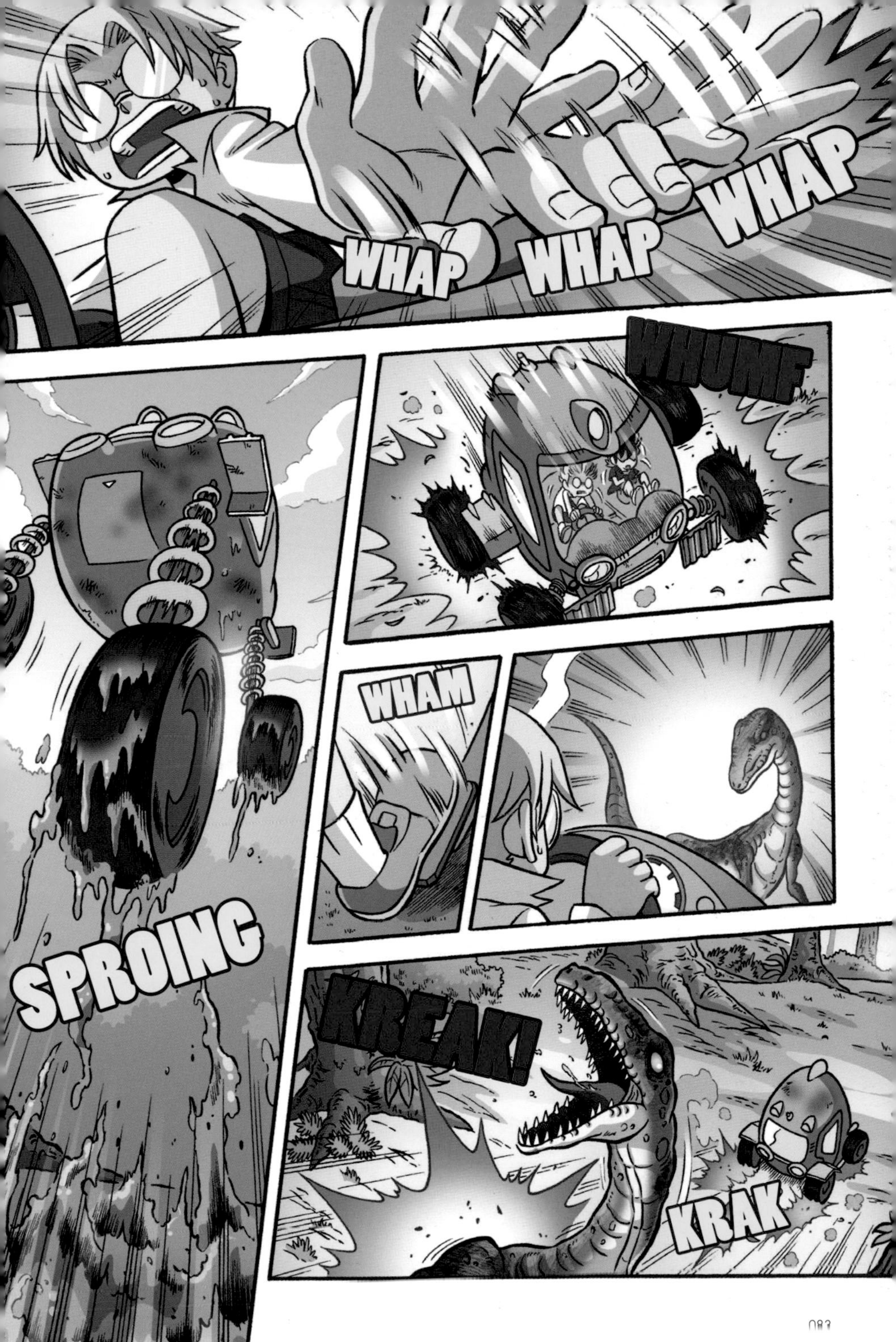
WHAP
WHAP
WHAP
WHUMF
WHAM
SPROING
KREAK!
KRAK

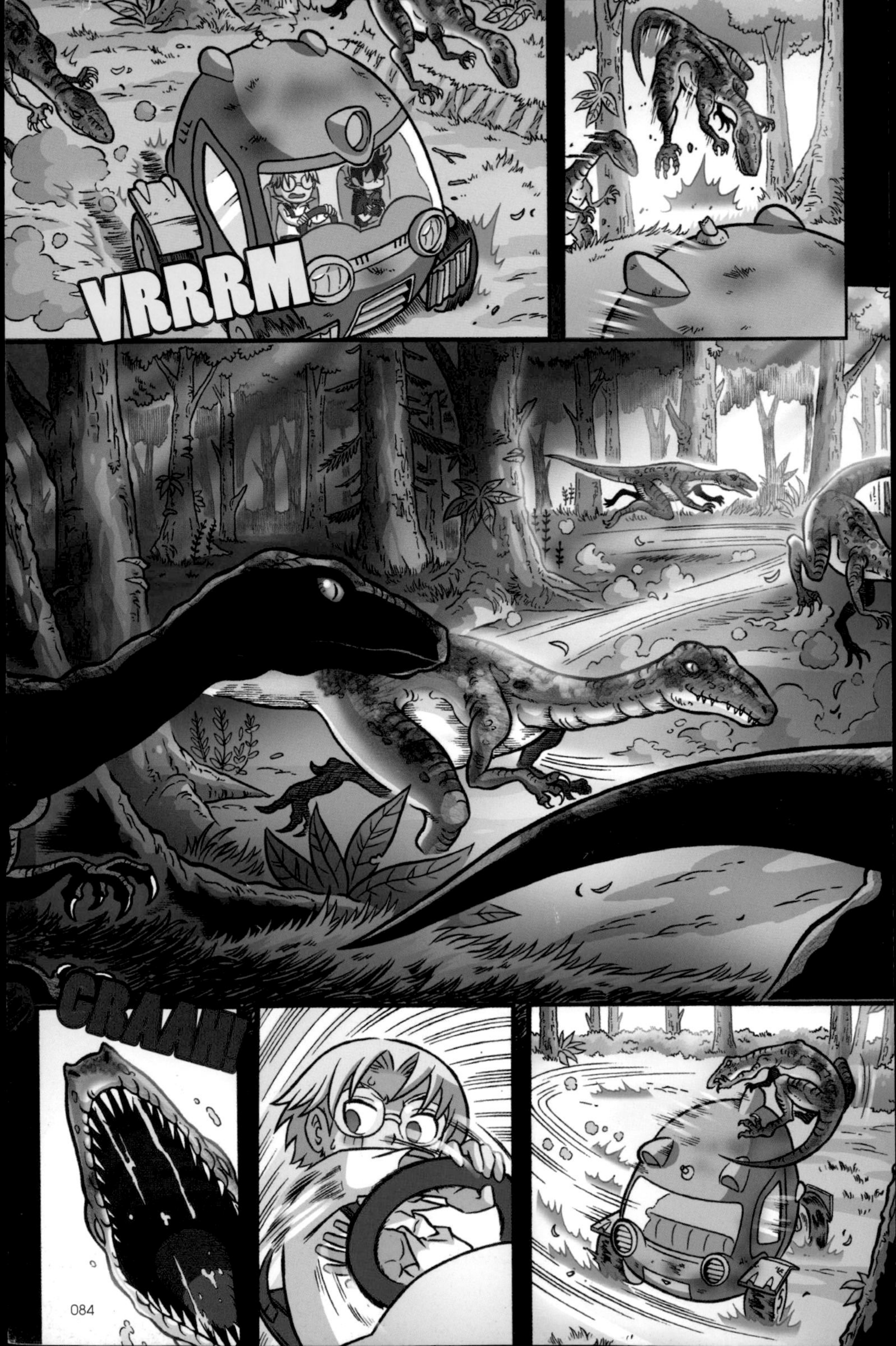
VRRRM
CRAAAH!

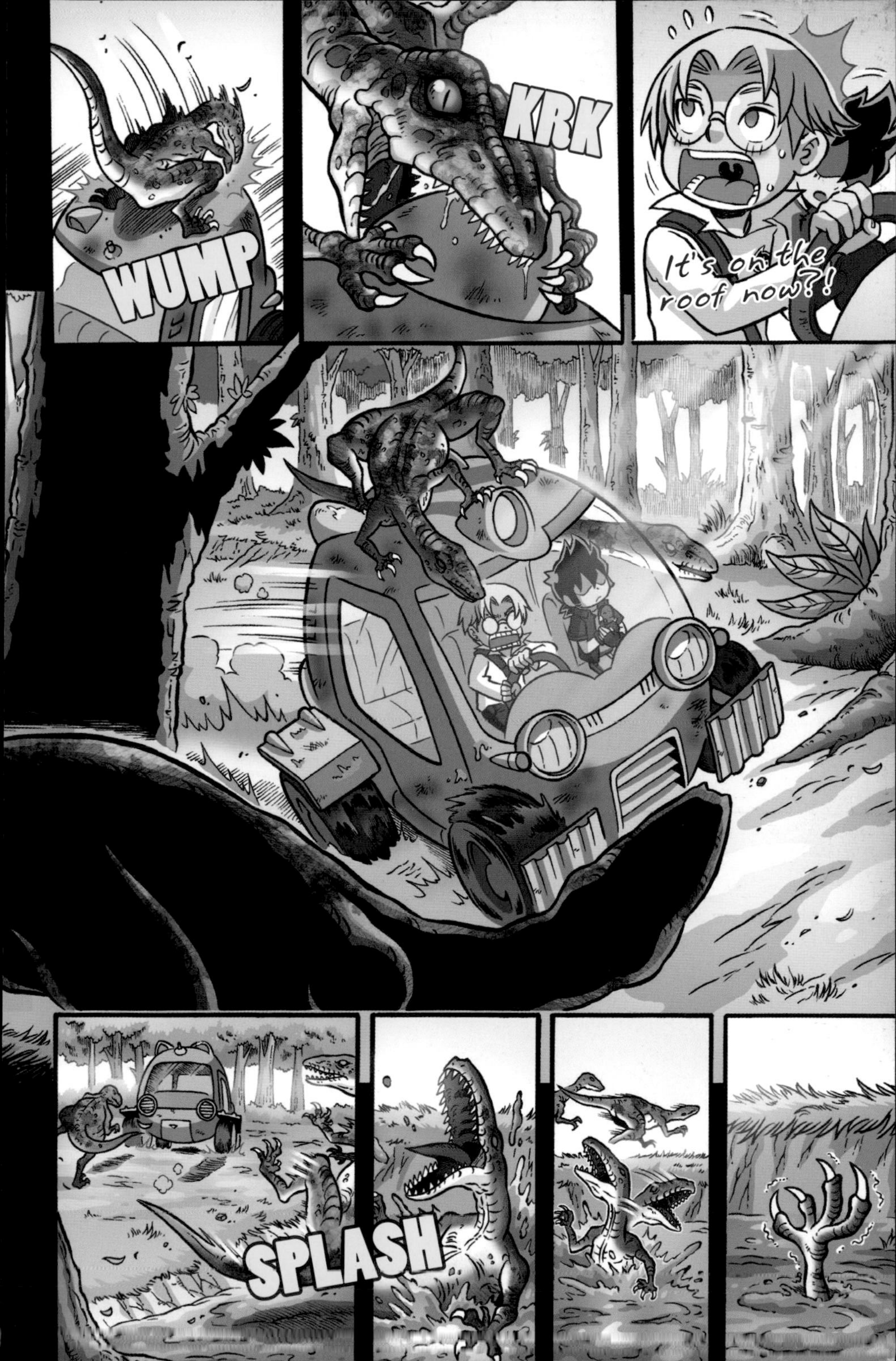
WUMP
KRK
It's on the roof now?!
SPLASH

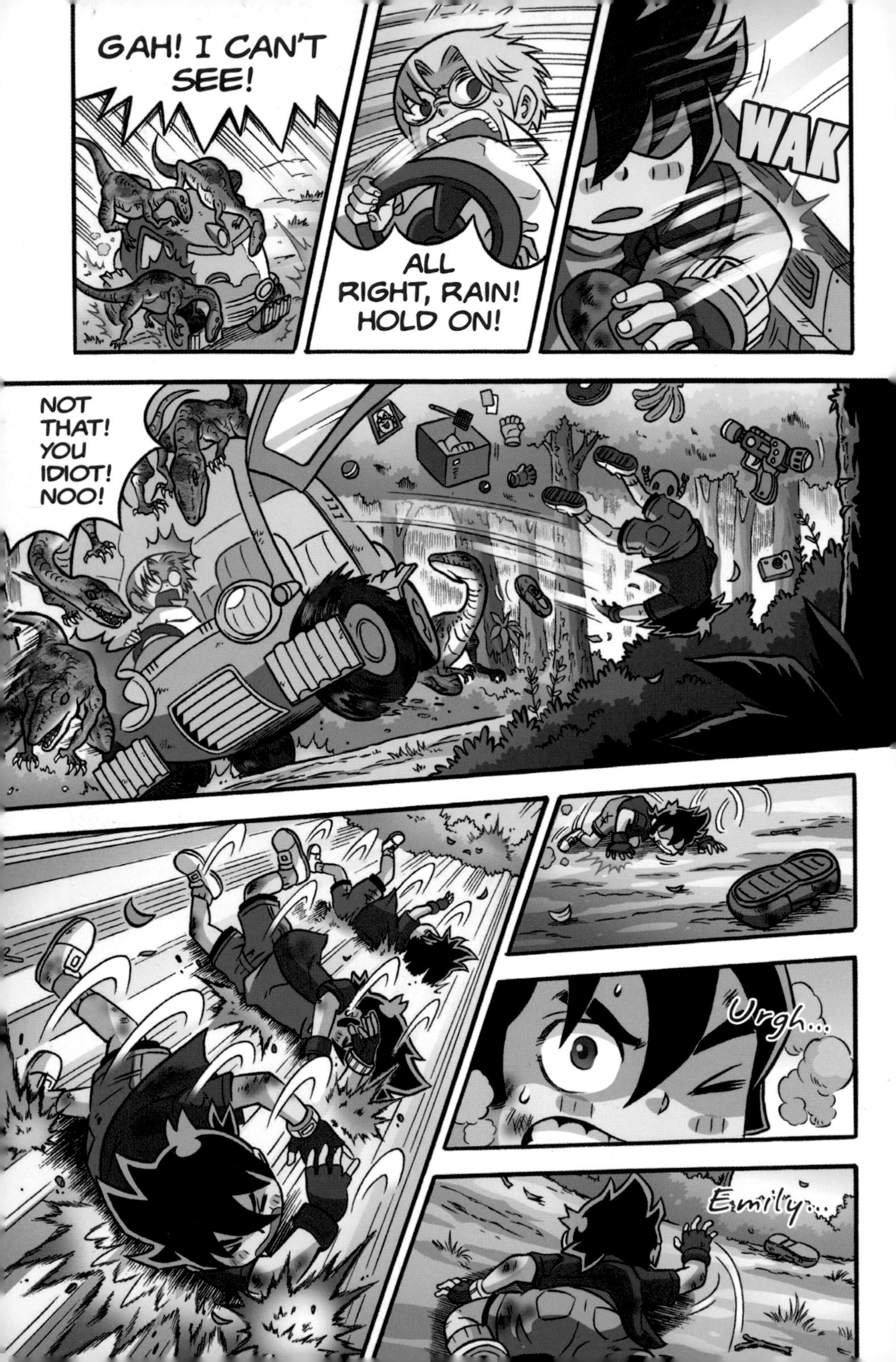
GAH! I CAN'T SEE!
ALL RIGHT, RAIN! HOLD ON!
WAK
NOT THAT! YOU IDIOT! NOO!
Urgh...
Emily...

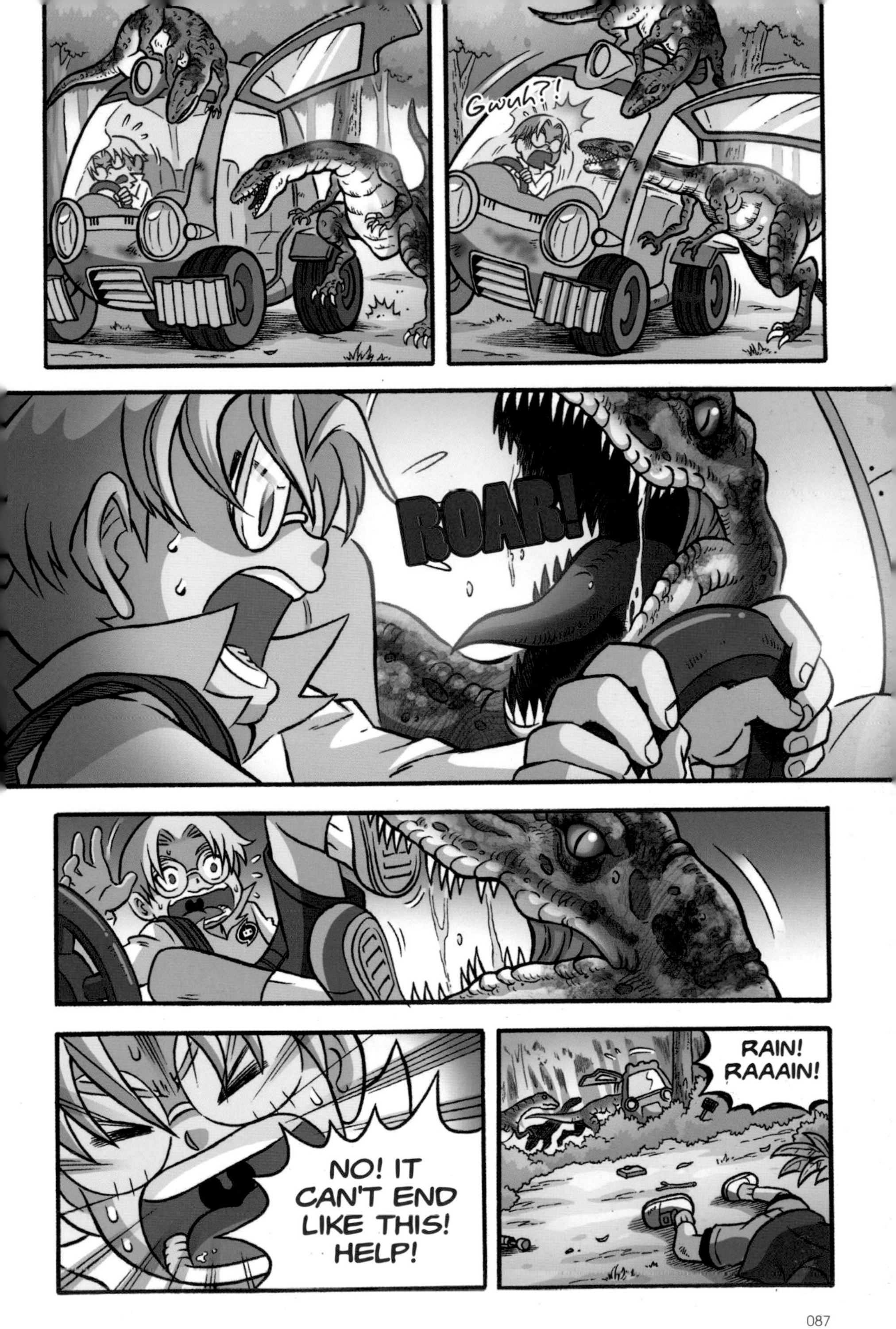
Gwuh?!
ROAR!
NO! IT CAN'T END LIKE THIS! HELP!
RAIN! RAAAIN!

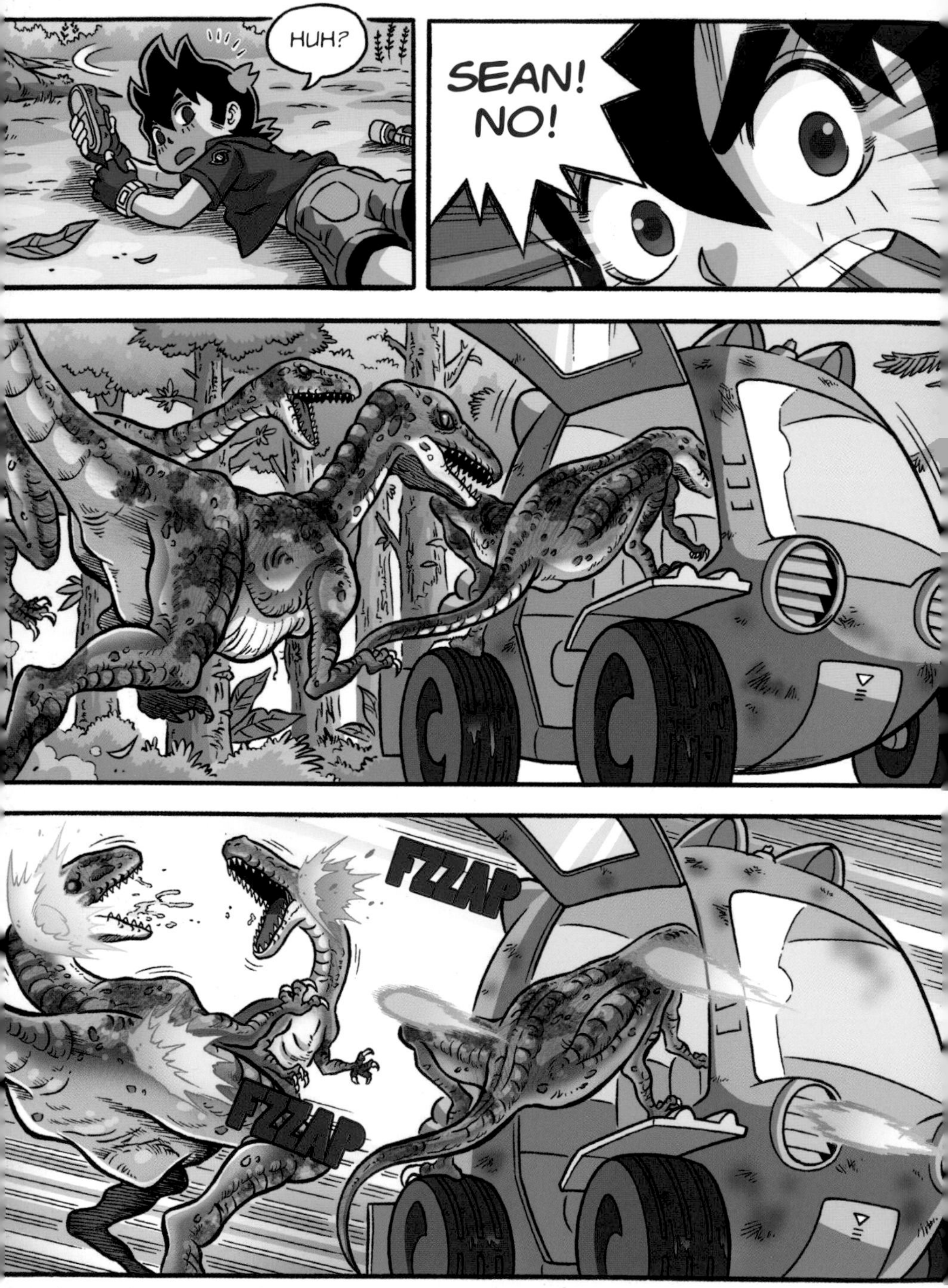
HUH?
SEAN! NO!
FZZAP
FZZAP

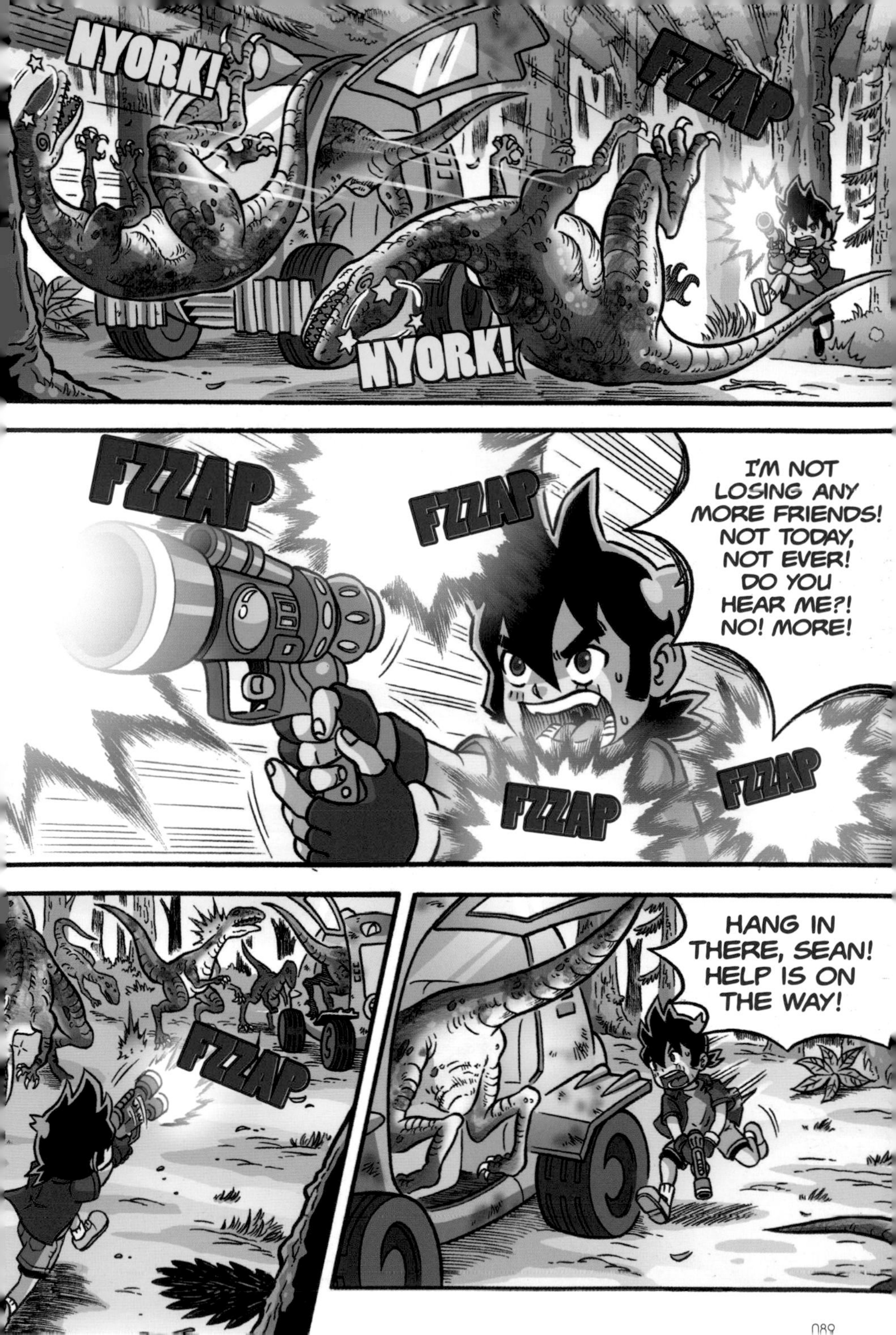
NYORK!
FZZAP
NYORK!
FZZAP
FZZAP
I'M NOT LOSING ANY MORE FRIENDS! NOT TODAY, NOT EVER! DO YOU HEAR ME?! NO! MORE!
FZZAP
FZZAP
FZZAP
HANG IN THERE, SEAN! HELP IS ON THE WAY!

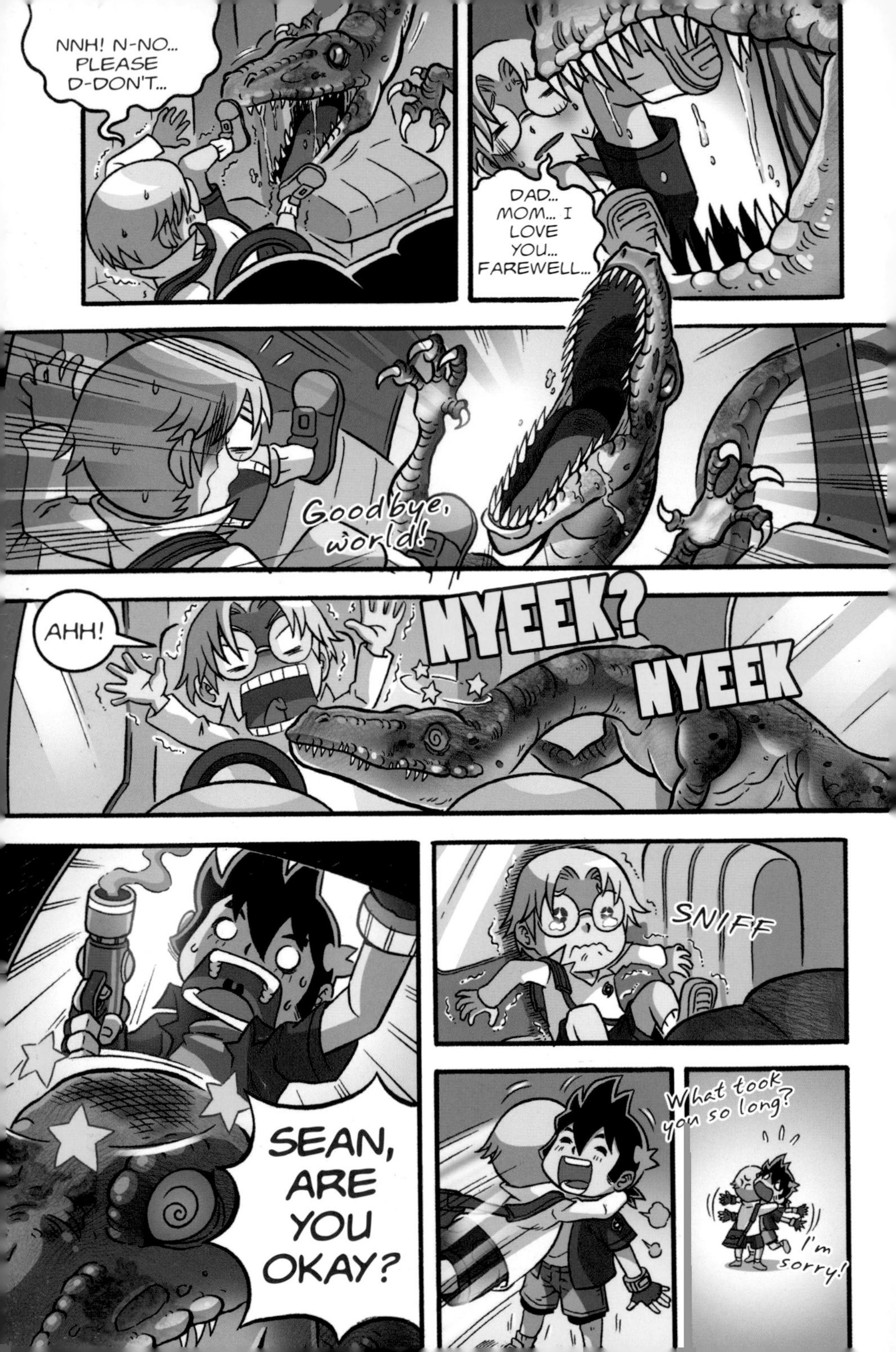
NNH! N-NO... PLEASE D-DON'T...
DAD... MOM... I LOVE YOU... FAREWELL...
Goodbye, world!
AHH!
NYEEK?
NYEEK
SEAN, ARE YOU OKAY?
SNIFF
What took you so long?
I'm sorry!

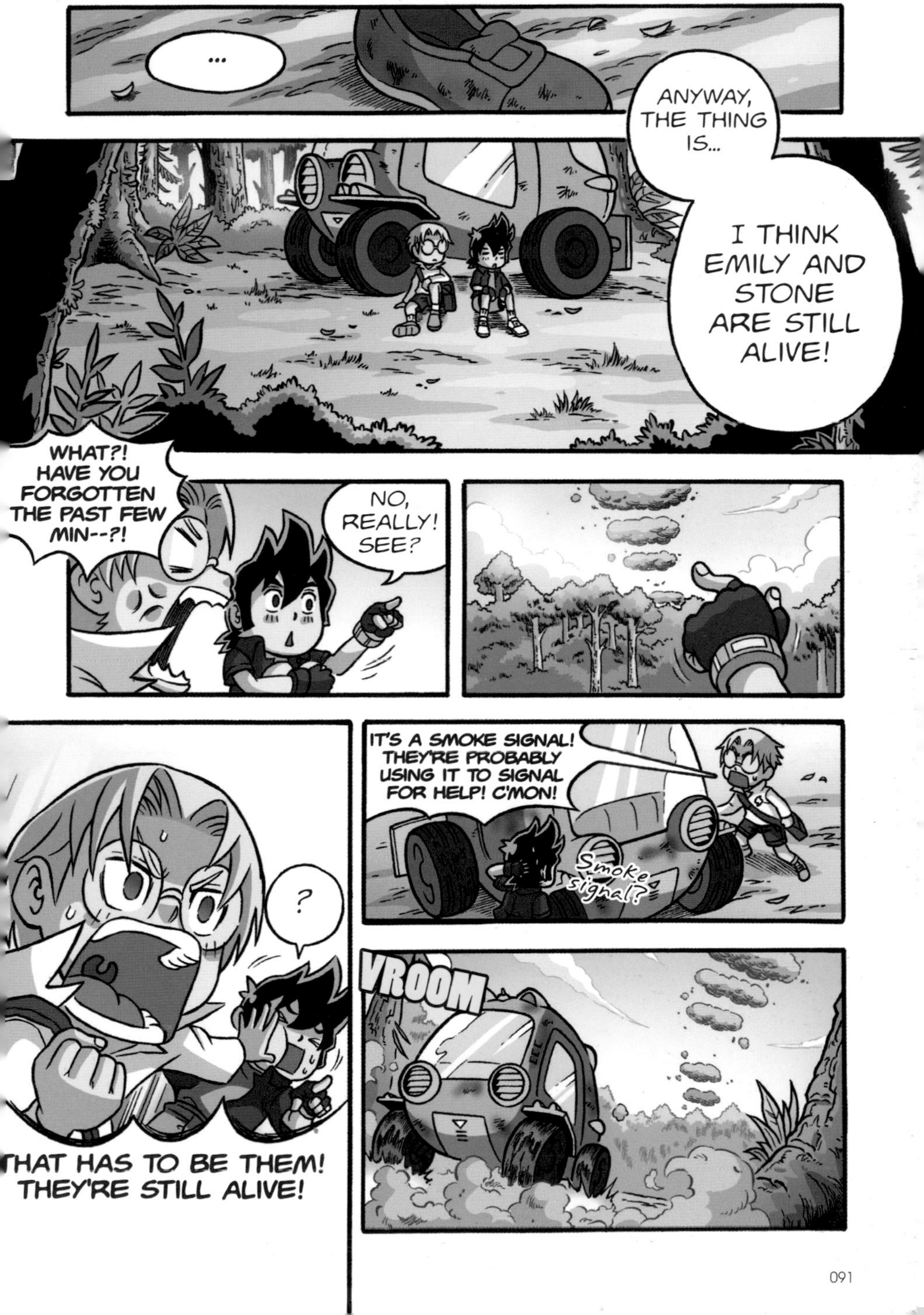
...
ANYWAY, THE THING IS...
I THINK EMILY AND STONE ARE STILL ALIVE!
WHAT?! HAVE YOU FORGOTTEN THE PAST FEW MIN--?!
NO, REALLY! SEE?
THAT HAS TO BE THEM! THEY'RE STILL ALIVE!
?
IT'S A SMOKE SIGNAL! THEY'RE PROBABLY USING IT TO SIGNAL FOR HELP! C'MON!
Smoke signal?
VROOM

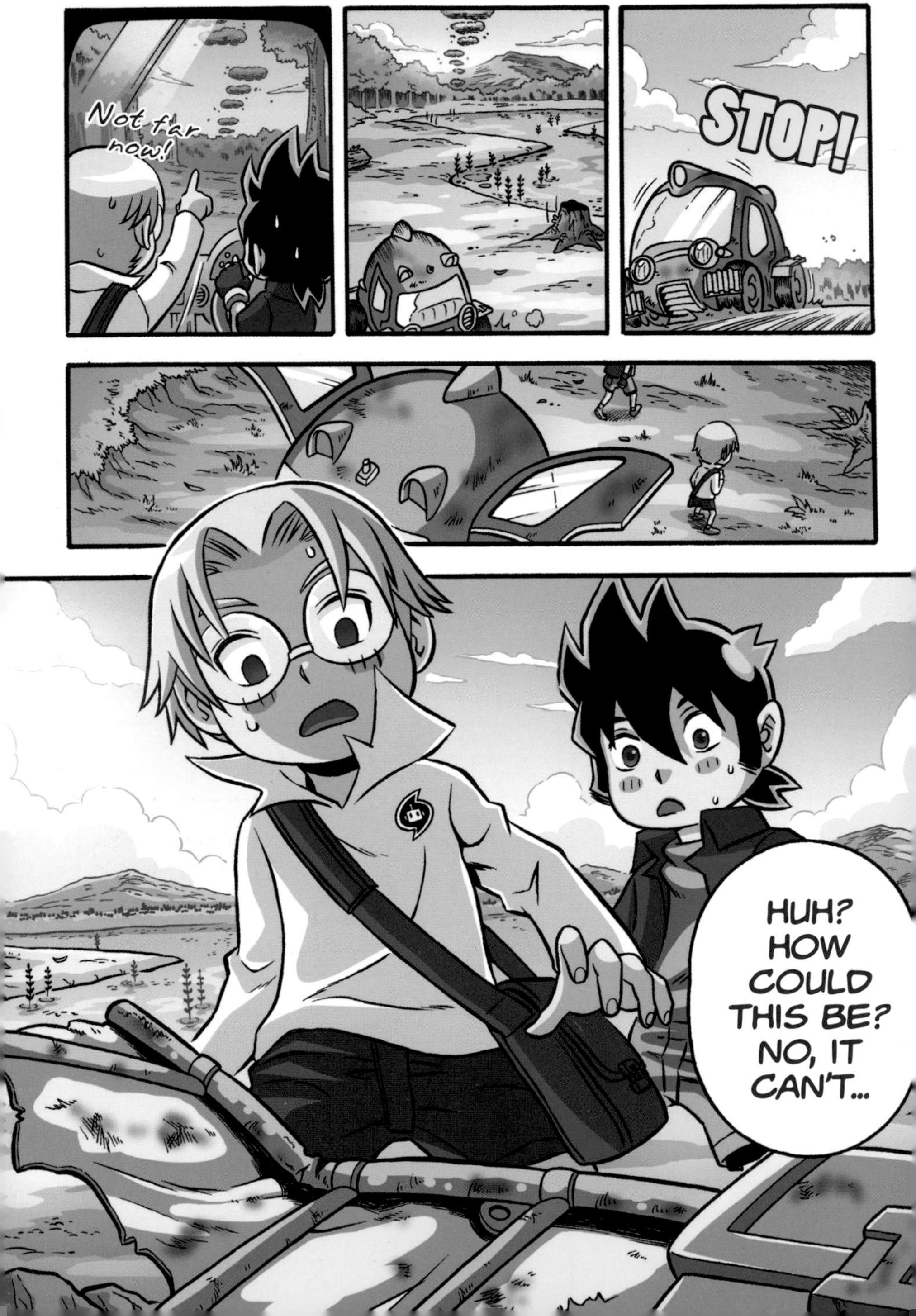
Not far now!
STOP!
HUH? HOW COULD THIS BE? NO, IT CAN'T...

Eoraptor

Eoraptor lunensis, which means "dawn plunderer from the Valley of the Moon," earned its fanciful name as a result of where its first fossil was discovered, in north-western Argentina. It was one of the earliest carnivorous dinosaurs, and its discovery changed views on when dinosaurs first appeared. It was not exceptionally large, but had strong hind limbs which helped it chase prey while its forelimbs had sharp claws which would have been powerful enough to capture and overpower creatures of similiar size.

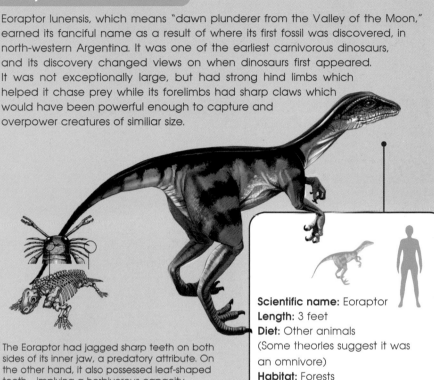

The Eoraptor had jagged sharp teeth on both sides of its inner jaw, a predatory attribute. On the other hand, it also possessed leaf-shaped teeth—implying a herbivorous capacity, leading to its classification as an omnivore.

Scientific name: Eoraptor
Length: 3 feet
Diet: Other animals (Some theorles suggest it was an omnivore)
Habitat: Forests
Discovered: Argentina
Era: Mid Triassic

Which was the first dinosaur?

The answer will continue to change as new species are discovered. In the mid-20th century, it was generally believed that Coelophysis was the earliest dinosaur, but this theory was debunked after the discovery of the Herrerasaurus when a complete fossil was excavated in the late 90s. In 1993, the Eoraptor was unearthed, and the current theory is that both Herrerasaurus and Eoraptor were the earliest dinosaurs.

I'M THE FIRST DINOSAUR!
BALONEY! I GOT HERE FIRST!
STOP ARGUING. WE ALL KNOW I'M THE FIRST!

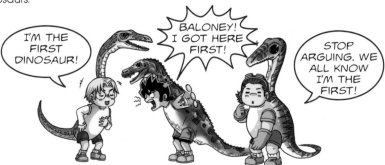

TAKING IN THE TRIASSIC

Coelophysis

Coelophysis was one of the earliest known dinosaurs; its name means "hollow form," referring to its hollow bones, similiar to a bird's, making it incredibly light, capable of easily outrunning heavier prey and its predators. It had similar attributes to smaller animals, and relied on its powerful hind limbs to sprint. When running, it tucked in its fore limbs to its chest and raised its tail to maintain its balance.

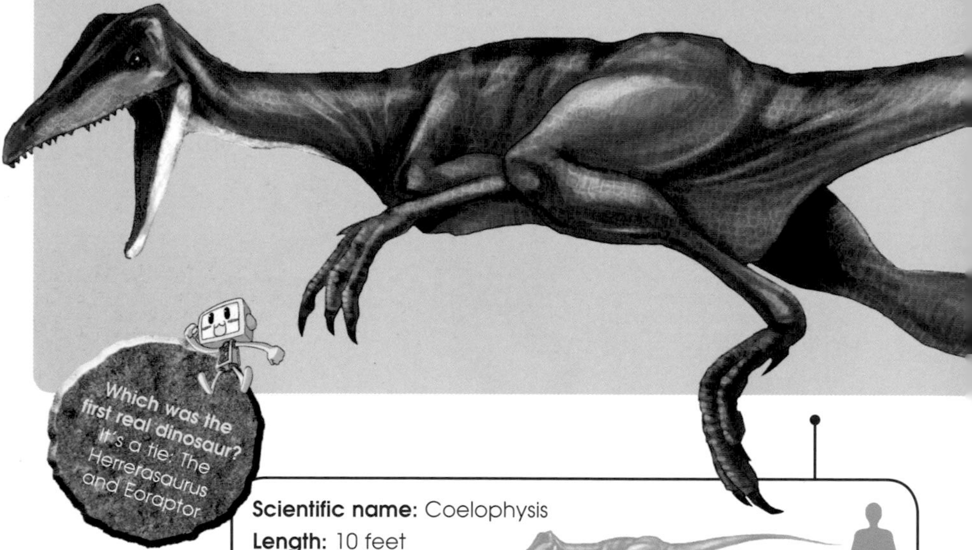
Which was the first real dinosaur?
It's a tie: The Herrerasaurus and Eoraptor

Scientific name: Coelophysis
Length: 10 feet
Diet: Other animals
Habitat: Desert plain
Discovered: America and South Africa
Era: Late Triassic

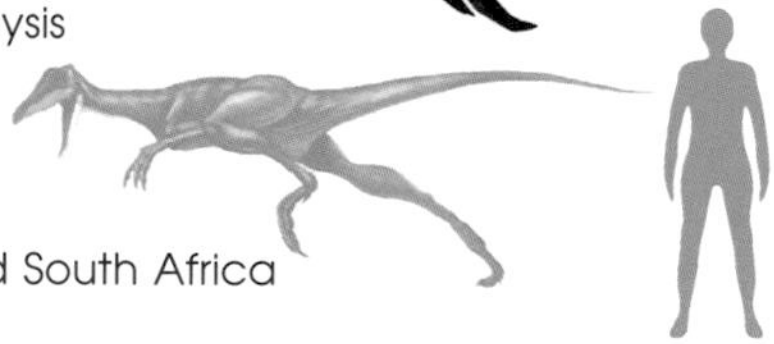

COELOPHYSIS BONE STRUCTURE

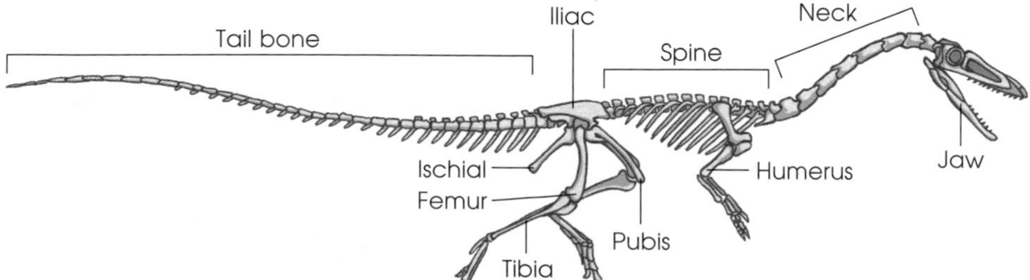
Tail bone
Iliac
Spine
Neck
Jaw
Ischial
Femur
Tibia
Pubis
Humerus

CHAPTER 5

TO THE RESCUE

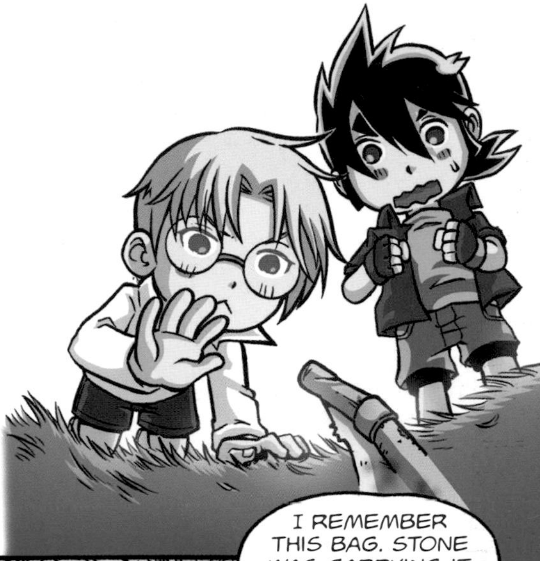
I REMEMBER THIS BAG. STONE WAS CARRYING IT WHEN HE LEFT THE CAR...

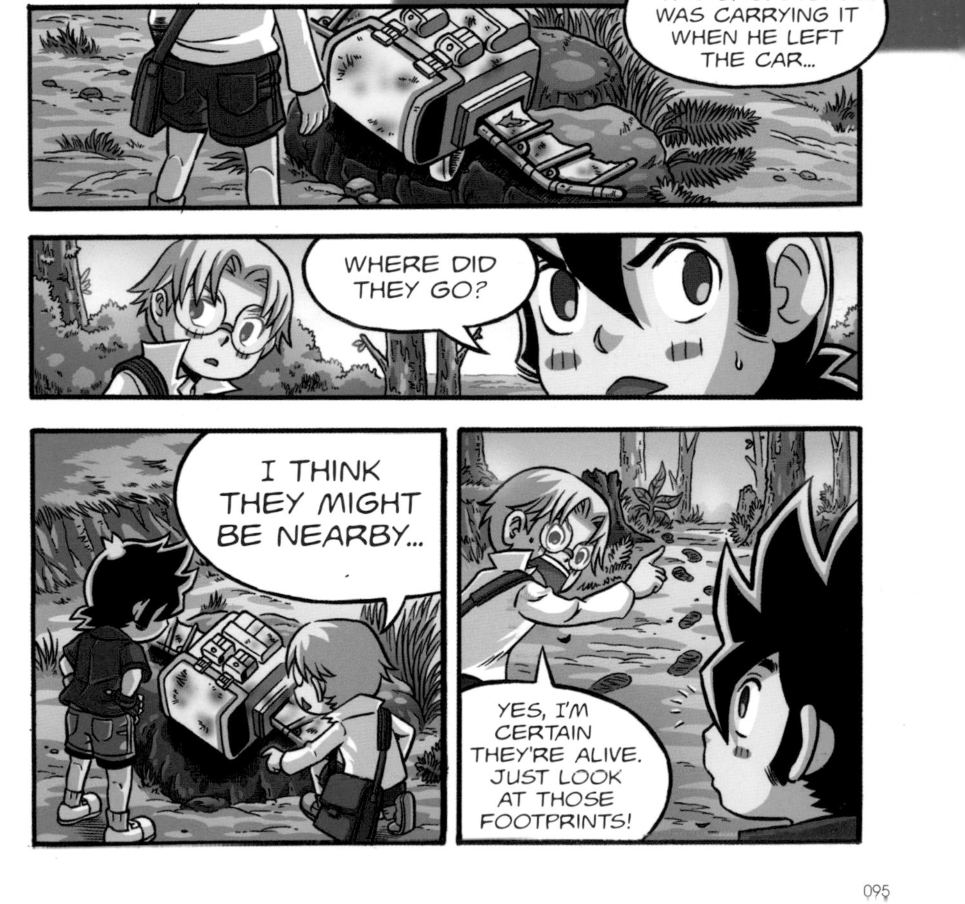
WHERE DID THEY GO?
I THINK THEY MIGHT BE NEARBY...
YES, I'M CERTAIN THEY'RE ALIVE. JUST LOOK AT THOSE FOOTPRINTS!

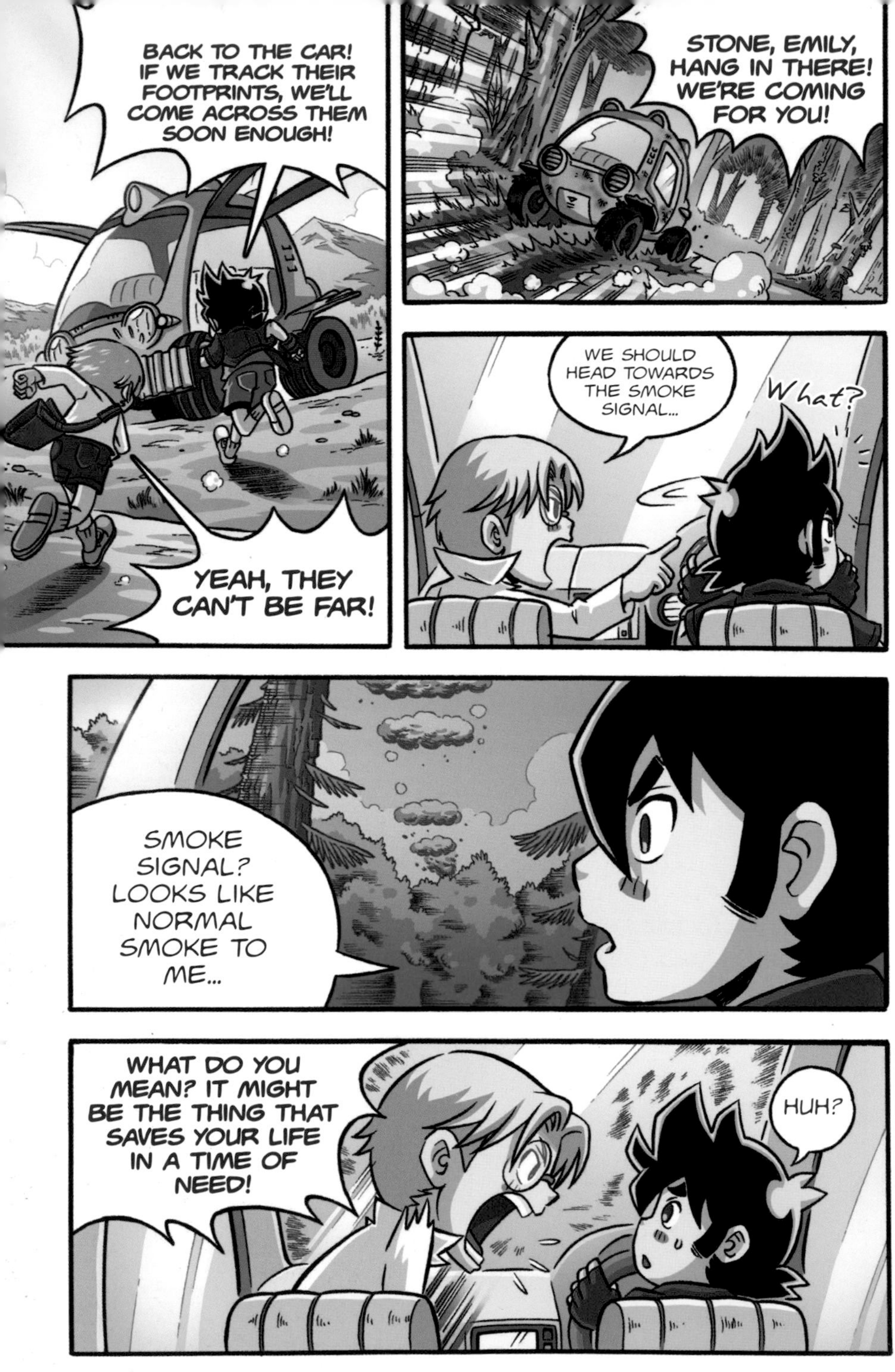
BACK TO THE CAR! IF WE TRACK THEIR FOOTPRINTS, WE'LL COME ACROSS THEM SOON ENOUGH!
YEAH, THEY CAN'T BE FAR!
STONE, EMILY, HANG IN THERE! WE'RE COMING FOR YOU!
WE SHOULD HEAD TOWARDS THE SMOKE SIGNAL...
What?
SMOKE SIGNAL? LOOKS LIKE NORMAL SMOKE TO ME...
WHAT DO YOU MEAN? IT MIGHT BE THE THING THAT SAVES YOUR LIFE IN A TIME OF NEED!
HUH?

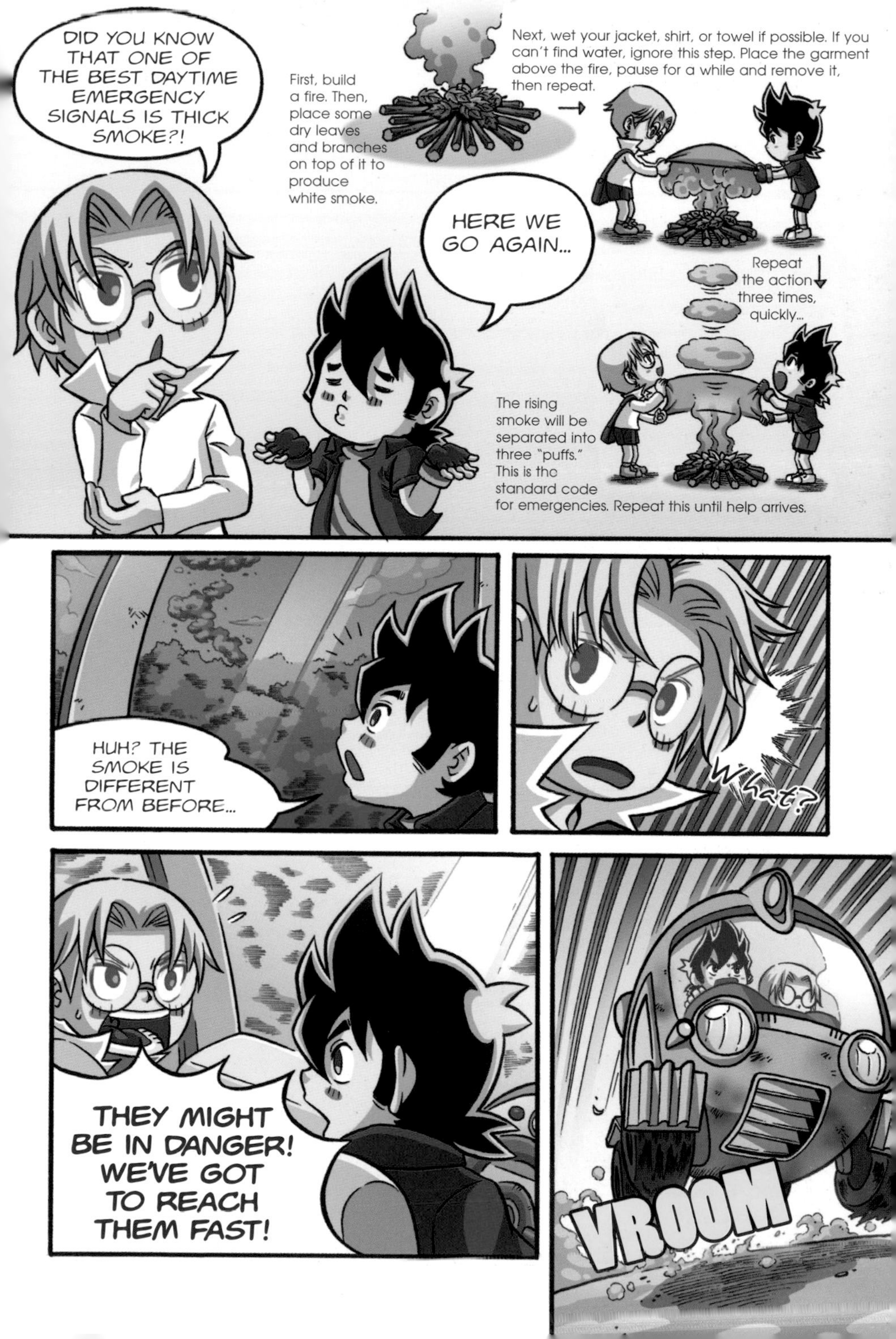
DID YOU KNOW THAT ONE OF THE BEST DAYTIME EMERGENCY SIGNALS IS THICK SMOKE?!
First, build a fire. Then, place some dry leaves and branches on top of it to produce white smoke.
Next, wet your jacket, shirt, or towel if possible. If you can't find water, ignore this step. Place the garment above the fire, pause for a while and remove it, then repeat.
HERE WE GO AGAIN...
Repeat the action three times, quickly...
The rising smoke will be separated into three "puffs." This is thc standard code for emergencies. Repeat this until help arrives.
HUH? THE SMOKE IS DIFFERENT FROM BEFORE...
What?
THEY MIGHT BE IN DANGER! WE'VE GOT TO REACH THEM FAST!
VROOM

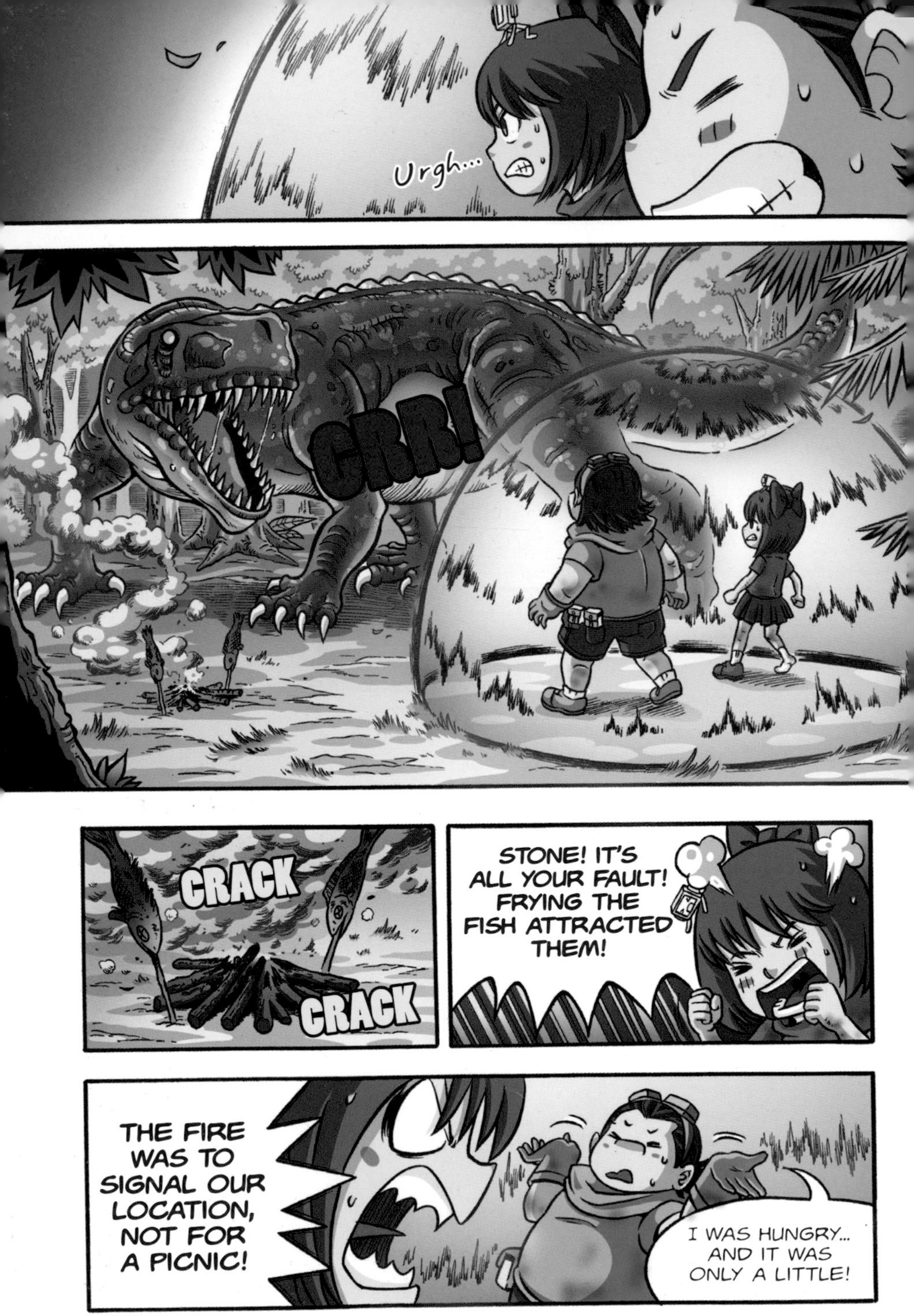
Urgh...
CRR!
CRACK
CRACK
STONE! IT'S ALL YOUR FAULT! FRYING THE FISH ATTRACTED THEM!
THE FIRE WAS TO SIGNAL OUR LOCATION, NOT FOR A PICNIC!
I WAS HUNGRY... AND IT WAS ONLY A LITTLE!

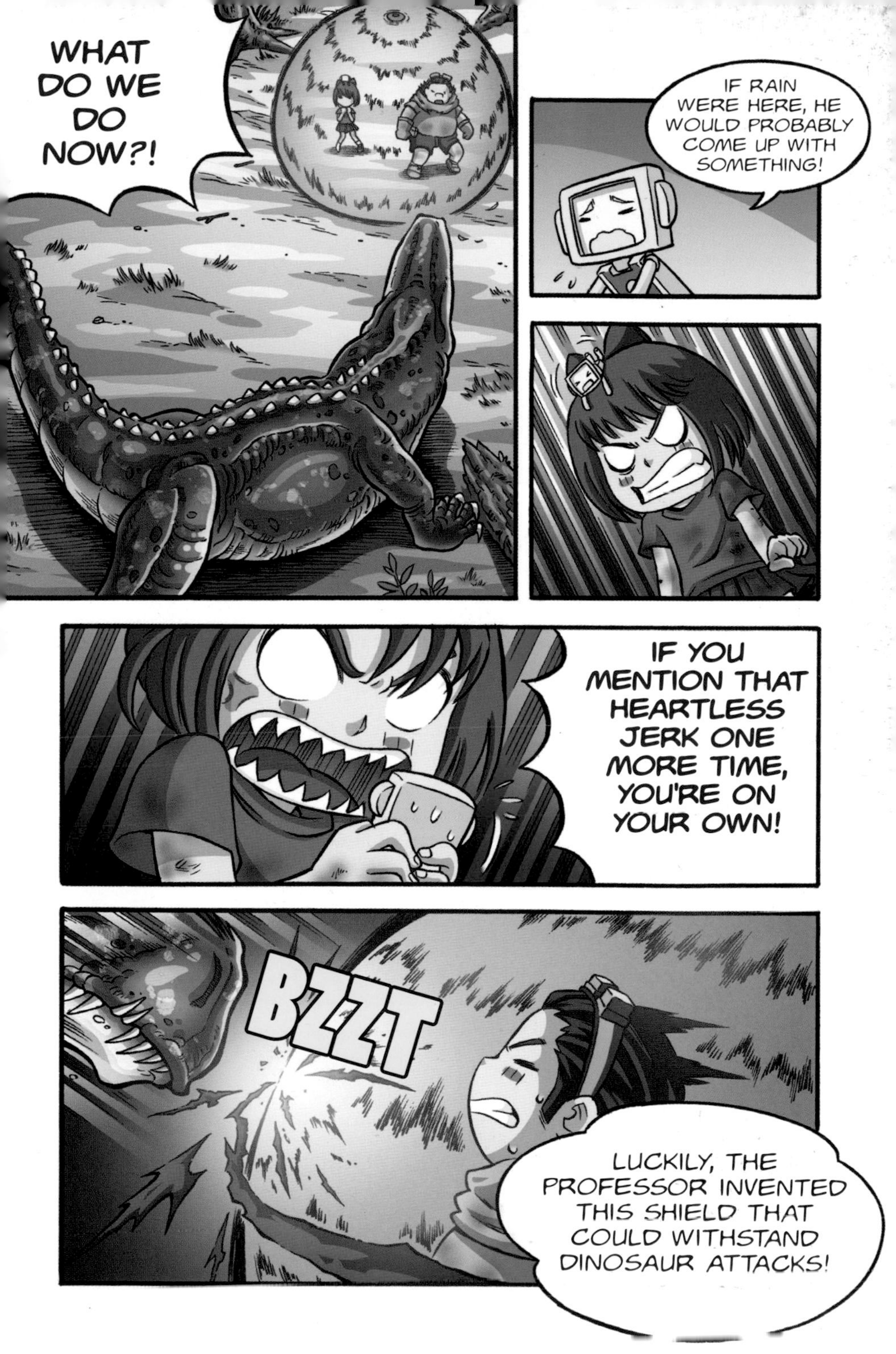
WHAT DO WE DO NOW?!
IF RAIN WERE HERE, HE WOULD PROBABLY COME UP WITH SOMETHING!
IF YOU MENTION THAT HEARTLESS JERK ONE MORE TIME, YOU'RE ON YOUR OWN!
BZZT
LUCKILY, THE PROFESSOR INVENTED THIS SHIELD THAT COULD WITHSTAND DINOSAUR ATTACKS!

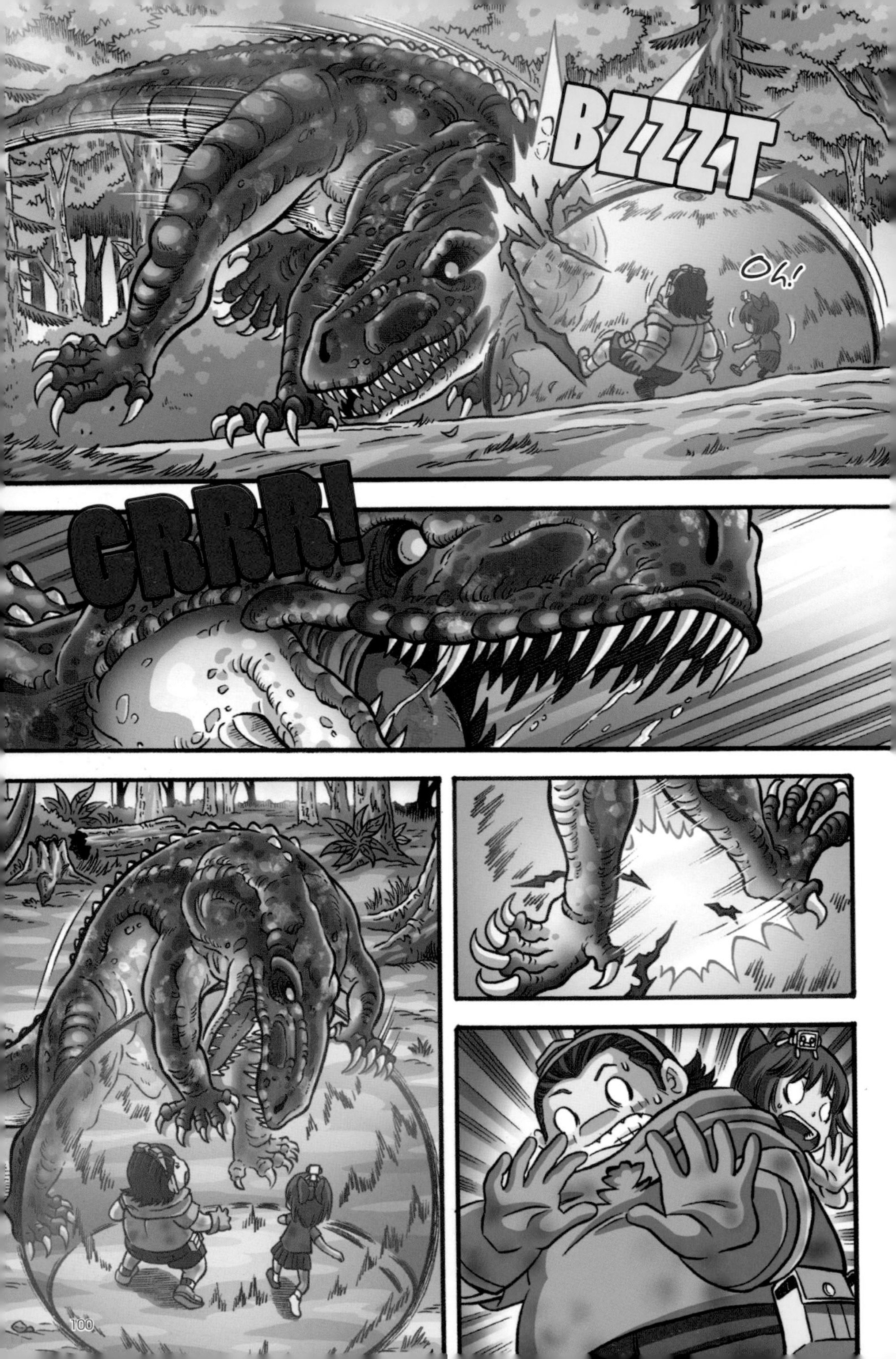
BZZZT
Oh!
CRRR!

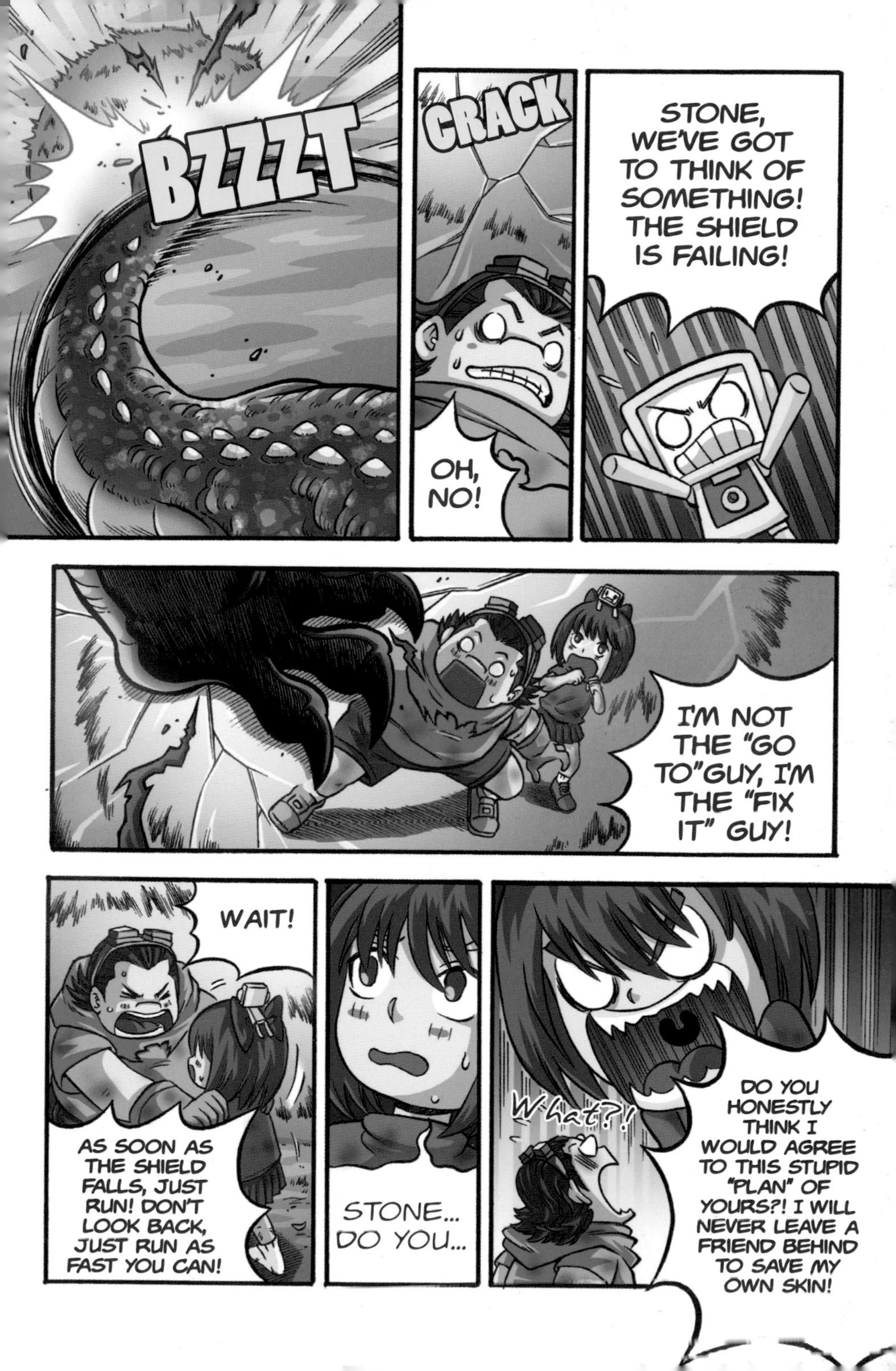
BZZZT
CRACK
OH, NO!
STONE, WE'VE GOT TO THINK OF SOMETHING! THE SHIELD IS FAILING!
I'M NOT THE "GO TO"GUY, I'M THE "FIX IT" GUY!
WAIT!
AS SOON AS THE SHIELD FALLS, JUST RUN! DON'T LOOK BACK, JUST RUN AS FAST YOU CAN!
STONE... DO YOU...
What?!
DO YOU HONESTLY THINK I WOULD AGREE TO THIS STUPID "PLAN" OF YOURS?! I WILL NEVER LEAVE A FRIEND BEHIND TO SAVE MY OWN SKIN!

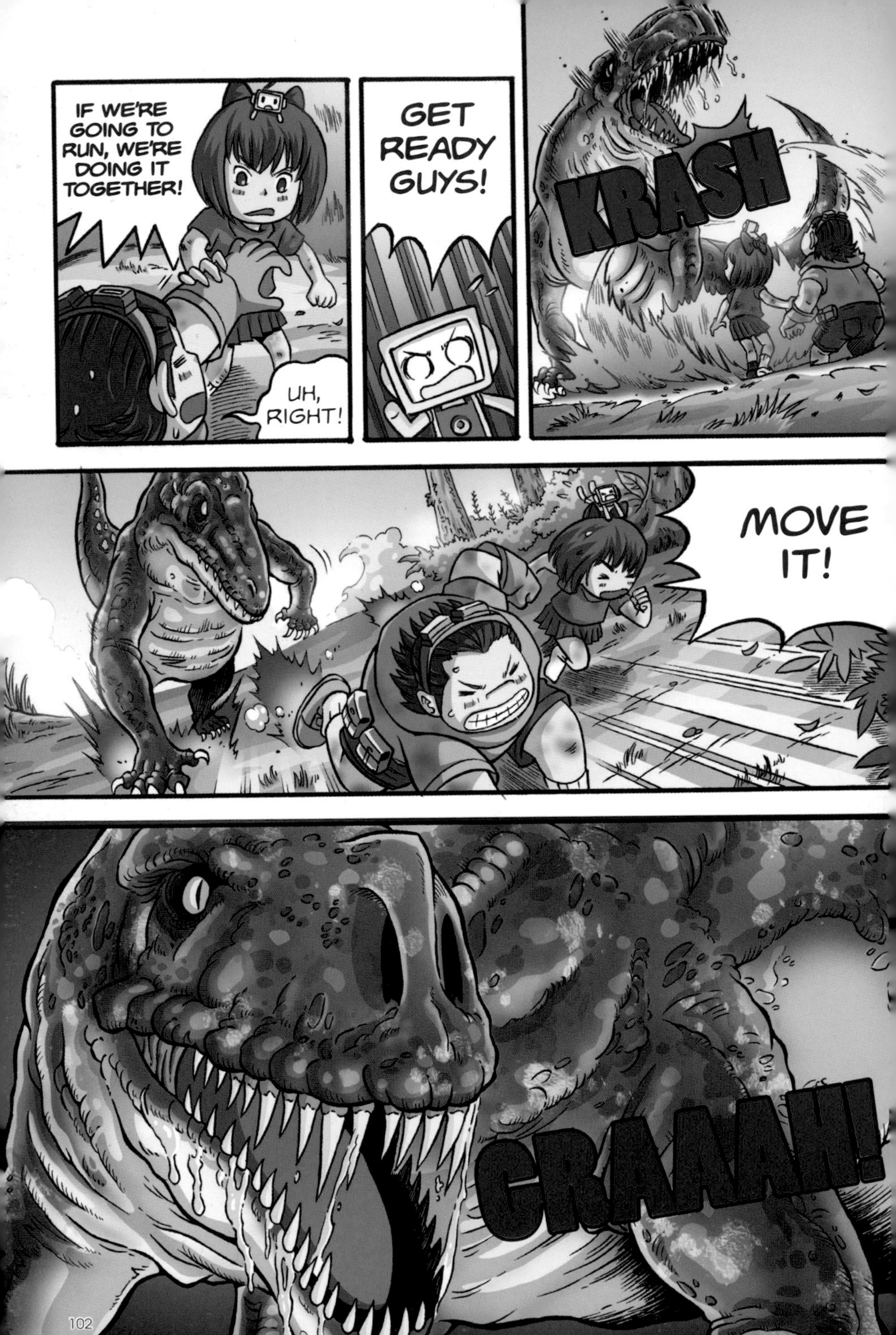
IF WE'RE GOING TO RUN, WE'RE DOING IT TOGETHER!
UH, RIGHT!
GET READY GUYS!
KRASH
MOVE IT!
CRAAAH!

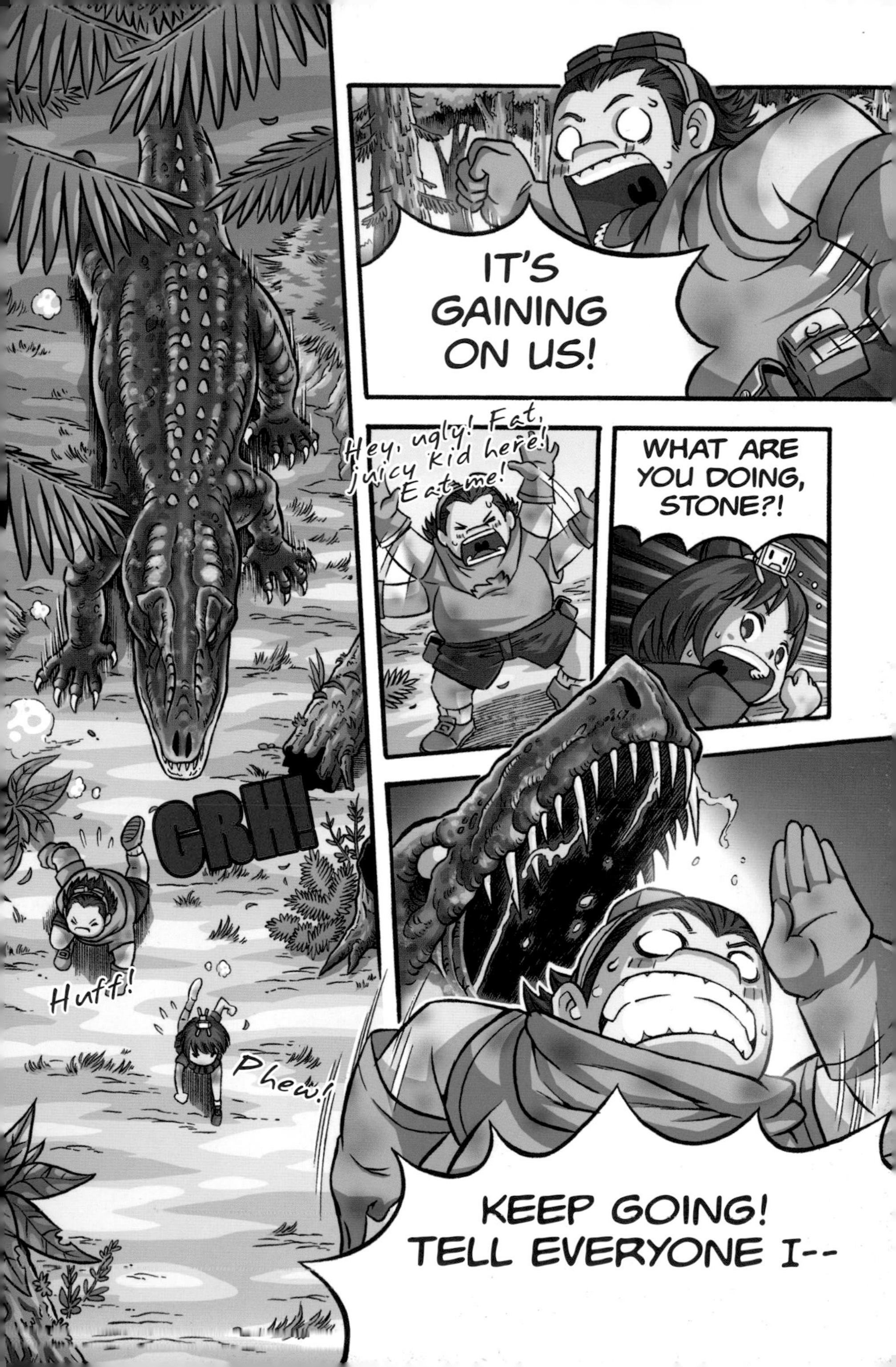
IT'S GAINING ON US!
Hey, ugly! Fat, juicy kid here! Eat me!
WHAT ARE YOU DOING, STONE?!
KEEP GOING! TELL EVERYONE I--
CRH!
Huff!
Phew!

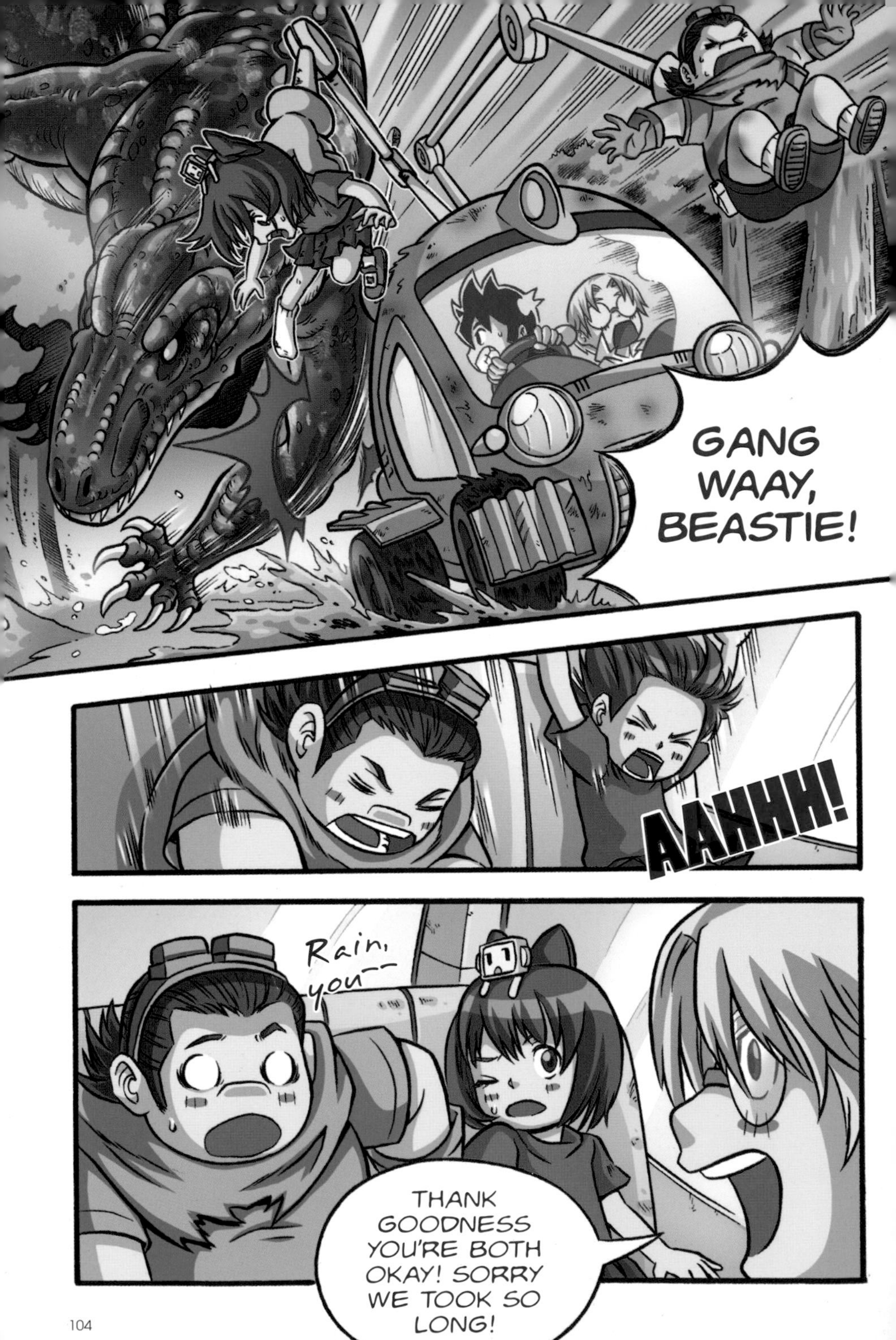
GANG WAAY, BEASTIE!
AAHHH!
Rain, you--
THANK GOODNESS YOU'RE BOTH OKAY! SORRY WE TOOK SO LONG!

RAIN, WHAT ARE YOU DOING? WHY ARE YOU TURNING BACK?!

SKREECH

BEFORE WE LEAVE, THERE'S ONE MORE THING THAT NEEDS TO BE DONE-- NO, TWO.

FIRST IS, WELL, ...

I'M SORRY, EMILY! I WAS STUPID AND ANGRY AND I RAN MY MOUTH OFF AND I'M SORRY!

HMPH!

I SWEAR I'LL NEVER DO THAT TO YOU AGAIN!

Geez, I...

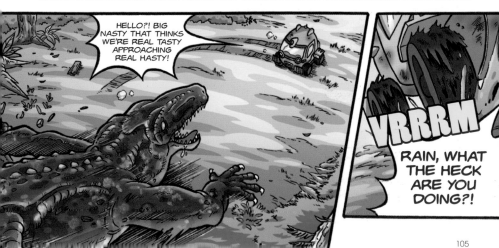

HELLO?! BIG NASTY THAT THINKS WE'RE REAL TASTY APPROACHING REAL HASTY!

VRRRM

RAIN, WHAT THE HECK ARE YOU DOING?!

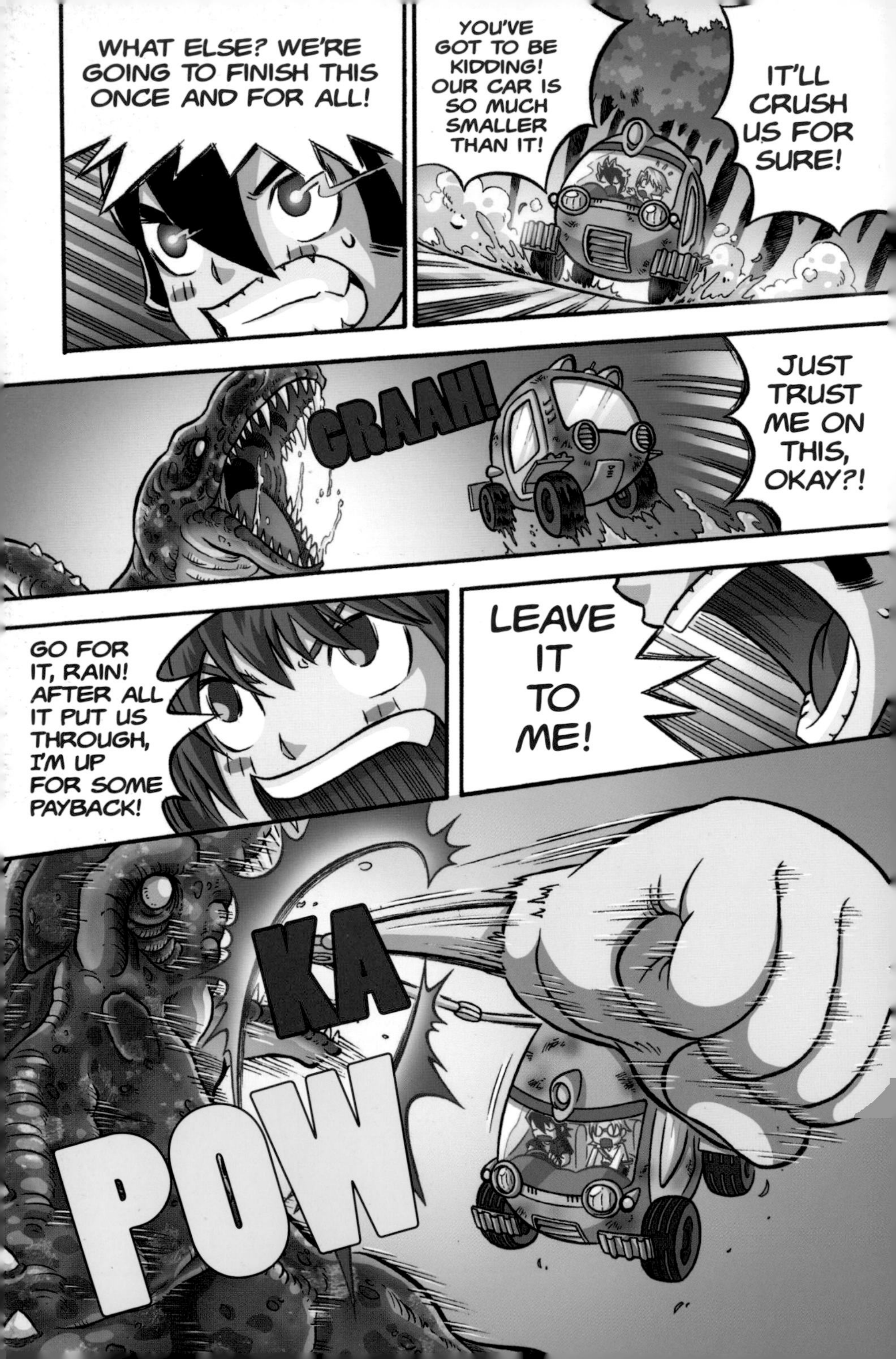
WHAT ELSE? WE'RE GOING TO FINISH THIS ONCE AND FOR ALL!
YOU'VE GOT TO BE KIDDING! OUR CAR IS SO MUCH SMALLER THAN IT!
IT'LL CRUSH US FOR SURE!
CRAAAH!
JUST TRUST ME ON THIS, OKAY?!
GO FOR IT, RAIN! AFTER ALL IT PUT US THROUGH, I'M UP FOR SOME PAYBACK!
LEAVE IT TO ME!
KA
POW

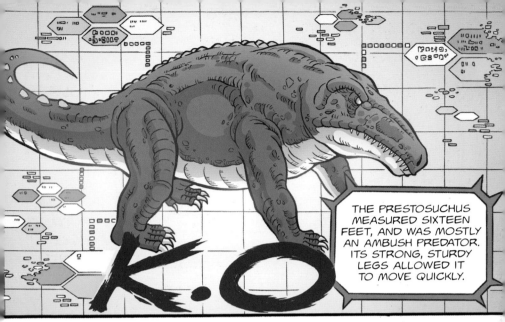

THE PRESTOSUCHUS MEASURED SIXTEEN FEET, AND WAS MOSTLY AN AMBUSH PREDATOR. ITS STRONG, STURDY LEGS ALLOWED IT TO MOVE QUICKLY.

WHUMP

WE... WE ACTUALLY BEAT IT!

Rocky, eat your heart out!

No way!

HRM!

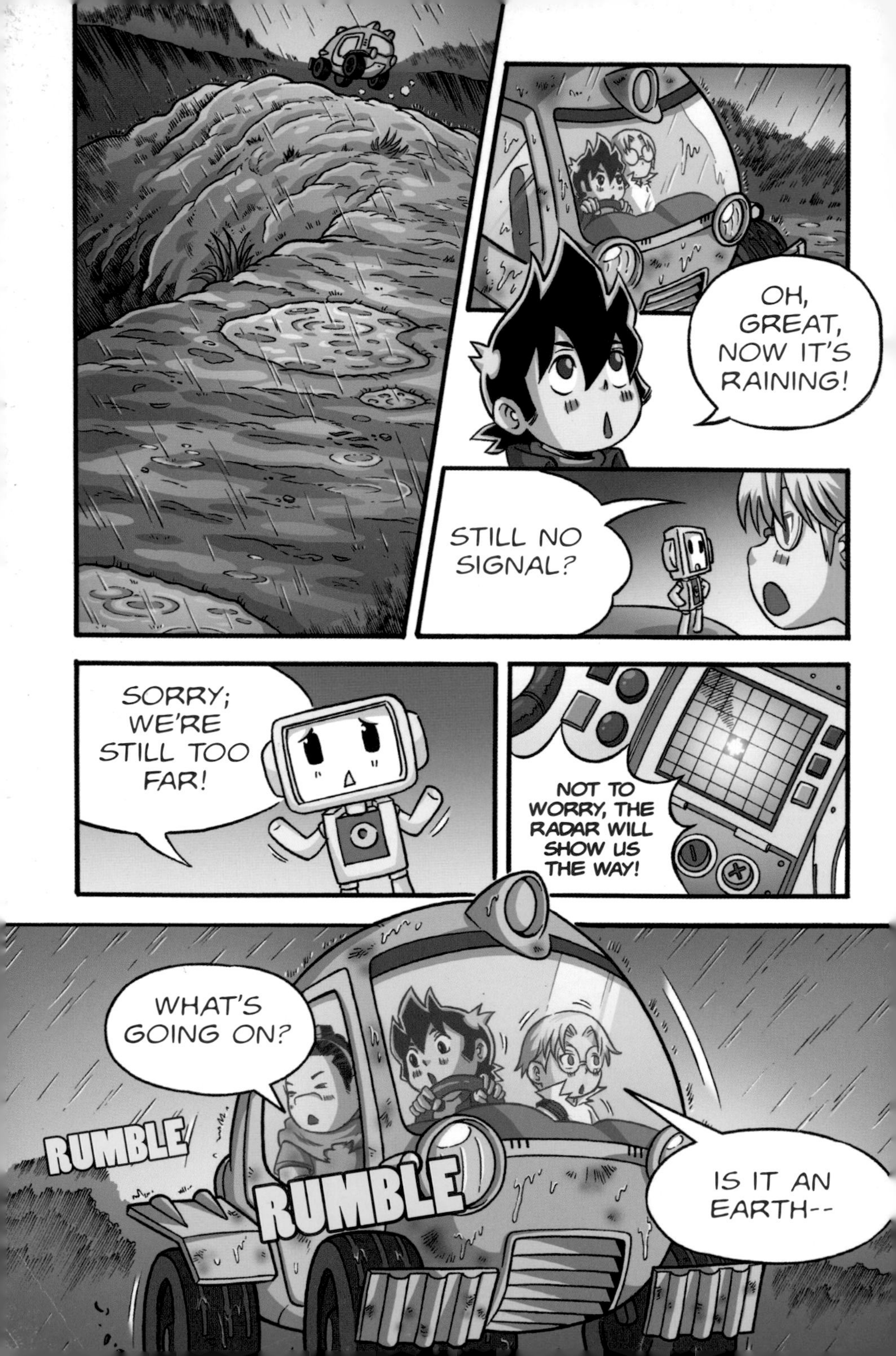
OH, GREAT, NOW IT'S RAINING!
STILL NO SIGNAL?
SORRY; WE'RE STILL TOO FAR!
NOT TO WORRY, THE RADAR WILL SHOW US THE WAY!
WHAT'S GOING ON?
RUMBLE
RUMBLE
IS IT AN EARTH--

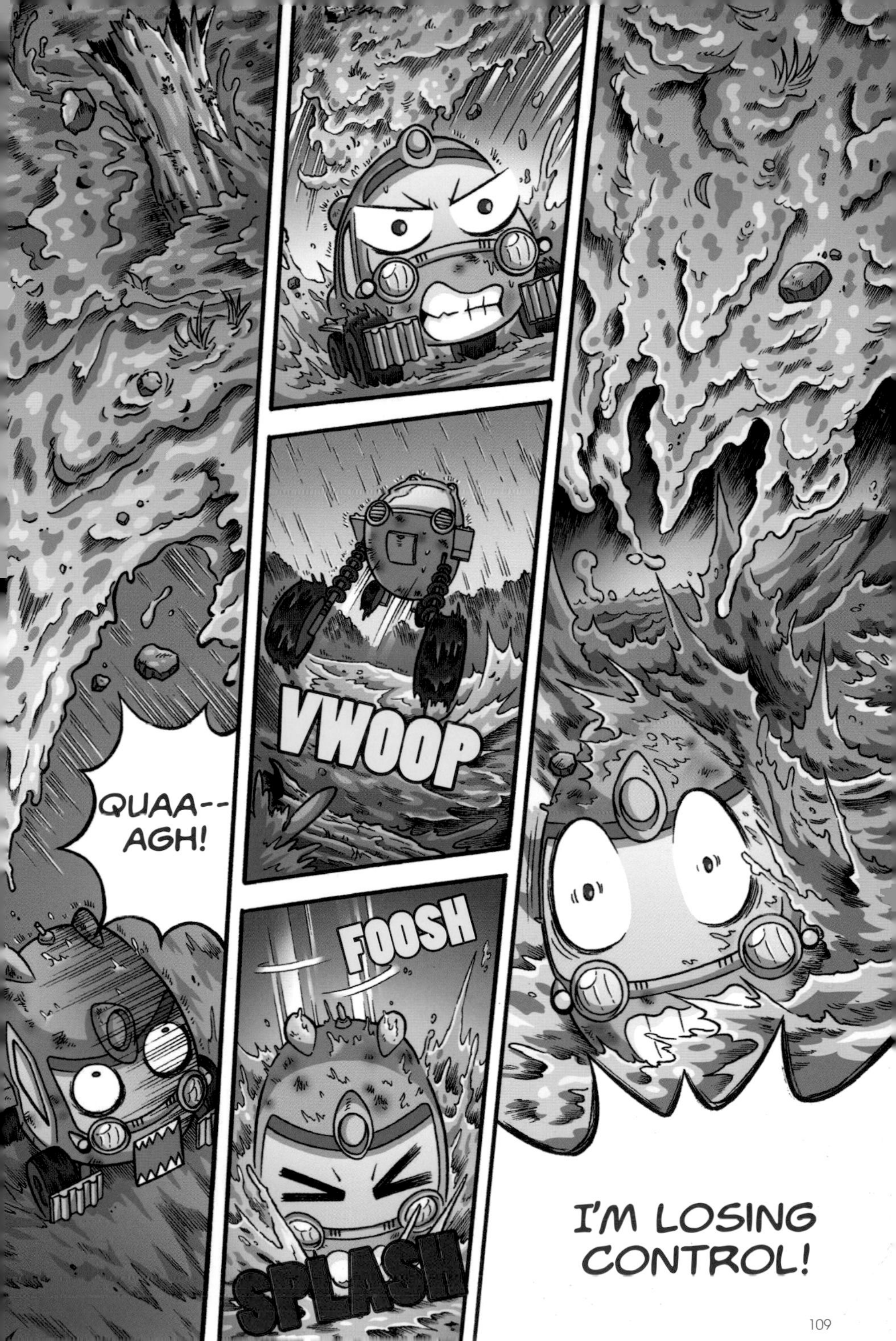
VWOOP
QUAA--
AGH!
FOOSH
SPLASH
I'M LOSING
CONTROL!

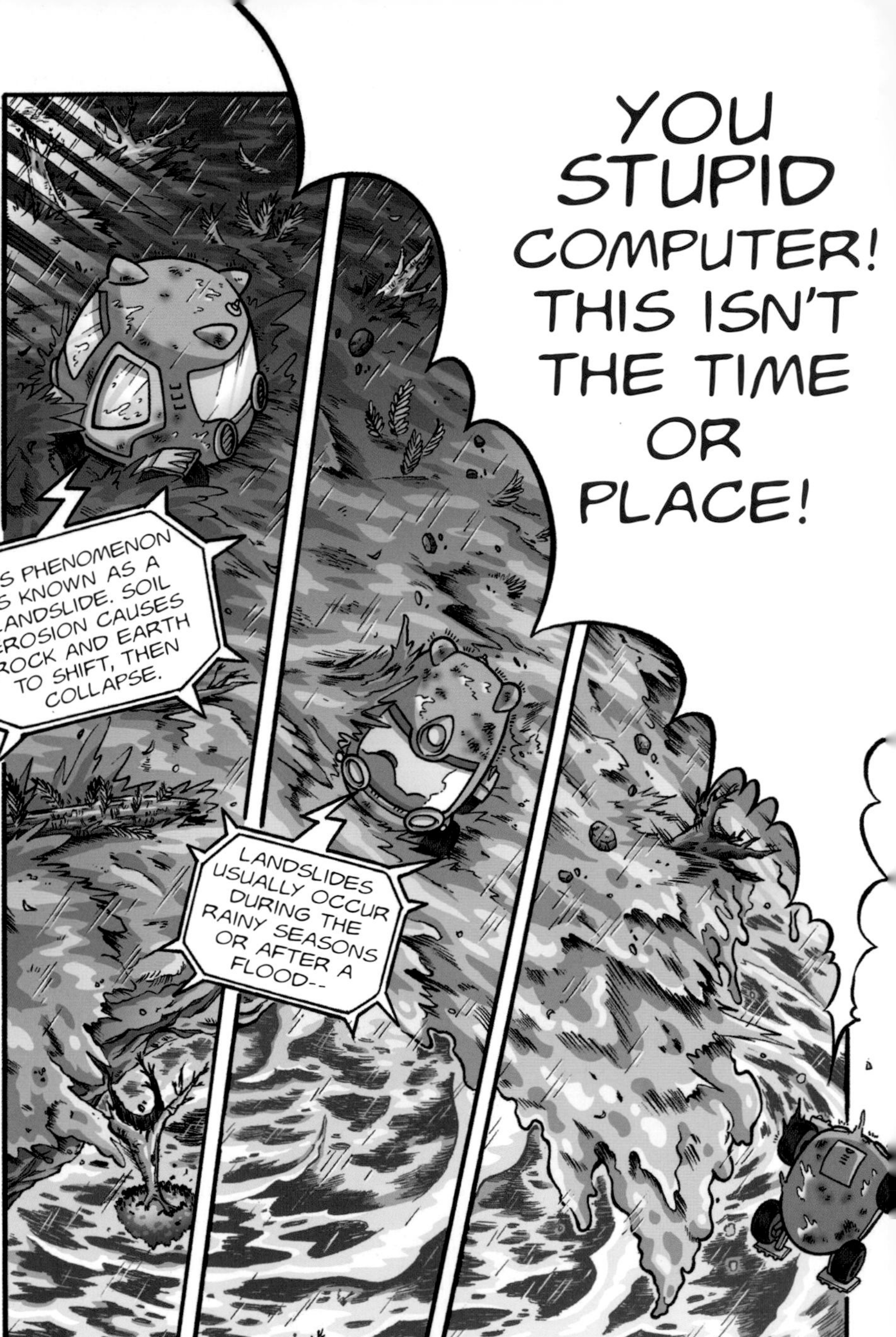
YOU STUPID COMPUTER! THIS ISN'T THE TIME OR PLACE!
THIS PHENOMENON IS KNOWN AS A LANDSLIDE. SOIL EROSION CAUSES ROCK AND EARTH TO SHIFT, THEN COLLAPSE.
LANDSLIDES USUALLY OCCUR DURING THE RAINY SEASONS OR AFTER A FLOOD--

TAKING IN THE TRIASSIC

Proterosuchus

Proterosuchus was one of the largest predatory land reptiles of the Triassic. Its body was massive and heavy and even though it shared similiar characteristics and lifestyle with modern crocodiles, paleontologists do not believe both species are directly related and that it was a coincidence they shared similiar lifestyles. If anything, it only proved that Proterosuchus was a primitive species with a splayed four-legged movement pattern.

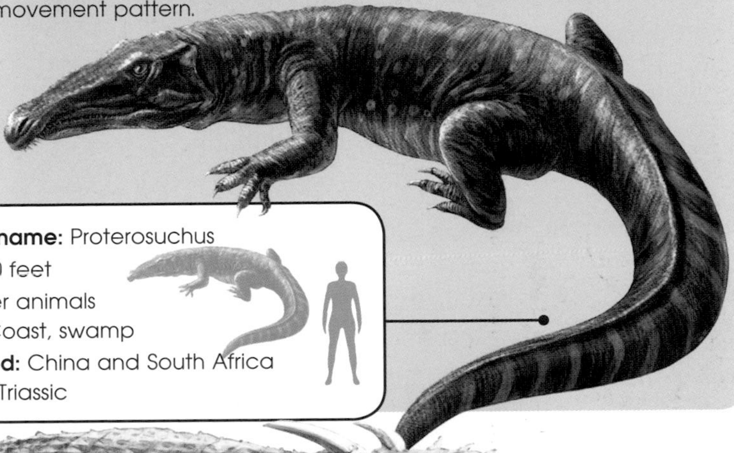

Scientific name: Proterosuchus
Length: 10 feet
Diet: Other animals
Habitat: Coast, swamp
Discovered: China and South Africa
Era: Early Triassic

TAKING IN THE TRIASSIC

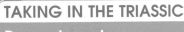

Desmatosuchus

Scientific name: Desmatosuchus
Length: 16 feet
Diet: Herbivore
Habitat: Forest
Discovered: North America
Era: Mid to Late Triassic

Desmatosuchus had short limbs, but a long tail and body covered in bony plate armor. It had a pair of 1 foot horns on the back of its shoulders along with two rows of spikes. The Desmatosuchus might have looked fierce and dangerous, but its formidable armor was purely defensive.

A SCENE FROM THE TRIASSIC

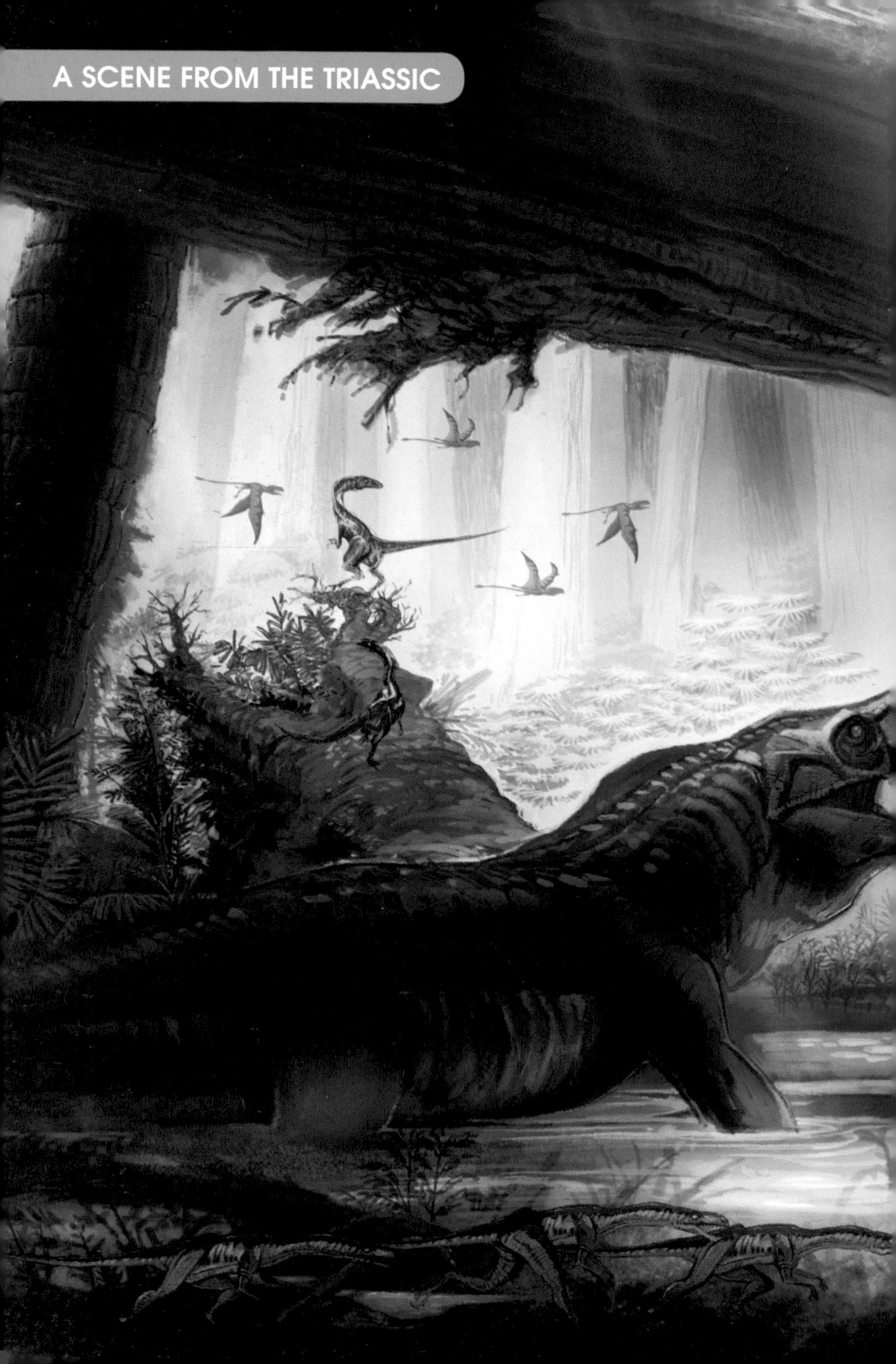

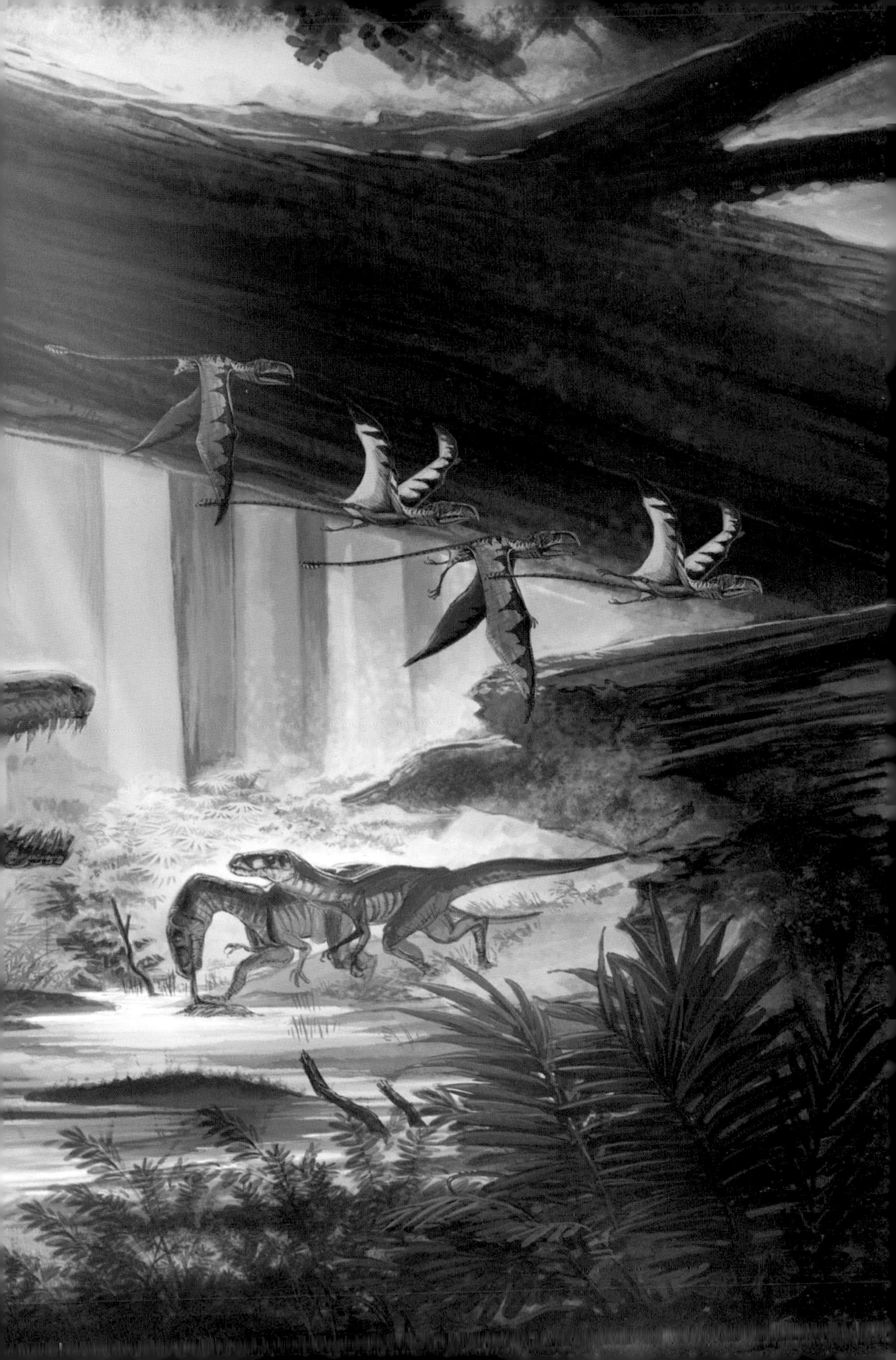

TAKING IN THE TRIASSIC
Parasuchus

Parasuchus was an amphibious predator that belonged to the order Phytosauria. It was closely related to crocodiles, its whole body was covered with thick scales with an underside supported by strong ribs. Furthermore, with nostrils situated on the top of its snout like modern crocodiles, it could submerge while keeping its nose above the surface to breathe—as modern crocodiles do.

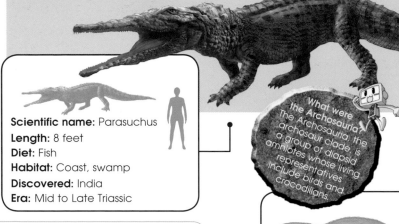

Scientific name: Parasuchus
Length: 8 feet
Diet: Fish
Habitat: Coast, swamp
Discovered: India
Era: Mid to Late Triassic

What were the Archosauria? The Archosauria, the archosaur clade, is a group of diapsid amniotes whose living representatives include birds and crocodilians.

TAKING IN THE TRIASSIC
Prestosuchus

Even though its body shape and upright posture resembled that of dinosaurs', it actually belonged to the order Archosauria. With strong limbs, it could sprint at high speed, making Prestosuchus one of the most fearsome predators during the Triassic.

Scientific name: Prestosuchus
Length: 17 to 23 feet
Diet: Other animals
Habitat: Coast
Discovered: Brazil
Era: Late Triassic

Prestosuchus skull
The Prestosaurus had a long pair of jaws with jagged teeth.

CHAPTER 6

OCEAN OVERLOAD

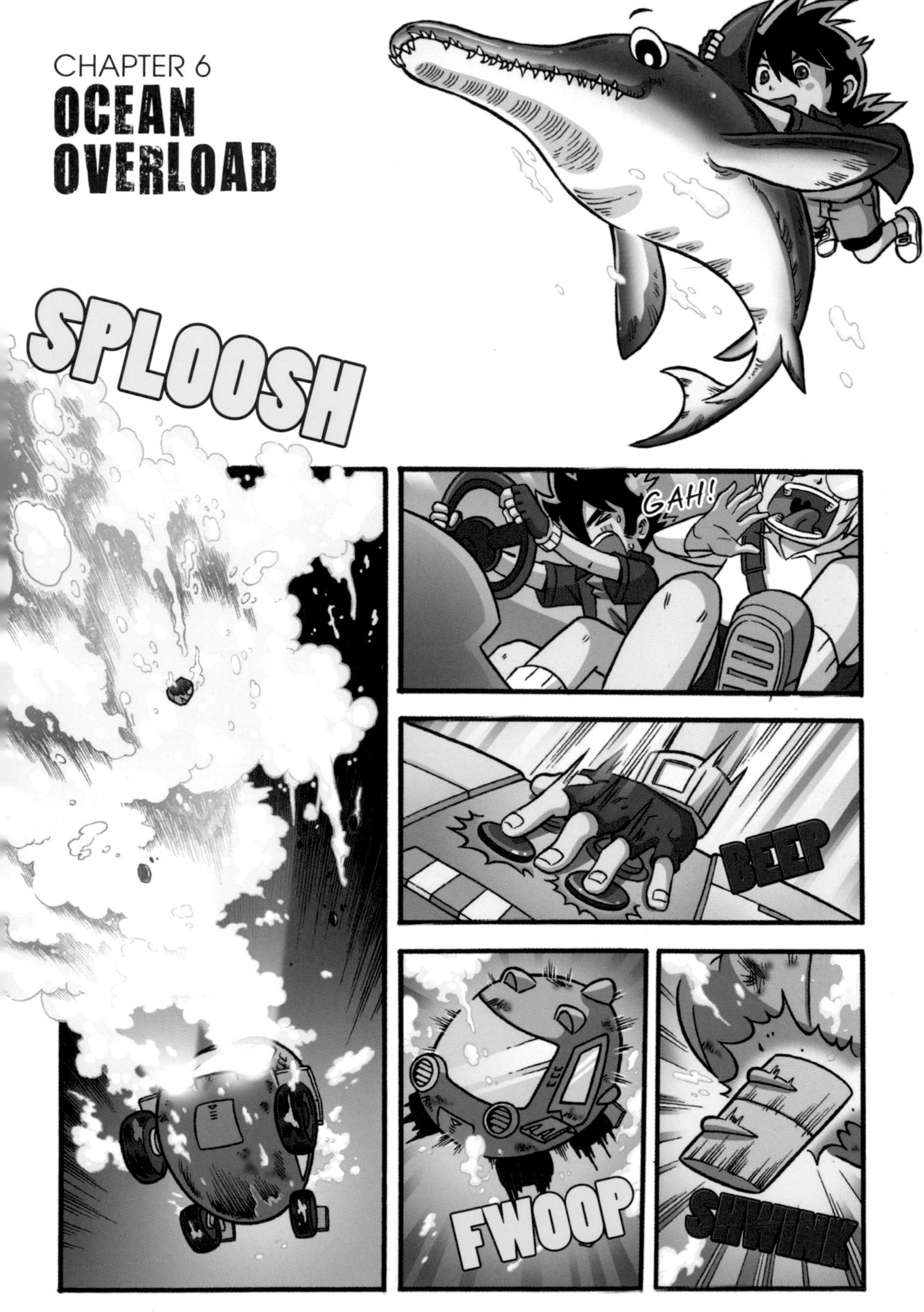
SPLOOSH
GAH!
BEEP
FWOOP
SHWINK

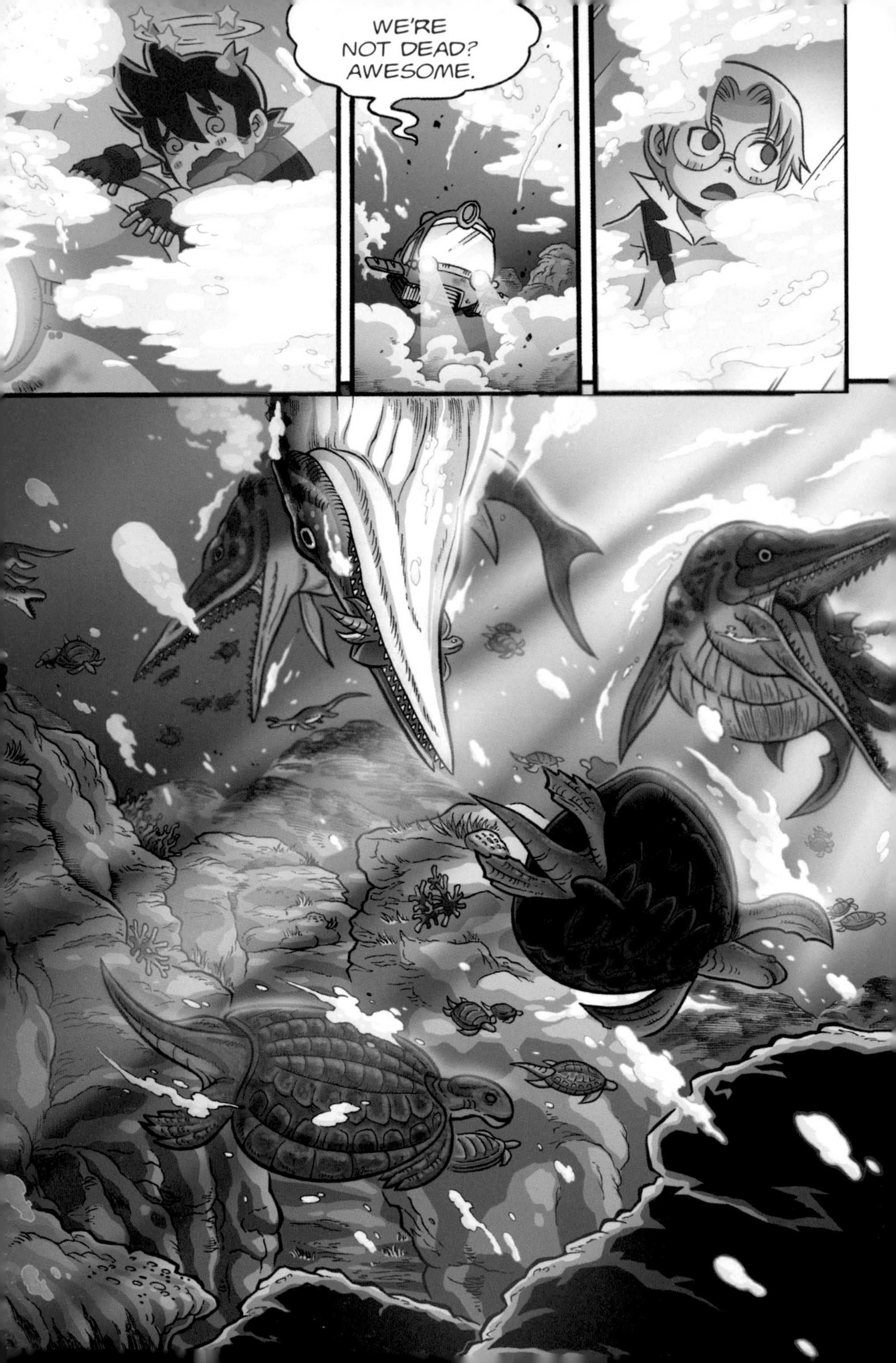
WE'RE NOT DEAD? AWESOME.

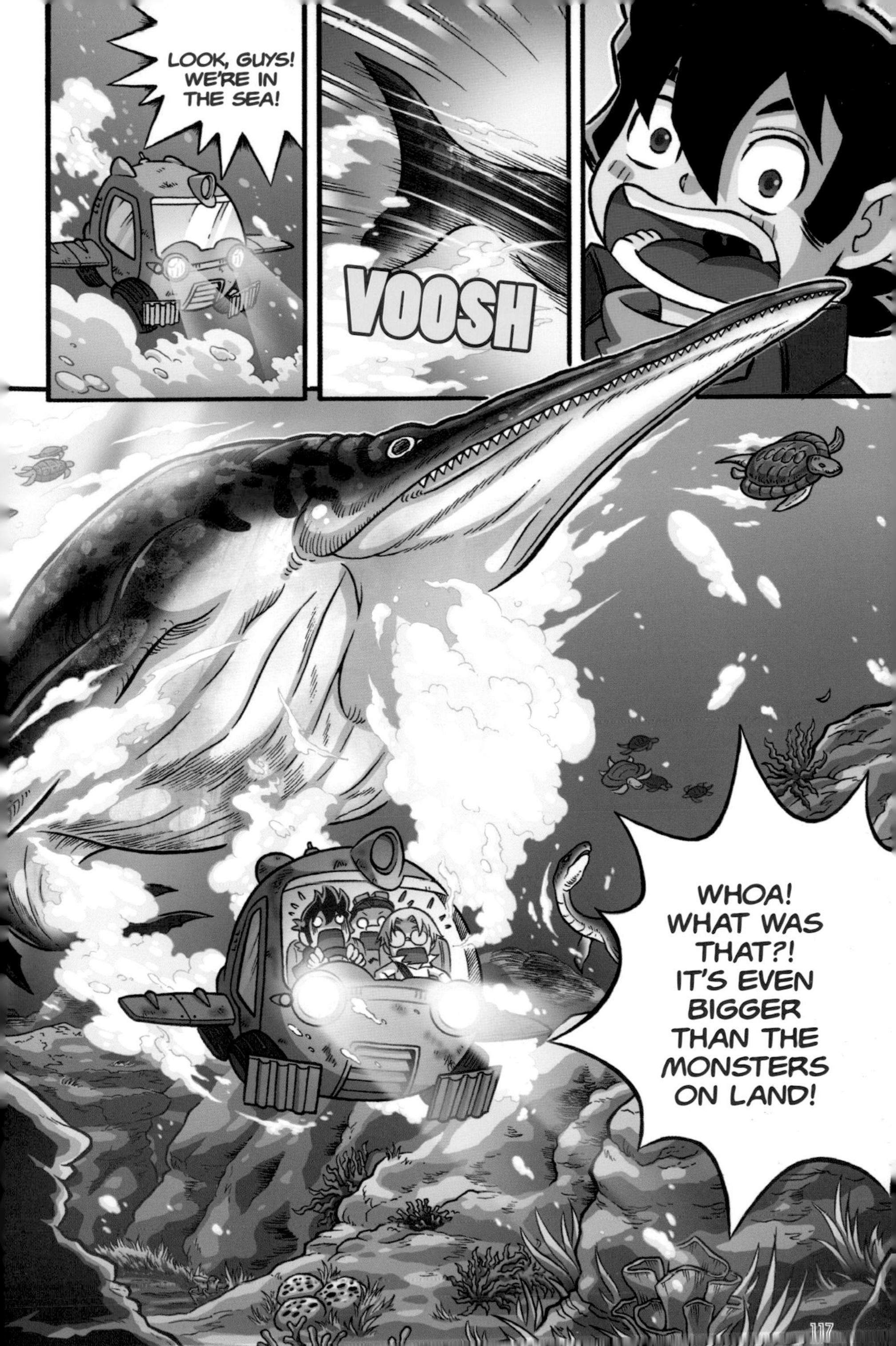
LOOK, GUYS! WE'RE IN THE SEA!
VOOSH
WHOA! WHAT WAS THAT?! IT'S EVEN BIGGER THAN THE MONSTERS ON LAND!

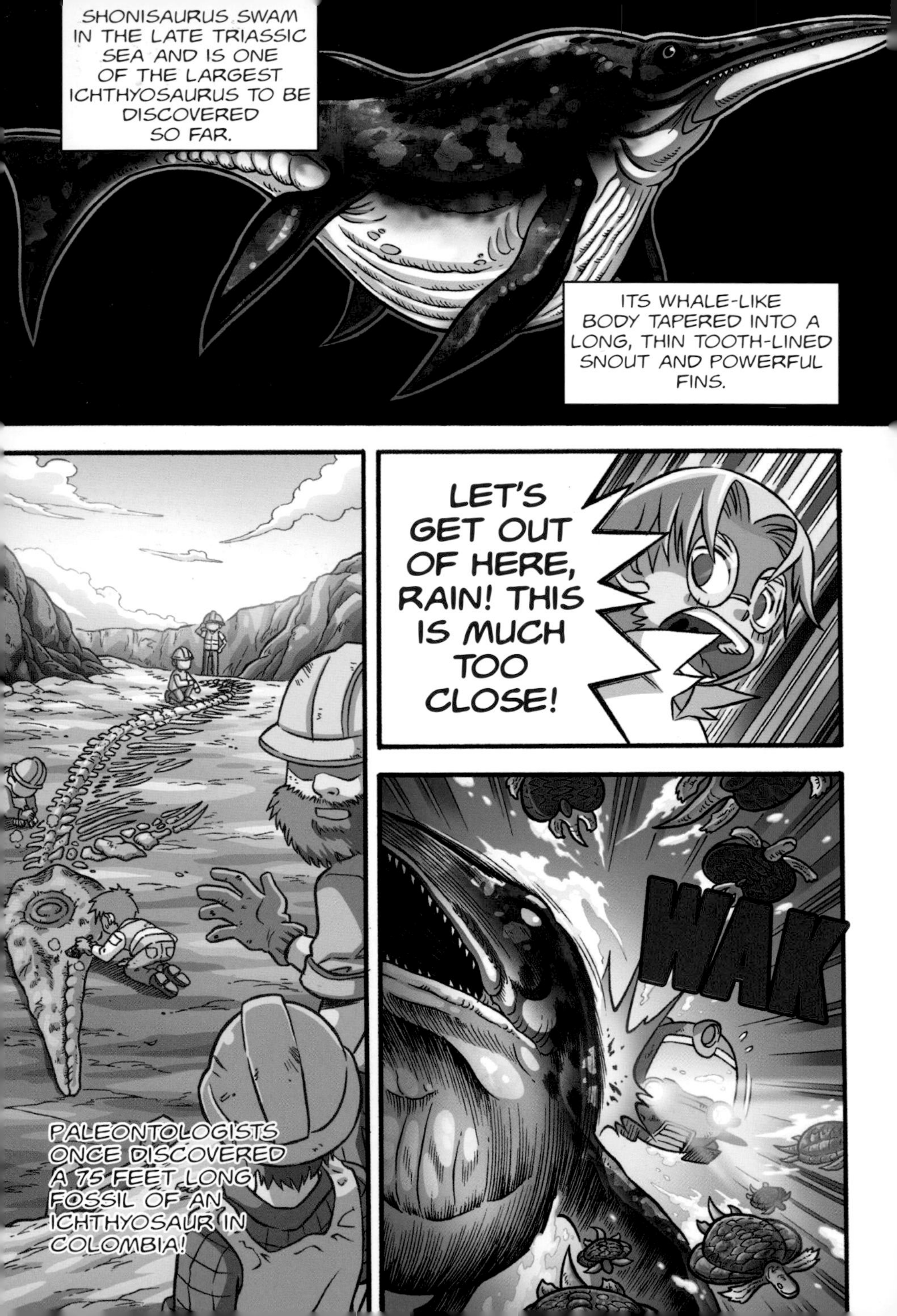
SHONISAURUS SWAM IN THE LATE TRIASSIC SEA AND IS ONE OF THE LARGEST ICHTHYOSAURUS TO BE DISCOVERED SO FAR.
ITS WHALE-LIKE BODY TAPERED INTO A LONG, THIN TOOTH-LINED SNOUT AND POWERFUL FINS.
PALEONTOLOGISTS ONCE DISCOVERED A 75 FEET LONG FOSSIL OF AN ICHTHYOSAUR IN COLOMBIA!
LET'S GET OUT OF HERE, RAIN! THIS IS MUCH TOO CLOSE!
WAK

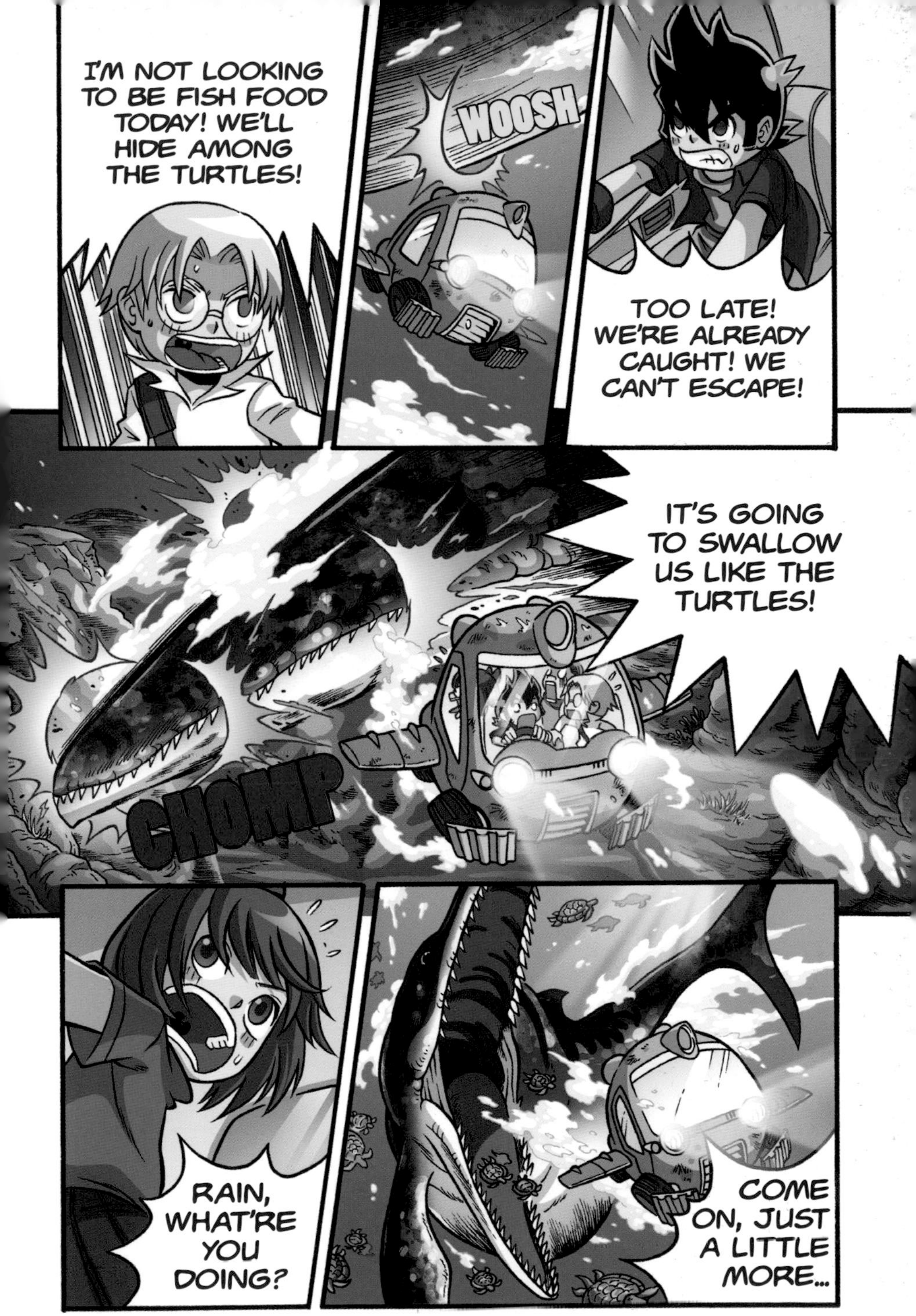
I'M NOT LOOKING TO BE FISH FOOD TODAY! WE'LL HIDE AMONG THE TURTLES!
WOOSH
TOO LATE! WE'RE ALREADY CAUGHT! WE CAN'T ESCAPE!
IT'S GOING TO SWALLOW US LIKE THE TURTLES!
CHOMP
RAIN, WHAT'RE YOU DOING?
COME ON, JUST A LITTLE MORE...

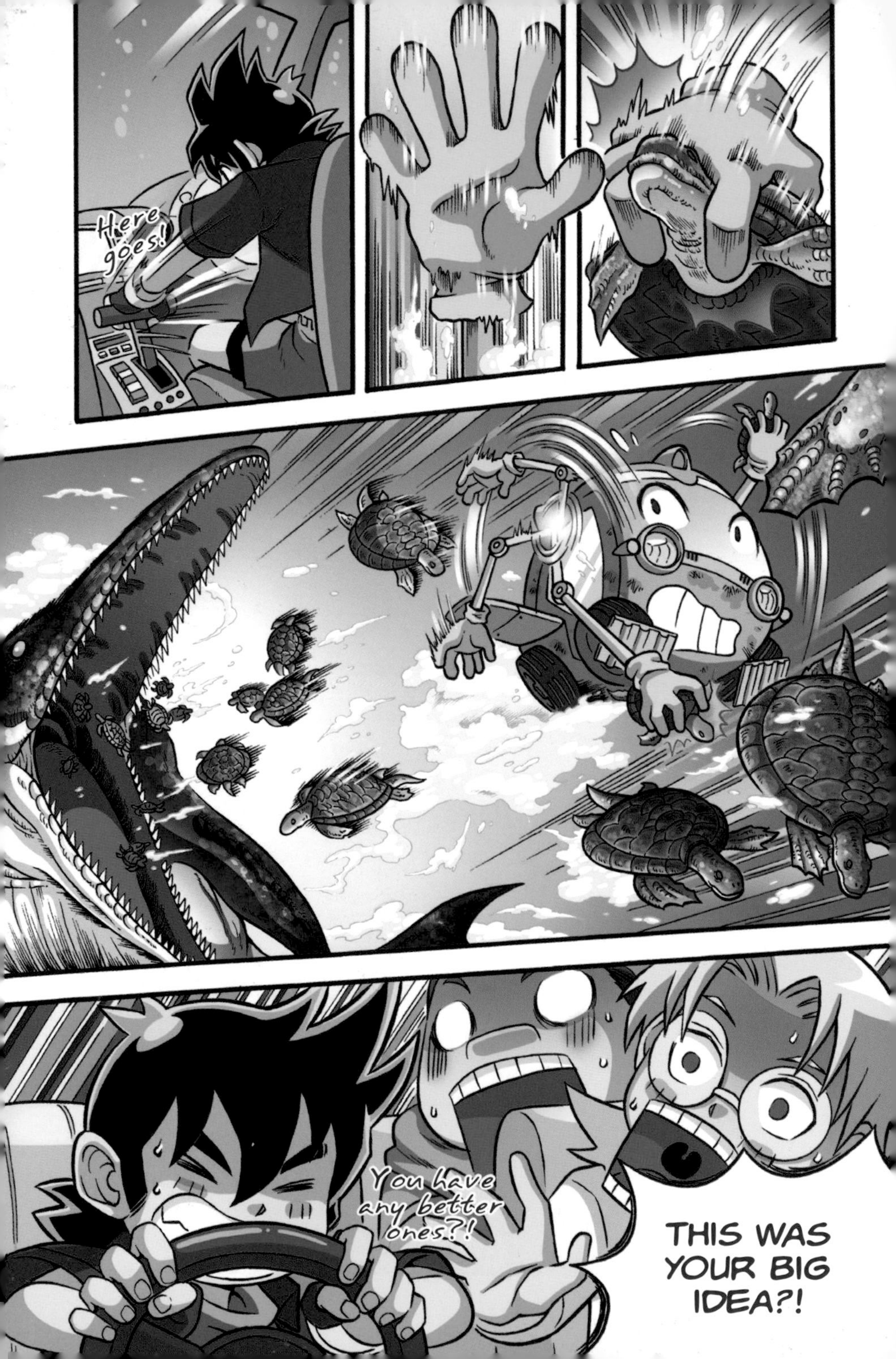
Here goes!
THIS WAS YOUR BIG IDEA?!
You have any better ones?!

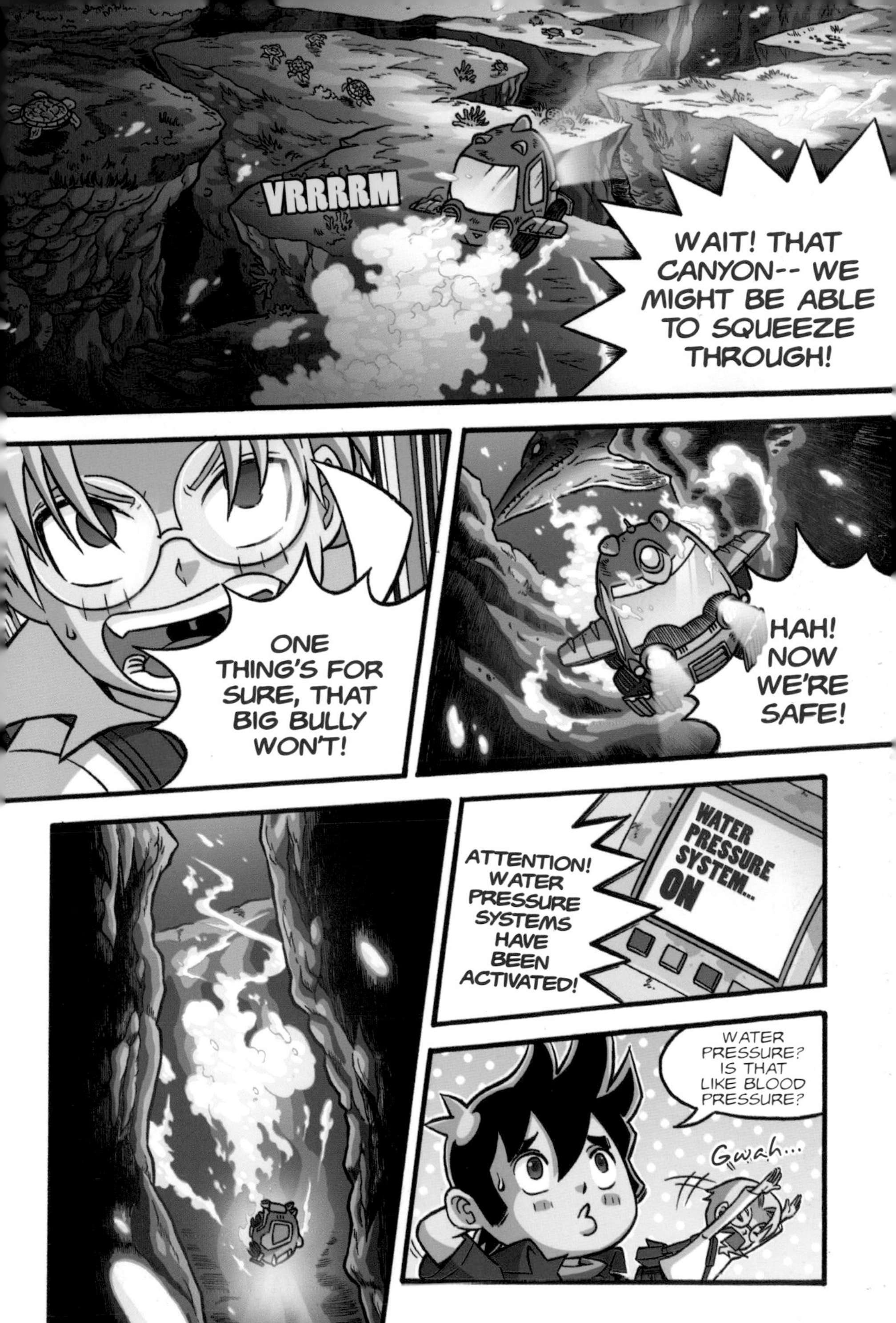
VRRRRM
WAIT! THAT CANYON-- WE MIGHT BE ABLE TO SQUEEZE THROUGH!
ONE THING'S FOR SURE, THAT BIG BULLY WON'T!
HAH! NOW WE'RE SAFE!
WATER PRESSURE SYSTEM... ON
ATTENTION! WATER PRESSURE SYSTEMS HAVE BEEN ACTIVATED!
WATER PRESSURE? IS THAT LIKE BLOOD PRESSURE?
Gwah...

Water pressure refers to the pressure in water. To illustrate this, we can conduct an experiment to see water pressure in action. First, fill a barrel with water and then poke three holes at a height of 1 inch, 1.5 inches, and 2 inches above the ground.

Results?:

The water from the 1 inch hole will expel water the farthest, followed by the 1.5 inches hole, with the water spurting from the 2 inches hole closest to the barrel.

Basically, the deeper the water, the higher the pressure, due to all the water above it.

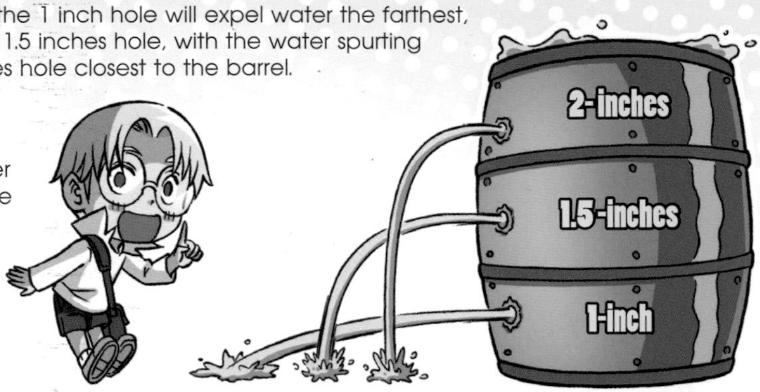
2-inches
1.5-inches
1-inch

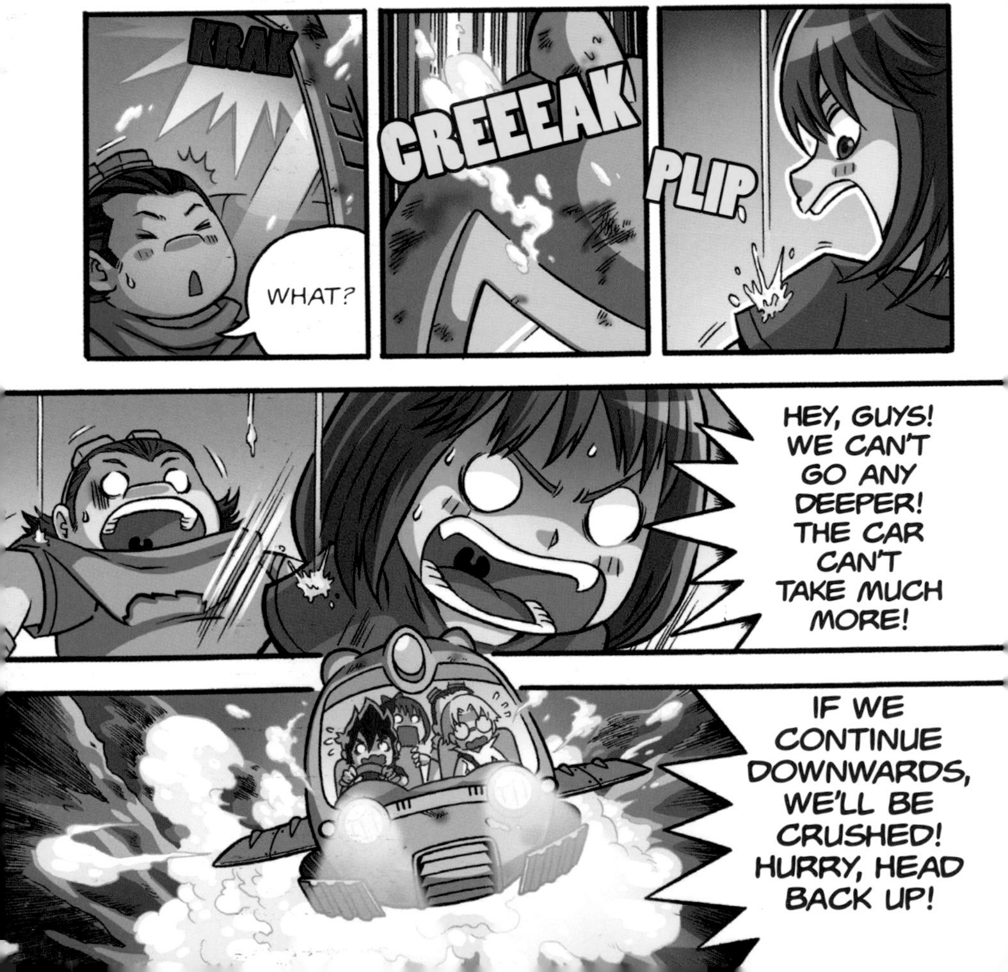
KRAK
WHAT?
CREEEAK
PLIP
HEY, GUYS! WE CAN'T GO ANY DEEPER! THE CAR CAN'T TAKE MUCH MORE!
IF WE CONTINUE DOWNWARDS, WE'LL BE CRUSHED! HURRY, HEAD BACK UP!

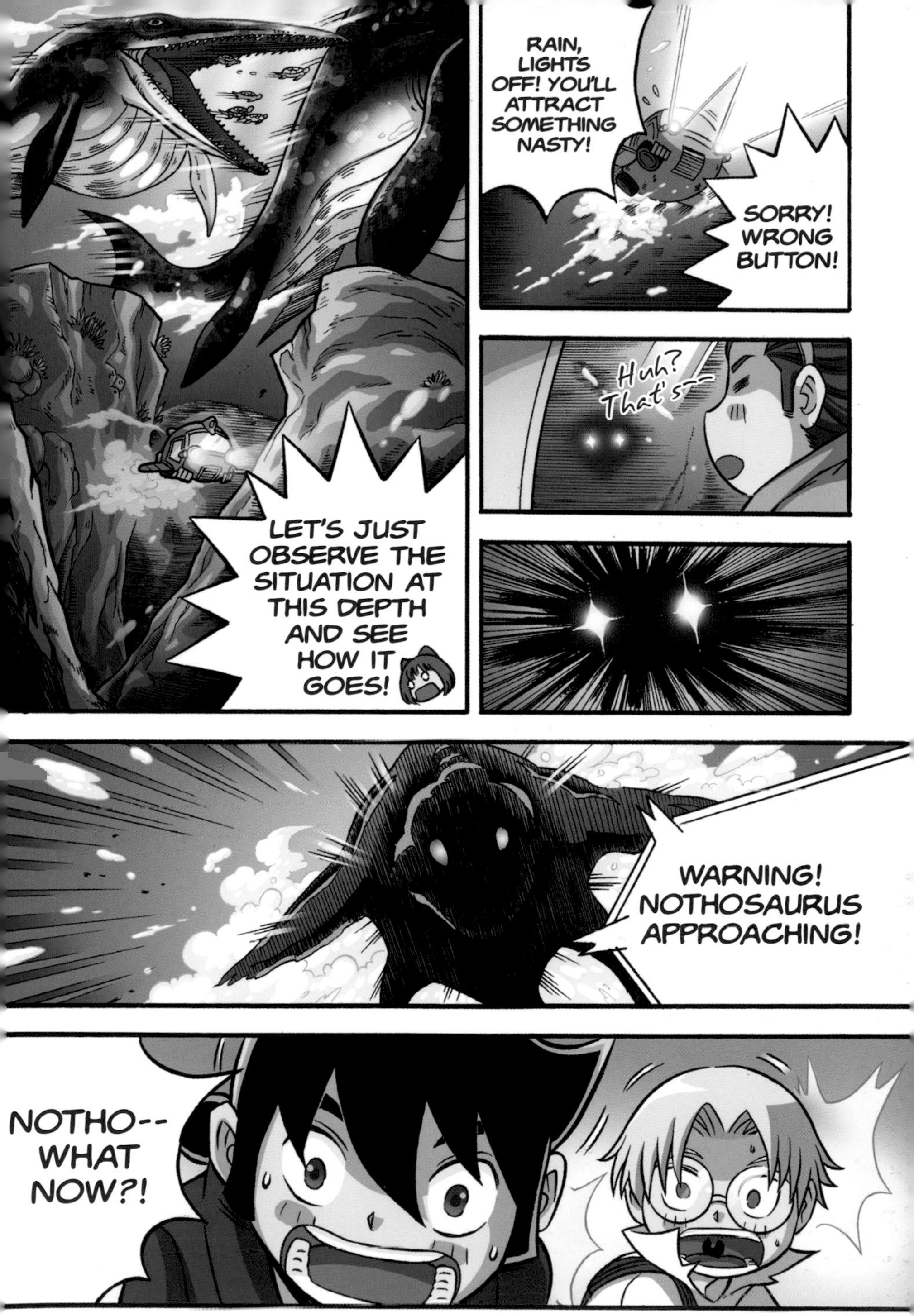
LET'S JUST OBSERVE THE SITUATION AT THIS DEPTH AND SEE HOW IT GOES!
RAIN, LIGHTS OFF! YOU'LL ATTRACT SOMETHING NASTY!
SORRY! WRONG BUTTON!
Huh? That's--
WARNING! NOTHOSAURUS APPROACHING!
NOTHO-- WHAT NOW?!

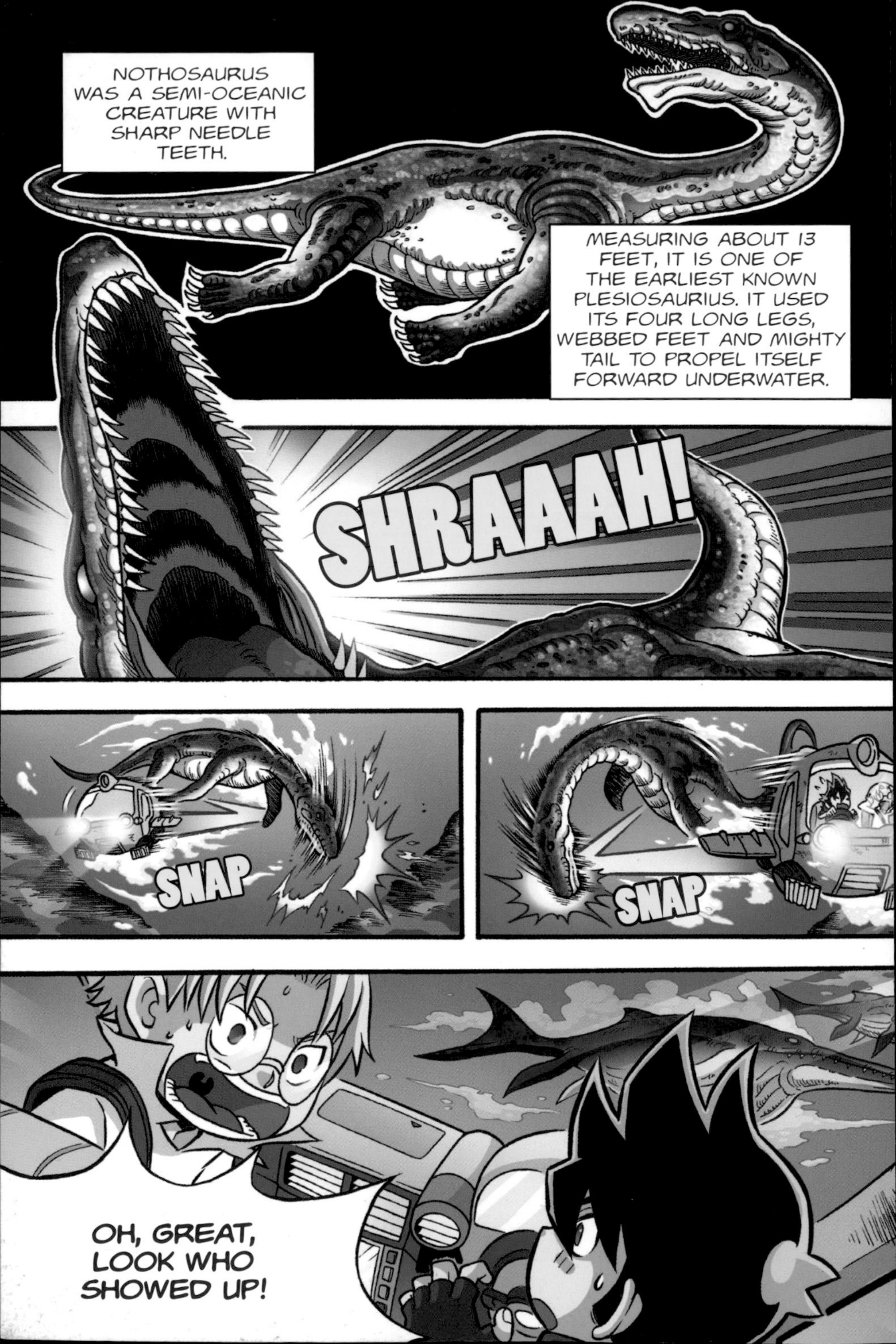
NOTHOSAURUS WAS A SEMI-OCEANIC CREATURE WITH SHARP NEEDLE TEETH.
MEASURING ABOUT 13 FEET, IT IS ONE OF THE EARLIEST KNOWN PLESIOSAURIUS. IT USED ITS FOUR LONG LEGS, WEBBED FEET AND MIGHTY TAIL TO PROPEL ITSELF FORWARD UNDERWATER.
SHRAAAH!
SNAP
SNAP
OH, GREAT, LOOK WHO SHOWED UP!

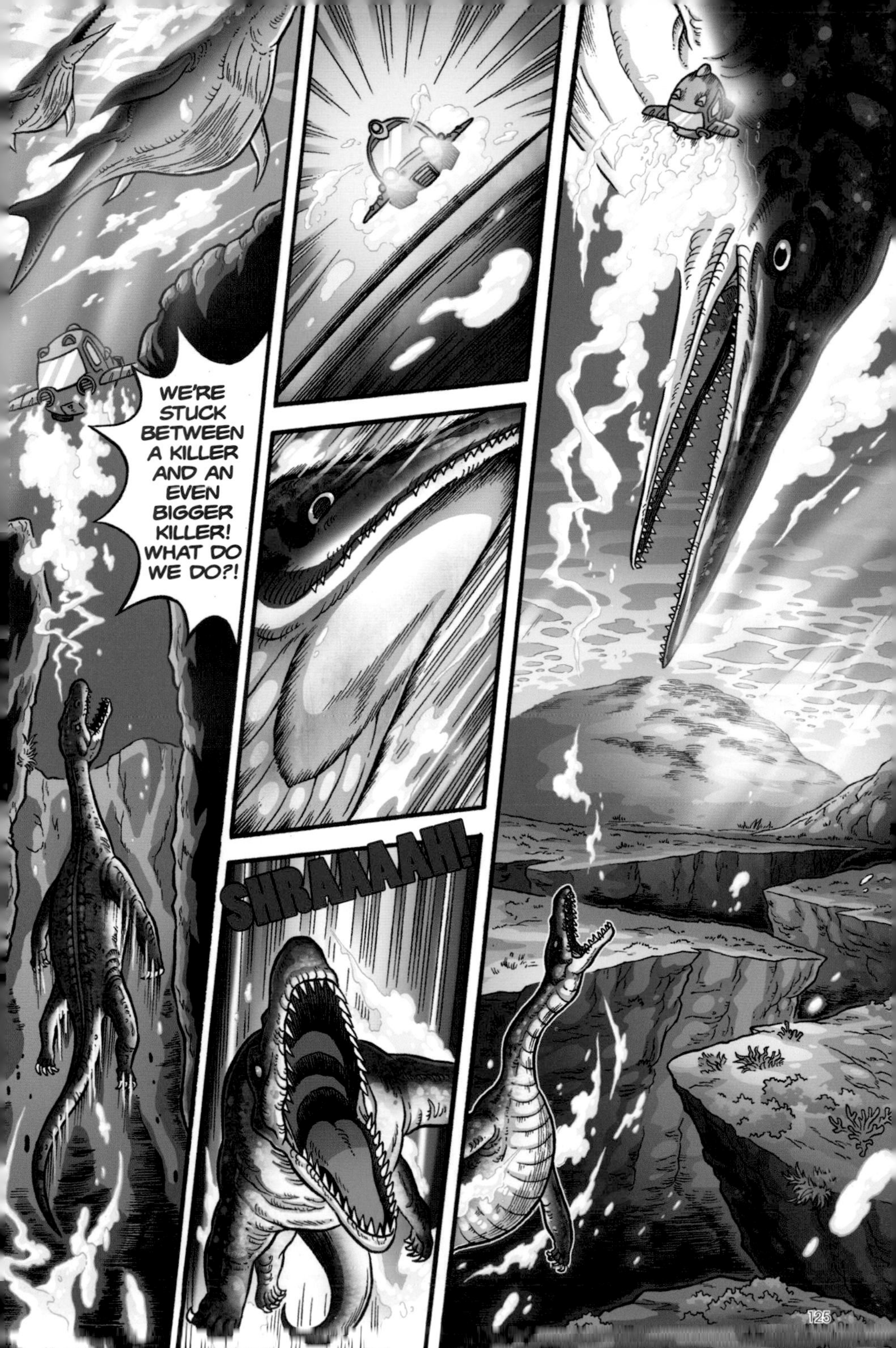
WE'RE STUCK BETWEEN A KILLER AND AN EVEN BIGGER KILLER! WHAT DO WE DO?!
SHRAAAAH!

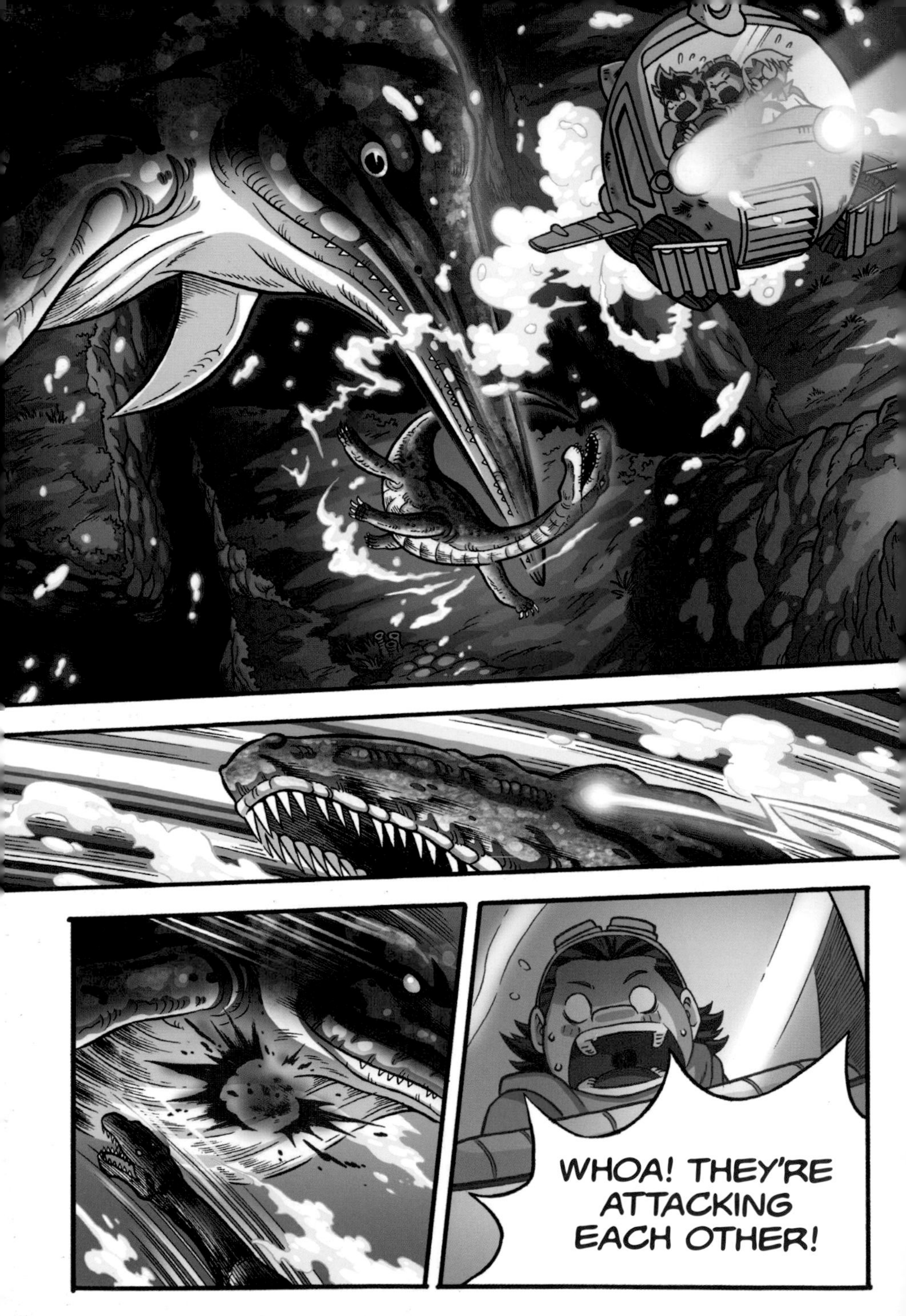
WHOA! THEY'RE ATTACKING EACH OTHER!

HUH-- THE NOTHOSAURUS MIGHT BE SMALLER, BUT IT'S FASTER TOO!

MAYBE IT'S TRYING TO TIRE ITS OPPONENT OUT, THEN GO FOR THE KILL!

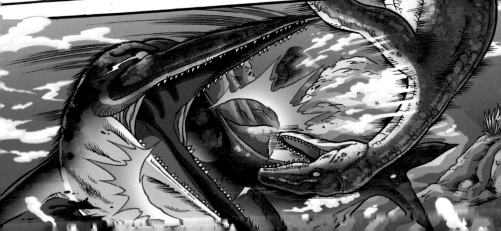

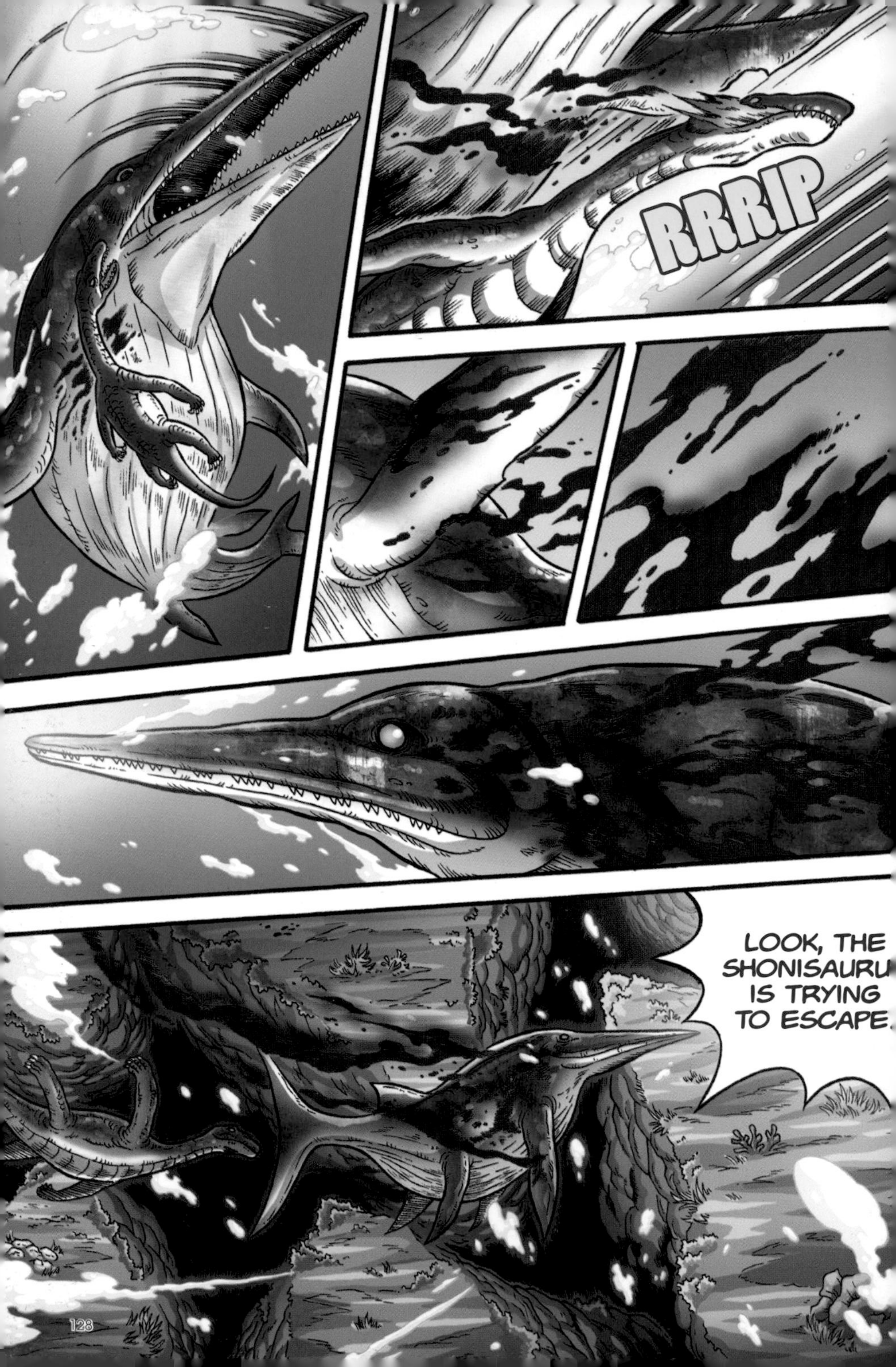
RRRIP
LOOK, THE
SHONISAURU
IS TRYING
TO ESCAPE.

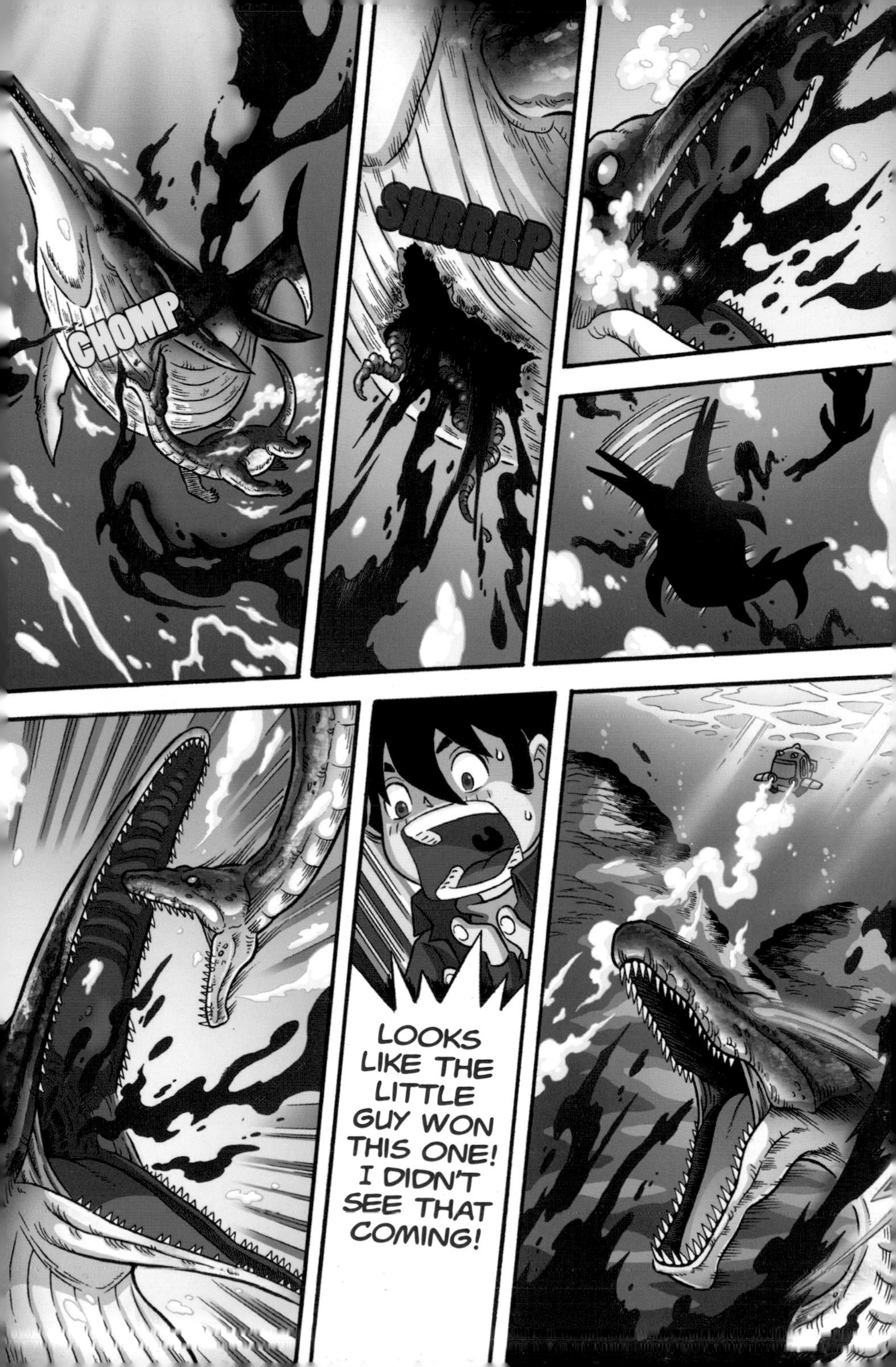
CHOMP
SHRRRP
LOOKS LIKE THE LITTLE GUY WON THIS ONE! I DIDN'T SEE THAT COMING!

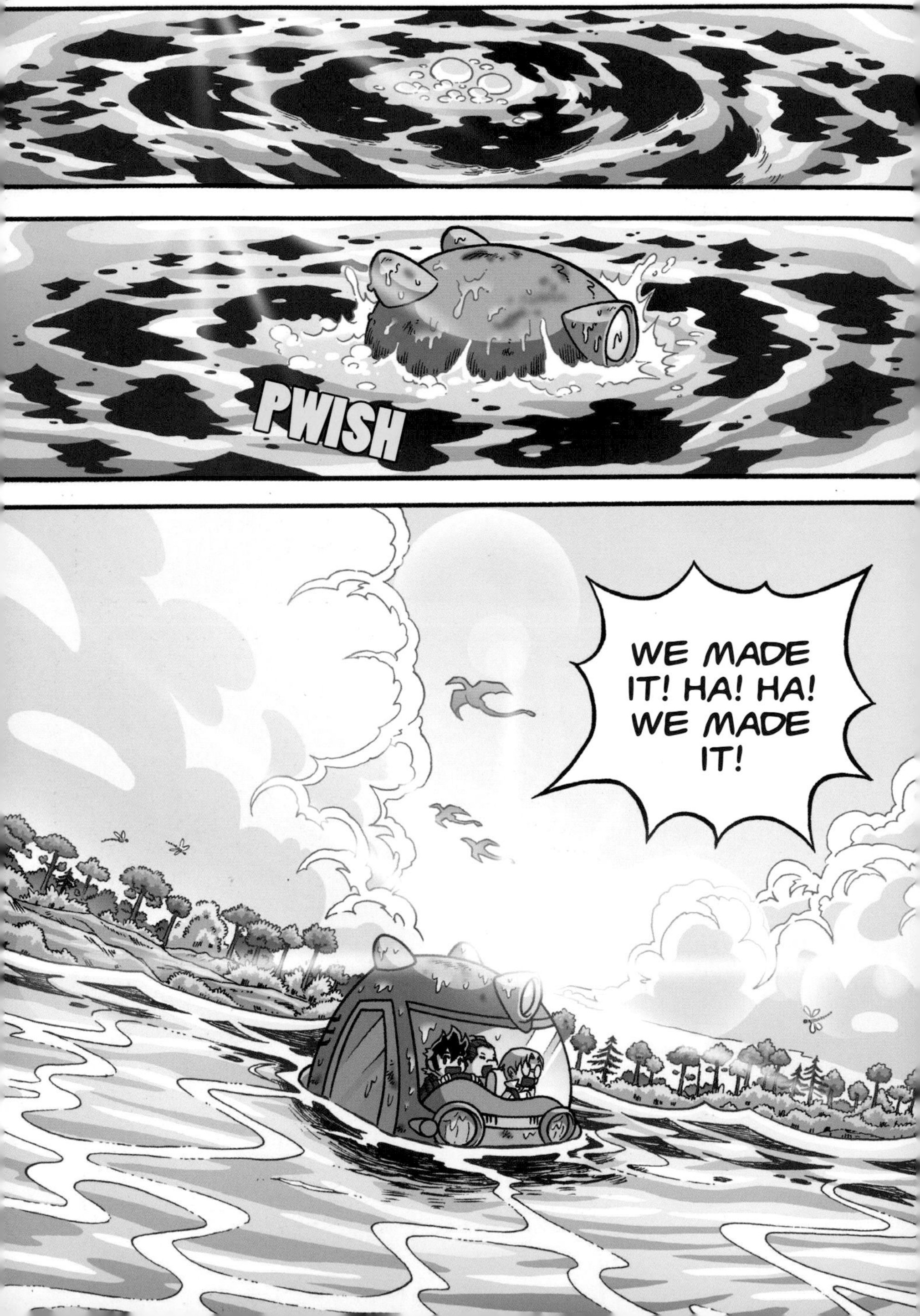
PWISH
WE MADE IT! HA! HA! WE MADE IT!

TAKING IN THE TRIASSIC

Nothosaurus

Nothosaurus shared similar physical attributes to modern crocodiles, such as long, tapering jaws with intercrossing teeth that allowed it to clamp down on prey. Nothosaurus mostly remained underwater, using its sinuous body and flexible tail to propel it through the water; its four webbed feet were only used to increase speed and maneuvrability when hunting.

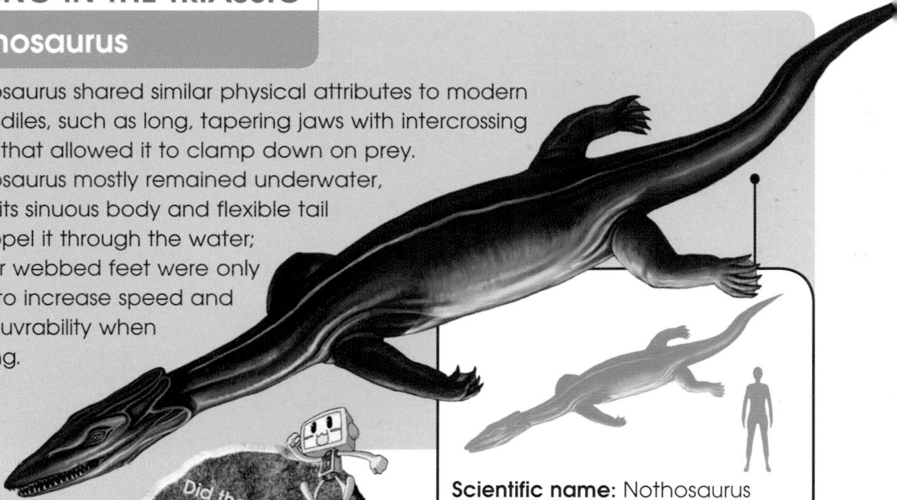

Scientific name: Nothosaurus
Length: Roughly 20 feet
Diet: Fish and prawns
Habitat: Coast
Discovered: Europe
Era: Triassic

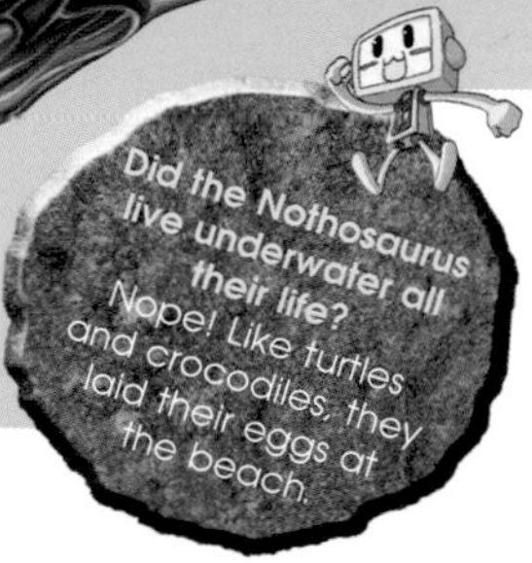
Did the Nothosaurus live underwater all their life?
Nope! Like turtles and crocodiles, they laid their eggs at the beach.

TAKING IN THE TRIASSIC

Cymbospondylus

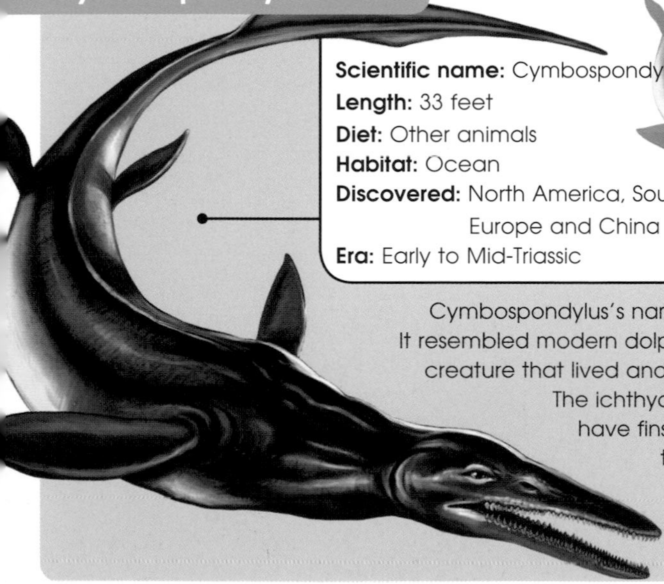

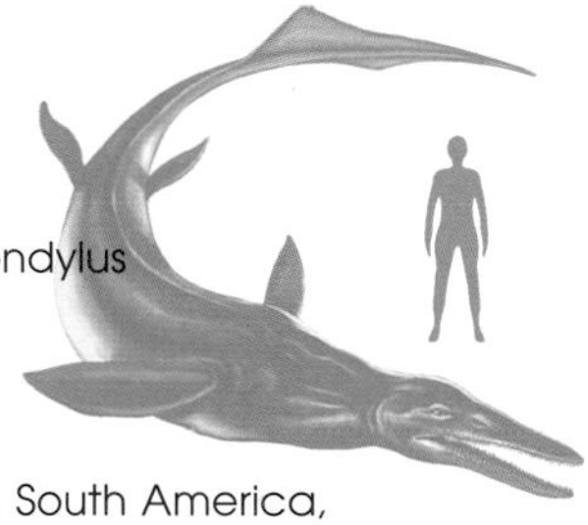

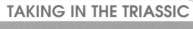

Scientific name: Cymbospondylus
Length: 33 feet
Diet: Other animals
Habitat: Ocean
Discovered: North America, South America, Europe and China
Era: Early to Mid-Triassic

Cymbospondylus's name means "Boat Spine," It resembled modern dolphins, and was a marine creature that lived and reproduced in the sea. The ichthyosaurs of this era did not have fins; instead, they relied on their four limbs and long tail fin to navigate underwater.

A SCENE FROM THE TRIASSIC

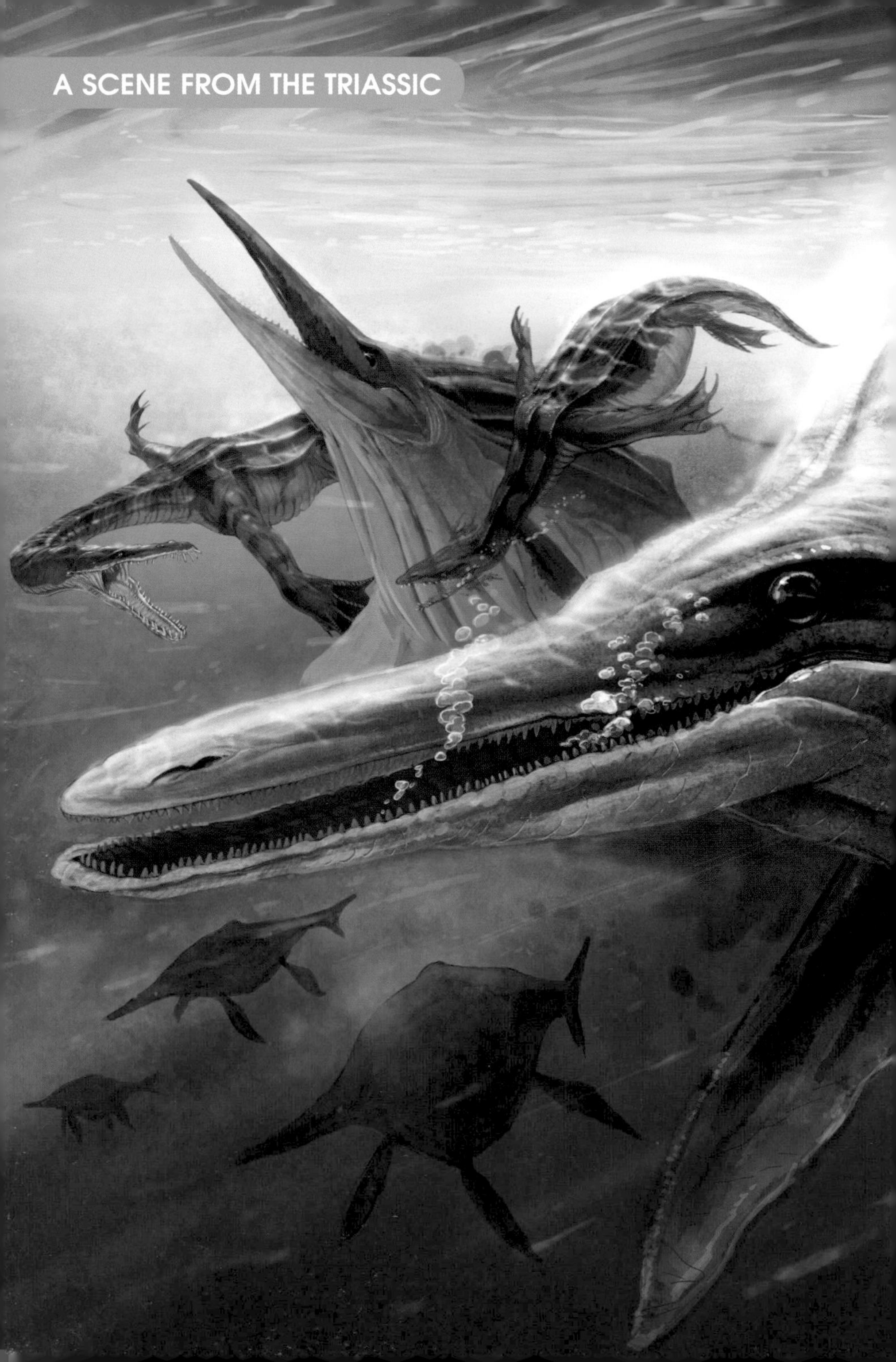

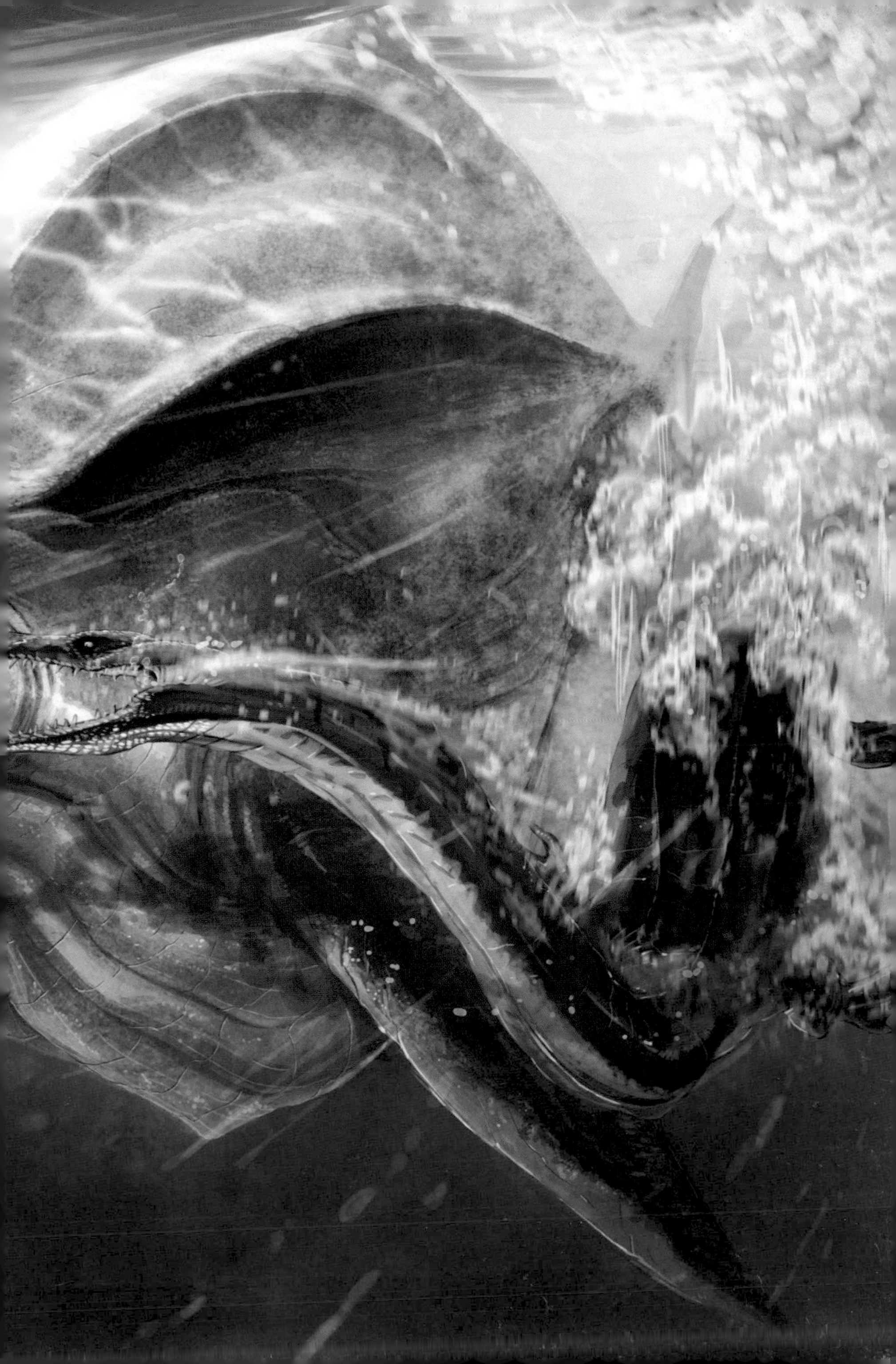

Shonisaurus

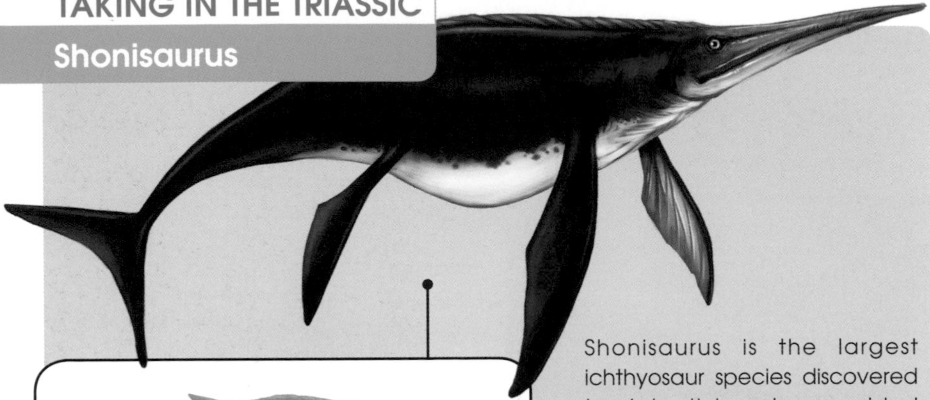

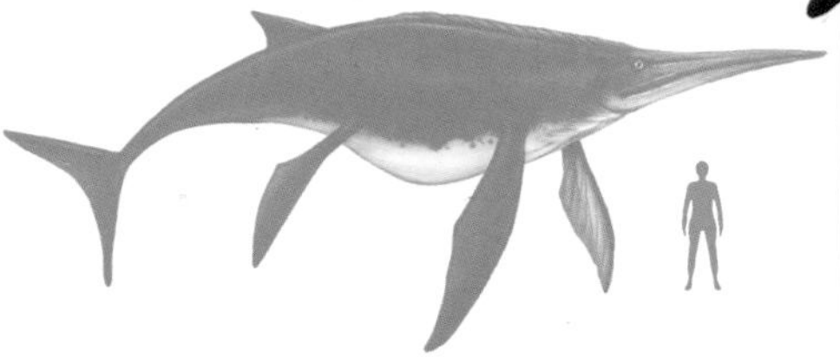

Scientific name: Shonisaurus
Length: 49 feet to 69 feet
Diet: Other animals
Habitat: Ocean
Discovered: North America
Era: Late Triassic

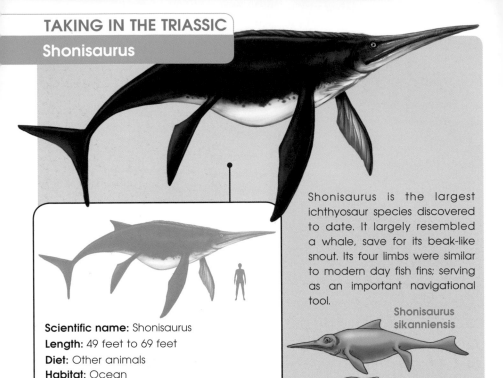

Shonisaurus is the largest ichthyosaur species discovered to date. It largely resembled a whale, save for its beak-like snout. Its four limbs were similar to modern day fish fins; serving as an important navigational tool.

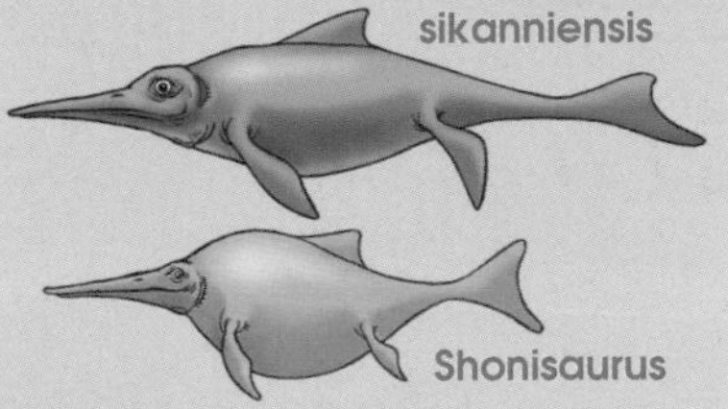
Shonisaurus sikanniensis
Shonisaurus

Most Shonisaurs measured about 49 feet and were considered large animals even by the standards of the Triassic ocean. In recent years, however, a new species, Shonisaurus sikanniensis, was found—it boasted a 69 feet, making it the new overlord of the ocean.

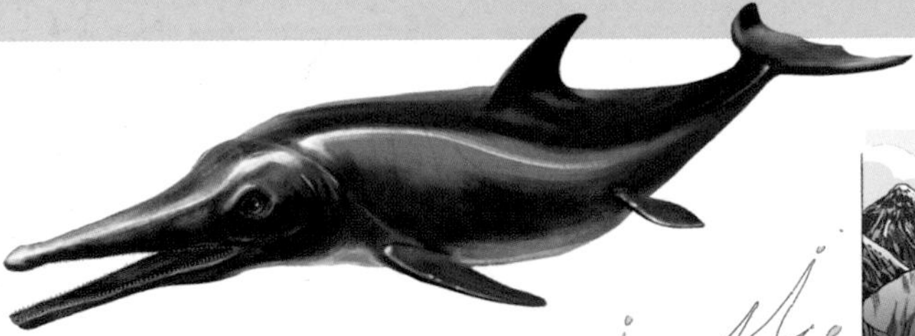

Himalayesaurus

Himalayasaurus was first discovered at the "roof of the world," (the Himalayas). Paleontologists suspect that it might be related to the Shonisaurus. In any case, these fossils prove that the Himalayas were once underwater during the Triassic.

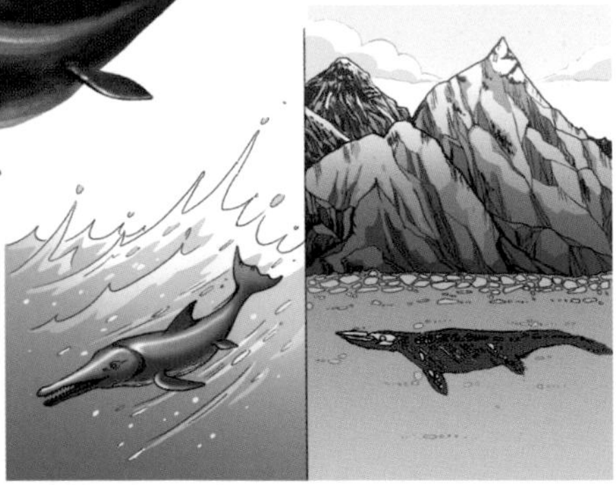

Himalayasaurus, which once dwelled in the Triassic ocean, is now a fossil beneath the Himalayan mountains.

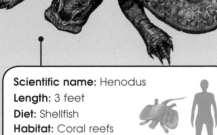

Henodus's body was covered by a carapace, much like modern day tortoises. Its back and belly had horn-plated scales which protected it from larger predators. It did not have teeth, but its lower and upper jaws formed hard beaks, which allowed it to pry shellfish off rocks and crush them in its mouth.

Scientific name: Henodus
Length: 3 feet
Diet: Shellfish
Habitat: Coral reefs
Discovered: Europe
Era: Late Triassic

Are the Henodus and Psephoderma early ancestors of the tortoise? Even though they shared similar attributes, these two species are not related to the modern tortoise

Scientific name: Psephoderma
Length: 3 feet
Diet: Conches and crustaceans
Habitat: Shallow waters
Discovered: Europe
Era: Late Triassic

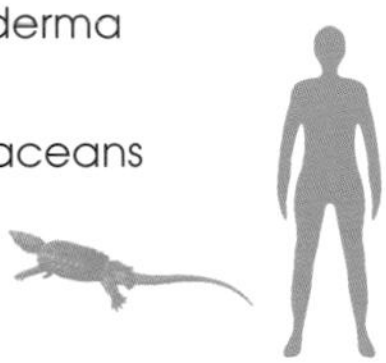

Psephoderma had a carapace, but unlike most of its kind, its shell was divided into two parts: one to protect the back and belly, while the other guarded its rear end. Furthermore, its carapace was shaped unevenly with its body being flat and large. It had rounded teeth in its jaw which allowed it to crush shellfish.

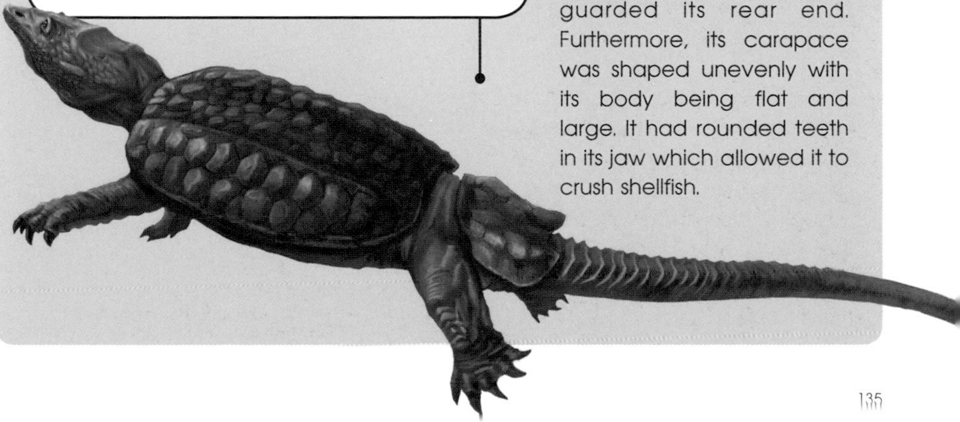

TAKING IN THE TRIASSIC

Peteinosaurus

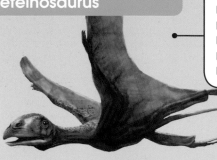

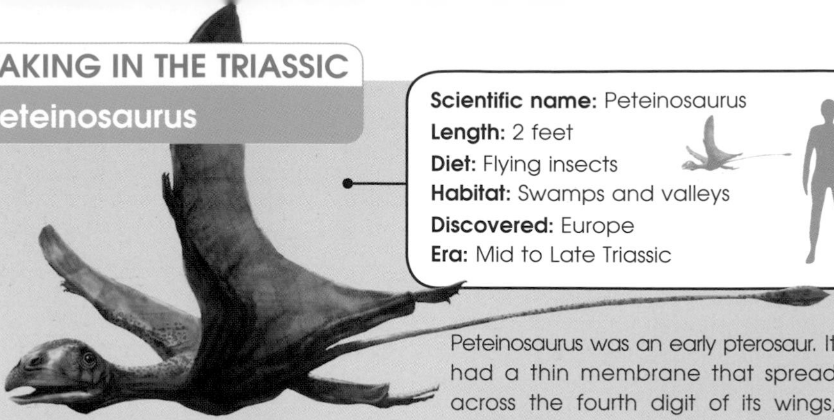

Scientific name: Peteinosaurus
Length: 2 feet
Diet: Flying insects
Habitat: Swamps and valleys
Discovered: Europe
Era: Mid to Late Triassic

Peteinosaurus was an early pterosaur. It had a thin membrane that spread across the fourth digit of its wings, and a sturdy but light bone structure. Given its 2 feet wingspan, it took to the skies quite easily relying on the bones in its long tail to maintain balance.

Comparison with other flying animals

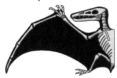

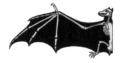

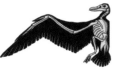

Peteinosaurus
Peteinosaurus had a thin membrane that spread across the fourth digit of its wings.

Bat
The thin membrane on its wings is spread between their second and fifth digit.

Bird
Its wings are covered with feathers.

Even though their wings were similar to those of a bat, the bone structures were quite different, and even more so compared to birds.

TAKING IN THE TRIASSIC

Eudimorphodon

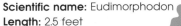

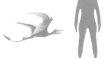

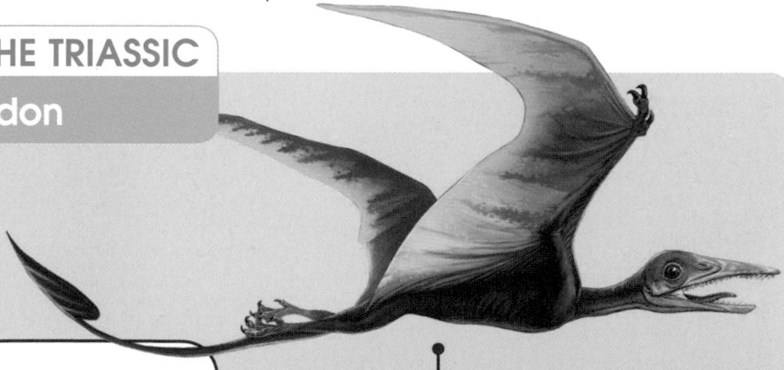

Scientific name: Eudimorphodon
Length: 2.5 feet
Diet: Fish
Habitat: Coast
Discovered: Italy
Era: Late Triassic

Eudimorphodon had a wing span of 3 feet and a spade-shaped flap at the end of its tail to help navigate, much like a boat rudder. Even though its head was only 2.5 inches in length, it contained 114 teeth!

CHAPTER 7

DALLYING WITH DANGER!

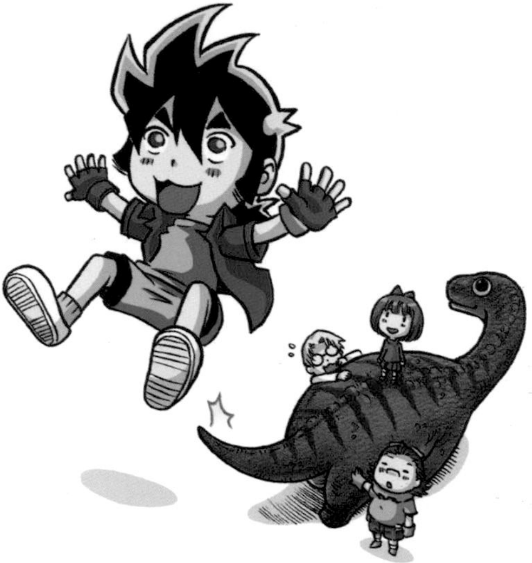

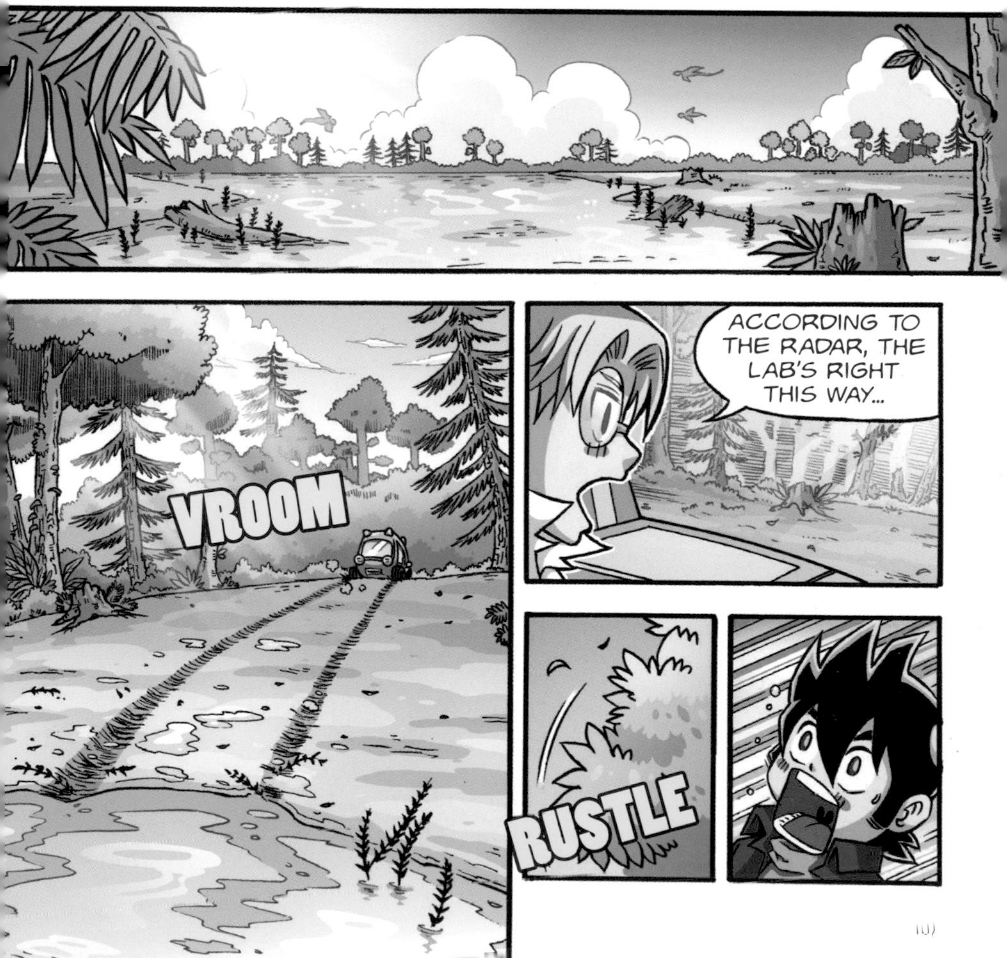
VROOM
ACCORDING TO THE RADAR, THE LAB'S RIGHT THIS WAY...
RUSTLE

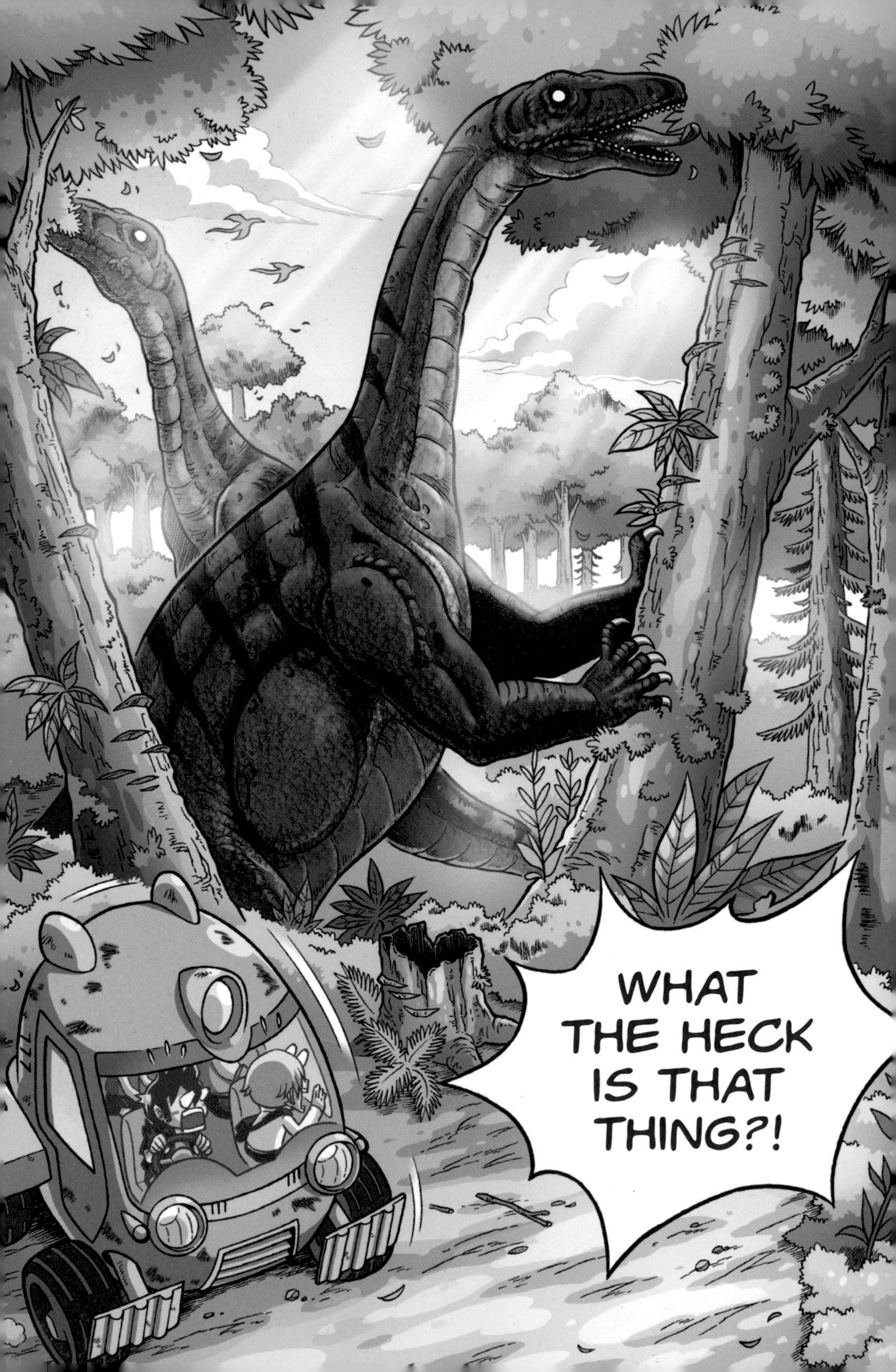
WHAT THE HECK IS THAT THING?!

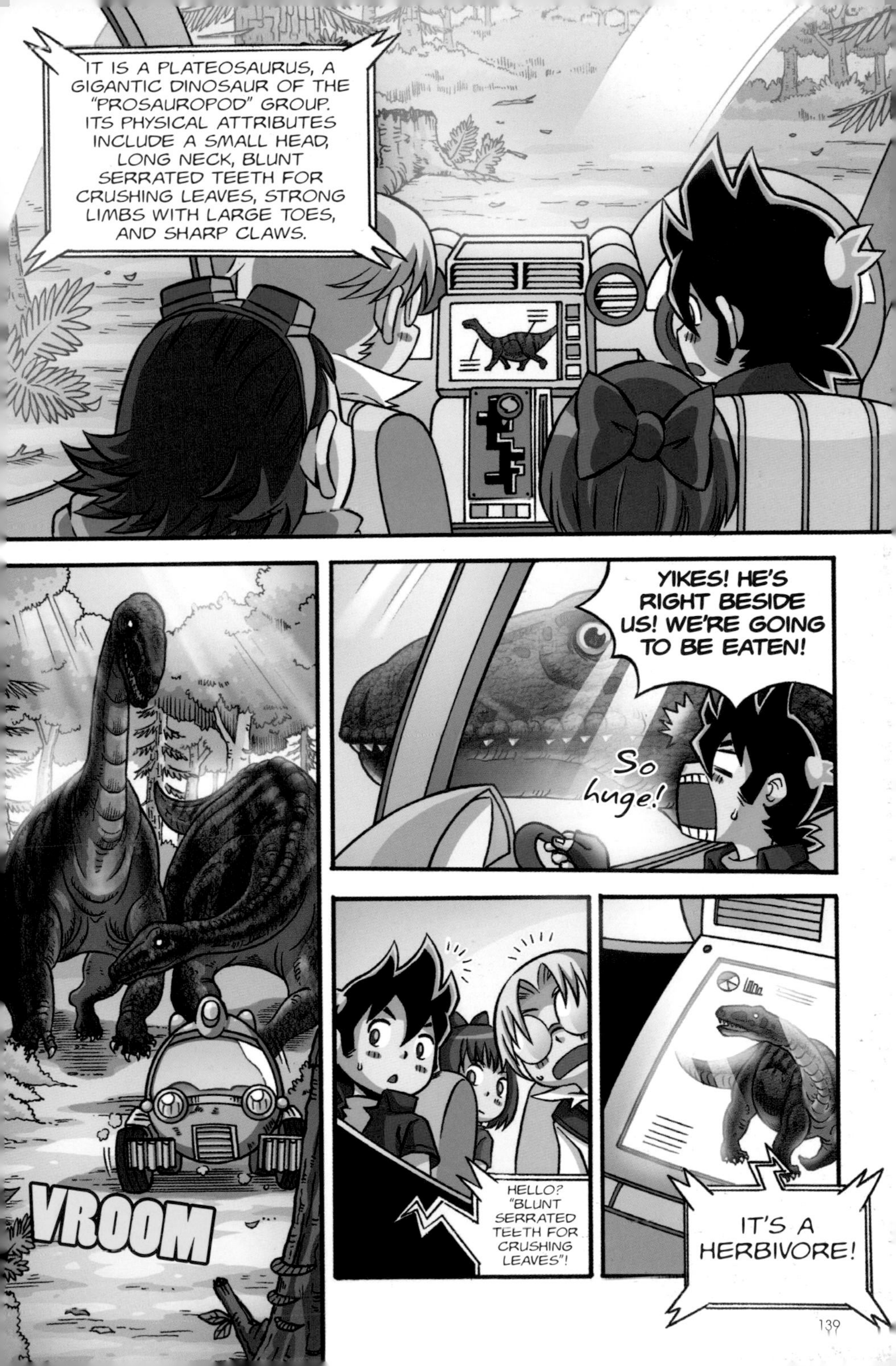
IT IS A PLATEOSAURUS, A GIGANTIC DINOSAUR OF THE "PROSAUROPOD" GROUP. ITS PHYSICAL ATTRIBUTES INCLUDE A SMALL HEAD, LONG NECK, BLUNT SERRATED TEETH FOR CRUSHING LEAVES, STRONG LIMBS WITH LARGE TOES, AND SHARP CLAWS.
VROOM
YIKES! HE'S RIGHT BESIDE US! WE'RE GOING TO BE EATEN!
So huge!
HELLO? "BLUNT SERRATED TEETH FOR CRUSHING LEAVES"!
IT'S A HERBIVORE!

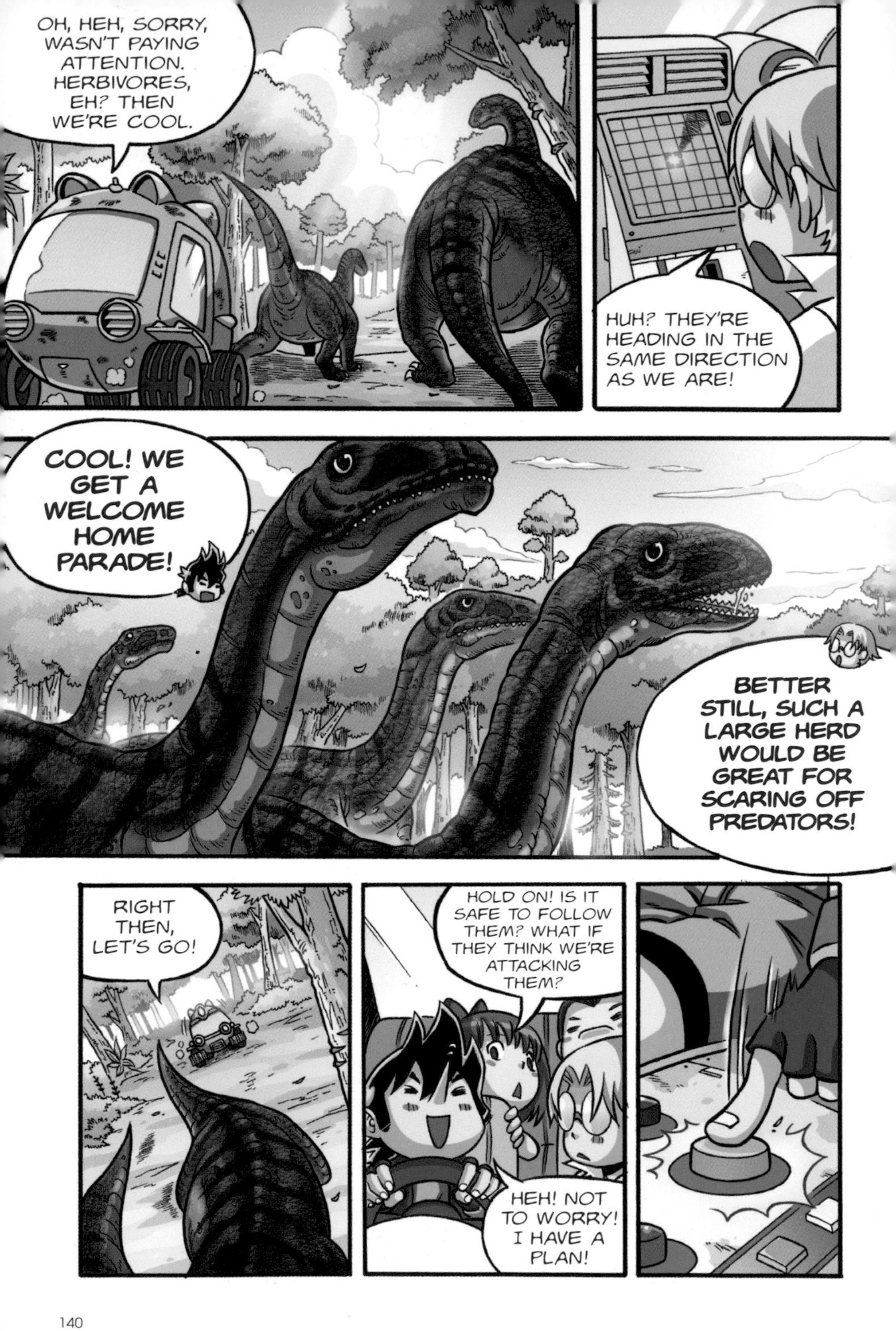
OH, HEH, SORRY, WASN'T PAYING ATTENTION. HERBIVORES, EH? THEN WE'RE COOL.
HUH? THEY'RE HEADING IN THE SAME DIRECTION AS WE ARE!
COOL! WE GET A WELCOME HOME PARADE!
BETTER STILL, SUCH A LARGE HERD WOULD BE GREAT FOR SCARING OFF PREDATORS!
RIGHT THEN, LET'S GO!
HOLD ON! IS IT SAFE TO FOLLOW THEM? WHAT IF THEY THINK WE'RE ATTACKING THEM?
HEH! NOT TO WORRY! I HAVE A PLAN!

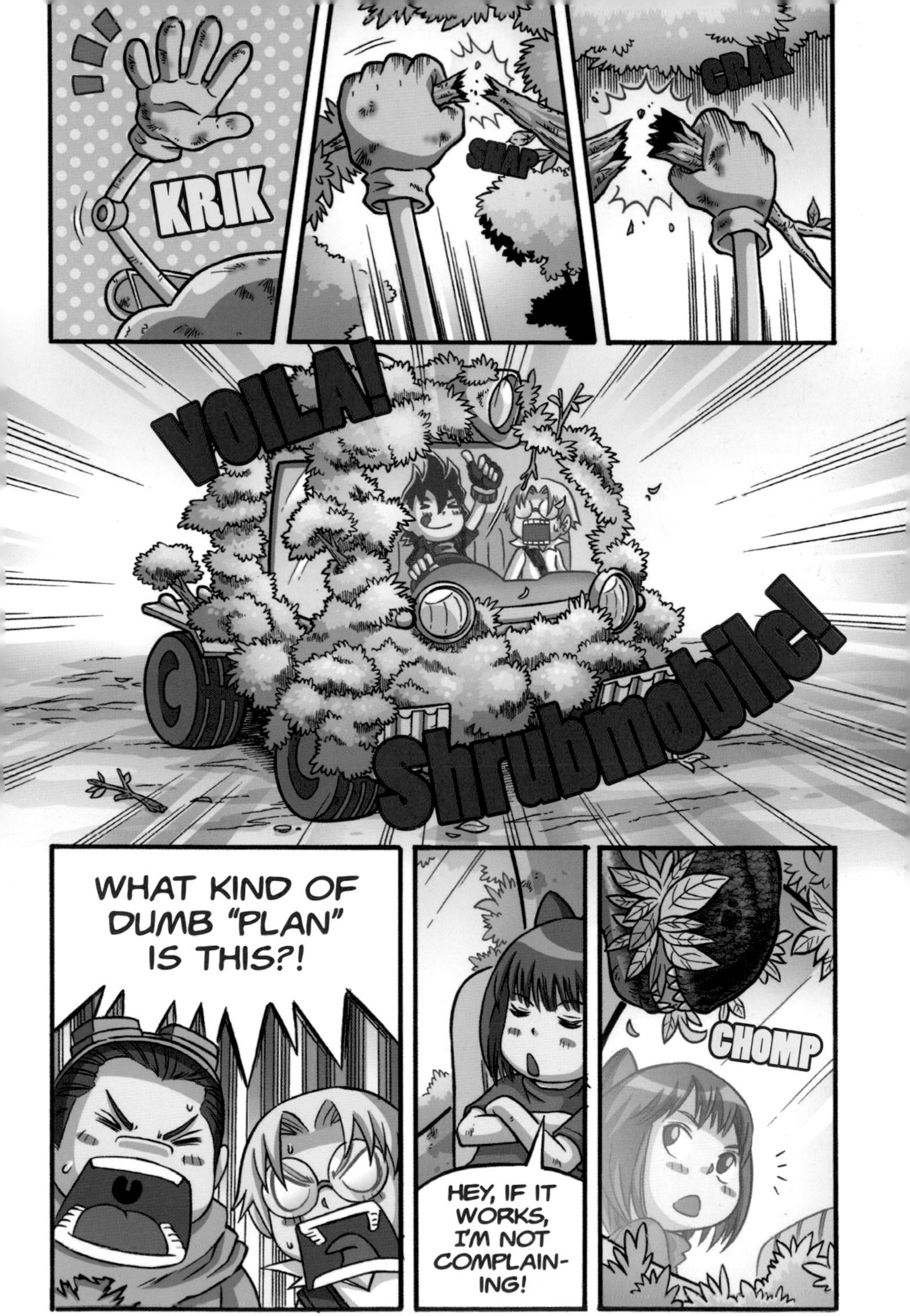
KRIK
SNAP
CRAK
VOILA!
Shrubmobile!
WHAT KIND OF DUMB "PLAN" IS THIS?!
HEY, IF IT WORKS, I'M NOT COMPLAIN-ING!
CHOMP

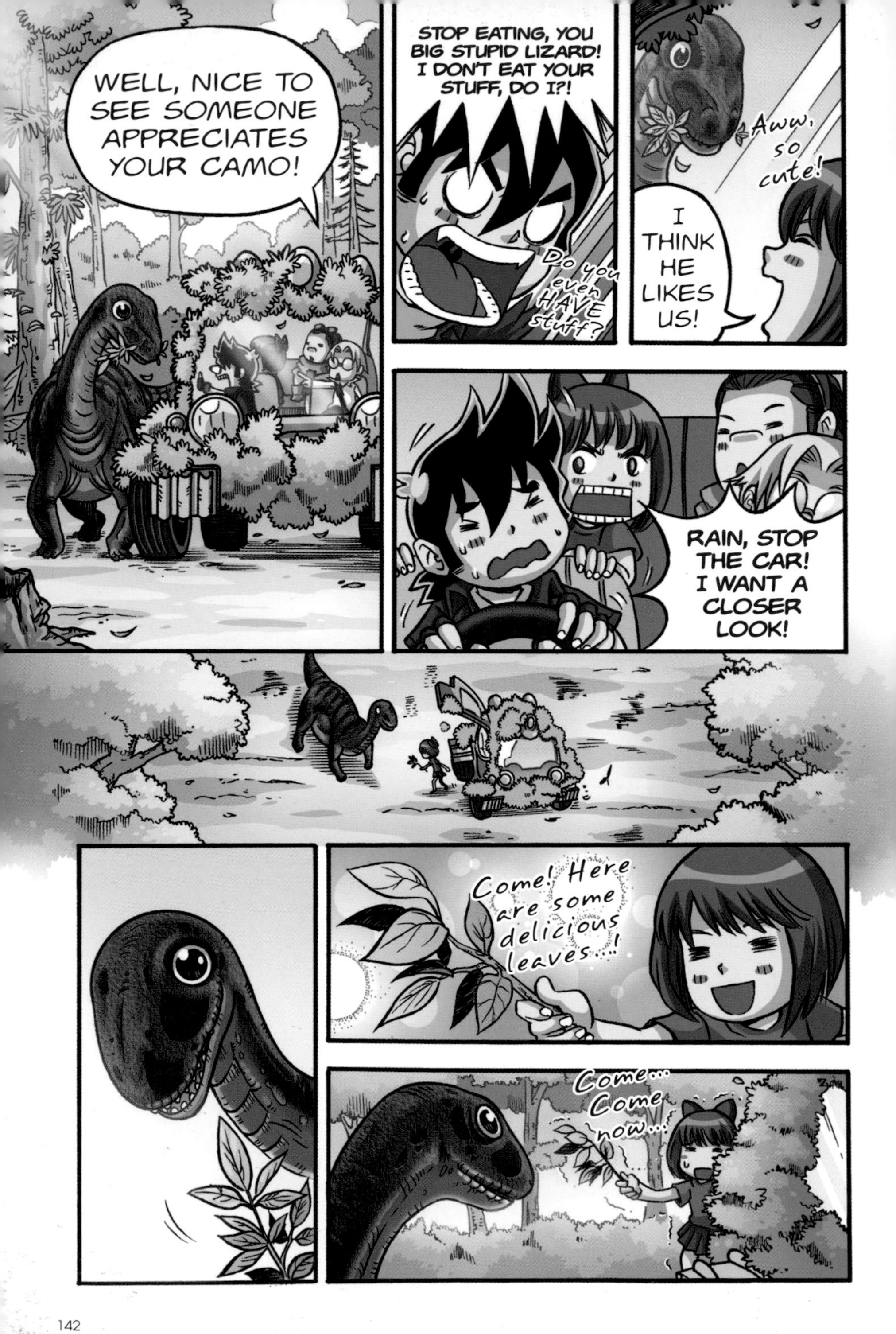
WELL, NICE TO SEE SOMEONE APPRECIATES YOUR CAMO!
STOP EATING, YOU BIG STUPID LIZARD! I DON'T EAT YOUR STUFF, DO I?!
Do you even HAVE stuff?
Aww, so cute!
I THINK HE LIKES US!
RAIN, STOP THE CAR! I WANT A CLOSER LOOK!
Come! Here are some delicious leaves...!
Come... Come now...

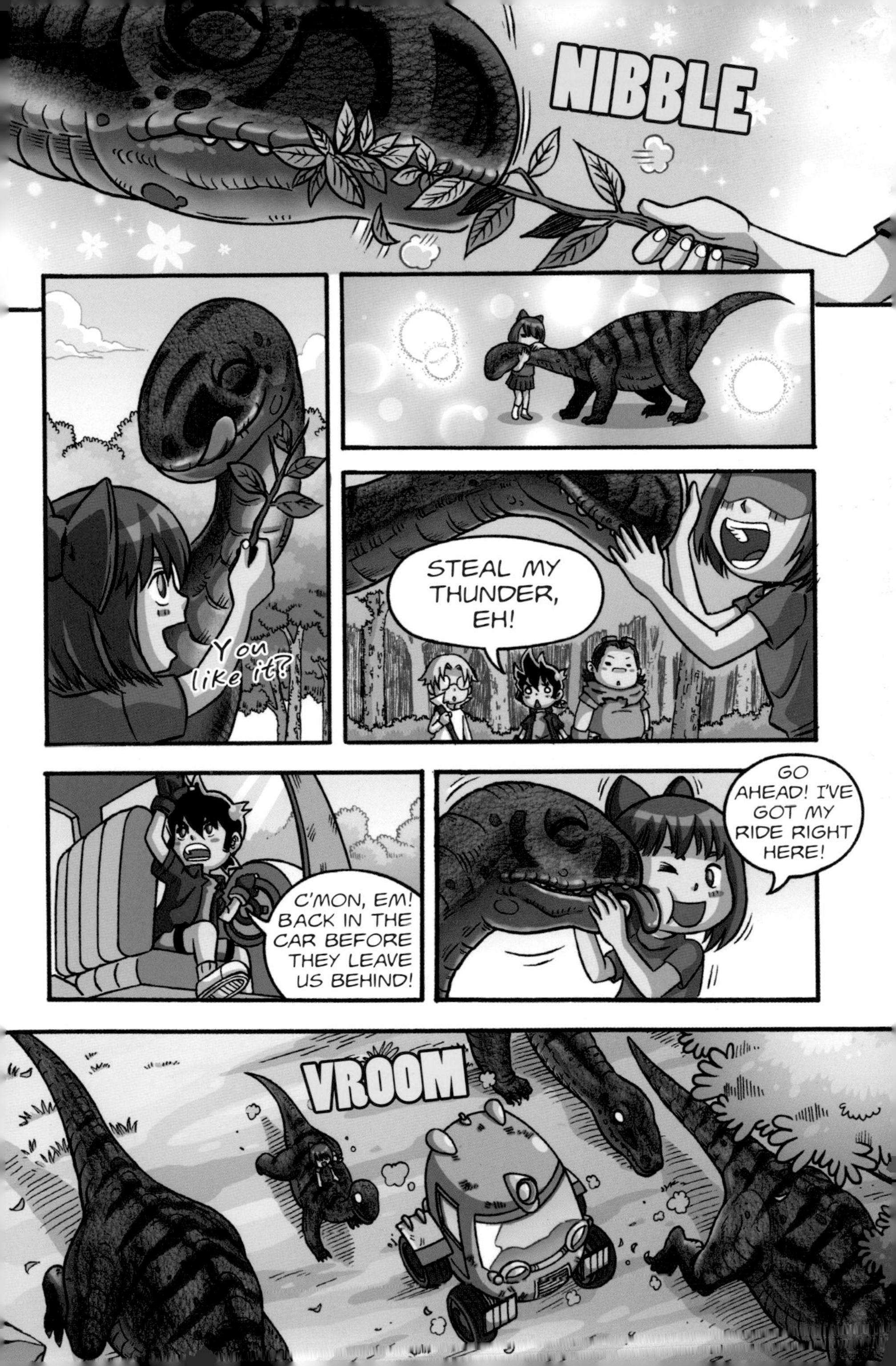
NIBBLE
You like it?
STEAL MY THUNDER, EH!
C'MON, EM! BACK IN THE CAR BEFORE THEY LEAVE US BEHIND!
GO AHEAD! I'VE GOT MY RIDE RIGHT HERE!
VROOM

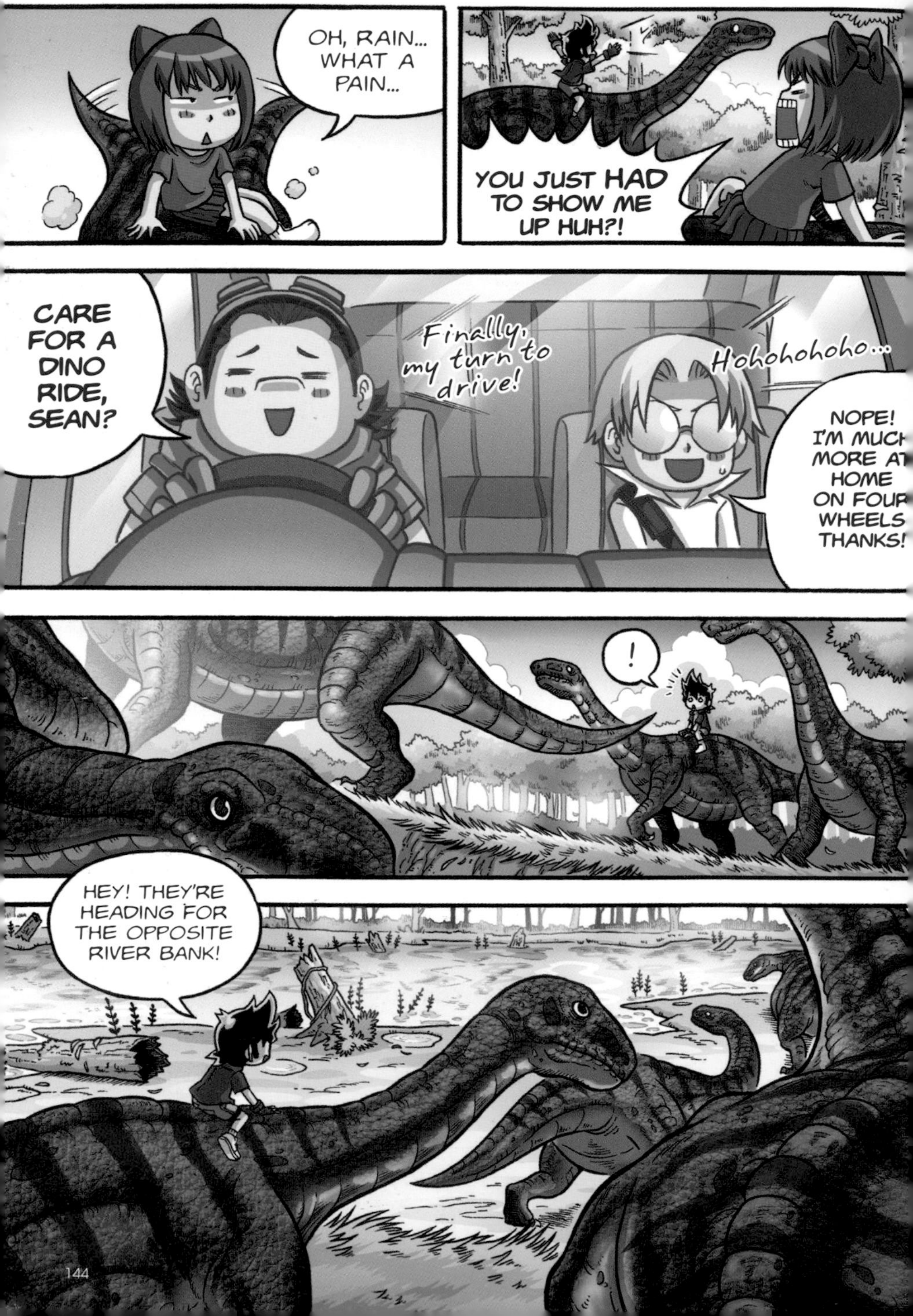

OH, RAIN... WHAT A PAIN...
YOU JUST HAD TO SHOW ME UP HUH?!
CARE FOR A DINO RIDE, SEAN?
Finally, my turn to drive!
Hohohohoho...
NOPE! I'M MUCH MORE AT HOME ON FOUR WHEELS THANKS!
!
HEY! THEY'RE HEADING FOR THE OPPOSITE RIVER BANK!

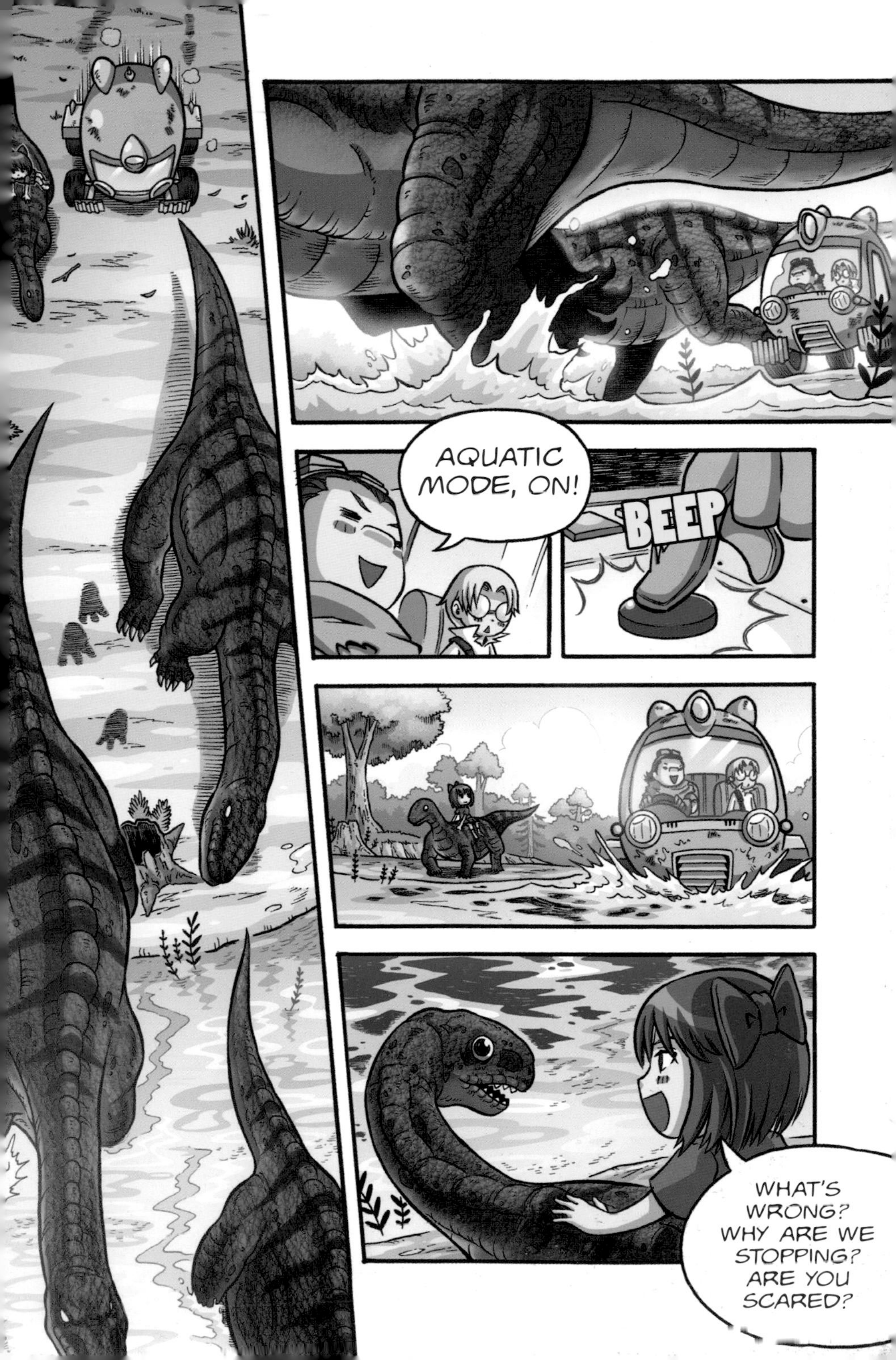
AQUATIC MODE, ON!
BEEP
WHAT'S WRONG? WHY ARE WE STOPPING? ARE YOU SCARED?

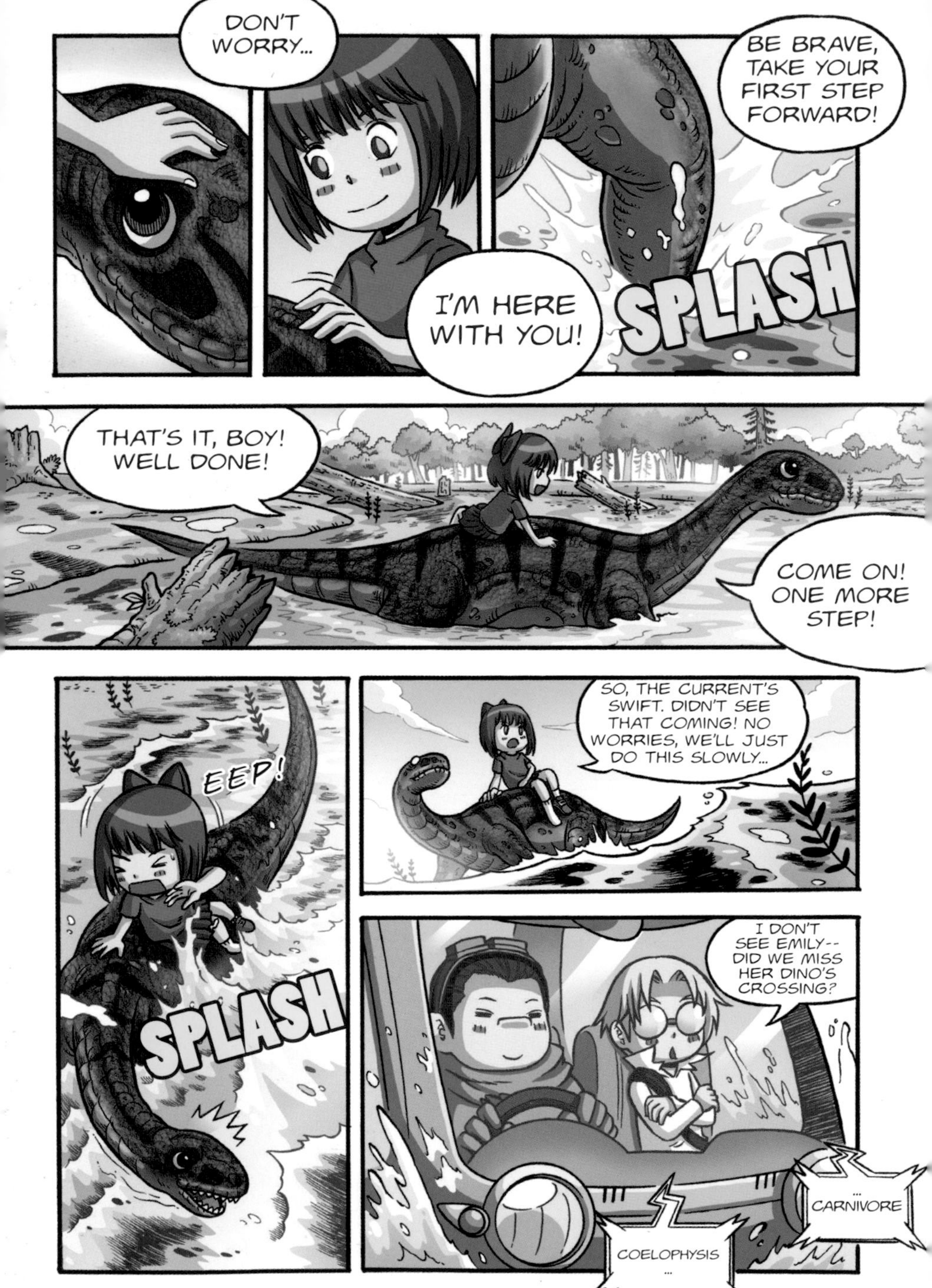
DON'T WORRY...
I'M HERE WITH YOU!
BE BRAVE, TAKE YOUR FIRST STEP FORWARD!
SPLASH
THAT'S IT, BOY! WELL DONE!
COME ON! ONE MORE STEP!
EEP!
SPLASH
SO, THE CURRENT'S SWIFT. DIDN'T SEE THAT COMING! NO WORRIES, WE'LL JUST DO THIS SLOWLY...
I DON'T SEE EMILY-- DID WE MISS HER DINO'S CROSSING?
COELOPHYSIS ...
... CARNIVORE

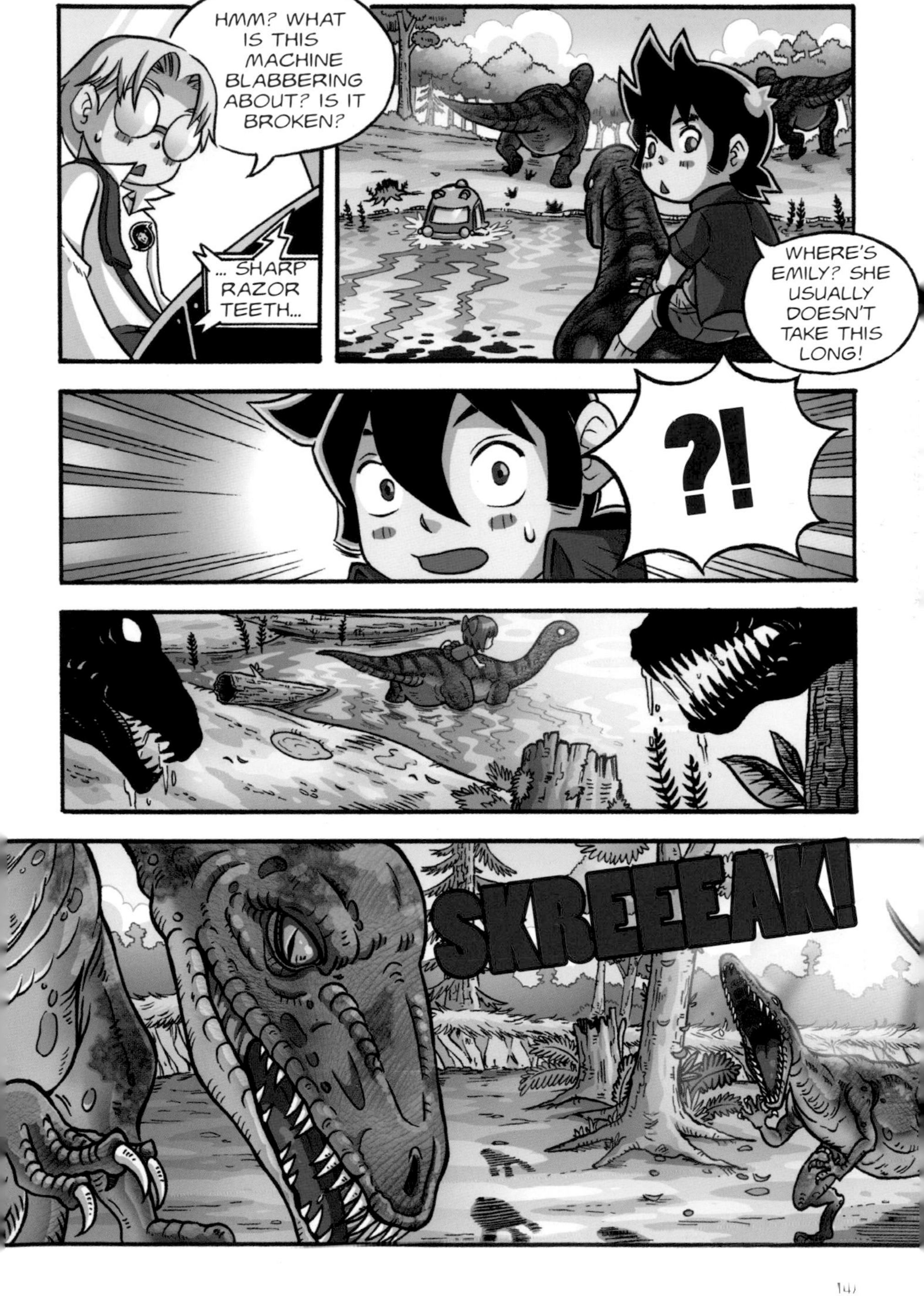
HMM? WHAT IS THIS MACHINE BLABBERING ABOUT? IS IT BROKEN?
... SHARP RAZOR TEETH...
WHERE'S EMILY? SHE USUALLY DOESN'T TAKE THIS LONG!
?!
SKREEEAK!

ALERT STONE AND SEAN! I'LL GET EMILY!

VVOOSH

ROGER THAT! YOU BE CAREFUL!

HIYAH!

COME ON, BOY! GENTLY DOES IT.

GRR! GRAAH!

NYEK!

OH, MY... PREDATORS... UHM, NO PRESSURE, BUT IF WE COULD CROSS RIGHT NOW THAT WOULD BE REALLY NICE THANKS...

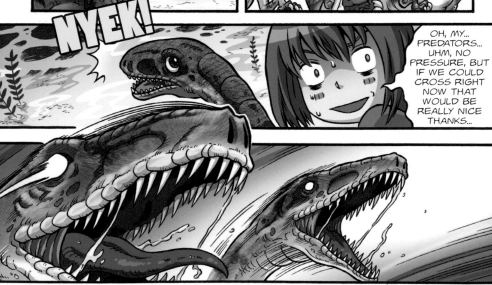

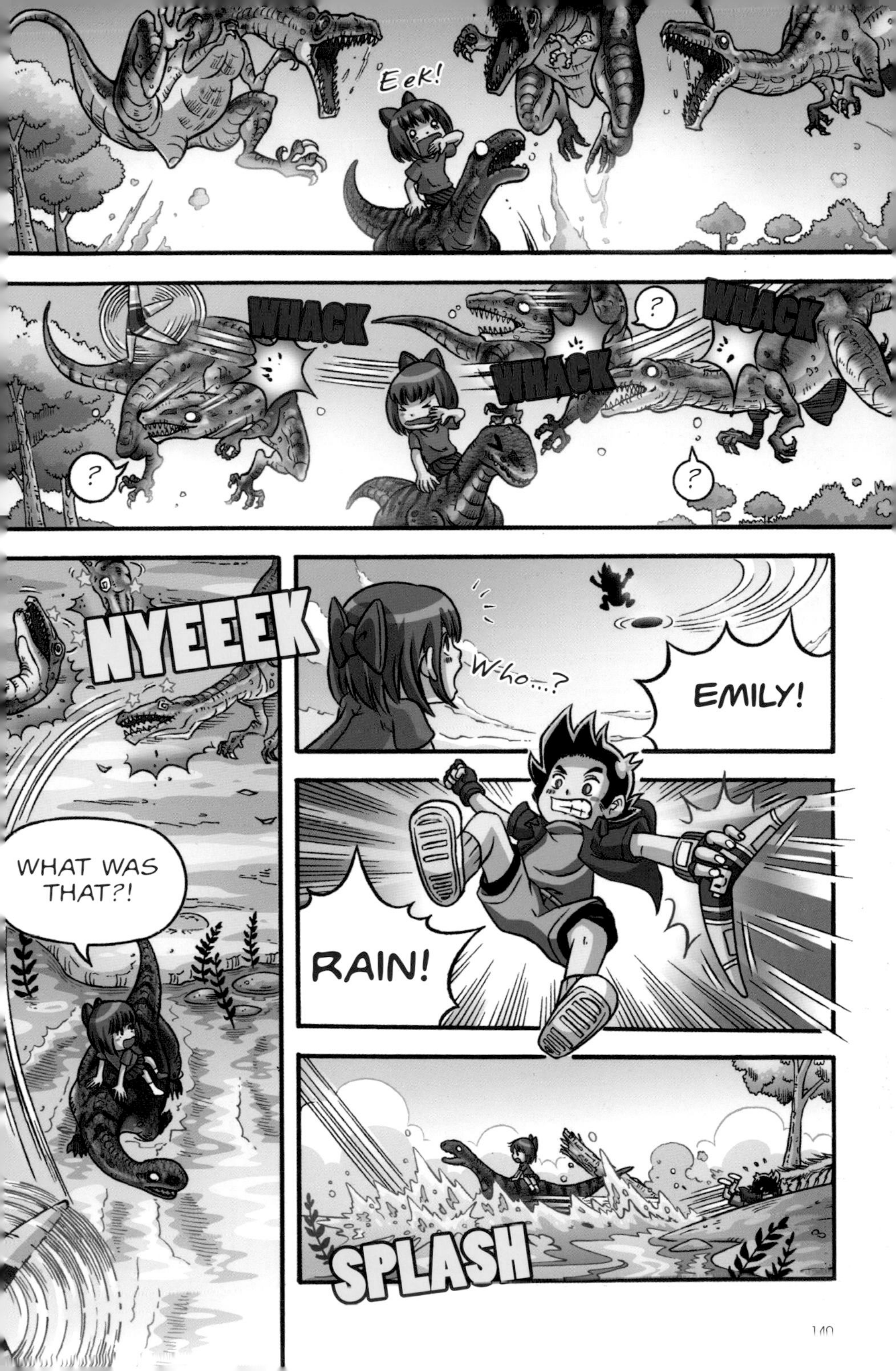
Eek!
WHACK
?
WHACK
WHACK
?
?
NYEEEK
WHAT WAS THAT?!
W-ho...?
EMILY!
RAIN!
SPLASH

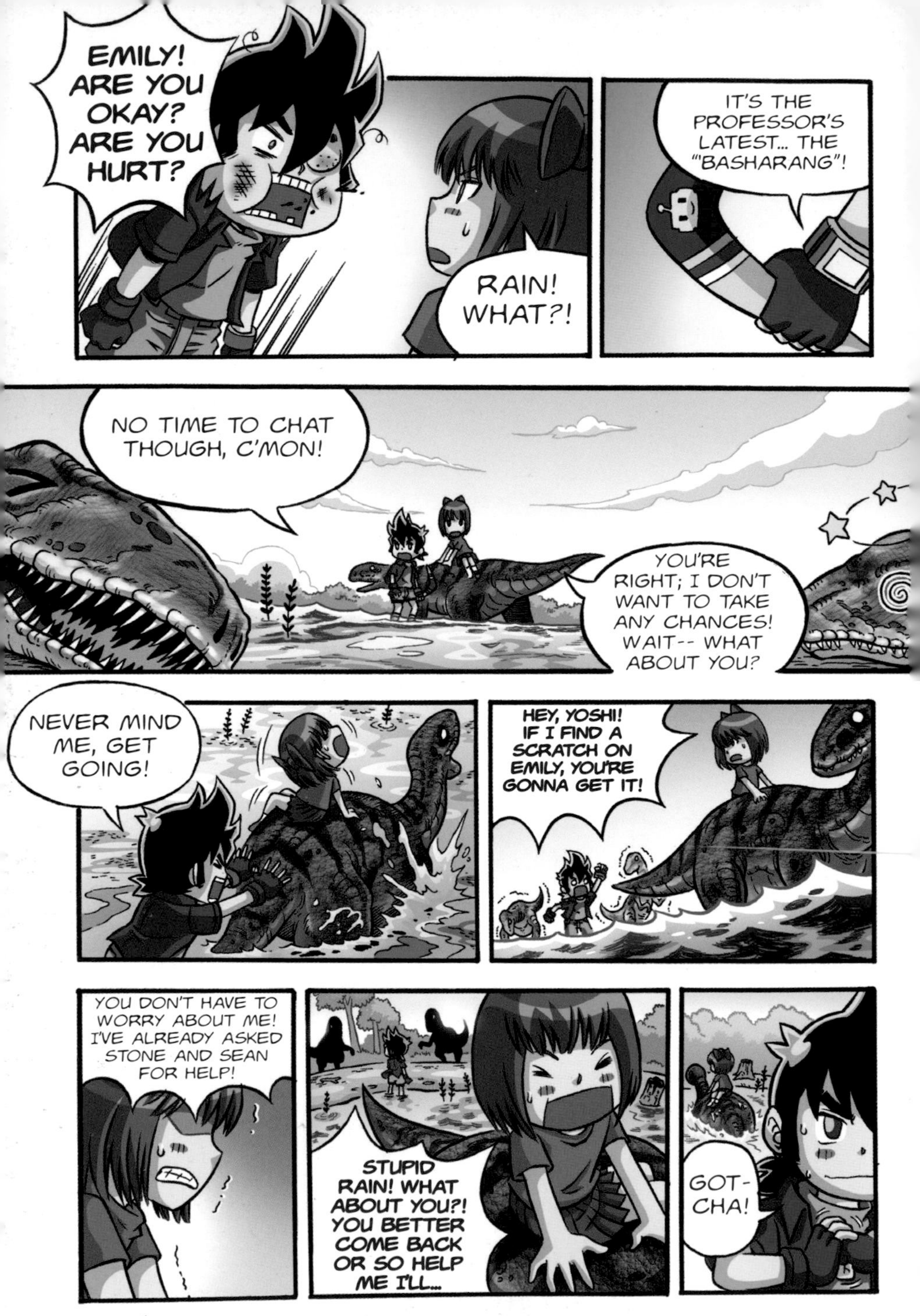
EMILY! ARE YOU OKAY? ARE YOU HURT?
RAIN! WHAT?!
IT'S THE PROFESSOR'S LATEST... THE "BASHARANG"!
NO TIME TO CHAT THOUGH, C'MON!
YOU'RE RIGHT; I DON'T WANT TO TAKE ANY CHANCES! WAIT-- WHAT ABOUT YOU?
NEVER MIND ME, GET GOING!
HEY, YOSHI! IF I FIND A SCRATCH ON EMILY, YOU'RE GONNA GET IT!
YOU DON'T HAVE TO WORRY ABOUT ME! I'VE ALREADY ASKED STONE AND SEAN FOR HELP!
STUPID RAIN! WHAT ABOUT YOU?! YOU BETTER COME BACK OR SO HELP ME I'LL...
GOT-CHA!

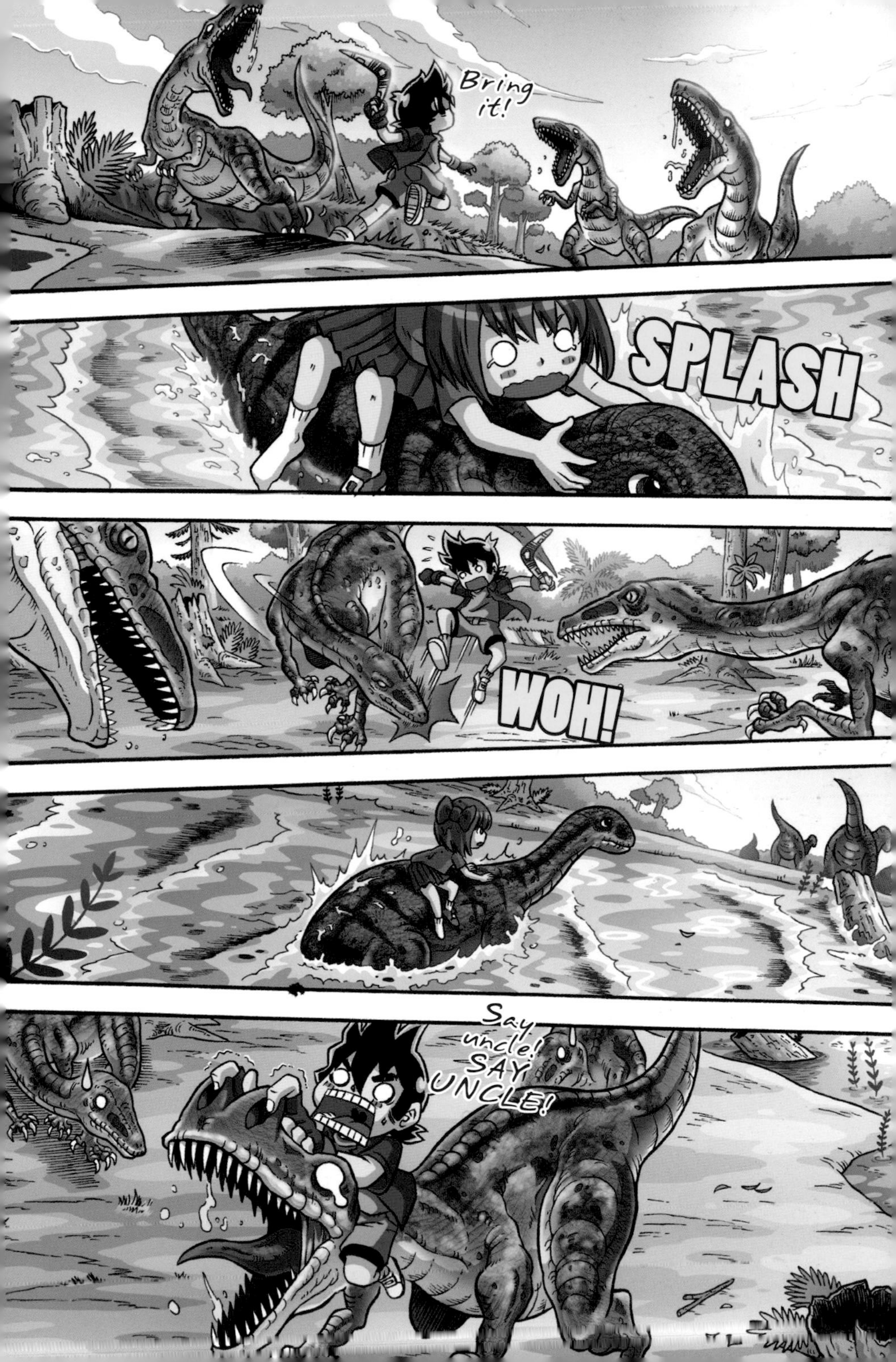
Bring it!
SPLASH
WOH!
Say uncle! SAY UNCLE!

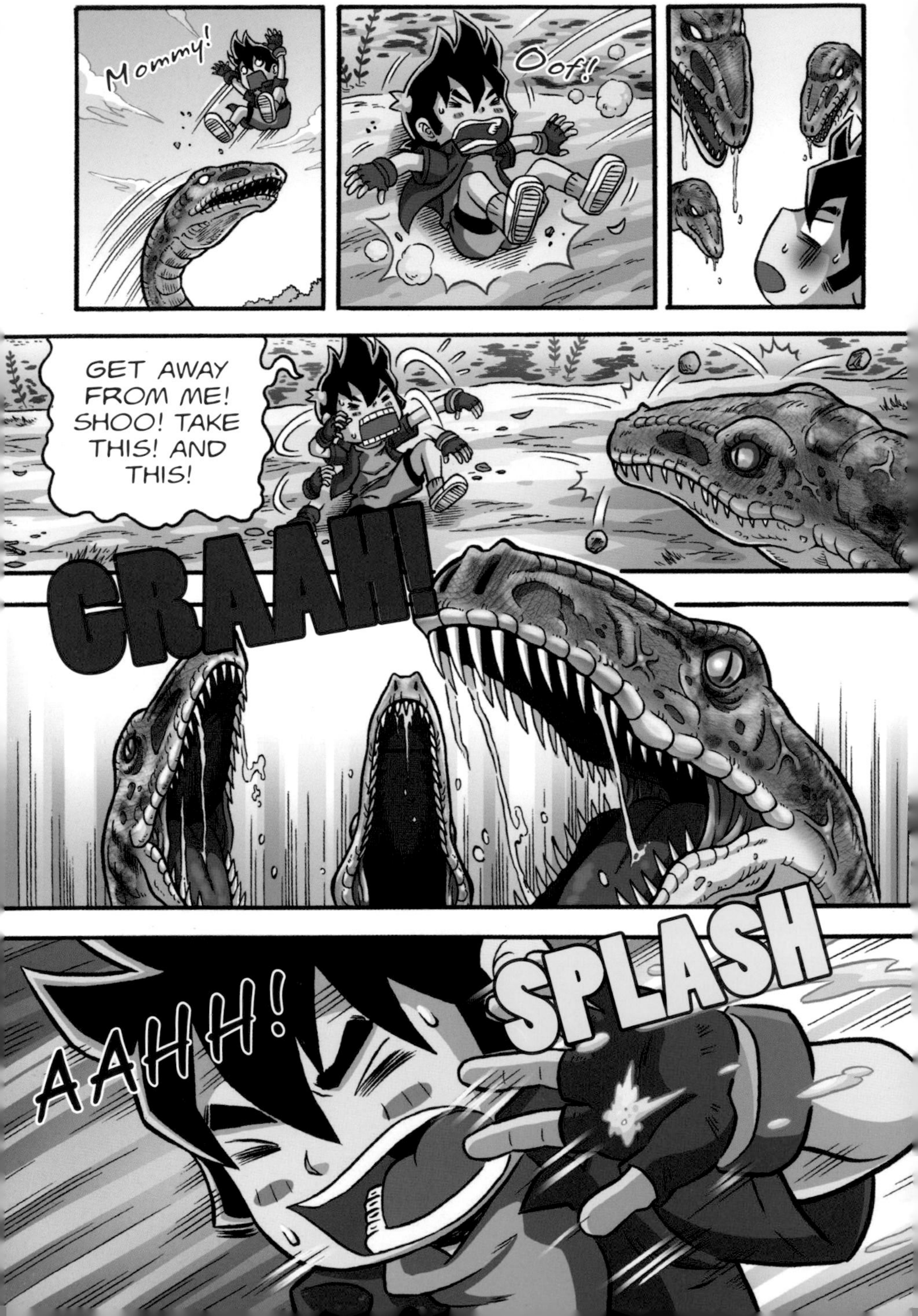
Mommy!
Oof!
GET AWAY FROM ME! SHOO! TAKE THIS! AND THIS!
CRAAAH!
AAHH!
SPLASH

TAKING IN THE TRIASSIC

Plateosaurus

Plateosaurus is one of the most famous prosauropods known today, and was one of the largest land dinosaurs of the Triassic. It had a long neck, but a very small head. Powerful hind limbs allowed it to stand upright for short periods of time, and coupled with a long neck, it was able to reach leaves on higher branches with relative ease.

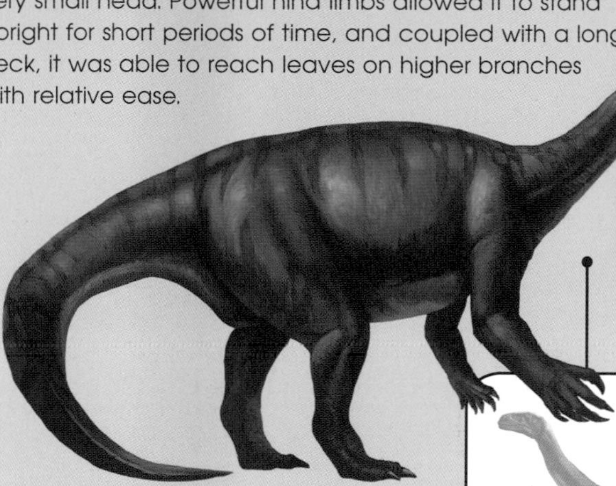

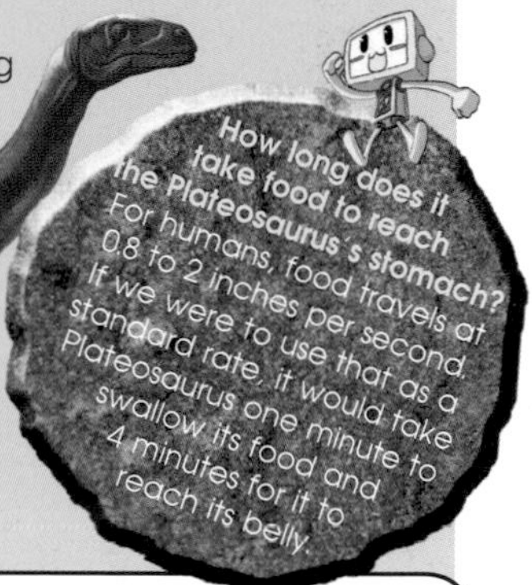
How long does it take food to reach the Plateosaurus's stomach?
For humans, food travels at 0.8 to 2 inches per second. If we were to use that as a standard rate, it would take Plateosaurus one minute to swallow its food and 4 minutes for it to reach its belly.

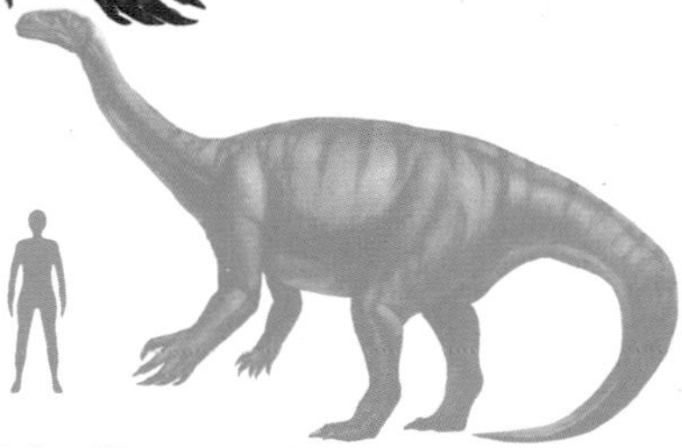

Scientific name: Plateosaurus
Length: 26 feet
Diet: Herbivore
Habitat: Plain
Discovered: Europe
Era: Late Triassic

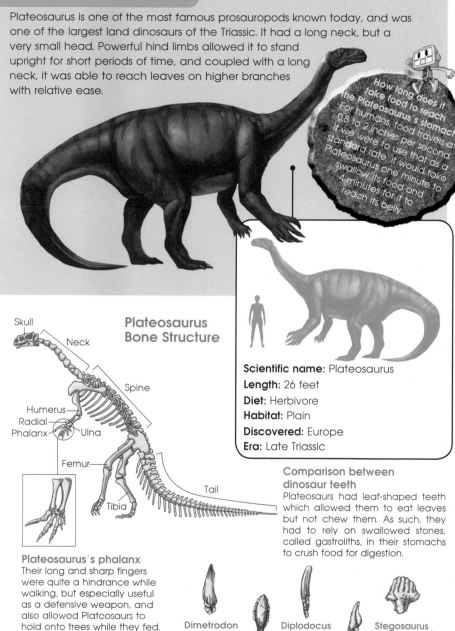

Plateosaurus Bone Structure

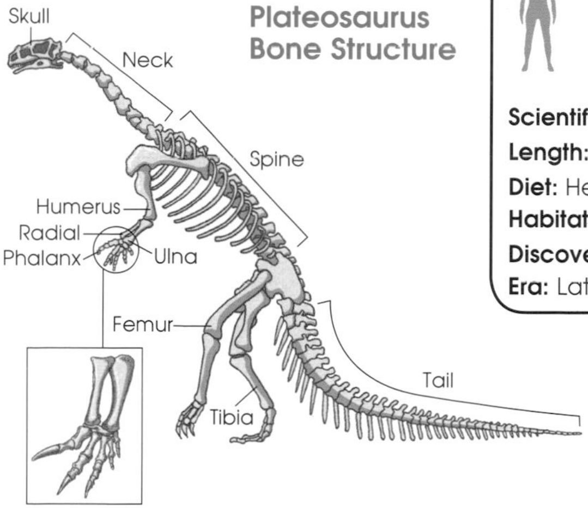
Skull
Neck
Spine
Humerus
Radial
Phalanx
Ulna
Femur
Tail
Tibia

Plateosaurus's phalanx

Their long and sharp fingers were quite a hindrance while walking, but especially useful as a defensive weapon, and also allowed Platcosaurs to hold onto trees while they fed.

Comparison between dinosaur teeth

Plateosaurs had leaf-shaped teeth which allowed them to eat leaves but not chew them. As such, they had to rely on swallowed stones, called gastroliths, in their stomachs to crush food for digestion.

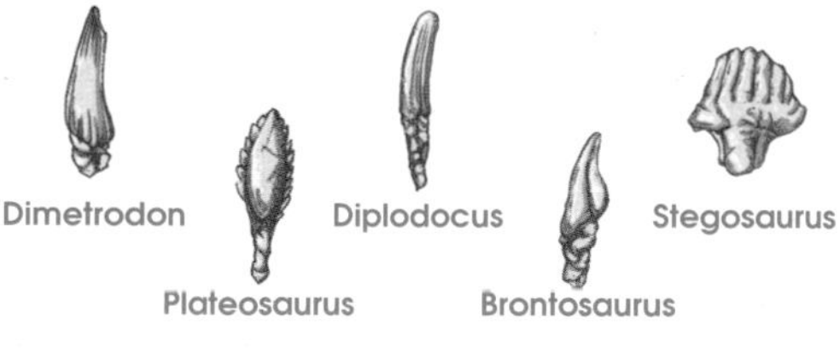
Dimetrodon
Plateosaurus
Diplodocus
Brontosaurus
Stegosaurus

TAKING IN THE TRIASSIC

Euskelosaurus

Euskelosaurus was one of the largest prosauropods around, and was closely related to Plateosaurus. The shaft of its thigh bone was twisted outwards, and paleontologists suggest that this was necessary to accommodate food that entered its large belly.

Scientific name: Euskelosaurus
Length: 30 feet
Diet: Herbivore
Habitat: Unknown
Discovered: South Africa
Era: Late Triassic

TAKING IN THE TRIASSIC

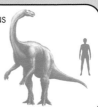

Jingshanosaurus

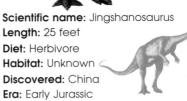

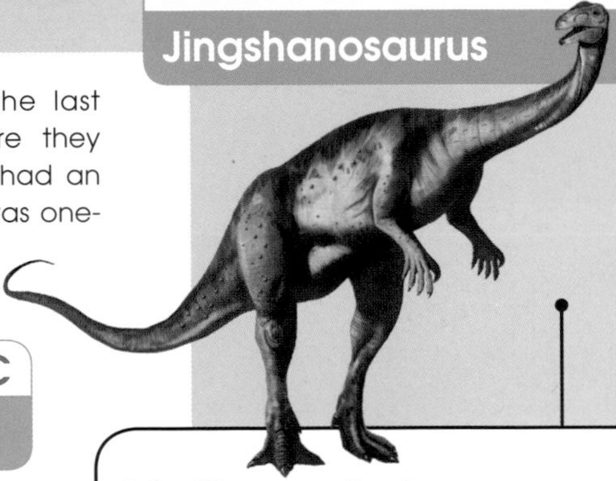

Jingshanosaurus was one of the last prosauropods to emerge before they were replaced by sauropods. It had an exceptionally long neck which was one-third of its actual height.

Scientific name: Jingshanosaurus
Length: 25 feet
Diet: Herbivore
Habitat: Unknown
Discovered: China
Era: Early Jurassic

TAKING IN THE TRIASSIC

Unaysaurus

Unaysaurus was closely related to Plateosaurus, just much smaller. As they were also discovered in different continents, however, paleontologists believe that plateosaurs migrated across the Pangaean supercontinent from South America to Europe.

Scientific name: Unaysaurus
Length: 8 feet
Diet: Herbivore
Habitat: Unknown
Discovered: Brazil
Era: Late Triassic

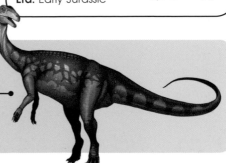

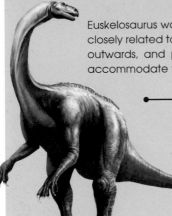

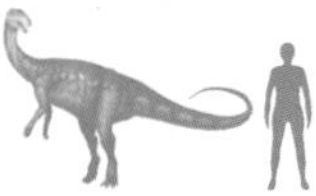

CHAPTER 8

'TIL WE MEET AGAIN, TRIASSIC

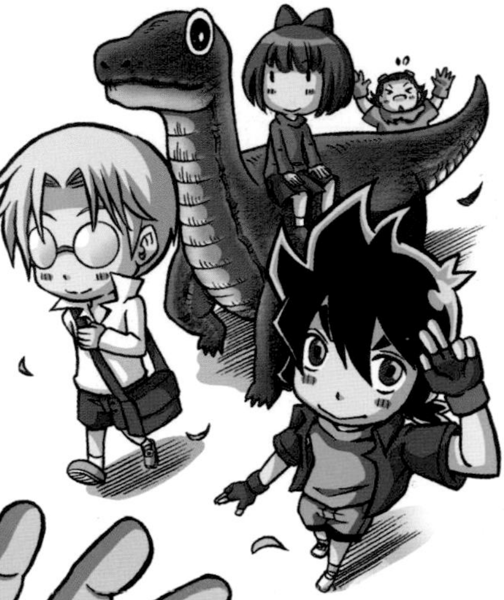

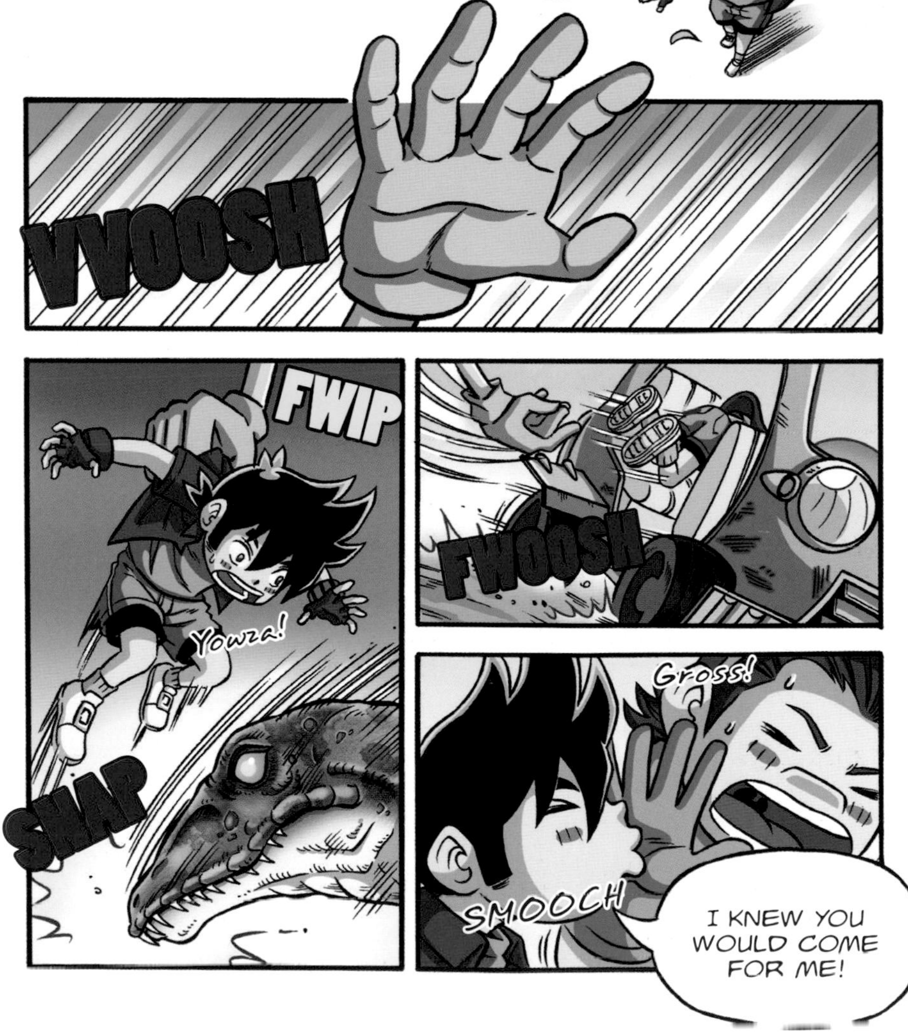
VVOOSH
FWIP
Yowza!
SNAP
FWOOSH
Gross!
SMOOCH
I KNEW YOU WOULD COME FOR ME!

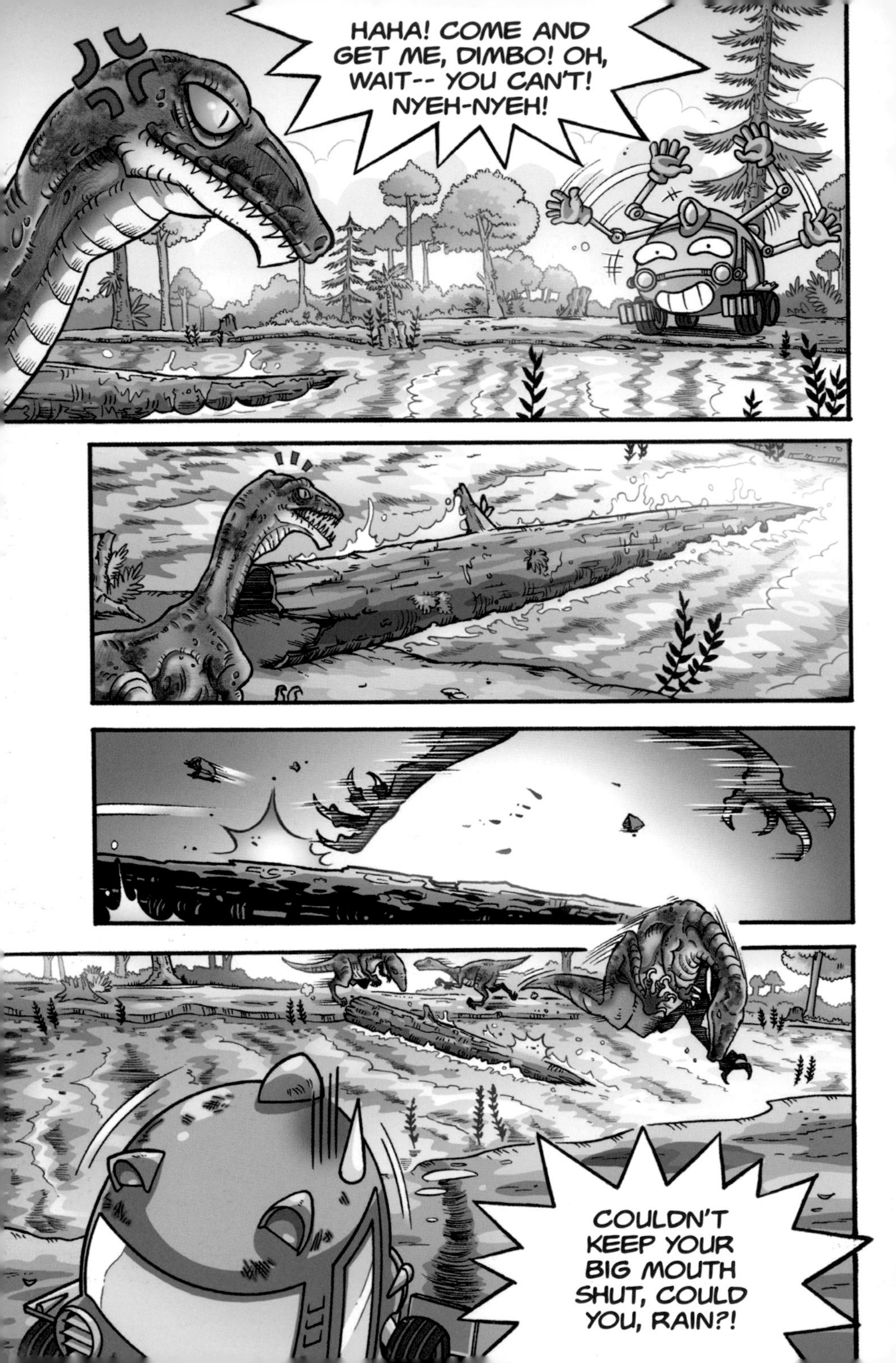
HAHA! COME AND GET ME, DIMBO! OH, WAIT-- YOU CAN'T! NYEH-NYEH!
COULDN'T KEEP YOUR BIG MOUTH SHUT, COULD YOU, RAIN?!

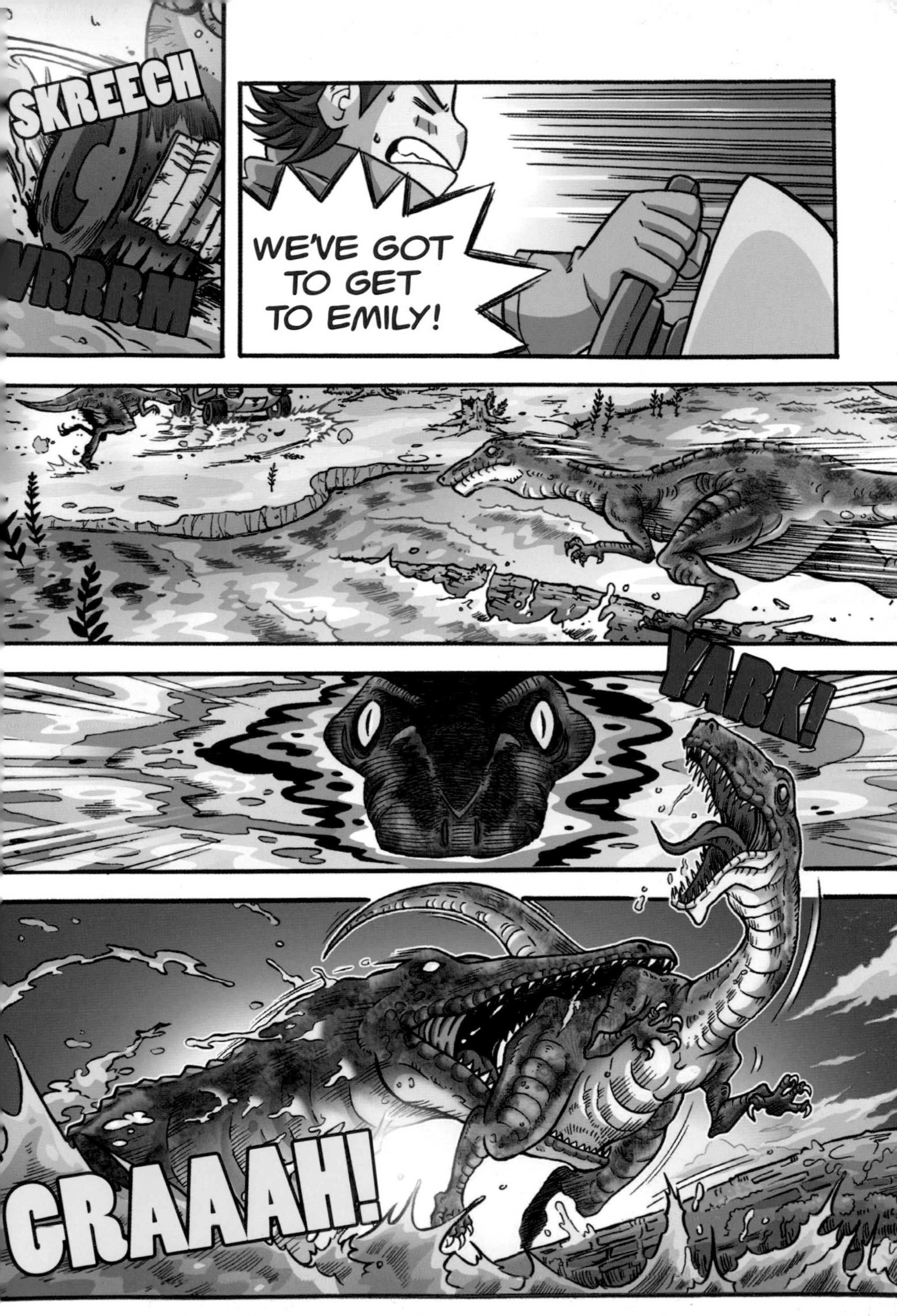
SKREECH
VRRRRM
WE'VE GOT TO GET TO EMILY!
YARK!
CRAAAH!

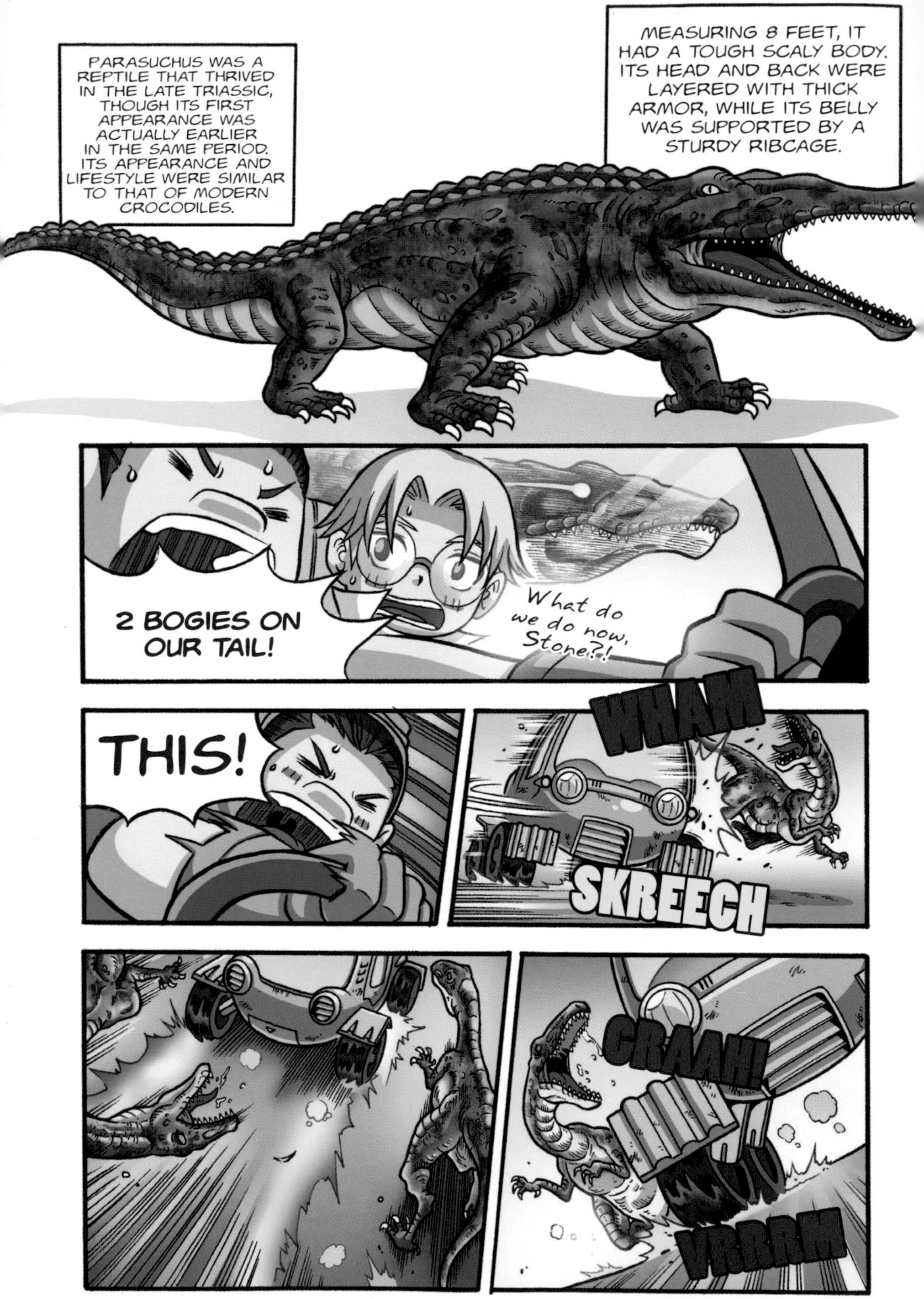
PARASUCHUS WAS A REPTILE THAT THRIVED IN THE LATE TRIASSIC, THOUGH ITS FIRST APPEARANCE WAS ACTUALLY EARLIER IN THE SAME PERIOD. ITS APPEARANCE AND LIFESTYLE WERE SIMILAR TO THAT OF MODERN CROCODILES.
MEASURING 8 FEET, IT HAD A TOUGH SCALY BODY. ITS HEAD AND BACK WERE LAYERED WITH THICK ARMOR, WHILE ITS BELLY WAS SUPPORTED BY A STURDY RIBCAGE.
2 BOGIES ON OUR TAIL!
What do we do now, Stone?!
THIS!
WHAM
SKREECH
CRAAH!
VRRRM

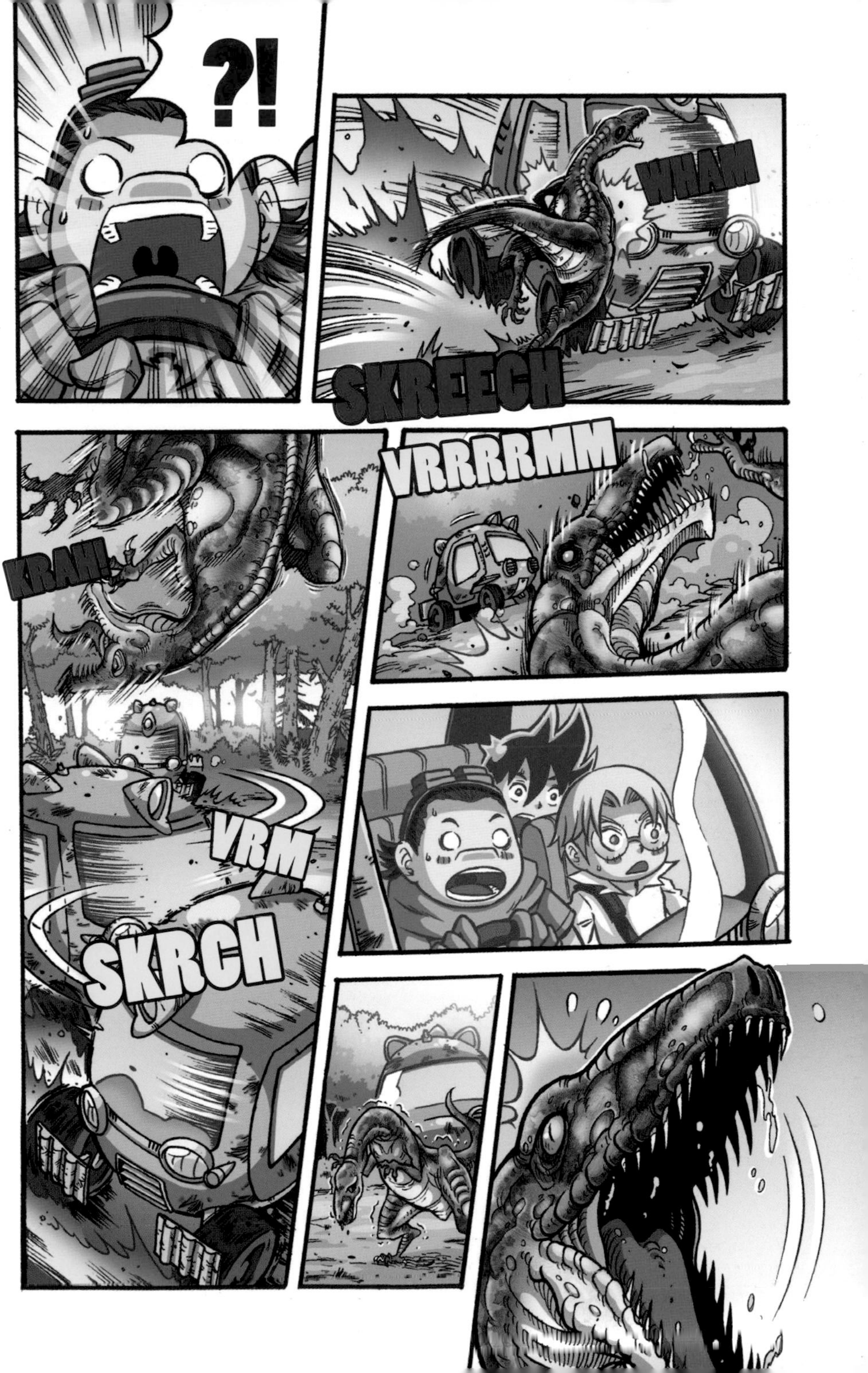
?!
WHAM
SKREECH
KRAH!
VRM
SKRCH
VRRRRMM

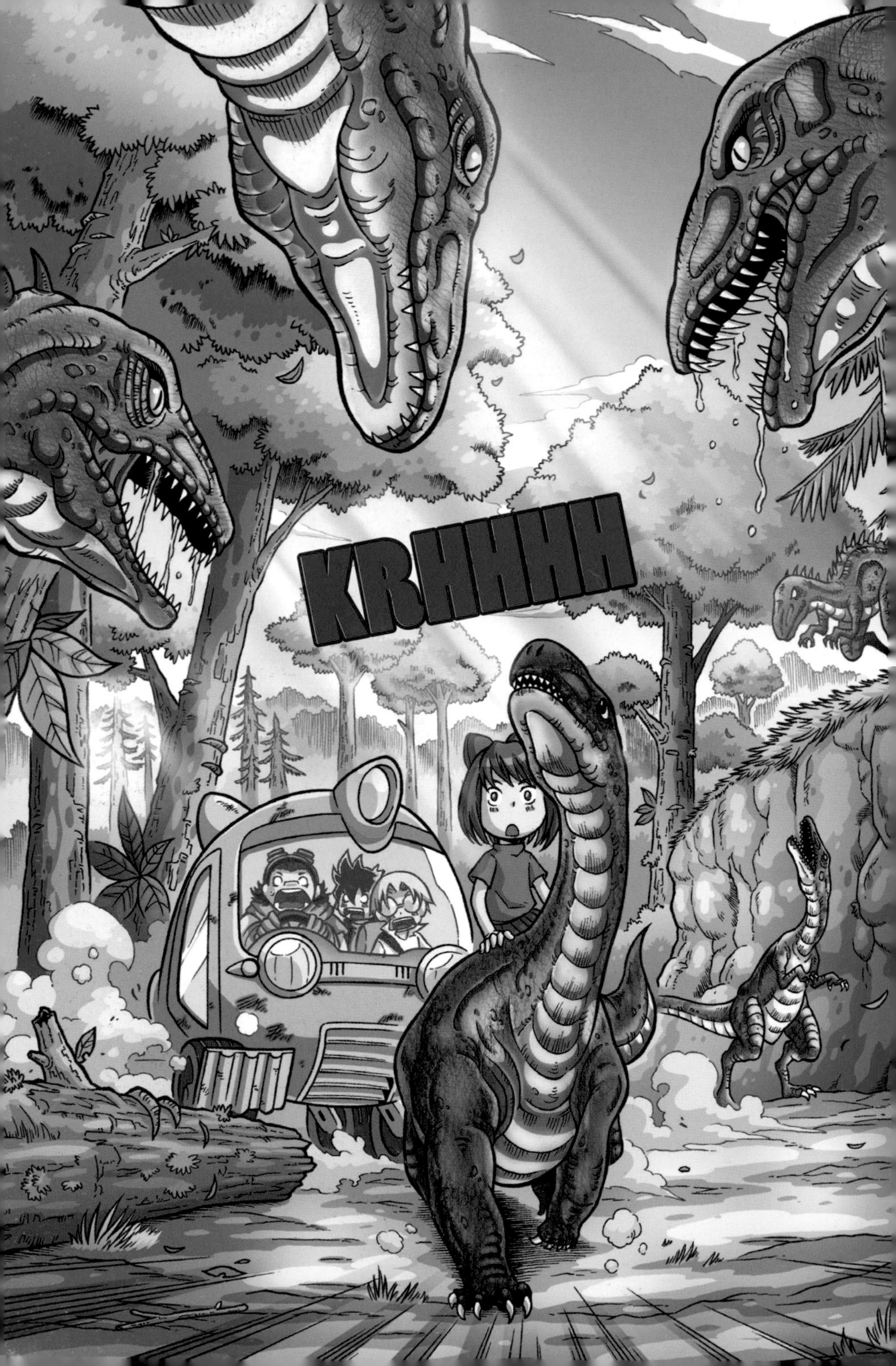
KRHHHH

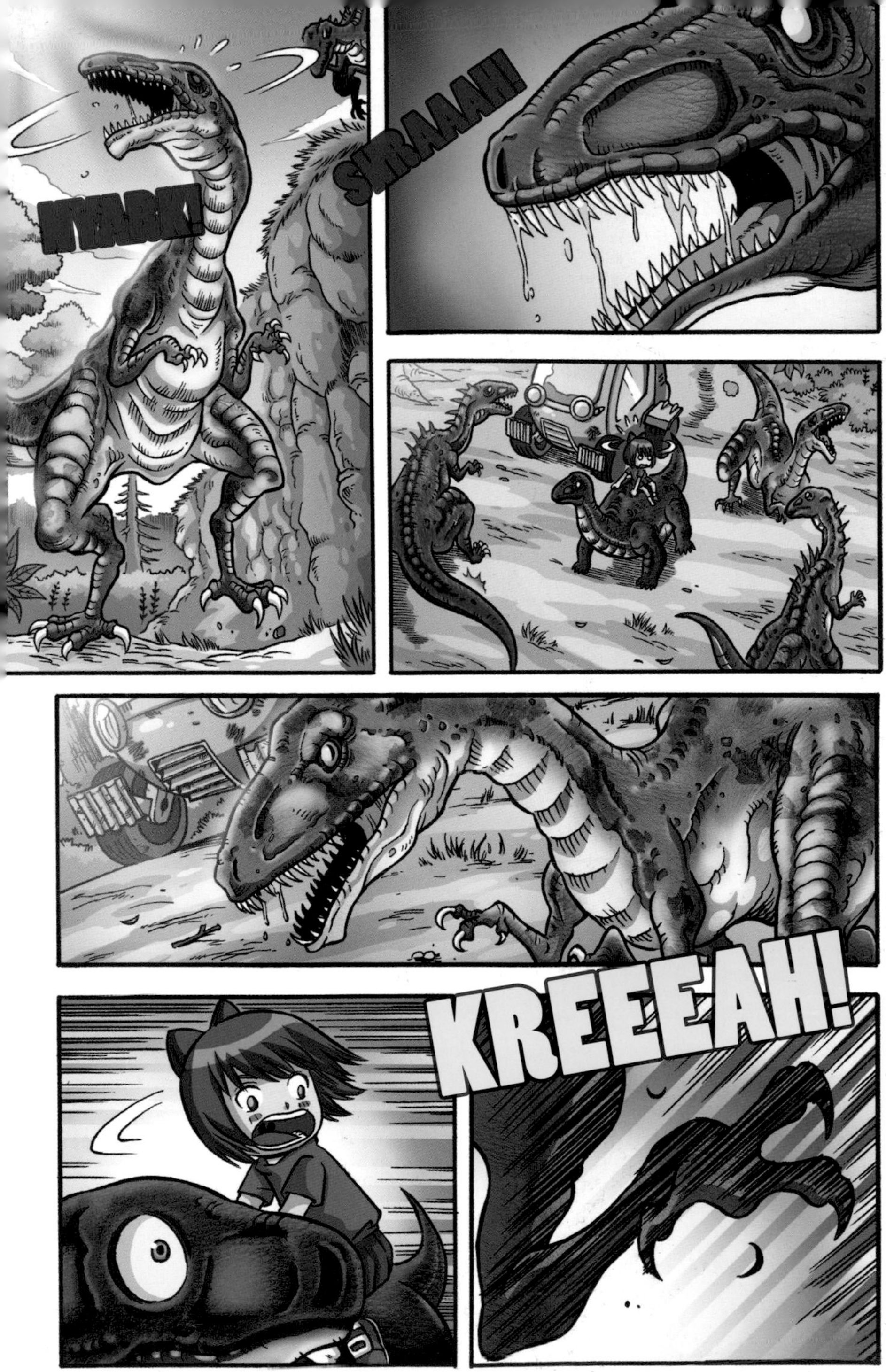
HYARK!
SHRAAAAH!
KREEEAH!

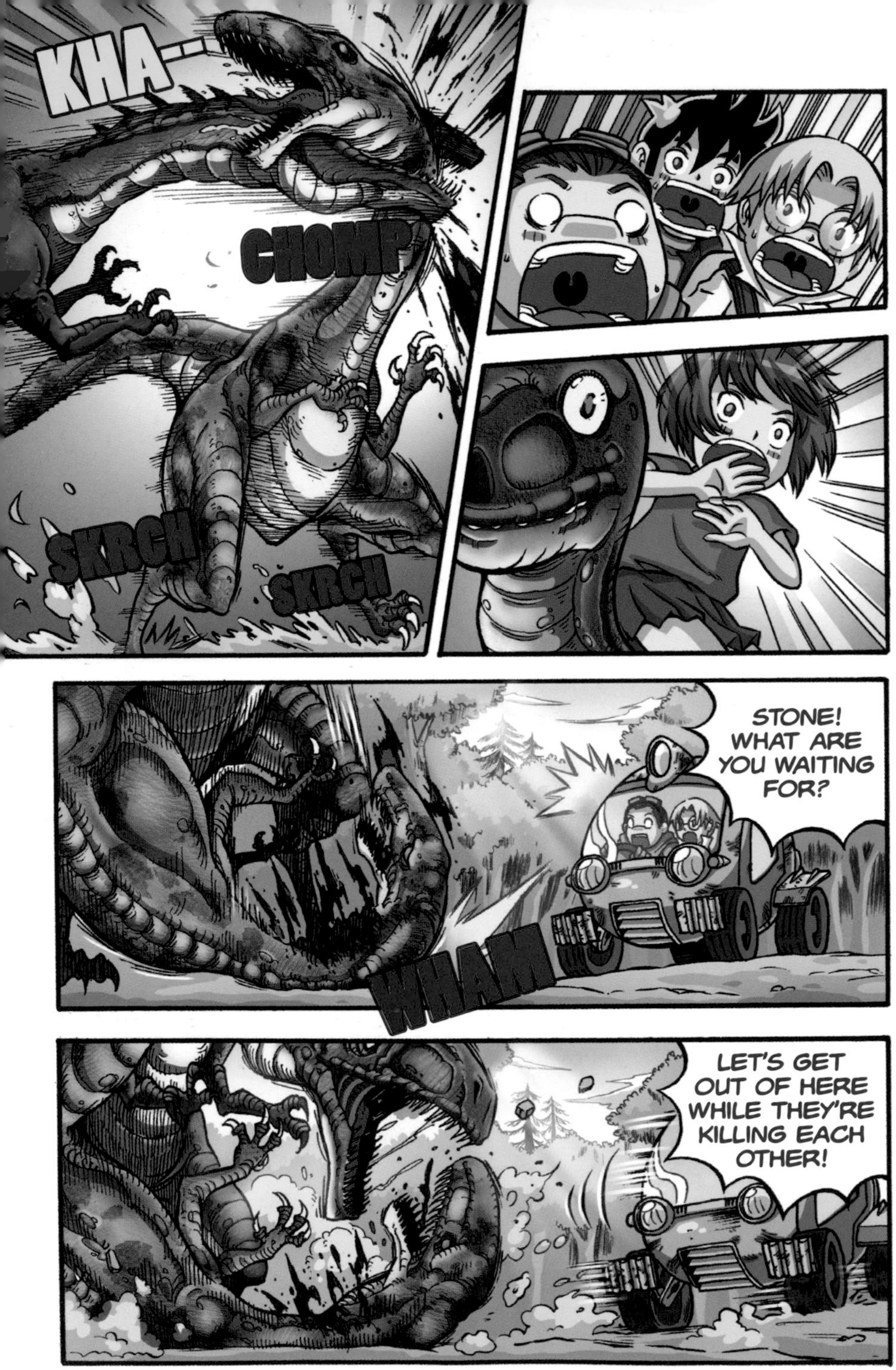
KHA---
CHOMP
SKRCH
SKRCH
STONE! WHAT ARE YOU WAITING FOR?
WHAM
LET'S GET OUT OF HERE WHILE THEY'RE KILLING EACH OTHER!

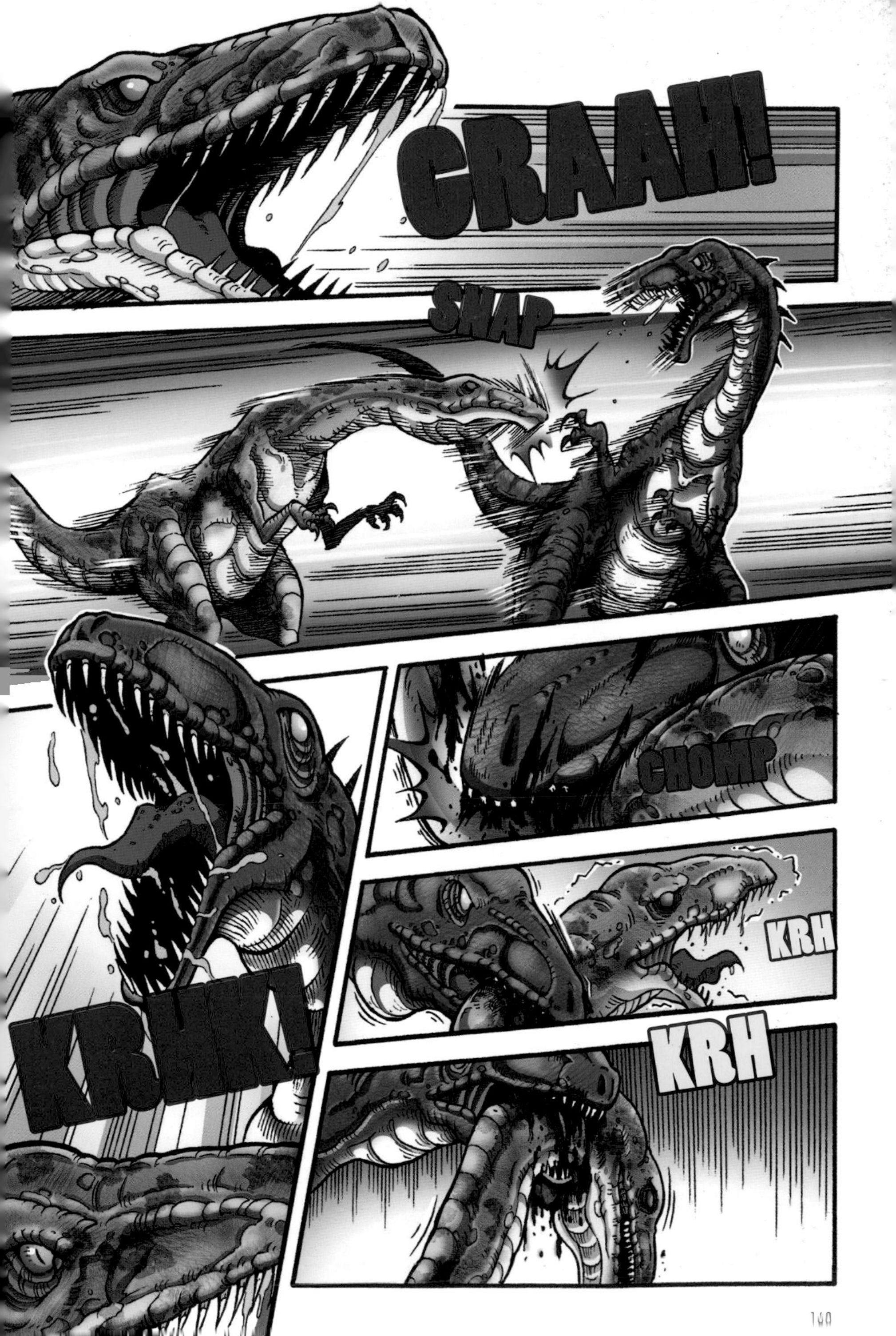
CRAAAH!
SNAP
KRHK!
CHOMP
KRH
KRH

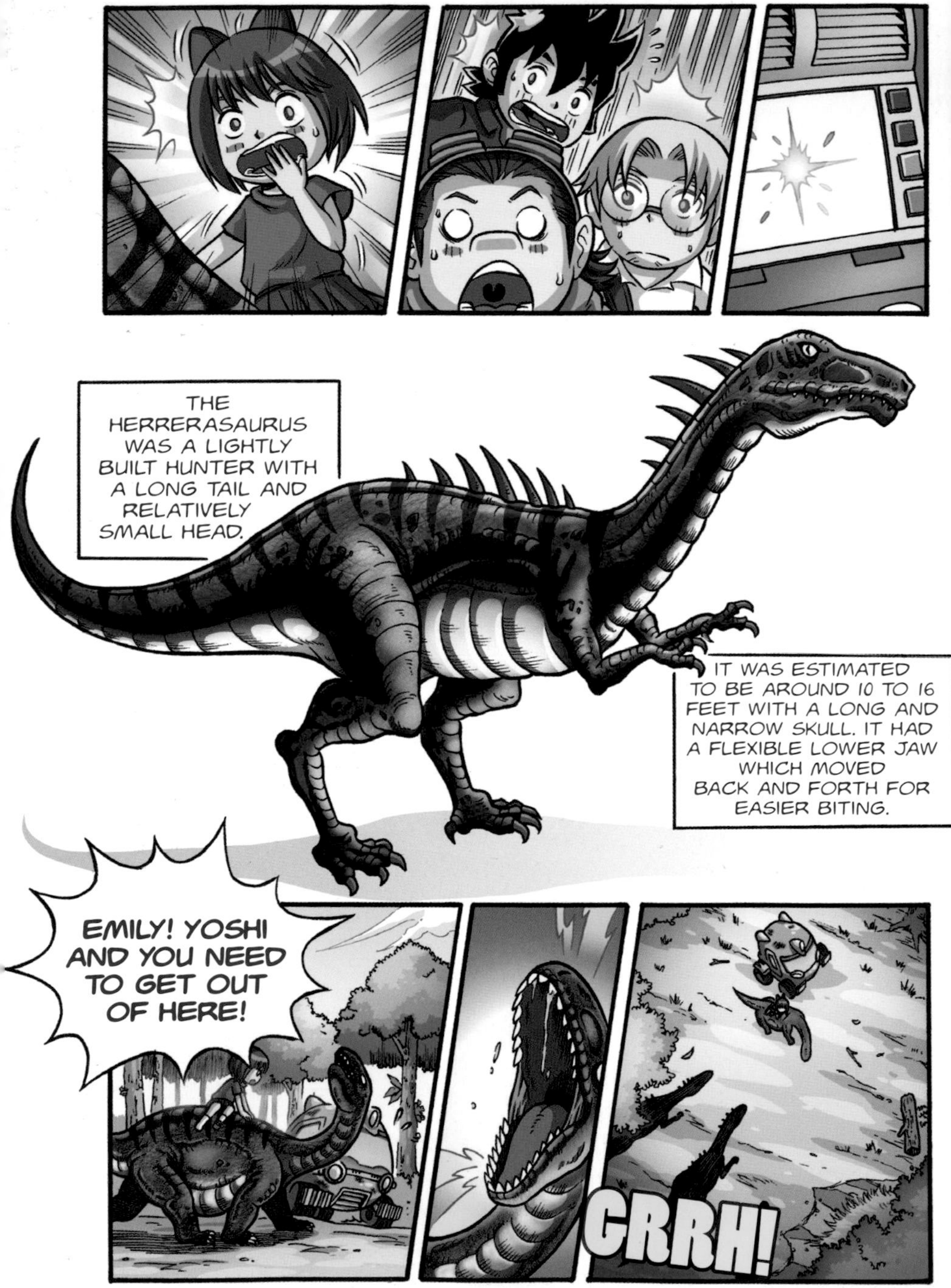
THE HERRERASAURUS WAS A LIGHTLY BUILT HUNTER WITH A LONG TAIL AND RELATIVELY SMALL HEAD.
IT WAS ESTIMATED TO BE AROUND 10 TO 16 FEET WITH A LONG AND NARROW SKULL. IT HAD A FLEXIBLE LOWER JAW WHICH MOVED BACK AND FORTH FOR EASIER BITING.
EMILY! YOSHI AND YOU NEED TO GET OUT OF HERE!
GRRH!

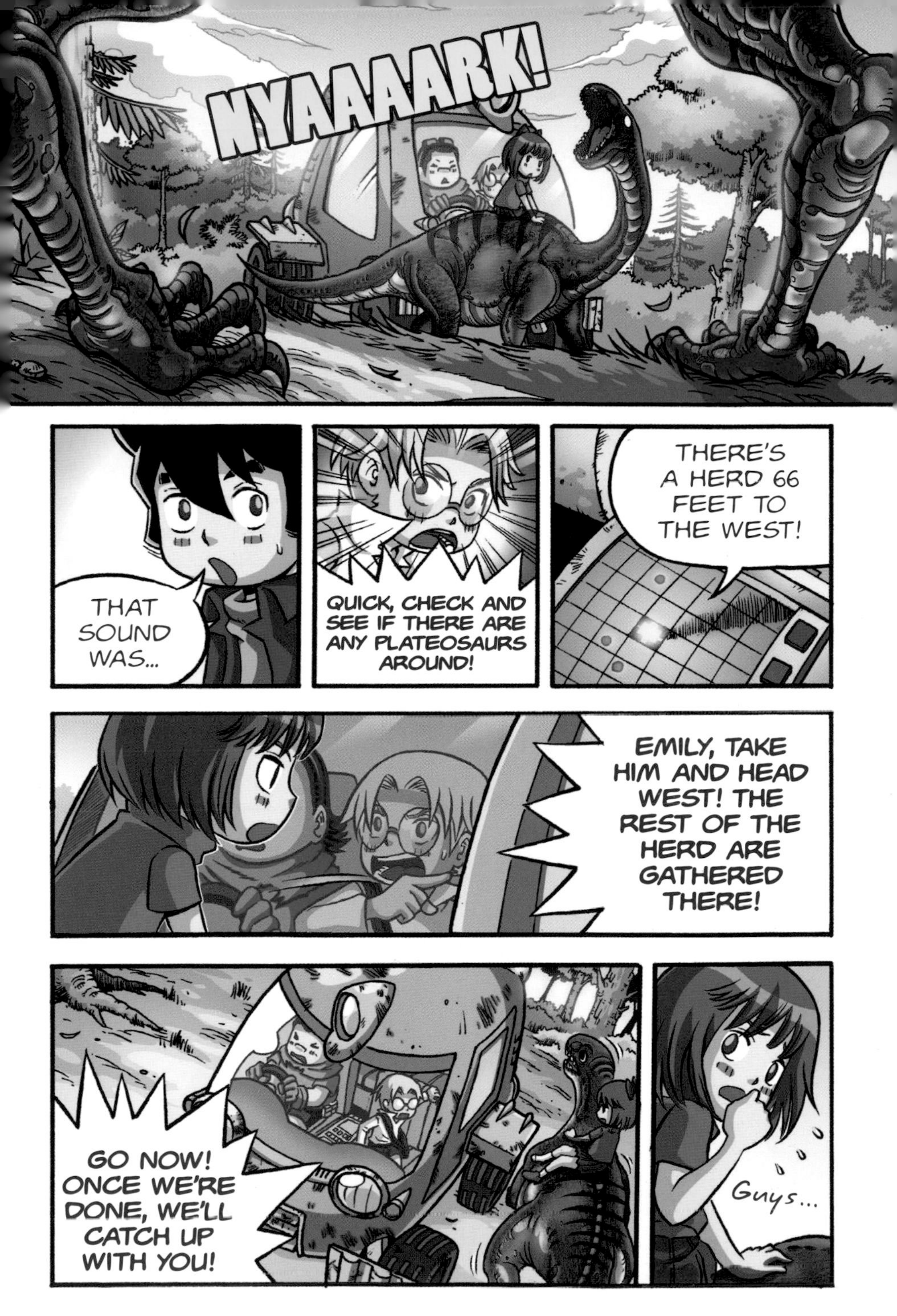
NYAAAARK!
THAT SOUND WAS...
QUICK, CHECK AND SEE IF THERE ARE ANY PLATEOSAURS AROUND!
THERE'S A HERD 66 FEET TO THE WEST!
EMILY, TAKE HIM AND HEAD WEST! THE REST OF THE HERD ARE GATHERED THERE!
GO NOW! ONCE WE'RE DONE, WE'LL CATCH UP WITH YOU!
Guys...

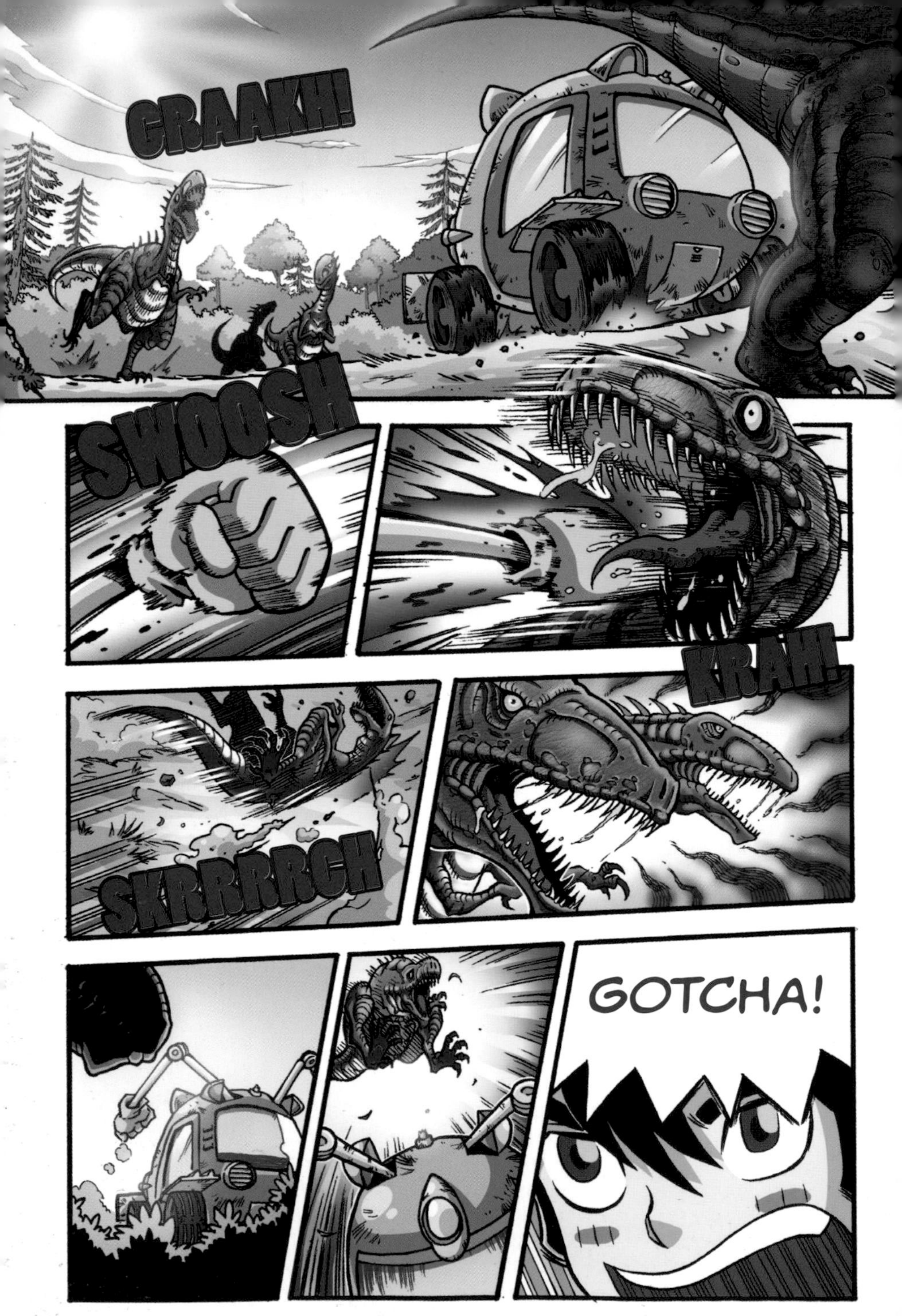
GRAAKH!
SWOOSH
KRAH!
SKRRRRCH
GOTCHA!

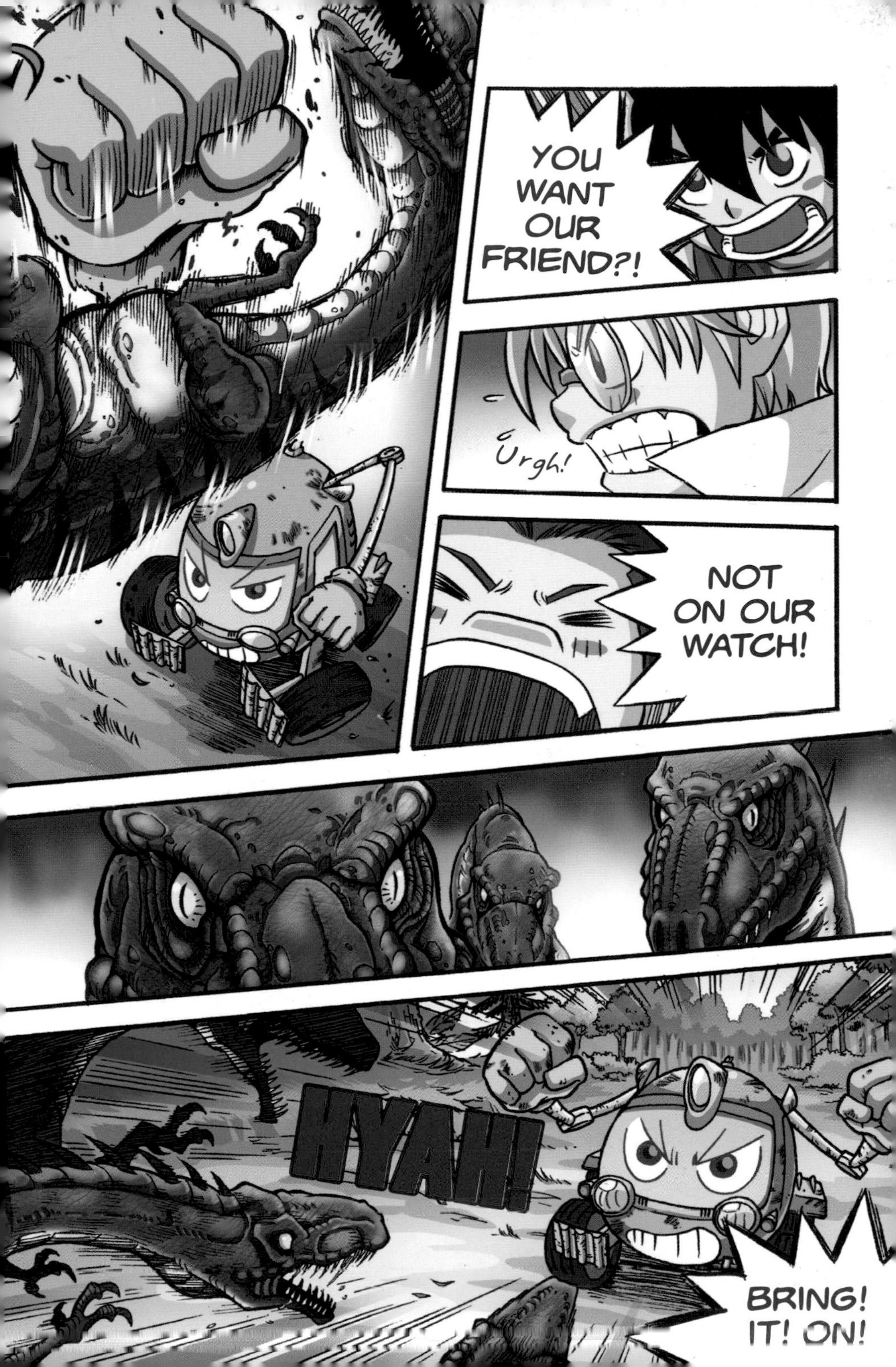
YOU WANT OUR FRIEND?!
Urgh!
NOT ON OUR WATCH!
HYAH!
BRING! IT! ON!

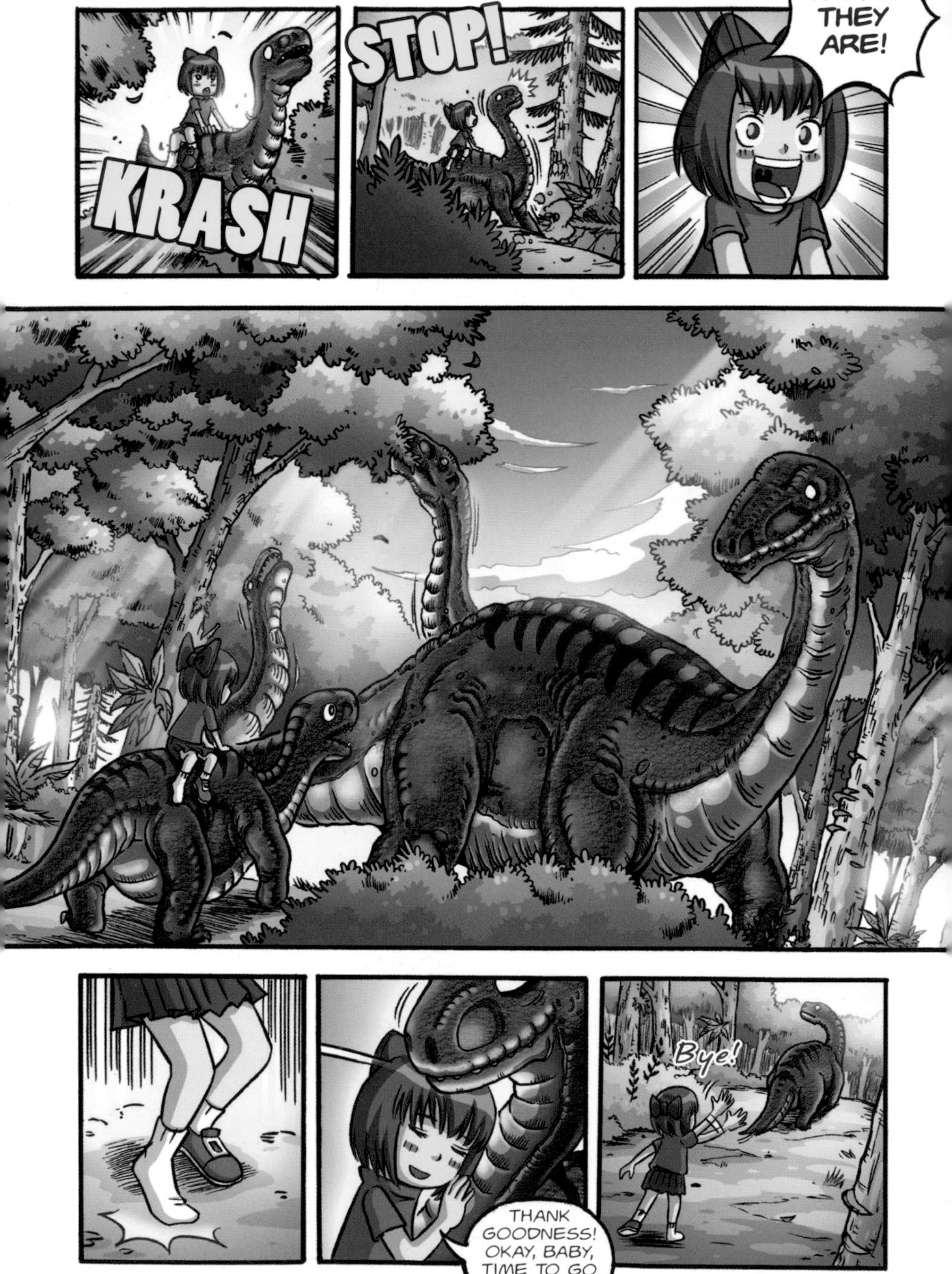
KRASH
STOP!
THERE THEY ARE!
THANK GOODNESS! OKAY, BABY, TIME TO GO HOME!
Bye!

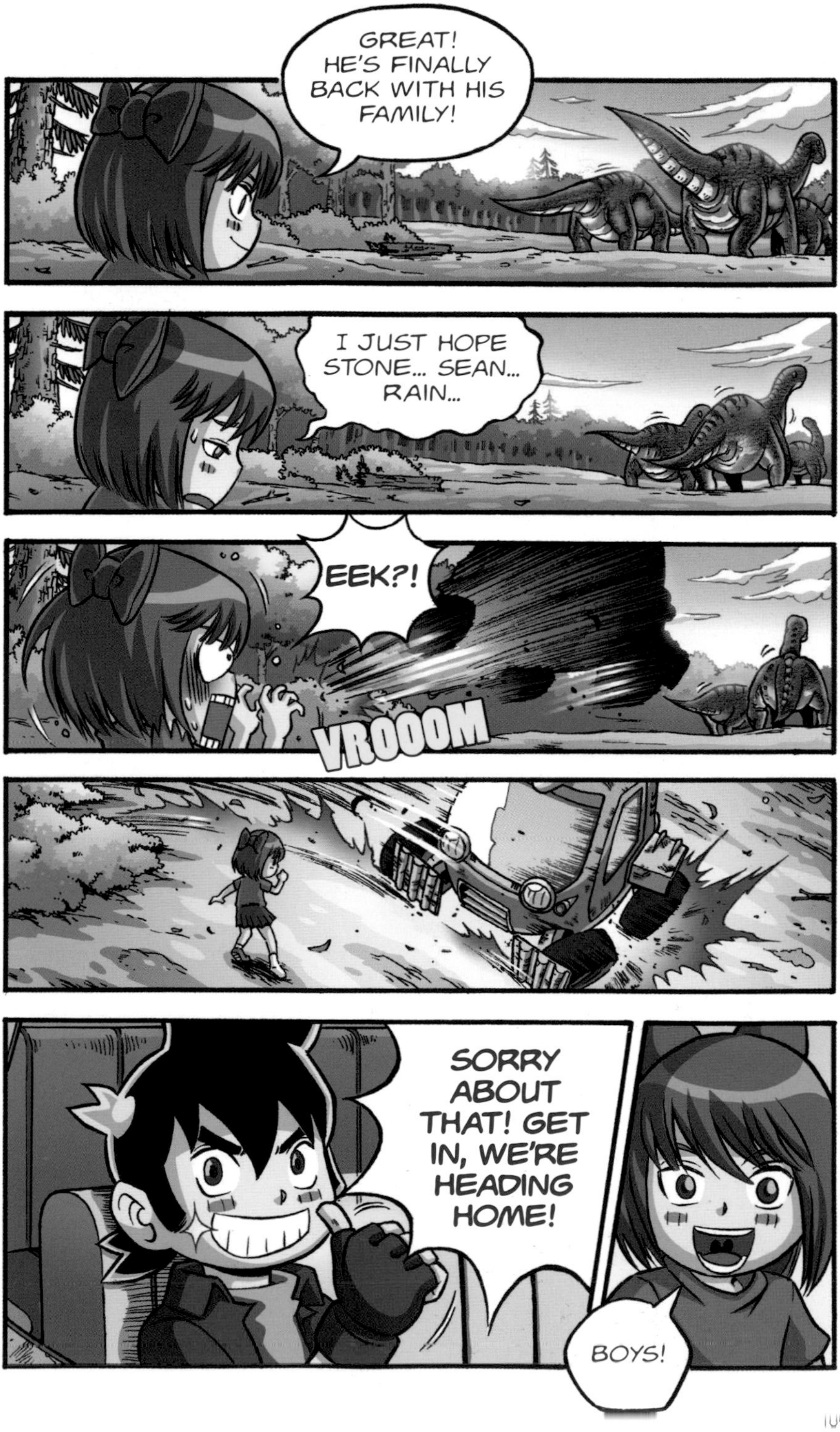
GREAT! HE'S FINALLY BACK WITH HIS FAMILY!
I JUST HOPE STONE... SEAN... RAIN...
EEK?!
VROOOM
SORRY ABOUT THAT! GET IN, WE'RE HEADING HOME!
BOYS!

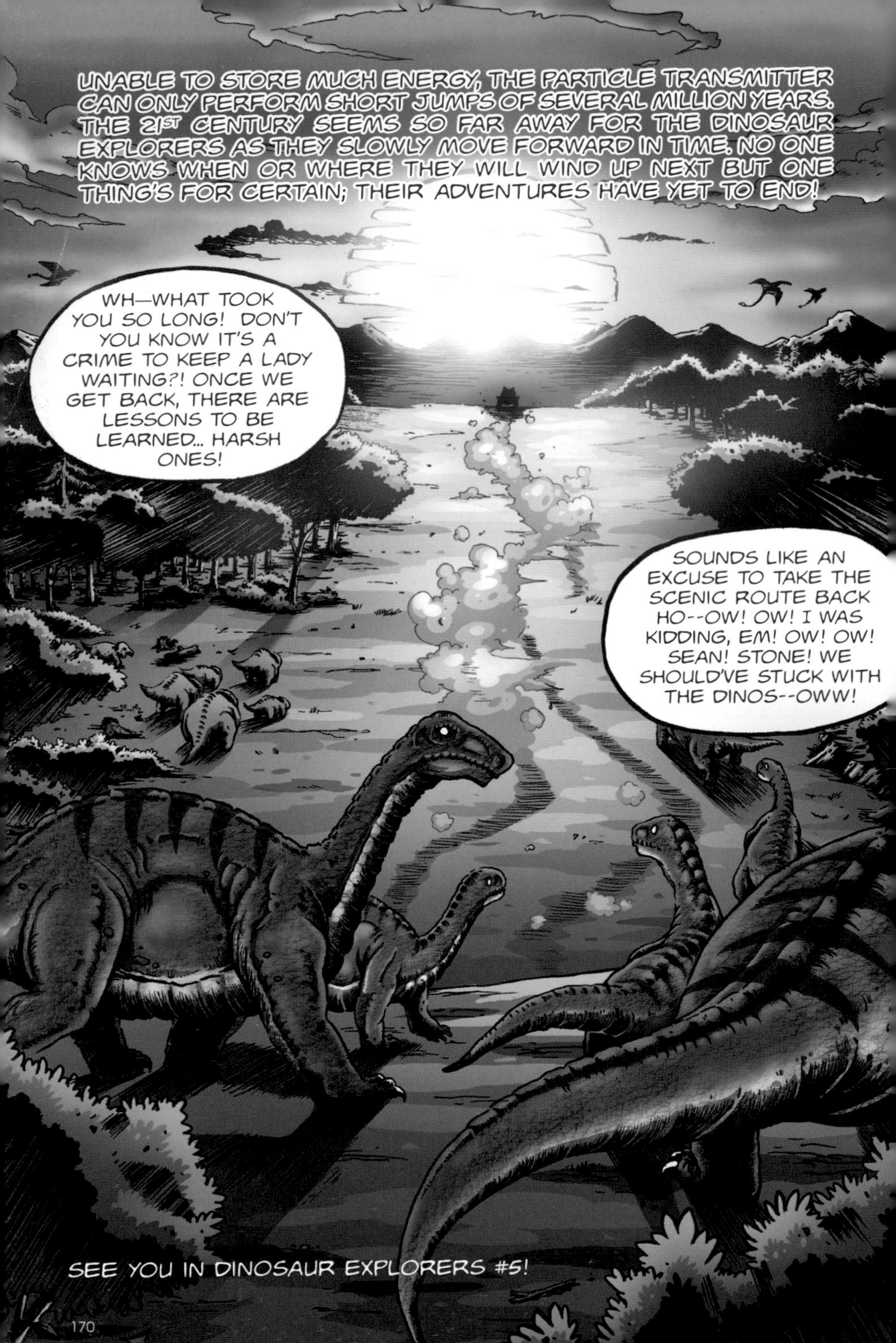
UNABLE TO STORE MUCH ENERGY, THE PARTICLE TRANSMITTER CAN ONLY PERFORM SHORT JUMPS OF SEVERAL MILLION YEARS. THE 21ST CENTURY SEEMS SO FAR AWAY FOR THE DINOSAUR EXPLORERS AS THEY SLOWLY MOVE FORWARD IN TIME. NO ONE KNOWS WHEN OR WHERE THEY WILL WIND UP NEXT BUT ONE THING'S FOR CERTAIN; THEIR ADVENTURES HAVE YET TO END!
WH—WHAT TOOK YOU SO LONG! DON'T YOU KNOW IT'S A CRIME TO KEEP A LADY WAITING?! ONCE WE GET BACK, THERE ARE LESSONS TO BE LEARNED... HARSH ONES!
SOUNDS LIKE AN EXCUSE TO TAKE THE SCENIC ROUTE BACK HO--OW! OW! I WAS KIDDING, EM! OW! OW! SEAN! STONE! WE SHOULD'VE STUCK WITH THE DINOS--OWW!
SEE YOU IN DINOSAUR EXPLORERS #5!

TAKING IN THE TRIASSIC

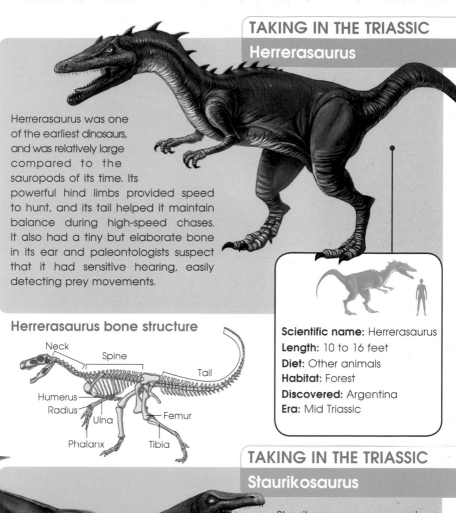

Herrerasaurus

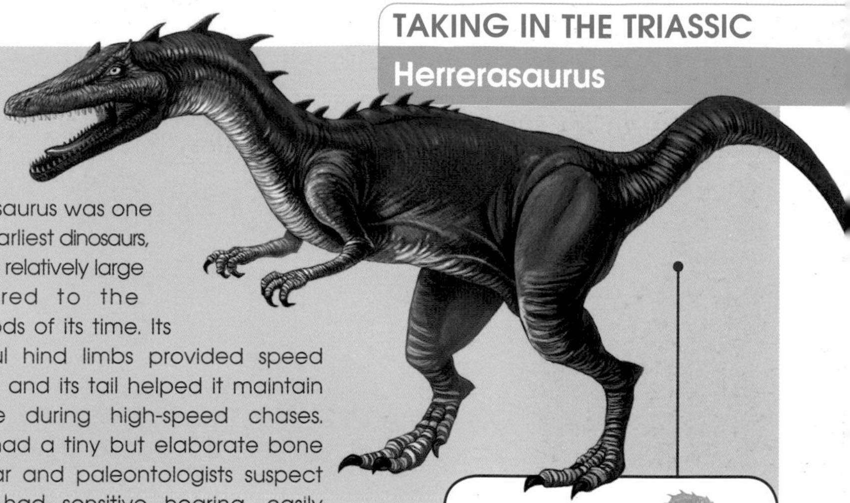

Herrerasaurus was one of the earliest dinosaurs, and was relatively large compared to the sauropods of its time. Its powerful hind limbs provided speed to hunt, and its tail helped it maintain balance during high-speed chases. It also had a tiny but elaborate bone in its ear and paleontologists suspect that it had sensitive hearing, easily detecting prey movements.

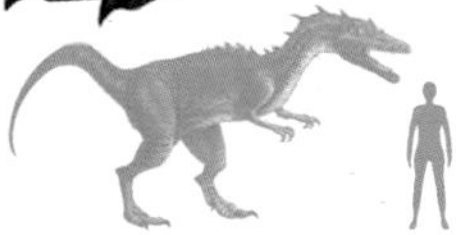

Scientific name: Herrerasaurus
Length: 10 to 16 feet
Diet: Other animals
Habitat: Forest
Discovered: Argentina
Era: Mid Triassic

Herrerasaurus bone structure

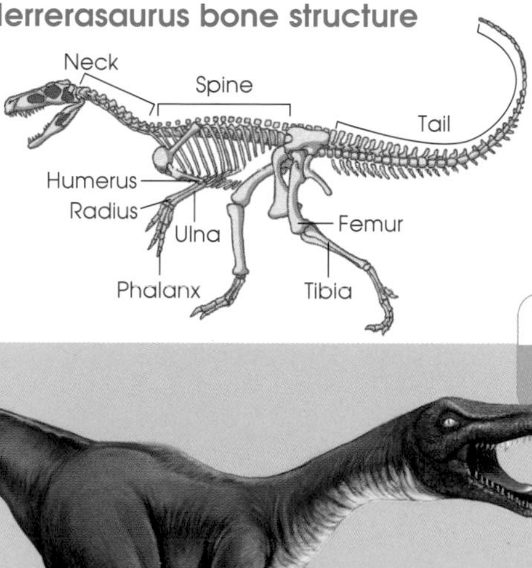

Neck
Spine
Tail
Humerus
Radius
Ulna
Femur
Phalanx
Tibia

TAKING IN THE TRIASSIC

Staurikosaurus

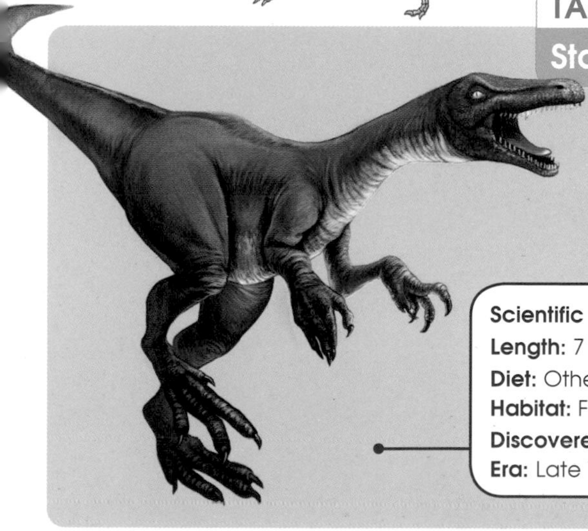

Staurikosaurus was an early therapod. It had a small but light body with long powerful hind limbs which effectively made it a speedy hunter.

Scientific name: Staurikosaurus
Length: 7 feet
Diet: Other animals
Habitat: Forest and bushes
Discovered: South America
Era: Late Triassic

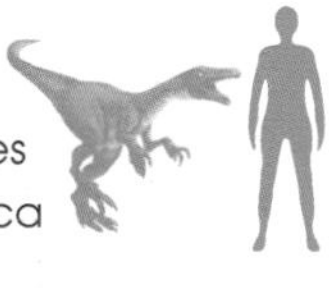

A SCENE FROM THE TRIASSIC

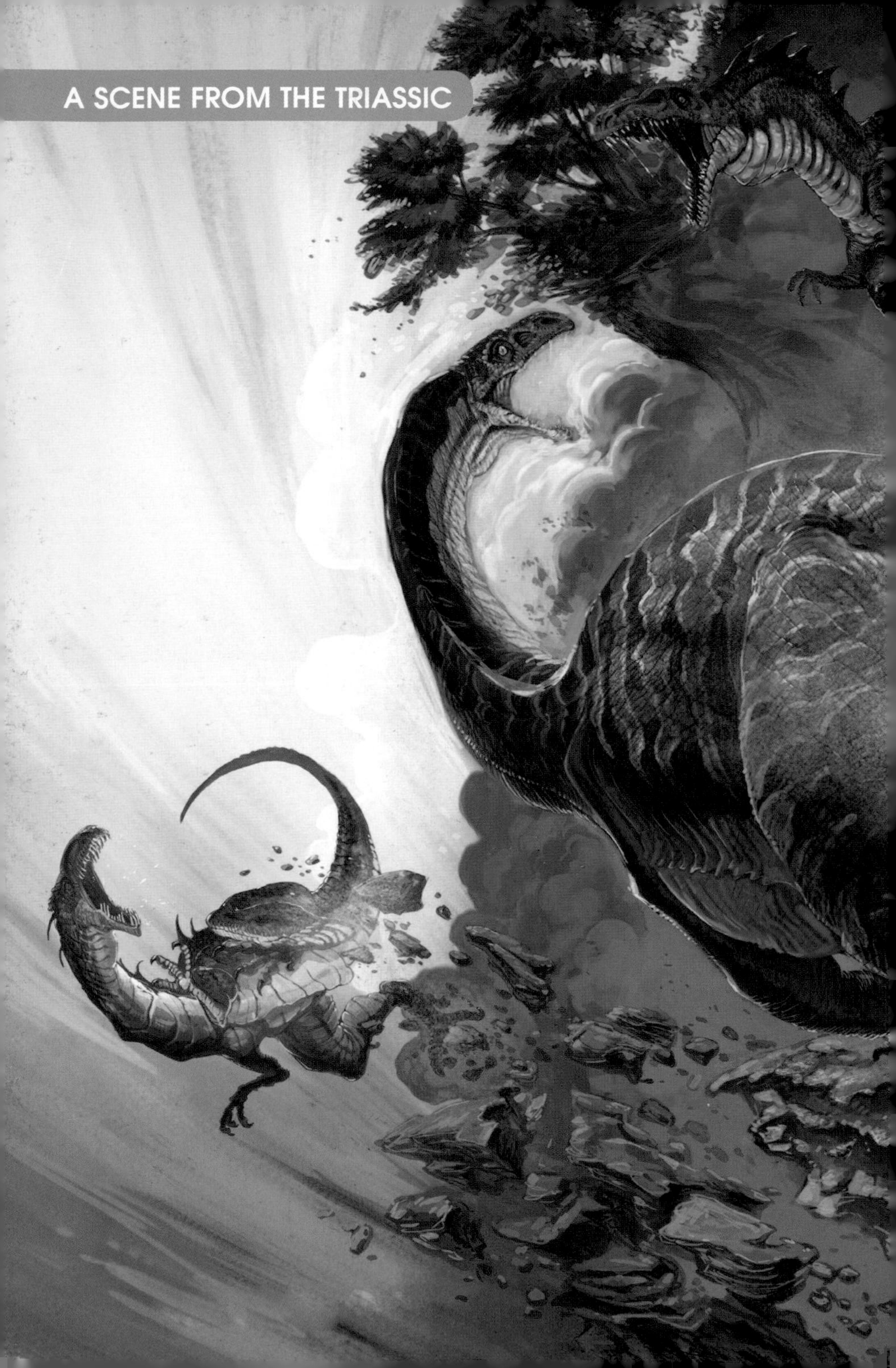

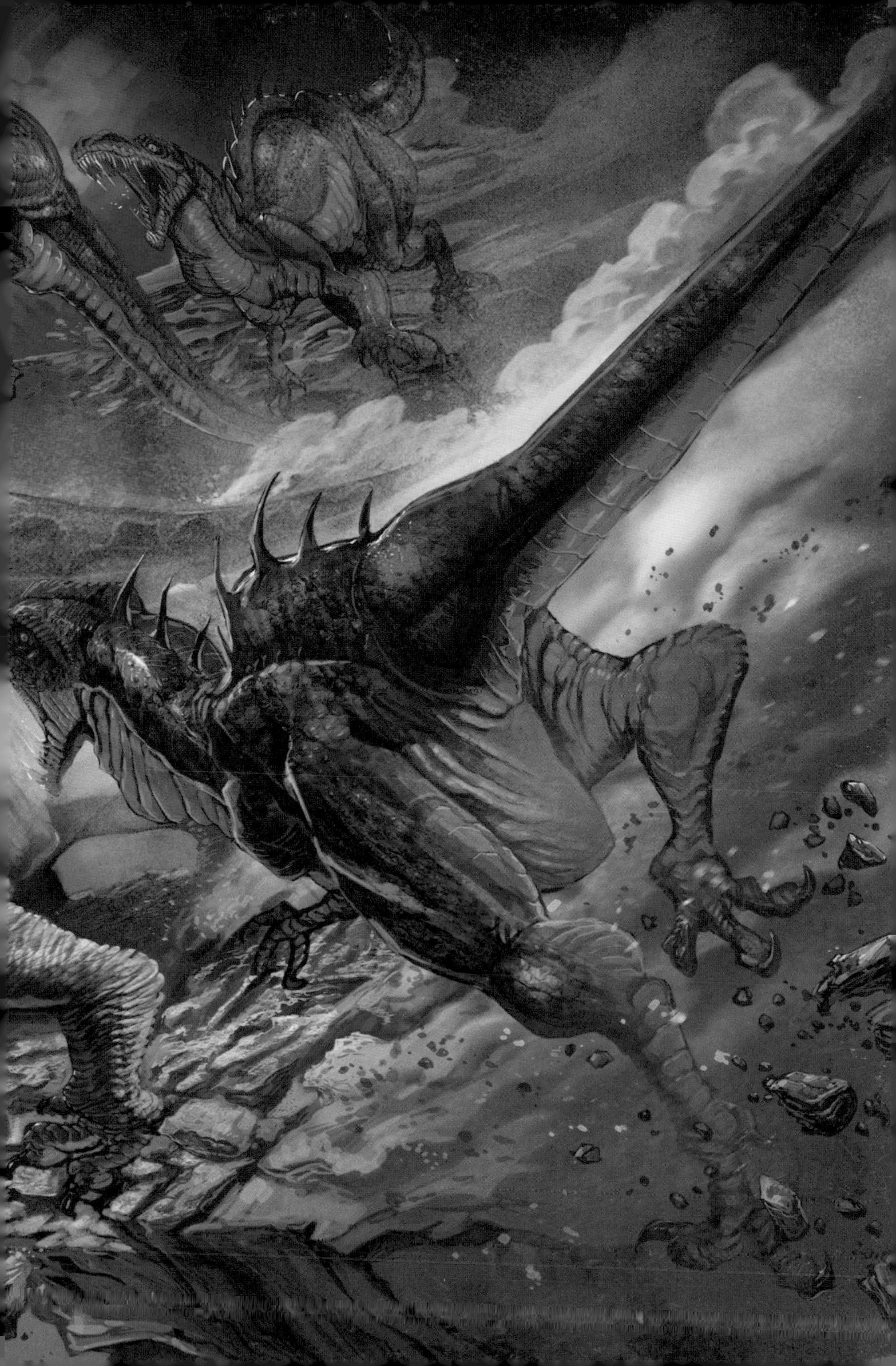

TAKING IN THE TRIASSIC

Gojirasaurus

Named after Godzilla, Gojirasaurus was one of the largest predatory dinosaurs of the Triassic, closely resembling Coelophysis. Some paleontologists, however, doubt its existence as a credible species, and no complete fossil, set has yet been found.

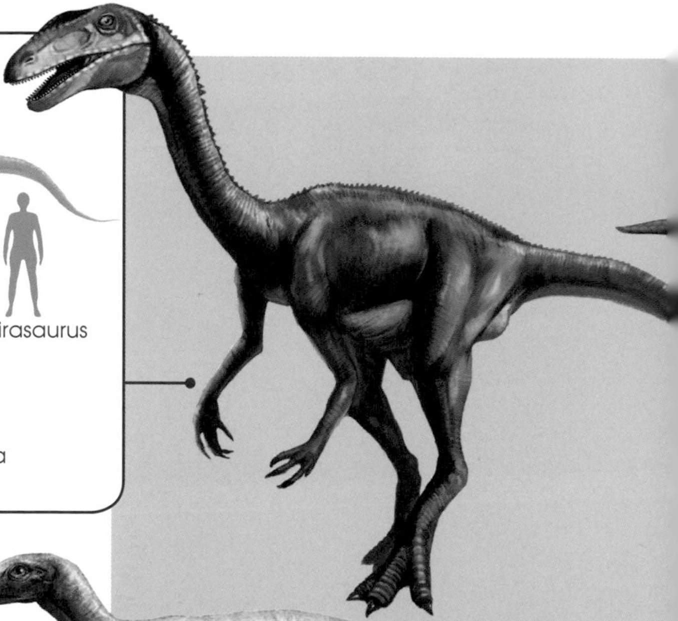

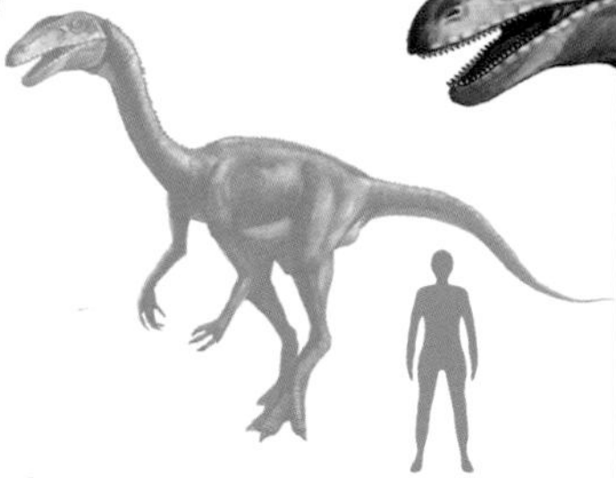

Scientific name: Gojirasaurus
Length: 18 feet
Diet: Other animals
Habitat: Unknown
Discovered: America
Era: Late Triassic

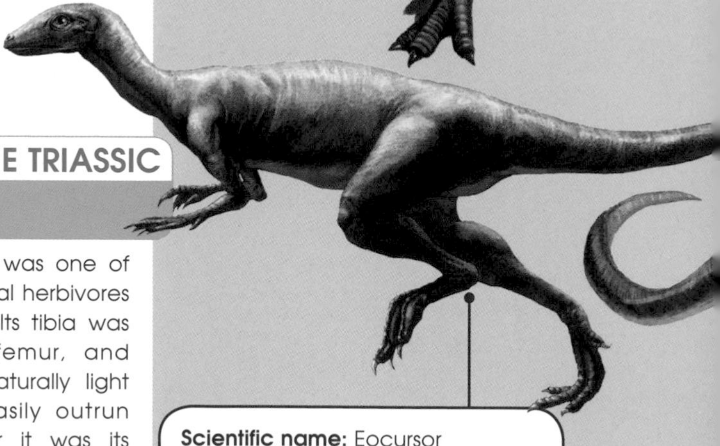

TAKING IN THE TRIASSIC

Eocursor

The "dawn runner" was one of the very few bipedal herbivores of the Triassic Era. Its tibia was longer than its femur, and coupled with a naturally light body, it could easily outrun predators. Whether it was its physical form or bone structure, it shared many qualities with the Jurassic Ornithischia, which led paleontologists to believe that the Eocursor could possibly be a precursor of Ornithischia.

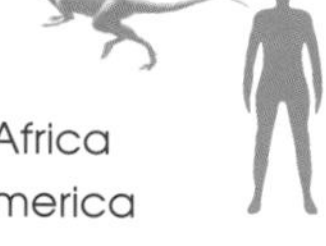

Scientific name: Eocursor
Length: 3 feet
Diet: Herbivore
Habitat: Unknown
Discovered: South Africa and America
Era: Late Triassic

TAKING IN THE TRIASSIC

Thecodontosaurus

Thecodontosaurus was one of the earliest discovered prosauropods. Its name means "socket-tooth" lizard, as its teeth were not rooted to the jaw bone but rather within sockets.

Scientific name: Thecodontosaurus
Length: 7 feet
Diet: Herbivore (Some omnivore)
Habitat: Dry highlands or desert plains
Discovered: America
Era: Late Triassic

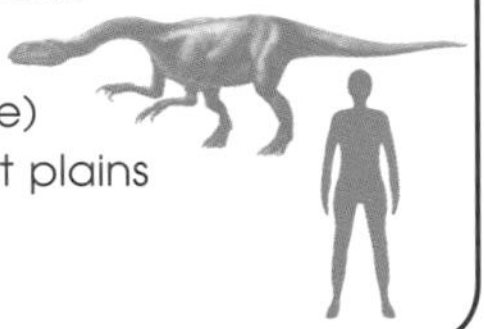

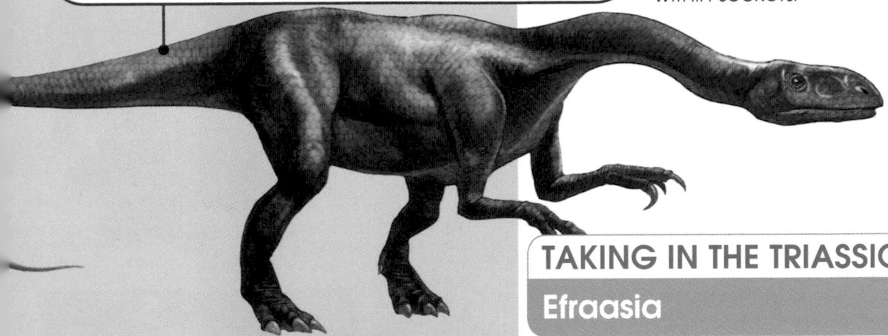

TAKING IN THE TRIASSIC

Efraasia

Efraasia had a small head and light body. Its hind limbs were longer than its forelimbs; it is thought that it walked on all fours most of the time but ran on two. It has been recently theorized that most Efraasia fossils excavated so far belonged to juveniles. If so, a mature specimen could have possibly been up to 20 feet long.

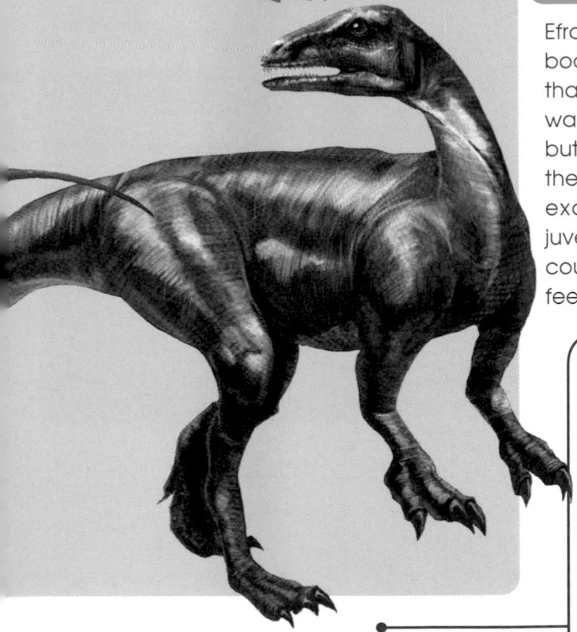

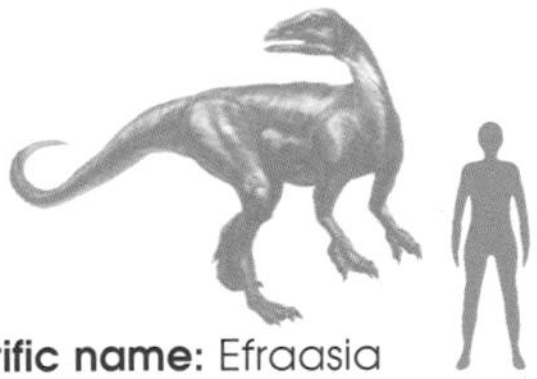

Scientific name: Efraasia
Length: 9 feet
Diet: Herbivore (Some omnivore)
Habitat: Dry highlands
Discovered: Europe
Era: Late Triassic

WATCH OUT FOR PAPERCUTZ

Welcome to the frenzied, fast-paced fourth DINOSAUR EXPLORERS graphic novel by Redcode and Albbie, writers, and Air Team, artists, from Papercutz, those Manosaurs dedicated to publishing great graphic novels for all ages. I'm Jim Salicrup, the Editor-in-Chief and someone who says "Smurftastic" more than anyone else, here to let you know a bit about what's going on behind-the-scenes here at Papercutz...

You've witnessed for yourself, in this very graphic novel, how dangerous life can be for Emily, Rain, Lil S, Sean, Stone, and the rest, millions of years ago back in the Triassic. But do you think things would be any safer in the far-flung future? Or on another world? For twelve-year-old Erik Farrel, who ran away from home and woke up without his memory on a patchwork planet, things are very, very dangerous. Of course, I'm talking about the award-winning Papercutz graphic novel series THE ONLY LIVING BOY, by David Gallaher, writer, and Steve Ellis, artist. Papercutz has recently collected the entire five-volume series in deluxe omnibus editions, available in either paperback or hardcover. Not only do you get all the comics from the five THE ONLY LIVING BOY graphic novels, but two bonus stories as well.

DAVID GALLAHER | STEVE ELLIS
THE ONLY LIVING BOY
OMNIBUS
THE COMPLETE SAGA
INCLUDES A NEW 20-PAGE STORY
PAPERCUTZ

In case you're thinking that you're lucky to be alive now, when there are no longer any dinosaurs around, think again. While they're not necessarily dinosaurs, there are all sorts of strange beasties lurking just below the ocean's surface. You can discover some of the wilder ones in SEA CREATURES #1 and #2, by Christophe Cazenove, writer, and Thierry Jytéry, artist, another great Papercutz graphic novel series, also available wherever books are sold (and in libraies too!). And here's the crazy part—in SEA CREATURES, you get to discover all the facts about these ocean dwellers from the SEA CREATURES themselves! While everything they tell you is based on fact, the creators of the series let the SEA CREATURES speak—to tell you their fascinating tales in their own words.

CAZENOVE
JYTÉRY
sea creatures
in their own words
1 REEF MADNESS
PAPERCUTZ

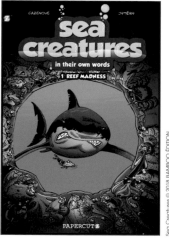

Oh, here's a real behind-the-scenes Papercutz story that proves what a dinosaur I am! When editing "Trapped in the Triassic," I was confused when on page 150 Emily's dinosaur friend is told, "Hey, Yoshi!" I won't tell you how long I spent poring over the previous 149 pages trying to figure out who Yoshi was! It wasn't until young Papercutz Managing Editor Jeff Whitman informed me that Yoshi was Mario and Luigi's dinosaur sidekick that I finally got the joke! I guess being older than Dr. Da Vinci can have its drawbacks...

So, on that slightly embarrassing note, I'll leave you to explore the future with THE ONLY LIVING BOY, search the present for SEA CREATURES, and return to the past for DINOSAUR EXPLORERS #5 "Lost in the Jurassic," coming soon!

Thanks, Jim

STAY IN TOUCH!

EMAIL:	salicrup@papercutz.com
WEB:	papercutz.com
TWITTER:	@papercutzgn
INSTAGRAM:	@papercutzgn
FACEBOOK:	PAPERCUTZGRAPHICNOVELS
FAN MAIL:	Papercutz, 160 Broadway, Suite 700, East Wing, New York, NY 10038

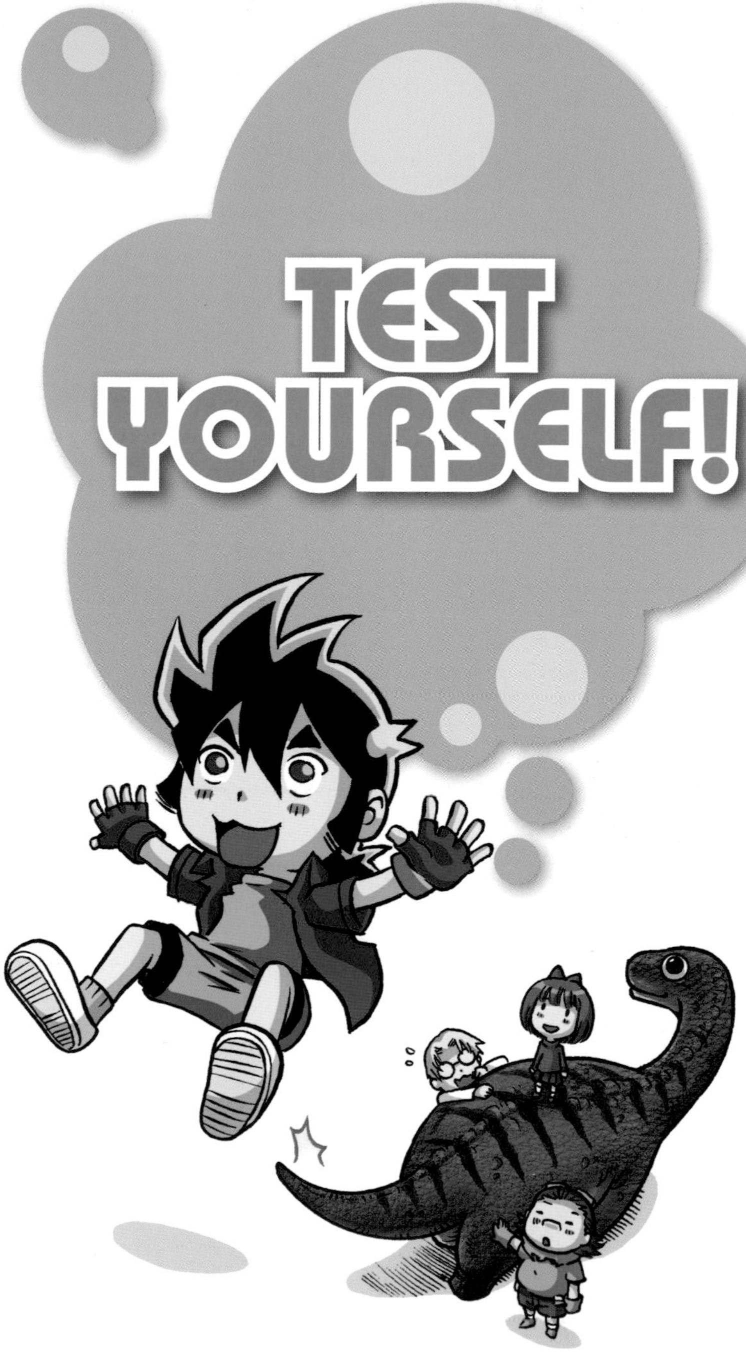
TEST YOURSELF!

ABOUT THE TRIASSIC...

01 **Which geological age did the Triassic belong to?**

A - 3rd

B - 5th

C - 7th

02 **What geographical phenomenon does the image below refer to?**

A - The union of lands and reduction of coastlines

B - The melting of glaciers and an increase of water levels

C - A strong earthquake that sank land under the sea

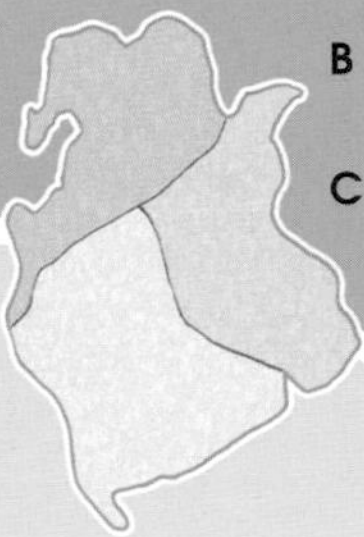

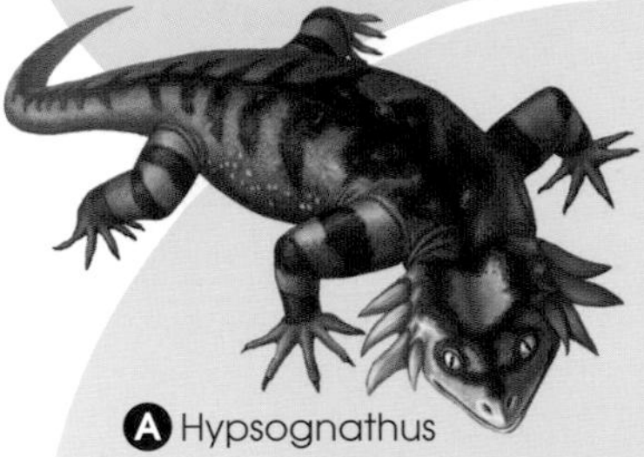

A Hypsognathus

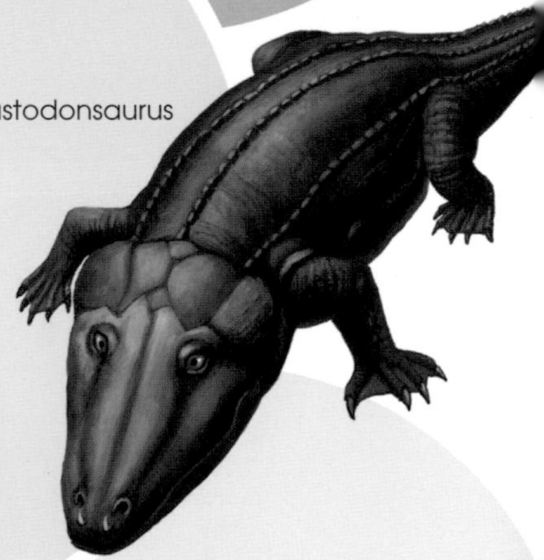

B Mastodonsaurus

03 **Which one of these is the earliest mammal?**

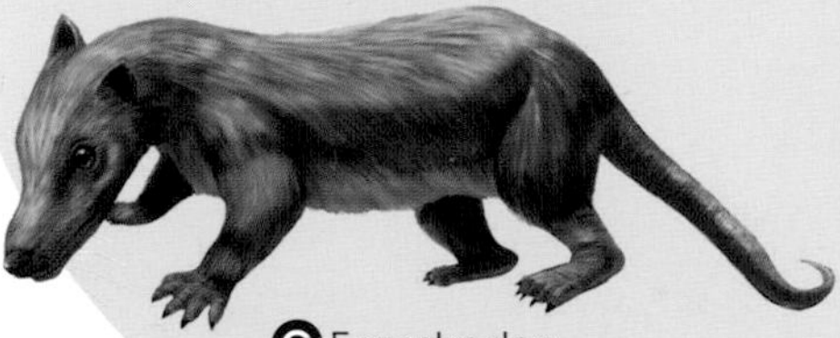

C Eozostrodon

04 **Which order did this pelvis structure belong to?**

A - Saurischia

B - Ornithischia

C - Therapoda

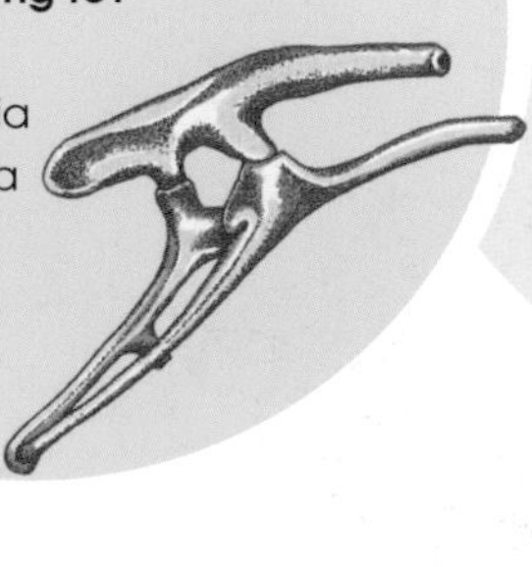

05 **Which was the most common species during the early Triassic?**

A - Lystrosaurus

B - Mastodonsaurus

C - Placerias

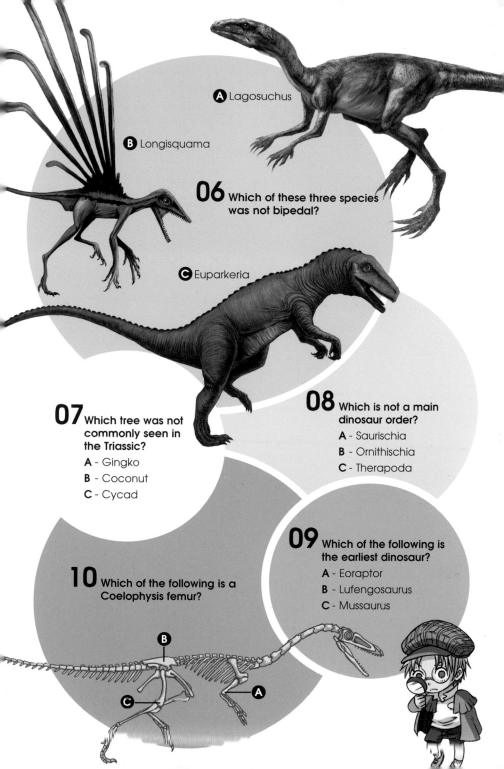

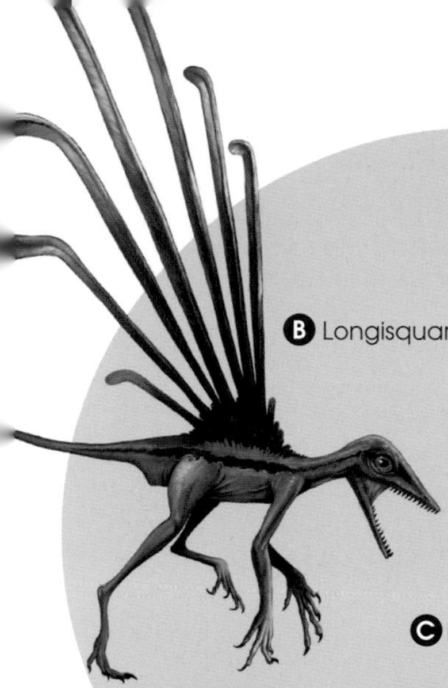
B Longisquama

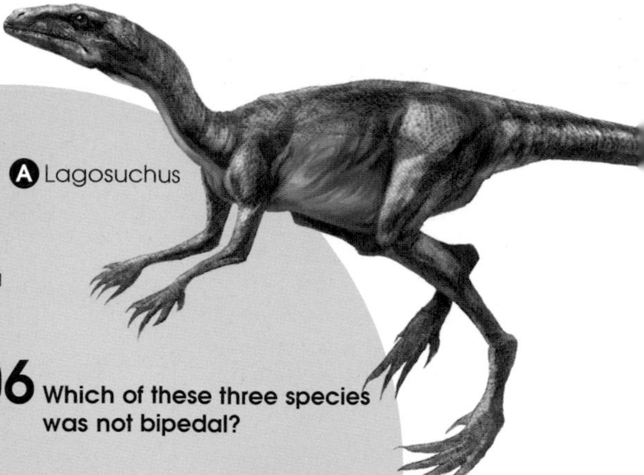
A Lagosuchus

06 Which of these three species was not bipedal?

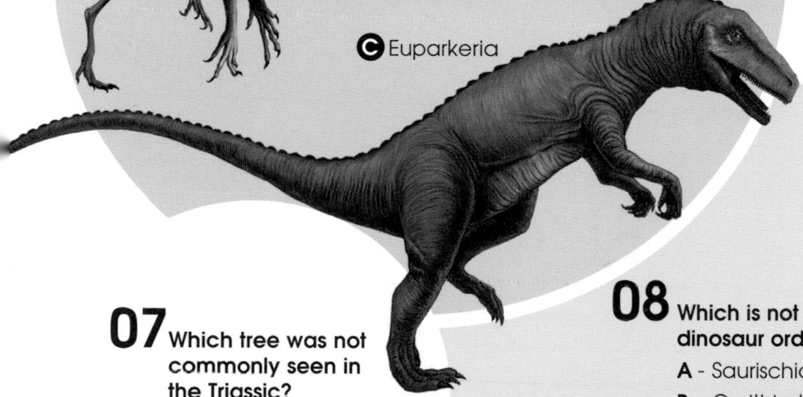
C Euparkeria

07 Which tree was not commonly seen in the Triassic?

A - Gingko

B - Coconut

C - Cycad

08 Which is not a main dinosaur order?

A - Saurischia

B - Ornithischia

C - Therapoda

09 Which of the following is the earliest dinosaur?

A - Eoraptor

B - Lufengosaurus

C - Mussaurus

10 Which of the following is a Coelophysis femur?

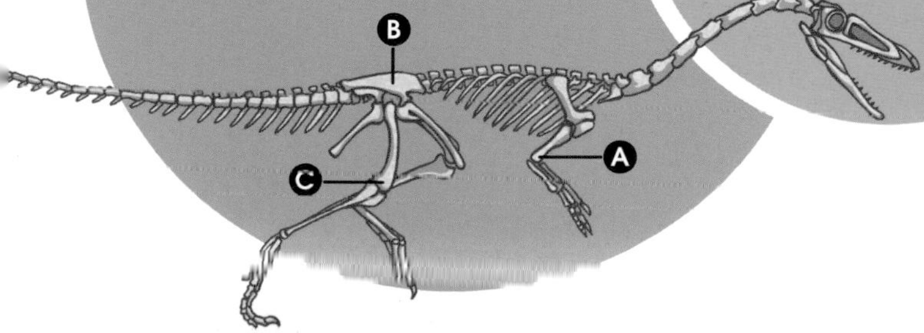
B
A
C

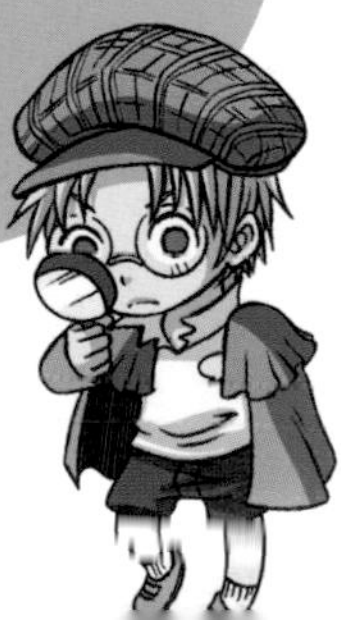

11 Which is a Staurikosaurus?

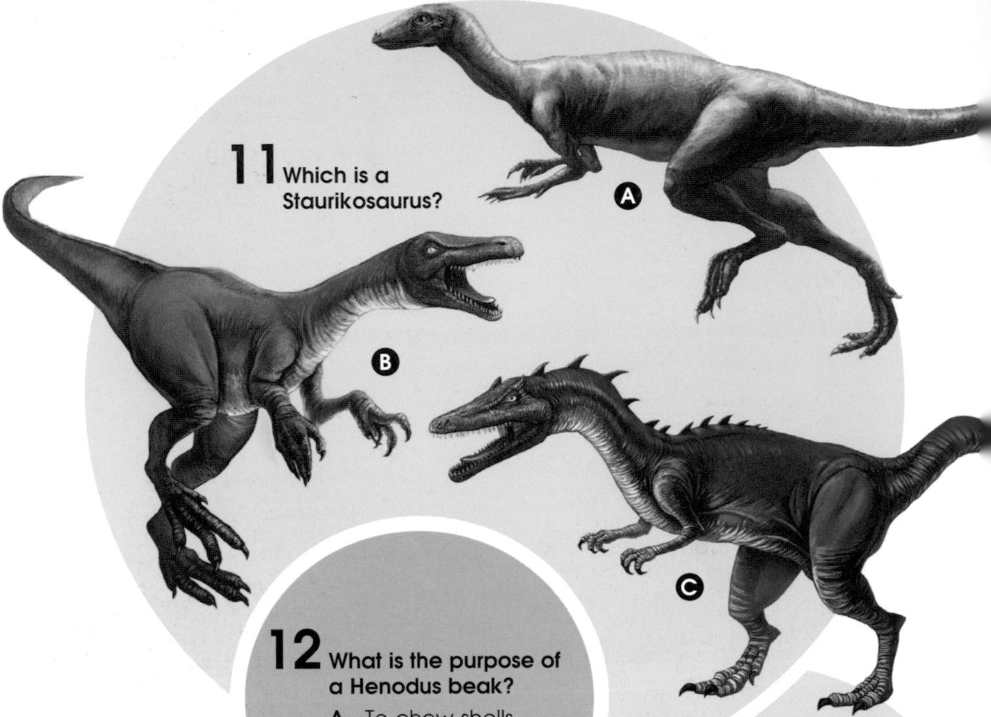
A
B
C

12 What is the purpose of a Henodus beak?

A - To chew shells

B - Decoration

C - To show off

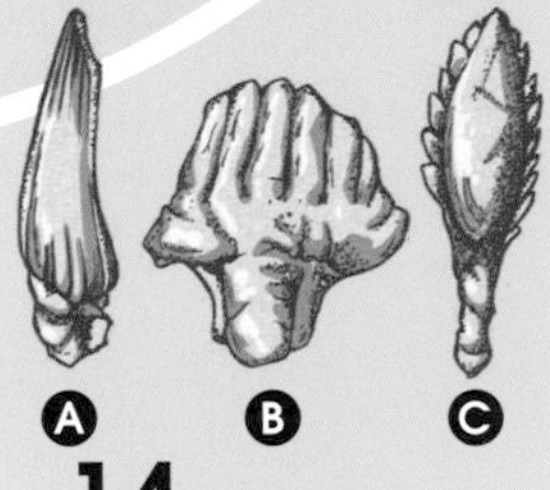
A
B
C

14 Which tooth belonged to the Plateosaurus?

13 Where is the Psephoderma's beak?

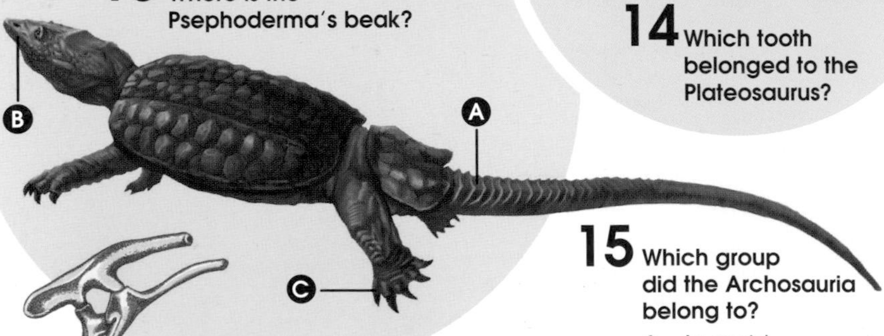
B
A
C

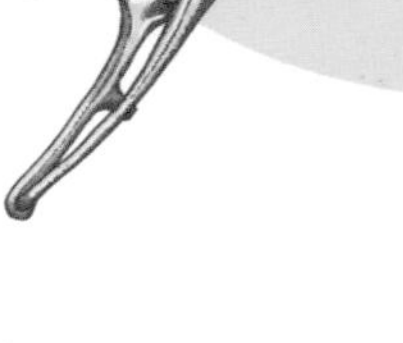

15 Which group did the Archosauria belong to?

A - Anapsid

B - Synapsid

C - Diapsids

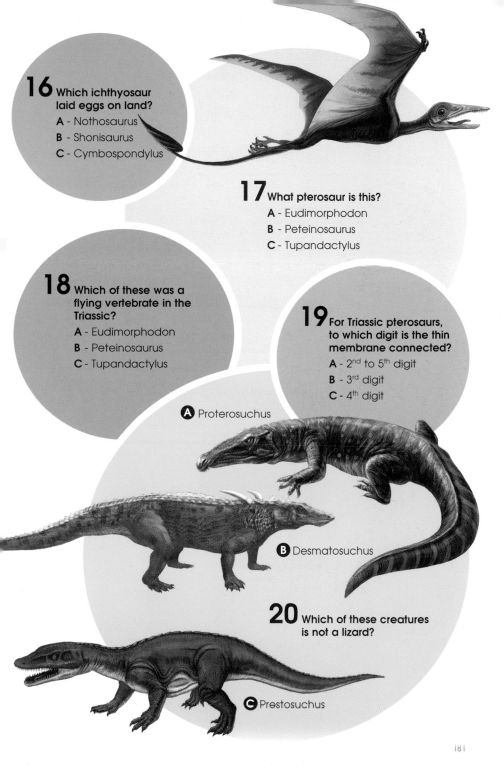

16 Which ichthyosaur laid eggs on land?
A - Nothosaurus
B - Shonisaurus
C - Cymbospondylus

17 What pterosaur is this?
A - Eudimorphodon
B - Peteinosaurus
C - Tupandactylus

18 Which of these was a flying vertebrate in the Triassic?
A - Eudimorphodon
B - Peteinosaurus
C - Tupandactylus

19 For Triassic pterosaurs, to which digit is the thin membrane connected?
A - 2nd to 5th digit
B - 3rd digit
C - 4th digit

A Proterosuchus

B Desmatosuchus

20 Which of these creatures is not a lizard?

C Prestosuchus

ANSWERS

01 C	02 A	03 C	04 B	05 A
06 B	07 B	08 C	09 A	10 C
11 B	12 A	13 B	14 C	15 C
16 A	17 A	18 B	19 C	20 B

All correct?

Congrats! You're as smart as I am! I think.

16 – 19 correct?

I'm actually smarter than the Doctor! Don't tell anyone!

12 -15 correct?

Don't just take in knowledge— apply it to real life!

8-11 correct?

What? You're smarter than me? Impossible!

4 – 7 correct?

Huh, looks like we both can use some work! Let's go to the library! Studying's better with friends!

0-3 correct?

Don't worry, you're as S-M-R-T smart as me!

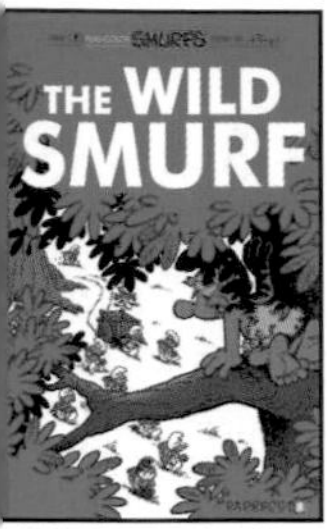
SMURFS
THE WILD SMURF
PAPERCUTZ

THE SMURFS #21

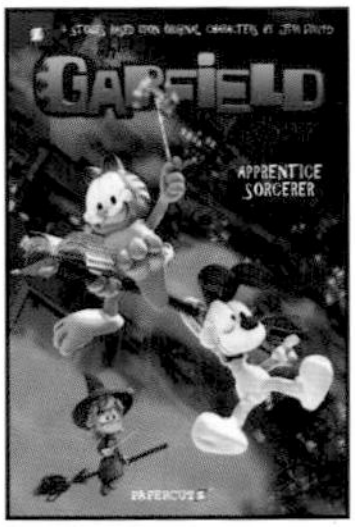
GARFIELD
APPRENTICE SORCERER

THE GARFIELD SHOW #6

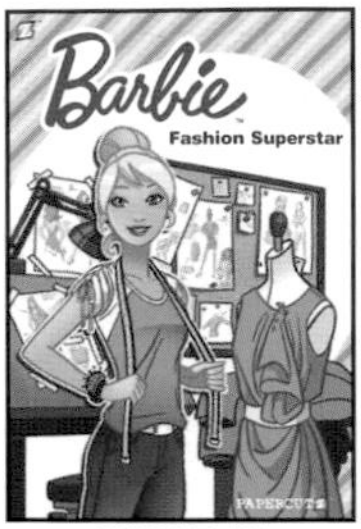
Barbie
Fashion Superstar
PAPERCUTZ

BARBIE #1

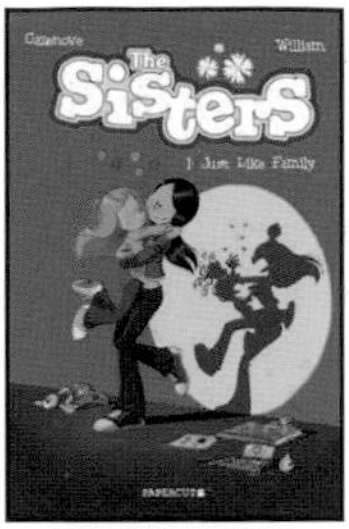
The Sisters
PAPERCUTZ

THE SISTERS #1

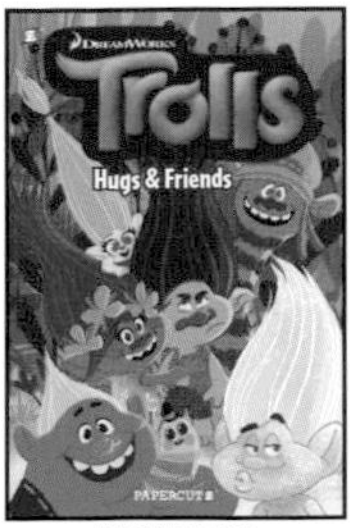
DreamWorks
Trolls
Hugs & Friends
PAPERCUTZ

TROLLS #1

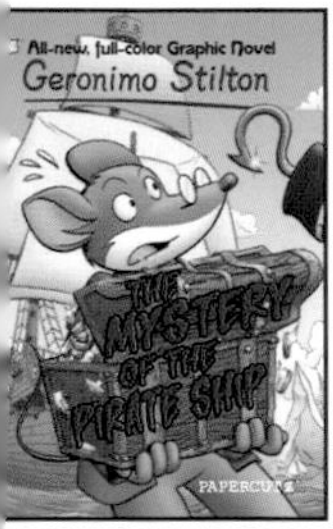
All-new, full-color Graphic Novel
Geronimo Stilton
THE MYSTERY OF THE PIRATE SHIP
PAPERCUTZ

GERONIMO STILTON #17

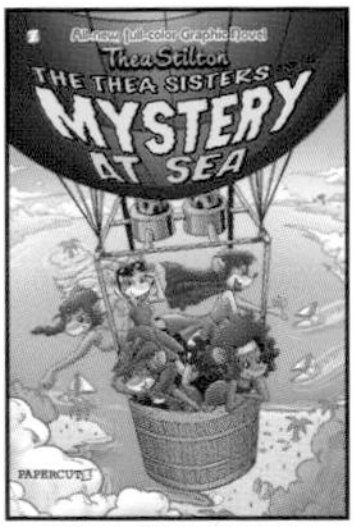
All-new full-color Graphic Novel
Thea Stilton
THE THEA SISTERS
MYSTERY AT SEA
PAPERCUTZ

THEA STILTON #6

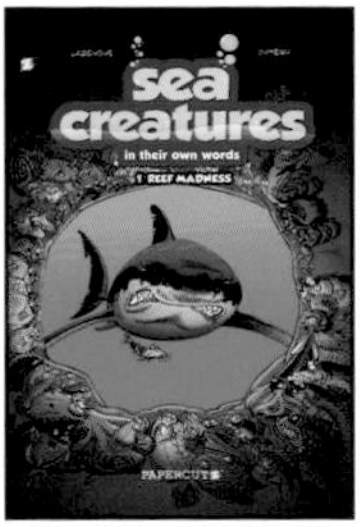
sea creatures
in their own words
REEF MADNESS
PAPERCUTZ

SEA CREATURES #1

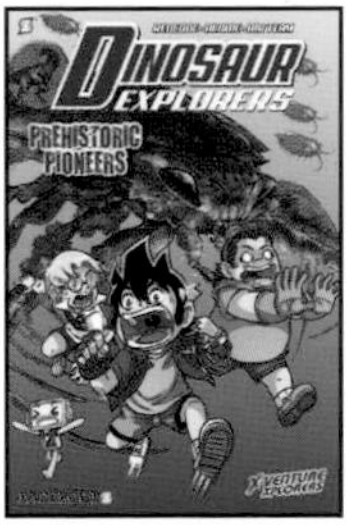
DINOSAUR EXPLORERS
PREHISTORIC PIONEERS

DINOSAUR EXPLORERS #1

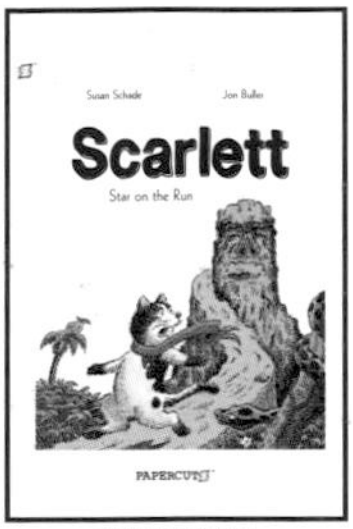
Susan Schade
Jon Buller
Scarlett
Star on the Run
PAPERCUTZ

SCARLETT

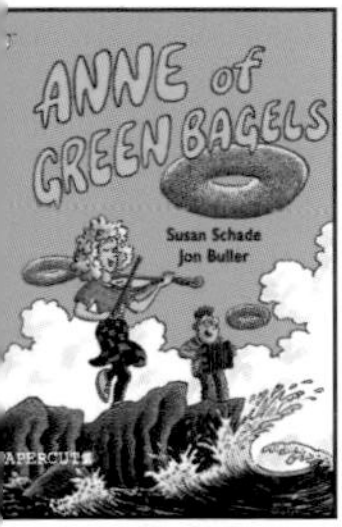
ANNE of GREEN BAGELS
Susan Schade
Jon Buller
PAPERCUTZ

ANNE OF GREEN BAGELS #1

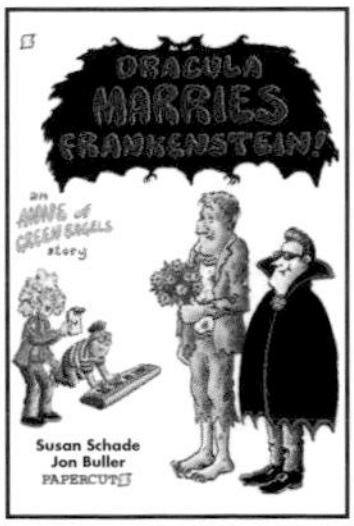
DRACULA MARRIES FRANKENSTEIN!
an ANNE of GREEN BAGELS story
Susan Schade
Jon Buller
PAPERCUTZ

DRACULA MARRIES FRANKENSTEIN!

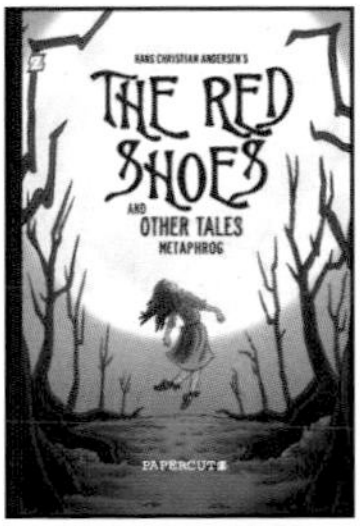
HANS CHRISTIAN ANDERSEN'S
THE RED SHOES
AND OTHER TALES
METAPHROG
PAPERCUTZ

THE RED SHOES

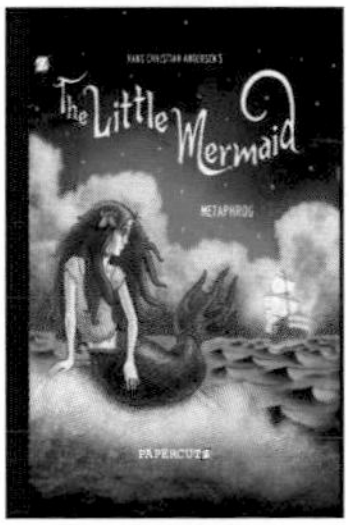
HANS CHRISTIAN ANDERSEN'S
The Little Mermaid
METAPHROG
PAPERCUTZ

THE LITTLE MERMAID

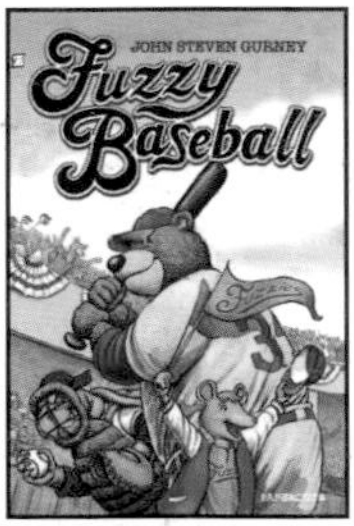
JOHN STEVEN GURNEY
Fuzzy Baseball

FUZZY BASEBALL

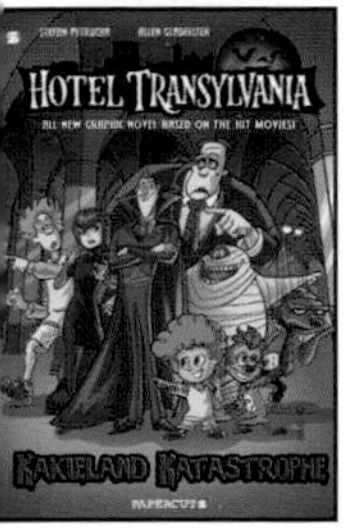
STEFAN PETRUCHA
HOTEL TRANSYLVANIA
KAKIELAND KATASTROPHE
PAPERCUTZ

HOTEL TRANSYLVANIA #1

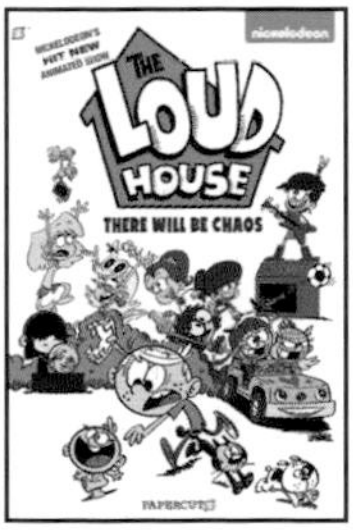
nickelodeon
THE LOUD HOUSE
THERE WILL BE CHAOS
PAPERCUTZ

THE LOUD HOUSE #1

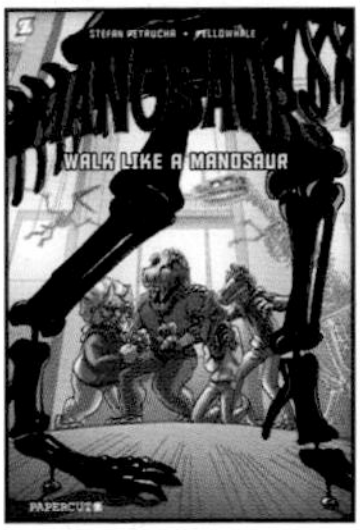
STEFAN PETRUCHA
WALK LIKE A MANOSAUR
PAPERCUTZ

MANOSAURS #1

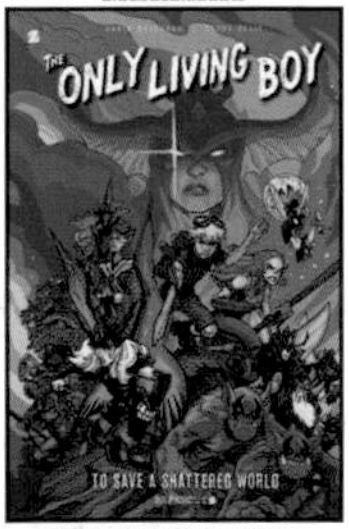
THE ONLY LIVING BOY
TO SAVE A SHATTERED WORLD

THE ONLY LIVING BOY #5

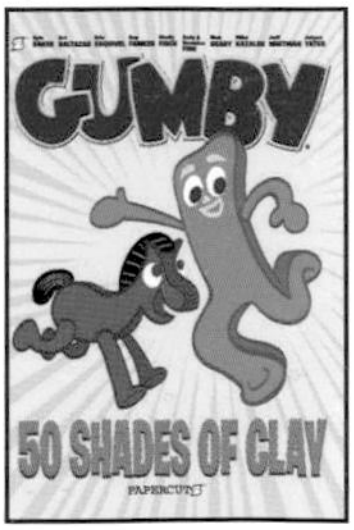
GUMBY
50 SHADES OF CLAY
PAPERCUTZ

GUMBY #1